The
Apprehensive
Prophet

By

Susan Davis Sandberg

SusanDavisSandberg@gmail.com

ISBN-13: 978-0-9849923-5-5
ISBN-10: 0984992359

To
My son Glen

For an insightful critique
on my first books that
has been a building block
for the others

Chapter 1

The octogenarian, tiny and thin, took the steps to the second floor law offices with an energy usually found in much younger woman. She was as unimpressive in dress as in stature. Her homemade pants were splattered with tiny smears of paint; her tennis shoes were equally dotted with color; her long-sleeved shirt, however, was checkered and clean. An old dark blue baseball cap with the Cubs logo on it hid her sparse straight hair.

The outer office was empty, so the old woman walked into the inner office. She had heard that the Praetzel law office had a gigantic aquarium; but, she never expected to see one that stretched along an entire wall. The light from the huge picture window revealed the renovated brick-faced buildings of a dozen small specialty shops which catered to the wealthy estate owners who frequented them looking for one-of-a-kind gifts, jewelry and wearing apparel. The shops did a brisk business even during harsh Illinois winters when the sheltered malls promised protection against strong winds and driving sleet.

The old woman herself had made several forays into the area, haunting the rare bookstore located there. She had spotted the small brass-plated sign above the hand-carved oak door leading to the second floor law offices of Stanley Davis Praetzel, Esquire and had resolved that if ever she needed a lawyer, she would come here first.

She hadn't however.

Stanley Praetzel was a children's advocate.

So she had gone elsewhere seeking help. No one held out any hope. Cases like hers were not winnable.

She smelled the fresh paint and noted that the wall opposite the fish tank held another tank, this one empty. She remembered reading that the assassin's bullet had hit it, shattering the glass and the onrush of water had flooded the office. The glass had been replaced, and it was obvious the tank was being restored.

One would have expected a variety of fish with such an elaborate setup, but the only fish in the water-filled tank were colorful orange and white Koi.

The old woman stood fascinated by the movement of the sweeping fins and tails of the large Koi. The aquarium had a natural feel to it, as much as an artificial environment could.

"It needs some dead wood or broken coral," she murmured.

"Exactly where?" came the soft voice of a woman from the doorway.

"Paper," the old woman requested, not taking her eyes from the fish. Her hand was held out.

A large legal pad was placed in it. The old woman waited and a pen was then handed to her. Quickly she sketched the tank minus the fish and rearranged the rocks, and took out the man-made additions of plastic tunnels and added coral, wood and several plants not currently in the tank and handed the sketch to the young woman without looking at her.

"I like it," the young woman said. "Now may I help you?"

"I'm here to see Aleta Locke Praetzel," the old woman said turning to face a lovely, slim young woman considerably taller than she and sporting a crown of auburn hair parted down the center by a scar.

"I'm not licensed yet to practice law in Illinois," Aleta said.

"You represent the Tontine Trust."

"As House Counsel only. I'm not legally permitted to help you in any way."

"What about your husband?"

"My husband is a children's advocate," Aleta said.

Recently married, Aleta carried the bloom of a happy new bride. The scar left by the bullet's path was untouched since the shooting two months ago. Aleta still hoped her hair would slowly cover the scar.

"I know," the woman said. "He can fill in until you can take over."

"I'm not currently taking clients," Aleta said politely. "When I do, I will be concentrating on corporate work."

"What a waste!" the old woman exclaimed. "You were born to be a trial lawyer."

"You don't know me," Aleta said, her voice pleasant because the woman's voice, while sharp and cutting, still carried a positive vibe of some magnitude.

"I was sent here," the woman said. "When do you take the bar exam?"

"The last Tuesday and Wednesday in February."

"But you're already a lawyer."

"Illinois accepted my MBE and MPRE scores from California, but I still need to take the essay portion. And the scores from that won't be posted until April."

"So long," the woman said, her voice shaky. "I need help now. What was He thinking?"

"Perhaps my husband can refer you to a lawyer who specializes in your legal issue."

"I want you!" the old woman said. She put her hand into her pocket, pulled out a single one dollar bill and laid it on the table.

Aleta felt pressed to explain. "Even if I wanted to help my husband prepare your case, I'm not acquainted enough with the Illinois statutes to be of much use. I'd have to spend too much time just doing basic research."

"Nonsense! the old woman exclaimed. "You've already done all the studying you need to do. Your corporate clients are all in Illinois, correct?"

"Yes, but…"

"So you're ready," the old woman said. "And I need you."

"I don't know your name," Aleta blurted out too unsettled at the persistence of the old lady to manage more. "Or why you need a lawyer."

"I signed the sketch," the old lady said. "You can come to my studio in Oakwood. That hell-hole of a town has decided to confiscate the home I've lived in all my life. Eminent domain is the jargon they used. It's only one house. But the government shouldn't be allowed to do that to a private citizen."

"I don't think I'm the lawyer for you," Aleta replied firmly.

"Of course, you are," the old woman said. "You're young and fresh from law school. You haven't been corrupted or beaten to a pulp yet. Your husband owns this whole block of stores, so you don't need the money, so I don't have to worry about you giving up because you can't afford to go on. You've got guts. That scar attests to that. And believe me, you'll need the latter. Oakwood isn't like Arborville or Willow Glen. The police are not your friends. Oakwood has lost its soul."

"Why not move?"

"Because I paint best at home."

"I'm sorry," Aleta began. "But I really... can't legally help you."

"I already told the mayor, I planned to hire you."

"That was premature."

"You'll figure out how to represent me," the old woman said. "I trust you."

"You don't understand 'can't', do you?"

"You will work it out," the old woman said with a finality that brooked no argument.

Aleta stared at the sketch long after the old woman was gone. She could barely make out the name. Why did artists and doctors always assume their signature was readable? No wonder the doctors were assigned numbers to put on their prescriptions as a means of identification.

She'd made a number of friends since arriving in Willow Glen, the closest one being Lauren West, the Arborville Police Chief's wife. Lauren wasn't a native, but perhaps she knew this artist.

Aleta called her.

"Bessie Dobbins," Lauren replied. "She lives on a farm outside Oakwood."

"She said she was from Oakwood."

"Oakwood's been trying to incorporate the farms to the west. I didn't know they'd won their fight," Lauren told Aleta. "Where did you meet her?"

"She showed up at the office and told me how to make the fish tank prettier."

"That's her!" Lauren said. "I have one of her paintings. So does your new mother-in-law."

Aleta was about to say more when she spotted the dollar on Stanley's desk. As long as Bessie thought she was a client, she had to honor privilege and not say anything about why Bessie Dobbins had visited her.

She switched the subject. "Ed did an ultra sound on Emma yesterday. She's got a bunch of pups in her."

Ed's black Lab had been bred to Lauren's champion black male. Aleta was in line for a show male.

"I've been studying the pedigree," Lauren responded. "Do you know Emma could be carrying chocolate?"

"Both parents have to carry the gene."

"Morgan has it."

"That'll surprise Ed. He's sold only blacks."

"You might wind up with a chocolate male."

"Stanley has his heart set on a black."

"He may just have to unset his heart," Lauren said. "Life is full of surprises."

Chapter 2

Driving along the road past Oakwood, Bessie Dobbins didn't know when her mind shut down. She remembered seeing the big red fire engine pushed under one of her hundred-year- old oaks. She remembered seeing white hoses crawling across her lawn, their thick upright heads being held up while water gushed from their throats. And she remembered the flames, the red and orange and yellow tongues of fire licking the corners of her family's white clapboard two-story farm house and reaching out to grab hold of the branches of the leafless oak.

The slap of a hand on the windshield of her slow-moving jeep shocked her into jamming her foot on the brake. She jerked forward and hit her chin on the steering wheel.

She glared at the police officer. "Why did you scare me like that!"

"You weren't stopping," Officer Kirk Boyes stated flatly.

"That's my house burning down," she shot back. "Now get your hand off my windshield."

"Sorry, Ma'am, you can't go any further on this road."

Bessie shoved the gear into reverse, and the hand came off the windshield as she backed down the road. Cars were turning onto the road to view the fire up close, so Bessie stopped and turned the wheel to the right. Her jeep took the ditch with ease, knocked down an old fence post, and bounced over a line of ridged rows of soil before turning toward the burning house.

The young officer shouted at her as she passed, but she ignored him as she bumped over the ridges and grooves in her headlong dash toward her house. She didn't have to squeal to a stop as a large clump of dirt halted her just a few feet from the fence. She left the car, scooted between the barbed wire and hurried toward the Arborville Fire Chief, Jack Hallihan.

The young cop, Kirk Boyes, caught up to her as she neared the chief and grabbed her arm. She tried to yank it from his grasp; but, his grip was firm.

"Let me go," she stormed, her old voice carrying her fury despite its thinness.

"I told you to stay away," he said roughly. "If you don't leave now, I'll have to arrest you."

"You told me I couldn't proceed down the road, so I didn't."

"You trespassed by driving through the farmer's field," Boyes said.

"It's my own field," Bessie said, still trying to extricate herself from Boyes' grasp.

"Well, leave the same way," Boyes ordered, tightening his grip.

Snatches of conversation between the Arborville Fire Chief, Jack Hallihan, and his Oakwood counterpart, Chuck Wicks, drifted to where Bessie stood. Despite her struggle with the police officer, Bessie heard most of it. Unnerved by Chuck Wicks's comments, Bessie resolved to insert herself into the decision-making process. First, however, she had to get rid of the cop holding onto her.

"Okay," she said suddenly. "You win."

She took off toward her jeep, and, as she expected, Kirk Boyes walked with her.

"So you're going to keep me away from the scene; but, let everyone else come and gawk," she observed bitterly. "The only one to keep away is the owner. Were those your orders?"

"What are you talking about?"

She pointed at the road behind him just as the first car skirted around the wooden barricade.

"Shit!" he exploded, running back toward the road, shouting at her to get in her car.

When he glanced back, she was ducking under the fence and climbing back into her jeep. He kept tabs on her until she backed away from the fence.

Bessie drove down the fence away from the house. At the far end of the field, she got out, opened a gate and drove through. Sometimes the quickest way is the longest route. She drove straight toward the fire engines and pulled up behind the two chiefs.

She jumped out and shouted at Oakwood's Chief Wicks, "Back off! Chief Hallihan is in charge."

"Sorry, lady," Wicks said, looking around for a cop. "You don't belong here."

"It's my house," Bessie pointed out.

"And it's my job to see that the fire's out!"

"By chopping my house to pieces."

"Electrical fires in the walls require extreme measures."

"This wasn't an electrical fire," Bessie claimed.

"We can't take any chances."

"I pulled the fuses," Bessie declared. "After the inspection two days ago."

"Then it couldn't be the wiring," Chief Hallihan observed.

"There could still be hot spots," his Oakwood counterpart argued irritably.

Bessie turned to Chief Hallihan. "Can't you override him?"

"It's his jurisdiction."

Bessie's face fell and tears began to roll down her cheek, "My paintings?"

"The roof caught fire over the studio," Hallihan said. "I'm afraid there's probably a lot of water damage, to say nothing of heat damage. I doubt any are salvageable."

"Can you move them out to the barn?" Bessie asked. She saw Wicks scowl and decided to put forth an argument he'd understand. "My insurance company will reimburse me for every ruined canvas I can produce."

"That can wait," Wicks said. "I can't spare the men."

Hallihan studied the despair on the face of the devastated old lady.

"I don't need all my men to pack up. I can spare a few to remove the paintings," he offered politely.

Wicks shrugged, "Yeah, sure, why not?"

As Hallihan had predicted the canvases were smeared. Still Bessie had the men prop each up carefully, tears streaming down her face as she did so.

Hallihan stood beside her. She was so tiny, so fragile. Wicks could have been kinder. One of the firemen carried not only a canvas but her brushes. Another lugged her tool box and palette. Their chief had been specific that they were to bring her painting tools as well. He was a man of experience.

When his men were done, Hallihan patted Bessie on the shoulder. "I'm so sorry."

"It wasn't just an old house." she murmured. "It has been my home since I was born. All my memories are between those walls."

Chief Hallihan took the frail hand in his and when her eyes met his, asked, "Do you have a lawyer?"

"Yes, why?"
"Call him."
"Why?"
"Just do it."

Chapter 3

Back in Willow Glen, Aleta was sitting at her husband's desk staring at the single dollar bill when her husband walked through the door. To the amazement of her ex-boyfriend, a fellow lawyer in a large San Francisco law firm, Aleta had, in his estimation, chosen to marry a homely man and move to a nowhere place. Aleta saw the marriage as one to a superior man and the move as one toward freedom.

"Good day?" she grinned, knowing the answer.

Stanley's eyes were twinkling and she could see the corners of his mouth holding back a smile. She remembered their first meeting. She, fresh off the plane from California, walking into a house to straighten out a messy situation, had been embarrassed by being called upon to comment upon whether Stanley should have a nose job. The woman who'd put her on the spot was an idiot trying to verify her own excursions under the knife. Aleta's reply had startled the woman who had expected someone so tastefully dressed and sporting a model's face and figure to agree. Aleta, however, had disagreed saying that Stanley's face had character. Now she would say it had strength as well. The close-set eyes were penetrating and missed nothing.

"So why are you staring at that bill?" Stanley asked, quickly switching to her wave length.

"How would you like a little change of pace?"

"Into what?" Stanley asked.

"Eminent domain."

"Take on the government? No way!"

"How about criminal defense?"

"Double no way!"

"How about being second chair?"

"To whom? This is a one lawyer office," Stanley pointed out. "And I like it that way."

Aleta waved the dollar. Stanley frowned slightly.

"Whom did you agree I would represent?"

"Her name's Bessie Dobbins and she wants me, but she'll allow you to represent her until I pass the bar exam despite it being months away."

"This is a no-brainer, Aleta," Stanley said and immediately realized he shouldn't have said that. "But I'm jumping to conclusions. Tell me why you have decided I'm going to take her on."

"They burned down her house and destroyed her paintings," Aleta said.

"We'll find her a good attorney," Stanley said. "But why criminal charges?"

"Arson."

"Did they arrest her?"

"No, but Chief Hallihan told her to call her lawyer."

"What's he doing in Oakwood?"

"Isn't he the fire chief?" Aleta asked.

"Yes, in Arborville."

"He told her to watch out for Wicks. Is he a cop?"

"No, he's Oakwood's fire chief." Stanley frowned. "Something's going on. Where's Ed Ornstein's number?"

Aleta rattled it off without looking it up.

"You're just like your grandmother, aren't you?" Stanley commented, as he tapped in the number.

"Yes, my brain likes numbers too," Aleta rejoined. "Why are we calling Ed?"

"We know him. We trust him. And he's not on a case right now."

"I mean, why are we calling in a private investigator?"

"Because we need one on this."

"We need to talk. I have a couple of important things to… someone's coming," Aleta said. "I thought you didn't have any appointments until next week."

"I don't. Must be another Bessie Dobbins," he commented. "You handle him. I'll be in your office… Hello, Ed. I've got a case for you."

The connecting door shut softly and Aleta realized that because she couldn't hear him, he couldn't hear her. Why fear rode in on that observation, she didn't understand. Later she would say it was the heavy footfall on the stairs that gave her a sense of danger.

She opened her cell and punched in Chief Milani's private number. The footsteps hesitated outside her door.

"Tom Milani here," came the cheerful voice of Willow Glen's police chief.

"This is Aleta Locke… I mean Praetzel. Just listen."

Tom almost said, "I am," when he heard a rough voice demand. "Where's your boss."

"Who are you?" Aleta asked setting the open phone on the desk.

"Don't matter none," the rough voice said. "We came to warn him that he don't want Bessie Dobbins as a client."

"Mr. Praetzel is a children's advocate," Aleta responded.

"Well, then he sure don't want her," the rough voice sneered. "She ain't no kid."

Tom Milani dispatched two units to Praetzel's law office while listening to every word. This was so blatant.

Why didn't the mayor send someone over to smooth talk the lawyers? Why the strong arm tactics?

"I have nothing to say regarding whom Mr. Praetzel chooses to represent," Aleta stated matter-of-factly.

Suddenly, it dawned on Milani that these jerks thought they were scaring Praetzel's secretary.

"If I was you, Lady," came a second higher-pitched voice, "I'd find me another job. No job is worth your life."

"What do you mean?" Aleta asked, the twinge of fear in her voice real. "I don't understand."

"We thinks you should tell Mr. Praetzel that if he insists on being old lady Dobbin's legal eagle, you quit. Is that clear enough?"

"I can't do that," Aleta said stiffly. "That's not my place. But if you'll give me your names and phone numbers, I'll have Mr. Praetzel contact you as soon as he returns."

"Screw you!" the rough voice said. "You see this?"

"Yes, I do," Aleta said. "It's a gun in a holster. So what?"

The tremulous tone had suddenly hardened.

In his office across town, Chief Milani sucked in a lungful of air. Damn her! Didn't Aleta know she was playing with fire.

"So what?" charged the rough voice. "I'll show you so what."

The discharge blasted over the phone. Milani jumped.

"Hell, you shot her!" the high-pitched voice squeaked. "The mayor ain't gonna like this. We was just supposed to scare Praetzel off."

"Shut up!" the rough voice said. "I was scaring her. Who'd figure she'd try to protect that damn tank of fish. Who does that? The lady's crazy."

"She can finger us," the high-pitched voice squealed. "You gotta finish her."

A strong voice came from the doorway.

"Police! If you don't drop that gun, you're a dead man."

Milani heard the thump as the gun hit the floor. A second thump followed the first. Then he heard his officer arrest the pair. He kept listening. Protocol was followed to the letter. He had it all on tape.

Smart girl, that Aleta, Tom Milani thought and wondered briefly if she was a psychic like her grandmother. They say such abilities run in families.

Of course, Harriet Locke denied she was a psychic claiming she couldn't see past events at all. She insisted she was a prophet sent to change the future if her warnings were heeded. To date, Aleta had shown no predisposition toward seeing into the future or the past. Still, despite the generation gap, both women were cut from the same mold. Aleta was a younger version of her grandmother down to her uncanny ability to handle dogs.

Maybe Aleta was spooked because she was alone in the office, Milani thought. She certainly had good instincts. But what was Stanley doing with an eminent domain case? It wasn't his bailiwick.

Stanley's yell startled Milani. Where had he been?

"It was an accident," the rough voice blasted out. "I was shooting at the fish and she jumped in the way. That's one crazy secretary you got."

"We only wanted to scare her to tell you to drop old lady Dobbins. That's all," said the other voice as Stanley ran to where Aleta lay. The two were so rattled by the events they themselves had brought about that their tongues came immediately to their defense.

"An ambulance is on the way," Milani's officer said as Stanley knelt down beside his wife.

"How is she?"

The second officer leaning over her replied, "Looks like a flesh wound."

Stanley took her hand, deep concern pushing his voice into harshness, "Aleta, what were you thinking?"

"He was going to kill your fish," Aleta replied with uncharacteristic meekness.

Stanley's exasperation boiled over. "Aleta, burn this into your memory. Never, never try to save my fish again!"

Aleta grinned. At their wedding ceremony where both had made up their own vows, she'd promised to obey. It was the only promise she made. He already had won her heart and respect. For her, obedience was the ultimate gift.

"You love your fish," she argued weakly. "We lost your mother last time."

The fish tank had been shattered by the assassin's bullet which had skimmed along the center of her scalp. A second bullet had nicked Stanley's ear.

The two had scrambled to rescue the fish that had cascaded to the floor with the sudden onrush of water. The bright orange and white Koi had laid flopping helplessly on the soaked rug. Aleta and Stanley, both bloody but mobile, hurriedly transferred all the large Koi to the other tank and lost only the one named after Stanley's mother.

The other tank had been rebuilt with bulletproof glass as had the window overlooking the street, but the new drainage system for the aquarium hadn't been completed, so it had no water. This time there would have been no rescuing the fish.

"You will take the case, won't you?" Aleta asked.

He took her hand and kissed it gently. "You don't get me so easily. I tell you what I will do. I'll bring you material to study for the bar exam while you recuperate and reflect on your foolishness in wanting to take on an eminent domain case."

"What are you going to do about Bessie?"

"I'll recommend a good lawyer," Stanley said as the two in handcuffs were escorted from the room.

"Will you at least speak to her personally?"

"I'll call her."

"A phone call isn't personal."

"Later," he said, getting up as the paramedics entered the room.

"Now!" she ordered. "And bring me everything covering eminent domain."

"Later," he said. "I'll call Ed and have him tell Bessie what happened here."

Aleta relaxed a bit. Stanley was beginning to think about Bessie. With him that was step one.

Chapter 4

Ed Ornstein, a short, rotund, balding man, was never taken seriously. And the fact that he took his dog with him wherever he went made him seem even less professional. Casualness disguised a sharp mind, and his perceptiveness was enhanced by his dog's reactions to people. Emma sorted out the good and the bad with a whiff. People used to tell him that she just instinctively sensed those that liked dogs; but, Ed believed it was more than that.

Emma had liked Aleta's grandmother, Harriet Locke, the second she walked into Ed's San Jose, California office. Harriet had petted the little black Lab on the head and ruffled her ears gently. That gesture alone won Ed over.

"Martha Cook referred you," she had said. "You did some work for a friend of hers."

"Here in California," Ed had clarified, knowing that Martha Cook lived in northern Illinois.

"Will you travel?"

"I ain't never ventured very far."

"I need someone to accompany my granddaughter to Illinois and help her."

"I'm not a bodyguard service."

Harriet had snapped, "I know that. I need you to investigate."

"Investigate what?" Ed had asked, prepared to turn her down. No family stuff was worth leaving home for.

"There's danger involve," Harriet said, sensing that the man was withdrawing from the project. "Two of my friends are in trouble. I'm sending Aleta along as the Tontine's lawyer. There will be another lawyer at the other end that will work with her; however, Martha didn't know a single private detective. She said the police are quite competent, but I need to find out who's threatening my friends."

"Threaten? How?"

"This morning I shot a man to death. He'd come to kill me."

Ed's interest had perked up the minute he realized how serious this could be.

"So what does this have to do with your friends in Illinois?"

"We are all members of a large trust fund—a Tontine," Harriet had explained. "If you will take the case, I'll tell you more."

Ed had taken the case and flown to Illinois with Aleta. Emma had come along as part of the deal. Harriet, whose dog had held the intruder at bay, understood a man's bond with his dog. She had one with her large male Chessie.

The Illinois trip proved to be a turning point in his life. He'd fallen in love with one of the Tontine members, all of whom showed dogs as a hobby. It was their common bond. Beatrice bred Scotties. Emma had taken to Beatrice instantly. The four Scotties loved the gentle black Lab and so Ed proposed.

When one of his operatives, Dean Lundgren, had agreed to move, Ed moved his office, which consisted of one of the most sophisticated computer set-ups of any P.I. on the West Coast, to a small bungalow located behind an abandoned gas station in a tiny cluster of old homes next to a railroad line that had been abandoned. With its abandonment went the tiny town's last hope of growth. The county fire department kept the ancient tavern company on what had been destined to be the main street.

Dean liked the location. He could hang around with the fire boys and belt down a few at the tavern. What more could a man want, especially a gay man?

When Stanley's phone call came, Ed climbed into his car and called Dean, whom he told to approach from the south while he approached from the north. It was an information gathering foray. Each was armed with miniature cameras and tape recorders. They'd be late on the scene; but, sometimes when everything was winding down good bits of info could be had.

Ed, with his dog Emma, obviously pregnant, traipsed across Bessie's field straight toward the barn. Officer Kirk Boyes saw him but assumed he was a neighbor out walking his dog.

Ed entered the barn. Bessie was startled by the sight of a stranger with a very bloated black dog. Ed pulled his cap from his head and the dog, panting from the exertion of crossing the field, lay down at his side.

"Excuse me, Miss Dobbins," Ed said politely. "Stanley Praetzel told me to tell you that Aleta was shot."

He spoke so matter-of-factly that it took several seconds before the words penetrated.

"Was she hurt bad?"

"Not too bad. Could've been, but wasn't. He says she's gonna stay in bed while she researches your case."

"So her husband is going to represent me?"

"Mr. Praetzel said that would depend on what Aleta turns up in her research."

"I must go see her," Bessie determined. "I'll take one of these. It'll be a promise to paint her one like it when I can. Which one do you think she'd like?"

Ed looked at the paintings scattered around the barn.

"Don't matter. They're all good. Can I buy one?" He pointed to one. "That one."

"I don't need charity," Bessie huffed.

"I ain't offering any," Ed said. "I hear you get a couple thousand a painting. Ain't that so?"

"It's ruined!" Bessie exclaimed.

"I like it. Two thousand be a fair price? I don't wanna gyp you."

"But you want me to fix it, right?" Bessie muttered. "As if I could."

"It's perfect just like it is."

"What is it you see?" Bessie asked, puzzled.

"We got a deal?" Ed asked.

"Yes, but you're paying too much."

"I never pay too much for anything," Ed retorted.

Bessie pondered his statement as she stared at the painting. Finally she agreed.

Ed smiled.

"Good. Now I'll get to work."

"Doing what exactly?"

"I'm a private investigator," Ed explained.

"And who's paying for your services?"

"I imagine they'll be included in Praetzel's bill," Ed said evenly.

"I'm not a wealthy woman," Bessie said.

"I know exactly what you're worth," Ed told her. "You can afford me."

"You pried?" Bessie croaked.

"That's what I do," Ed replied. "I have local references if you want any."

"I don't know many people," Bessie said. "You could rattle off a number of names and I probably wouldn't know any of them."

Ed punched in a number on his speed dial and handed the phone to Bessie Dobbins.

"Martha Cook here," came the crackly voice over the phone.

"Bessie Dobbins, here," the startled woman returned. Recovering she asked, "What do you know about Ed Ornstein?"

"He has my private number. Only half a dozen people have that."

That said it all as far as Bessie was concerned. Martha was as private a person as she and they both were old-timers in the area.

"Let me talk with Mr. Ornstein, please," Martha said.

Bessie handed over the phone. She listened to the short tubby man's half of the conversation.

"Please don't be angry. We got some bad shit going down. Aleta was shot an hour ago... Yes, Stanley's with her. It happened at their office. I don't have all the details, but it has something to do with the Bessie Dobbins case... Yes, I know... Thank you... Yes, I'll tell her."

"Tell me what?" Bessie said.

"That we are artists in our field and deserve just compensation."

"Does she think I'll quibble?"

"She knows you will. So do I. It's your nature. I see it in the original painting underneath the damage."

"That's evident in my work?" Bessie queried discomforted.

"It's not a negative," Ed said kindly. "It's just a statement of fact. You're careful."

"Quibble," Bessie said, chewing on the word.

Ed switched topics. He was evidently hired.

"Tell me how you think the fire started."

"Someone set it."

"Not you?"

Bessie looked genuinely shocked. "Me? Never! I love that house. I need to be completely relaxed to paint well. My house gives me that."

"An accident?"

"When the fire inspector told me my wiring could short out and start a fire, I thought about my house and my paintings. I asked him what I could do that very moment to prevent a fire. He said the only sure way was to remove all the fuses and go without electricity until the wiring was redone. So I did."

"No heat?"

"I have a fireplace."

"Cooking?"

"I used my grandmother's wood stove to heat water," Bessie said. "And I didn't leave a fire going in either when I left the house."

"Where did you go?"

"To hire Aleta Praetzel to represent me."

"You mean Stanley."

"No. He represents children. I wanted Aleta. Some stupid Illinois law says she can represent corporations but not me," Bessie explained. "I told her Stanley could fill in until she got her license. This take-over has been going on for months. I figure we can delay it some more."

"Stanley agreed to do that?"

"She took my money," Bessie said, "but I never expected her to get hurt. I suppose the man who shot her got away."

"There were two. They were caught in the act."

Bessie's shock exploded as a single word, "How?"

"You hired yourself one sharp attorney," Ed said. He looked down at his dog.

"Come on, Emma, we got work to do."

Ed went into the garage turned studio first. Only the skylight in the roof gave evidence from the outside that this wasn't a garage.

He shivered slightly as the cool October air settled down upon him from the hole in the roof. The still wet floor added dampness to the chill.

He took pictures of the heaters sitting in various locations, their cords neatly tucked on top of each. Even with the fuses pulled, she was taking no chances.

He entered the house through the door to the kitchen. Emma puffed up the two steps behind him. Quickly he snapped photos of the kitchen and most of the living room Then Emma's growl warned him to palm his tiny camera. The shout that came a second later was expected,

"What the hell are you doing here?"

"Just looking around," Ed said casually. "Some fire, huh?"

"Who the hell are you?"

"Name's Ed. I told Bessie I'd come in and see if you guys left anything intact. She's too upset to come see herself."

"This is still a fire scene!"

"You don't need to yell. I didn't touch nothing."

The fire chief took a step toward Ed, and Emma growled. She bared her teeth and moved toward the man who was yelling.

"That dog gonna bite me?" Wicks charged, taking a step back.

"She don't like your attitude," Ed said. "She's pregnant. Makes her touchy."

"If you don't get the hell outta here, I'll have you arrested and that damned dog taken to the pound."

Ed called to Emma, "Come on, Girl. Let's go."

"Whoa!" Chief Wicks said. "Why are you coming this way?"

"Front door's the quickest way out. Emma won't bite you unless you touch me."

"Go!" Chief Wicks yelled, stepping back, "Just get the hell outta here."

Ed left the house and headed straight toward Wicks's crew. "You guys saved the house. That must've been some battle.

"We weren't here first," one of the younger firemen said. "Arborville's crew did most of the saving."

"Shut up!" hissed an older man.

"What? What did I say? It's the truth, ain't it?"

"Why is there so much damage?" Ed asked the young man who'd spoken first.

"Checking for hot spots in the wall," the young man replied. "That's a real danger with electrical fires."

"So, bad wiring caused the fire?"

"Yeah," the young fire fighter said. "It's the usual cause in these old houses."

"Gonna take a lot of fixing to get this house livable again."

"Oh, nobody's gonna live in it. It was gonna be torn down anyways."

"So why save it?"

"We weren't saving it. It was the trees we were saving."

"And the old lady's stuff," chimed in the older man.

"Good reasons!" Ed said as he stepped back and shot the crew working with the half-burned house as background. Those shots would pinpoint the time the first photos were taken. Years of court appearances had taught him that much.

Emma had growled at the Chief Wicks. That meant Wicks was giving off the same vibes as someone with something to hide. The fact that he was too busy inside the house to chase Ed away from his crew added to Ed's suspicion.

Stanley was right. This needed investigating.

Chapter 5

A couple hours later Bessie showed up at the hospital, and Aleta gave permission for her to visit.

The little old woman entered with a large leather case. "I got something for you. I'm sorry you were hurt on account of me. I didn't think they'd do that."

"Aleta can't represent you," Stanley said firmly, "but I can recommend several attorneys who specialize in eminent domain cases."

"They don't want to touch my case," Bessie said. "No chance of winning, they said. Nobody gets their land back. All they could do was get me more compensation. I don't want compensation. I want to keep my home—even though most of the house is now burned down. It's still my home. The trees are still there. I can rebuild the house."

"But why Aleta?"

"Cause she's sweet," Bessie said, "and she's not afraid of a fight. I need a really smart lawyer. I want someone who can help me keep my land."

"I thought you were in the assessment phase," Stanley said.

"Yes, that's where we are alright."

"It's pretty much over, I think," Stanley observed matter-of-factly.

"Hey, do you treat the kids you represent this way? Do you tell them there's no hope or do you keep fighting for what they need."

"This isn't a case of need…," Stanley began.

Bessie's eyes lit up. "You're wrong! It is! I can't paint anywhere else. It's not just my home they're taking away. It's my life."

"Fighting city hall is a waste of money," Stanley finished a bit lamely.

"Fighting city hall is always a waste of money, but sometimes it's got to be done," Bessie proclaimed. "Government has got to be accountable for the killing it does."

Stanley shrugged. He and Aleta would talk later. They were not taking the case.

"Can I see the painting?" Aleta asked.

"Sure," Bessie said unzipping the case and pulling out the canvas. "If you like it, I'll repaint it for you."

"Why?" Aleta breathed, taken by the uniqueness of the work.

"What do you mean 'why'? This one's ruined. You don't think I would apologize with a damaged piece of art, do you?"

"But it's perfect!"

Bessie scowled. "I don't need you to pretend to like it. I will paint another."

"How do we frame it?" Aleta asked. "I'm not good at that sort of thing."

"Frame it?" Bessie gasped. "You can't hang it up!"

"Of course, I can hang it up. You gave it to me."

"I said I'd paint you another," Bessie said setting the canvas back into the large leather carrying case.

"I don't want another!" Aleta said. "Stanley, buy it for me. Your mother can help me find a frame."

Stanley recognized a decisiveness in his wife's tone that was best not to argue with. He could well afford the painting.

"Mother paid five thousand for hers," Stanley said.

"Ed just paid me two for one of these," Bessie murmured.

"He got a bargain," Aleta said. "Ed is one sharp cookie. Don't you see how great this one is?"

Bessie shook her head.

"It's like looking through a window on a day when the rain is coming down so hard it sheets down the pane and outside it's all blurry and misty. And the water on the pane takes the colors from outside and drags them down. You caught that moment."

Bessie set the painting on the arms of the chair and stepped back and looked at it.

"The frame could act as the window frame," she said pensively.

"You've got to move the paintings off your property!" Aleta said suddenly.

"Whatever for?"

"I have a bad feeling," Aleta said. "Stanley, she could store them in our barn, couldn't she?"

"Well, er, yes…but, Aleta, are you sure?"

"About the barn? You don't think they'd be safe there?"

"No. I mean, are you sure about your feeling?"

"It's not just instinct," Aleta said. "We're dealing with violent people. It's insurance."

"I think my paintings will be safe enough," Bessie said.

"Please do it my way," Aleta begged. "I need time to research the glimmer of an idea I have; but, you need to move those paintings."

Stanley, seeing how agitated Aleta was, turned to the old woman and said softly, "I can't explain why this is so important to my wife; but, if you do this, I will represent you in court until she is licensed."

"Seems a bit foolish to me," Bessie said. "But, I'll arrange for them to be moved tomorrow."

Surprisingly, it was Stanley who objected to waiting.

"Ed's wife has a van. He can start transporting the paintings tonight. There'll be no paper trail so that should keep them safe for a while. You can bunk with Aleta's grandmother tonight. She lives in an RV on our property. You'll only be a stone's throw from your paintings. How does that sound?"

"I don't like owing," Bessie said a tad sourly.

"It's quid pro quo," Stanley said. "If you do what my wife asks, she'll relax and sleep well. We'll be even."

Bessie smiled. "Okay, then, I'll do it."

The Tri City Register's newest reporter, Justin Conway, waited until both visitors were in the elevator before entering Aleta's room.

Aleta half-recognized the tall black man. "Where do I know you from?"

"I'm the reporter who interviewed you after you won Best in Show."

Aleta nodded remembering. "I liked your story. You write well."

The man grinned broadly showing an even set of straight teeth.

"I know. So how about another interview?"

"Sure, why not?"

"Who shot you?"

"I don't know their names, but they were arrested."

"So they were strangers?"

"They thought I was Stanley's secretary."

"Is that a dangerous job?" he quipped.

"Not until today, it wasn't," she rejoined.

"What made today different?"

"They wanted me to tell Stanley not to take on a certain client."

"What client?"

Aleta just smiled.

"Okay," Justin backed up. "How badly were you hurt?"

"I won't be using my left arm for a couple weeks at least. It'll hamper my winning another Best in Show." Aleta smiled.

The young reporter however brushed aside her comment and focused on the shooting. "Did the men tell you who they were working for?"

"They mentioned a person by title only," Aleta replied.

"A government official?"

Again Aleta was silent.

Justin pressed on.

"Is Bessie Dobbins your client?"

"I'm a House attorney and I only represent the people in the Tontine. I'm not licensed to represent anyone else."

"Wasn't she just here?"

"She brought me a painting," Aleta said, pointing at the chair in the corner.

Justin glanced over and his eyes stayed fixed on the painting. "That's not her usual style."

"No, it's not. I like it. What do you think?"

"Much more impressive," Justin commented as he walked over for a closer look. He whipped out his tiny digital camera and snapped a shot of the painting.

Before Aleta could object, Justin snapped out, "So your husband is taking on the Oakwood city council, huh?"

"I didn't say that," Aleta said emphatically. "And I suggest you don't speculate. If you do, however, you need to do it in the form of a question in order to save us both a court appearance."

"Thanks for the tip."

"I want you to be on my side. I plan to use you."

"I wish you knew something about the fire at Bessie's place."

"It was arson."

"Rumor has it that it was the wiring."

"All the fuses were removed by the fire inspector at Bessie's request."

"So the wires couldn't have shorted."

"She told the fire chief that the fuses were pulled. Wicks still sent in his men to chop into the walls that hadn't been touched by the fire. It was unnecessary."

Justin's eyebrows went up. His voice stayed even.

"So who set the fire?" he asked.

"Someone who evidently wanted Bessie Dobbins out of her house permanently."

"But why would the city council burn her out when they'd already won in court?"

"Good question," Aleta agreed. "It appears someone else has an agenda."

Chapter 6

Later that same day, Aleta was awakened from her nap by the gentle touch of her grandmother's hand.

"Where's Stanley?" Aleta asked, slightly worried.

"Helping Bessie arrange her paintings. She's planning on asking an art critic out to view her work," Harriet Locke said. "She has rearranged them three times so far."

"So, Ed managed to transport them all."

"Lyle West helped," Harriet Locke said. "So did Madge. Having friends with vans is important sometimes."

"But Grams, Lyle's the Arborville Chief of Police? He didn't go in uniform, did he?"

Harriet nodded. "Lauren told Lyle that no one would stop the others if he was there."

Aleta pointed at the chair in the corner. Perched on the arms was her painting. "Isn't it lovely?"

"It is indeed," Harriet agreed. She took her granddaughter's hand and her face sobered. "Why did you tell Bessie to move her paintings?"

"Just a gut feeling?"

"Why did you call Milani? He got every word on tape, you know."

"A premonition."

"I didn't get one, you realize," Harriet said. "I haven't had one in a while."

"How long a while?"

"Since I asked God to let me out of the prophet business."

"And you think He did?"

"I'm hoping He didn't choose you as my successor."

Aleta patted her grandmother's hand. "Don't worry. I've always had good instincts. I was worried that if whoever did this to Bessie realized she had assets left they might come after them. That's all. Just reasoning. Nothing supernatural. As for calling Milani, the footsteps were heavy. No one was supposed to be coming up those stairs. We were closed for repairs to the office. No appointments were scheduled until next week. I admit I was jumpy, but I figured Milani would understand considering all that happened in August. If it had turned out to be nothing, I would have apologized and he would have been nice about it."

"If nothing else, moving Bessie made her feel less alone," Harriet observed, relieved.

"Did Stanley send any material with you?"

"A briefcase full," Harriet said.

"Isn't he coming tonight?"

"He gave Bessie your bed, so he's either sleeping on the couch or here," Harriet said.

"Why'd he do that?"

"My dogs make her nervous."

"It's so odd to have a non-dog owner as a client," Aleta said.

"No left arm means you won't be showing dogs for a couple of months," Harriet pointed out.

"Months?" Aleta breathed in sharply. "I was thinking in terms of weeks."

"You need to let that arm heal."

"What'll I do about George Sciretta? He's been waiting until I finished with my honeymoon to show Maggie for him."

"Hasn't Tom Wilson been showing her?"

"Maggie's been pouting. She thinks she has a vote in this."

"Tom' will get her over of that," Harriet said. "He just needs a little time. Look we'll all miss you; but, we'll manage."

Aleta smiled wryly.

"Considering how my shoulder feels, you guys won't be the only ones missing me."

Stanley arrived two hours after Harriet left. When he came in carrying Aleta's favorite food, he found her asleep and the briefcase unopened. He set down the food and sat beside her bed and watched her breathe evenly and peacefully.

He hated that she'd been hurt. He'd hated leaving her for a moment; but, she'd been insistent that he help Bessie. He couldn't get over how concerned Aleta had become for the welfare of an old lady she didn't know. There was nothing to do but support his wife until she was able to carry her cases alone. He wondered if that time would ever come.

He shrugged imperceptibly. It was more of an inner shrug. It didn't matter if she messed up his orderly life as long as she remained a part of it. Her unpredictability was part of her attraction. Just when he thought he understood what moved her, something came along to show him she had an intricate mesh of switches in her brain.

He lay his head on the bed near her hand and took her hand in his. The rhythm of her breathing soothed him. He closed his eyes.

Aleta awoke several hours later. Before she opened her eyes, she felt a hand holding hers and knew she wasn't alone.

He'd come as promised. That thought came as a comfort she didn't even realize she needed.

Independence had been the life choice she'd thought she wanted as the cornerstone of her life; but, now that she tasted interdependence, she realized it was a better life goal.

She eased her hand from Stanley's grasp and would have tried to get out of bed had the nurse not entered the room to check on her. Thus Aleta had the tray moved nearer and the briefcase set upon it without disturbing Stanley's head which was resting against her thigh.

The nurse asked if she wanted a bed moved into the room; but, Aleta declined the offer.

"He won't use it," she said.

After the nurse left, Aleta pulled sets of papers from the briefcase and began to read.

There were newspaper articles, and editorials in the Tri City Register denouncing the abuse of the eminent domain procedure in general and condemnation of Oakwood's takeover of Bessie Dobbins' farm in particular.

Bessie's fight to stay unincorporated had resulted in her having no voice in the Oakwood city council's decision-making regarding the taking of her property. The strongest written opposition came from a city council member, Phillip Fleming who answered every editorial and letter with an written argument. Mayor Basil Liston was his verbal counterpart.

Aleta paused over the records of the public hearings of which there were five. The first two were well-attended and Bessie Dobbins' supporters were many. The number dwindled markedly by the fourth public hearing. At the fifth the council deemed it safe enough to call for a "resolution of necessity".

By then the Dobbins' case was more of a nuisance than a cause. Her supporters had returned to their everyday lives, resigned that "you can't beat city hall."

The resolution of necessity which was the city council's formal decision to acquire property by eminent domain passed unanimously. They then went to court.

The court documents showed that her property was being taken for public use which the council defined vaguely as economic development.

According to the documents Aleta was reviewing, the courts seldom found against the agency acquiring property by this method unless a technical procedure hadn't been followed. In such a case, the agency could always start over; therefore, arguing procedural errors didn't win more than a delay.

As Aleta perused the material, she remembered that the California eminent domain statutes had what was loosely termed a "goodwill" section that allowed special consideration for any business that would be irreparably harmed by relocation.

She remembered that Bessie had argued in the public hearings how necessary her home was to her as an artist. It could be reargued in court if Illinois, like California, allowed for that aspect to be considered.

It was two hours later when she moaned, "They've won."

Stanley stirred. "Who won?"

"The public despots."

Stanley didn't open his eyes when he murmured, "They always win. Absolute power…"

The words provoked Aleta. She withdrew her leg and let Stanley's head bounce on the mattress. It was a slight bounce, but the withdrawal was abrupt.

"How can you be mad about the definition of a word?" he said in his most reasonable half-awake tone.

"Don't change the subject!"

"What subject?"

"You know what subject."

Stanley, by now, was completely awake and aware that his wife was steaming. Aleta not angry could be difficult; Aleta, angry, was impossible. His eyes saw the mess of papers on the bed and realized she'd been deeply involved in Bessie Dobbins' case for hours. He'd never catch up.

"Exactly which despots are we angry with—the city council, the mayor, the fire chief, the U.S. government, the President or the Supreme Court?"

"The Illinois State Legislature!" she stormed. "They wrote an eminent domain law with no heart in it."

"I thought all eminent domain laws were heartless," Stanley countered, knowing full well that California's wasn't or she wouldn't have brought it up.

"There's no 'goodwill' provision!"

"What's that?"

"The peg we could hang our win on."

"Oh," Stanley murmured. "The case is in court. City governments never lose such cases. The only thing that's argued is compensation. Isn't their offer fair?"

"It's low," Aleta admitted, "but Bessie isn't in this for the money. She wants her home back."

"You know what I don't understand," Stanley put in thoughtfully, "is why muck up with a done deal?"

Aleta jumped on his thought. "They had to know that threatening you could be construed by the court as illegal interference, same as a bribe, and throw the verdict Bessie's way."

"So why do it?"

"It isn't as if some great arguments haven't been offered up in recent cases; but, the courts don't seem to even listen," Aleta said angrily sweeping the papers off her bed.

"As I said, so why threaten me?"

"They followed every procedure to the letter," Aleta went on, her anger unabated, but more controlled. Reason was taking over. "Bessie's hiring me… er, us… er you was an act of desperation. They must have known that. Why not just sweeten the pot with a better offer to save the trouble of a court battle?"

"Does the mayor strike you as stupid?"

"I don't know him."

"Well he's a slick political opportunist who is using his office for two purposes—to make money and to gain power. And he's accomplishing both quickly. He's a smart man."

"So sending hoods to threaten us is not something he would do."

"Not when it wasn't necessary. Brilliant as I may be as a child advocate, I'd bungle an eminent domain case. He's got two lawyers on the city council who would have told him that."

"So he didn't send the shooters," Aleta said. "But since they said he did, couldn't we ask for a continuance until we find out who's behind this?"

"I would think so. The courts don't like it when lawyers are threatened and their wives are shot."

"Who burned down Bessie's house?" Aleta asked.

"Not the mayor. No reason," Stanley answered.

"Not even to frame Bessie?"

"Whatever for? He's already won in everyone's eyes but Bessie's. In fact, it's the last thing he would do. Her home destroyed will garner up new sympathy for her. People don't think moving is a tragedy, but having all your possessions destroyed is another matter. Basil Liston wouldn't make that mistake."

"Someone trying to discredit him might," Aleta suggested.

"There's one more possibility," Stanley said thoughtfully. "What if someone just wanted Bessie to be unable to live in it for a while?"

"When she lost her case, she'd have to move."

"But if the land was turned over to a developer, what's the first thing he'd do?"

"Dig," Aleta replied. Then she smirked. "So you think there's a dead body buried there or a chest of gold?"

"That's not my idea."

"Then what is?" Aleta asked, now completely baffled.

Stanley grinned. "It's you who have an active imagination. I love to watch your brain work."

"Well, it's getting angry right now," Aleta warned. "I'd tread carefully."

"I have no idea who is doing this or why," Stanley confessed, "but I say we ask the police to investigate."

"And we ask for a continuance."

"And talk with Bessie."

Why?"

"With her house destroyed, she may not want to live there anymore."

"I know she will. You aren't getting off the hook that easily."

The nurse poked her head into the room. "You made the five o'clock news."

She flicked on the TV set and Aleta watched herself trotting around the ring with Evelyn's Golden Retriever, Topaz.

"It's my Best in Show win, they're showing," Aleta exclaimed. "Call Grams. Tell her to record it."

Stanley was on the phone when the station displayed footage of Aleta being carried out of Stanley's office on a stretcher.

"She can skip the stretcher part," Aleta noted aloud.

"She's going to catch it next newscast," Stanley reported. He turned back to the broadcast.

The reporter had shoved a microphone in the face of one of the handcuffed men and asked him why he shot Aleta Praetzel.

"Don't know who that is," the man said in a rough voice. "I was shooting at the fish tank, so's the secretary would take us serious and she jumped in front of the bullet."

"You shot Stanley Praetzel's wife," the reporter informed him.

"You hear that, Scotty," the smaller man said. "We're in big trouble now."

"You just shut up. It was an accident."

"We wasn't paid enough!" the smaller man complained.

"Shut the hell up!" Scotty roared.

That ended the interview but the newscaster had more information. The story was repeated every half hour and each report put a slightly different spin on it. By the seven o'clock news, Bessie Dobbins, her house, her fight with the city council and the fire were all tied into the shooting.

Stanley and Aleta watched every newscast until it was time for Stanley to leave for home. He had three juvenile cases in the morning.

"What about Bessie's case?" Aleta said.

"I'll get the continuance. Don't worry. Just rest."

Aleta used the remote for the bed to flatten it and, as she lay back, she closed her eyes. She didn't intend to sleep; but, her body didn't give her the choice.

Chapter 7

Her first dreams were pleasant ones. When she awoke she knew this for a fact although she hadn't the vaguest idea what any of them were about. Feeling pleasantly warmed by them, she reached for the newspaper and noted that it was today's date; however it was the Tri City Register which was an afternoon paper. Surely, she hadn't slept that long.

The nurse came in. "Ready for your bath?" she asked.

"What time is it?"

"Quarter to ten."

"Just bring me soap and a towel. I can bathe myself."

"Not a good idea. We don't want to strain that shoulder."

The nurse went into the bathroom to fill the basin with warm water.

Aleta glanced at the paper and this time her eyes widened with surprise. The headline read "Car Bomb Kills Mayor Liston."

She scanned the article quickly, then checked the paper's date. It was today's paper.

Suddenly, the date changed, and it was a week later. Boy Slain by Mother was the new headline. Again she scanned the article. She could hear the nurse turn off the water in the bathroom.

The date changed again, and there was a photo of Bessie Dobbins' smiling face.

Aleta began to read, "The city council has decided not to exercise the city's right to seize her farm under the eminent domain provision in the law. Her lawyers have successfully argued…"

The paper was plucked from her hand.

"Wait!" Aleta cried. "I was reading something important."

"I'll just put it over here," the nurse said. "Boy, this is an old one. I'll get you this morning's Chicago Trib."

"I want to finish that article," Aleta insisted.

But the nurse determined that old news could wait. She chatted cheerfully as she bathed the young woman. Aleta, her mind puzzling over what she had read, grappled with what steps she should take.

She couldn't call the mayor. He'd think she was behind the bomb if there even was a bomb.

Maybe it's just my imagination enjoying a fanciful solution to the Dobbins' mess; she thought. But if that's the case, why did I see the headline about the boy?

She remembered the article about the boy's death vividly. Four-year-old Kevin McCarran had been smothered by his mother because he wouldn't stop crying. Just a week before the court had awarded her custody because the boy had testified that his father abused him.

The child's lawyer, Stanley Praetzel, said the child was adamant about staying with his mother. Kevin vividly described the bruises he still had from his father beating him. There was hospital documentation that the child had suffered a broken arm and leg in the past year. The boy said his father had hit him.

The mother had backed the child's story. The father was held over on child abuse charges and the boy went home with his mother.

Neighbors reported that the child had screamed several times on the day of his death. Two of the neighbors had called the Oakwood police; but, no units had responded according to the neighbors.

Police Chief Herbert Ramage had refused to comment.

The coroner reported that both the boy's legs had been recently broken.

Aleta remembered that her husband was in court this morning with three cases. One of them could be the custody hearing for Kevin McCarran. She reached for the phone beside her bed and called her husband's beeper. She typed in the message "Kevin lying."

Stanley checked his beeper when it vibrated. He did so surreptitiously as he was in the middle of the McCarran custody battle.

He had no idea who sent the message; but, his instinct told him to believe it. Four-year-olds rarely dared to accuse an abusing parent in open court. In fact, they sometimes accused the opposite parent because they were too afraid to tell the truth. The non-abusive parent wouldn't punish them.

The mother's lawyer had put Kevin on the stand to confirm the mother's story. The father's lawyer had declined to cross-examine the young child.

The judge was about to excuse the child when Stanley stood up and asked permission to address his client. No one objected.

"You have done very well," Stanley said. "I'm proud of you. You didn't forget a single thing you were told to say."

The young boy nodded almost imperceptibly.

"It's scary up here, isn't it?"

The boy nodded.

"Remember what I told you about nodding?"

"Yes," the boy said. "I remember."

"When you broke your arm and leg it hurt a lot, didn't it?"

"Yes."

"What did the doctors do?"

"Fixed them."

"How?"

"Put a cast on."

"Did anybody sign your cast?"

The boy looked puzzled, so Stanley elaborated. "Write their name on it?"

The boy shook his head. Stanley waited and the boy realized he needed to talk.

"No," he said. "Mommy wanted it to stay clean."

"So, you had to be careful."

Kevin nodded.

"Use words, Kevin," Stanley said gently again.

"Yes. I had to sit still all the time."

"No playing?"

"I watched TV."

"That doesn't sound so bad," Stanley said. "Did you have snacks?"

"No. They're messy."

"So when did you eat?"

"When Daddy fed me."

The mother's counsel objected. Stanley was ready. Quietly, he asked the judge for a little time.

"I'm talking to a four-year-old in a courtroom, Your Honor. One can't rush this."

"Go on," the judge ordered. "No more interruption by either counsel."

"It was the hand that you used to eat with that was in the cast, right?"

"Yes. It was broke."

"But it was hard to get dressed with only one arm."

"Daddy dressed me."

"Who took you potty?"

"Daddy."

"What about during the day?"

"I holded it."

"Long time, huh?"

"Uh-huh."

"Is that a yes?"

"Yes."

"Now tell me what your Mommy said to tell the doctor about how you broke your arm."

"She said to say I fell down the stairs."

"And you did that, didn't you?"

"Yes."

"You are such a good boy for obeying your mother."

"Sometimes I'm bad."

"We want to talk about when you were good, okay?"

"Okay."

"Your Mommy said to tell a different story to me, didn't she?"

"Yes."

"So you obeyed your Mommy again, didn't you?"

"Yes."

"She wanted everyone to know you didn't fall, didn't she?"

"Yes."

"You obeyed again," Stanley said. "You are such a good boy."

"I did it right, Mommy, didn't I?" Kevin said looking toward his mother. Stanley quickly blocked Kevin's line of sight before he saw the angry scowl on his mother's face.

"Yes, you did, Kevin," Stanley hastened to assure the child

The boy settled back into the seat taking comfort in the words of the man who had so many fish in his wall.

Stanley went on. "When you had to go potty and your daddy was at work, did you ask your mommy to help you?"

"Yes."

"Why did she say no?"

"Because I was a bad boy. She said mommies don't help bad boys."

"Was it your fault your leg broke?"

"Yes."

"What did you do to make your mommy mad?"

"I runned away."

"Why did you run away."

" I was scared."

"Why were you scared?"

"I knocked over her bottle of stuff. And Mommy gets mad if I run away."

"What does she do when she gets mad?"

"She hits me."

"With her hand?"

The young boy shook his head.

"Does she always use the bat?" Stanley asked quietly.

"Not always," Kevin whispered. "Sometimes…"

Suddenly, a look of terror washed across his face.

"I love you, Mommy!" Kevin cried trying desperately to look past Stanley at his mother's face.

"Judge, may I remove the child from the courtroom," Stanley asked.

"Permission granted."

Stanley gathered Kevin in his arms and carried him, sobbing, through the courtroom doors.

At the time Stanley was questioning the young child, back in the hospital Aleta called the Oakwood police and asked to speak with Chief Ramage. The dispatcher asked her on what business.

"I've just received a tip that a bomb has been planted in Mayor Liston's car," Aleta said.

The dispatcher put her through.

Over the phone came the harsh voice of the pot-bellied gray-haired head of the Oakwood police department. He wasn't only old, he was sloppy and lazy.

"Chief Ramage here. You say you gotta tip? From who?"

"That doesn't matter. What matters is that I have a tip that there's a bomb attached to the mayor's car."

"Look, Lady, I ain't scaring the mayor without knowing who gimme the tip."

"Just check it out!" Aleta said and hung up.

The inquiry had been reasonable; but the tone had been abusive. It had scared Aleta.

Her stomach churned. She hadn't done the job. She debated calling again; but, couldn't bring herself to do so.

She sat back and tried to calm herself. She'd tried. She'd told two people. On top of that, she remembered the third headline had shown Bessie getting her property back. With the mayor gone, maybe the project had folded. That was a good result, wasn't it?

Her brain reminded her that even if the mayor had been killed, the developers wouldn't abandoned the project. The argument presented in court had been the telling factor. She wished she could have seen what argument it was. If it was based on the major being behind the shooting at their law office, then his death would preclude him from denying he was behind the attack and that might give them the winning argument.

What if it were Stanley and not the mayor in danger her mind asked. She pushed the question aside. An unbidden response crowded in.. If it were Stanley, she wouldn't quit trying to help.

Why did God have to complicate things? Saving one's enemy was something holy people did. She wasn't holy.

It's one thing to act kindly toward someone you hate. It's another to put yourself on the line for them. She'd be labeled a crazy woman. Or worse, yet, she'd be held accountable for the bomb. And why not? Revenge is one of the oldest motives in the world. It was too much to ask.

Her mind wouldn't let go. Eventually, she came upon a reasonable compromise. She didn't check with God because He might object.

She called Chief Lyle West.

"How are you doing?" he asked with obvious concern.

"Fine. Fine," she rejoined. "Something important has come up. I need your help."

"Go on," he said gently.

"I have a tip that there's a bomb planted in Mayor Liston's car that will go off at ten twenty-five unless something is done."

"Where'd you come up with this tip?"

"You wouldn't believe me if I told you."

"Try me," Lyle urged.

"I read it in today's paper," Aleta said. "Only today's paper hasn't been published yet."

"You're right. I don't believe you," Lyle said flatly. "You are in the hospital, after all, and pain medications can do funny things to a brain."

"How much trouble would it be to check it out?"

"For me, a lot. That's Ramage's jurisdiction. We don't cross lines."

"I called him. He says he won't scare the mayor for no reason!"

"I could call him," West said. "He might listen to me."

"Can you keep me out of it?"

"I guess I can do that."

"I owe you," Aleta said. "Thanks for believing me even when you don't."

West grinned. It was an odd statement. Martha Cook, the town's wealthiest citizen and only proven prophet, had said the same thing to him once. He never forgot it.

Immediately, West called Ramage and passed along the tip.

"That crazy lady called me too," Ramage chortled.

"Wouldn't hurt to check it out," West said calmly.

"You trying to embarrass me?"

"No, I'm not," West returned. "I just think this is one of those easy things to check out, so why not. It'd show you don't take chances."

"I don't take chances," Ramage shot back. "But I don't investigate every crackpot's claim either. I use my brain instead of wasting my manpower on bogus runs."

"This seems important to me," West said. "I can spare a unit if your men are engaged elsewhere."

"It's a wild goose chase," Ramage declared. "Embarrass yourself if you want."

West immediately dispatched two units and told both men to hold the mayor until he arrived.

The reporter Justin Conway was drinking coffee with two of Oakwood's finest, Rob Finch and Ernie Wilson, across from the Oakwood city hall. He was pumping them for information on the arson investigation and getting nowhere because neither of the patrolmen were in the loop.

When the two Arborville patrol cars slid into parking spaces in front and behind the mayor's car parked in front of city hall, Justin was the first to see them arrive.

He pointed them out to his companions.

"Why are they here?" Rob asked. He was the rookie.

"Probably here to escort the mayor to the meeting with the other mayors," Ernie surmised.

"Shouldn't we do that?"

"Ramage doesn't like us going out of the district," Ernie explained knowingly. "He says that escorting big wigs is a dumb-ass job and we ain't doing it."

"Suppose something's going on?" Rob asked. "Shouldn't we check?"

"Ramage would've called," Ernie replied. "He don't like us to call in unless we see a crime being committed."

Uncomfortable with the conversation, Ernie switched topics. "Have you met today's traffic ticket quota yet?"

"Hell, I never make it. Will he fire me for that?"

"No, but he'll ride you about it."

"Why's he so fired up about traffic violations?"

"Traffic accidents are lower here than in the other two cities," Ernie said. "The old man's proud of that."

"We don't catch many criminals." Rob complained.

"We don't have much crime," Ernie said. "Nobody's rich enough to rob in this town."

"But we've got homicides that nobody investigates," Rob pushed, ignoring the presence of the Tri City Register reporter sitting at their table.

Justin Conway was only half listening. Across the street the uniformed Arborville officers had gotten out of their cars. Why would police sent to escort someone get out of their cars? There was no crowd around to contain. In fact, the city hall steps were empty.

"The chief knows which ones are a waste of time," Ernie said. "That's how he keeps inside his budget. No unnecessary investigations into obvious accidents."

Justin Conway tucked that statement into his memory, but right now what was going on across the street intrigued him. Justin rose and left the cafe.

"What's wrong with you?" Ernie hissed at Rob when the reporter left. "We don't wash our dirty laundry in front of a reporter."

"Why's he going across the street?"

"To get a quote from the mayor," Ernie said. "You're just lucky he weren't paying no attention to what you was saying."

"Hey, isn't that the Arborville Chief's car?" Rob said. "Something's going on. Maybe we should go over there."

"You see a crime?"

"No."

"Then we stay put," Ernie said firmly.

Rob acquiesced to the senior officer.

Chief Lyle West approached Mayor Basil Liston and spoke to him quietly.

Justin Conway edged closer, but an Arborville police officer kept him away, telling him the conversation was private.

And important, Justin thought as he stepped back. Something was going down.

He saw a frown on Liston's face and the mayor tried to move around West, but the chief blocked him. His two officers stepped closer.

"Look," West said. "The delay will only take a few minutes. You can report me to my mayor if you like. If I'm wrong, you will have something that will embarrass him. If I'm right, the alternate reward is your life. It's a win-win situation."

Liston was a shrewd judge of character. West was going out on a limb here, but he didn't make stupid moves.

"Okay. Go ahead. Check. But if Chief Ramage had put any credence in the report, he'd be here," Mayor Liston proclaimed loudly enough for Justin Conway to hear.

West nodded at his men who went down the stairs and approached the mayor's car.

Liston kept talking. "Two of Ramage's officers are in the coffee shop across the street. They'd have been over here if anyone suspicious had been loitering around my car."

One officer dropped to the ground. He was up half a minute later.

"See!" Liston exalted. "Nothing!"

He whispered to the other officer who trotted up the stairs. "There's a bomb Sir."

"On a timer?" West asked.

"No timer," the man replied.

"Call the county bomb squad," West said. "And keep people back until the Oakwood police get here."

"Get here?" Liston raged. "They are here—I can see two of them through the window of the diner across the street."

West swallowed his smile as he returned to his car.

Chapter 8

After making the phone calls, Aleta was restless. She turned her attention to the remainder of the paperwork in the briefcase.

She couldn't call Stanley. He was in court. She wouldn't embarrass him that way.

She couldn't call Lyle West. She'd already presumed too much upon his friendship. She knew that eventually he'd call her. She needed to wait.

The minutes dragged by. Her ability to focus was gone. Her mind was trying to cope with sounding alarms that were foolish. The one thing she'd prided herself on was not being foolish. How was she going to live with what she'd done?

In retrospect, she didn't believe what had happened herself. Maybe it was just as well she hadn't read her winning court argument. It was probably just another bit of foolishness.

"Well, God," she murmured, "you trampled my pride to pieces. I know pride is wrong; but, was there no other way? How am I ever going to face Lyle West? He's so self-assured, so sophisticated, so mature. He'll treat me like a child after this, a child with a fanciful imagination, a child not to be taken seriously. You've destroyed my reputation.

"I'm not old enough to deal with prophecy. Grams can barely handle it and she's had years in which to establish herself as a woman of sound mind and great financial skill.

"But me. I'm not established. I've never even seen the inside of a courtroom. I've been at the bottom rung of a law firm for almost a year.

"How am I going to face Stanley? He believes in me. There's no way he won't know I beeped him that ridiculous message. Only a few people have his beeper number. His parents would never beep such a message. Only me.

"Why did You make me so uncomfortable? I know this is how You work, but I don't like it. Suppose I didn't act correctly. I know...I know...all things work together for good when You're obeyed; but there's nothing about the person You're using coming out looking good in the process."

There was no 'amen', just sudden resignation. What happened, happened. She'd have to live with it.

It won't happen again, she told herself. It can't. I won't let it.

With that resolve parked in the forefront of her thinking, she sorted through the papers in the briefcase and settled down to read the case studies first. In the past, they always fascinated her.

As usual, before ten minutes had passed, she was deeply involved.

The first call Aleta received was from Chief Lyle West.

"Was there a bomb?" she asked immediately.

"Yes, there was," he said happily.

Obviously, the mayor had been saved.

"Did Chief Ramage thank you?"

"The mayor did personally. I was standing next to him when it was found."

"Where was Ramage?"

"In his office."

"Figures," Aleta commented.

"Mayor Liston wanted to know why I didn't tell his chief of police," Chief West reported. "I told him I did. Then I added that Ramage had received the tip first."

"Wow!"

"It was a foolish slip of the tongue. Ramage won't forget. I'm not sure I won't regret it."

"You saved a man's life!" Aleta declared.

"People quickly forget," Lyle said with equanimity. "But it doesn't matter. I acted appropriately."

"Thank you!" Aleta enthused. "I appreciate what you did."

"He's your main enemy in the Bessie Dobbin case. Why didn't you let the bomb go off?"

"You know why," Aleta said. "But what's even worse, I saw another paper. Had he died, Bessie would have gotten her farm back.

"That one you can keep to yourself," West counseled. "Since one event was changed, so might the one that followed. By the way, there was a reporter there. Did you call the paper?"

"No."

"Good. See you later."

"Later?"

"At your coming home party," West said.

"Whose idea was that?"

"Lauren's."

"I love your wife," Aleta chuckled.

"So do I," Lyle agreed.

The second call Aleta received was from her grandmother.

"Hi Grams," Aleta said cheerfully. "I hear there's going to be a coming home party for me."

"What's going on?" Harriet asked abruptly.

"What do you mean?" Aleta hedged. How could she have heard about the mayor so soon?

"Stanley called and thanked me. Of course, I had no idea what he was talking about. Seems he got this message on his beeper during a court session. He assumed it was from me."

"Oh, that," Aleta said.

"Yes, that!" Harriet exclaimed. "Why did you call Stanley?"

"The paper said Stanley was the child's advocate."

"You were pretty cryptic," Harriet said bluntly.

"Stanley's pretty sharp," Aleta retorted.

"Well it worked," Harriet said. "Stanley said that knowing the truth made it possible to protect the boy's sense of morality while getting him to paint a devastating picture of his mother as a parent."

"So Kevin's father got custody."

"Yes, and Kevin's mother is in jail," Harriet said. "What did you see?"

"I didn't see anything. I read an account in a paper dated a week from today. In it, his mother broke both his legs and then smothered him because he cried."

"Your life has just gotten complicated," Harriet responded. "Don't tell anyone about the reading of a future edition of a newspaper."

"I already have."

"Who?"

"Chief West."

"Why did you tell him?" Harriet pressed.

"Because I saw two papers," Aleta explained. "And I did it to save someone else's life that was in jeopardy today."

"Well Lyle West is discreet."

"Anyone else?"

"I tried to tell Oakwood's police chief, but he wouldn't listen. But I didn't tell him who I was."

"Can't unring the bell. We'll just have to hope this doesn't go any further."

Lyle West could keep a secret; but, this one was in the category that he and Tom Milani had shared since they first were pressed into Martha Cook's private rescue service. Martha seemed tuned into her friends in various nursing homes in both towns. When new staff refused to check on certain patients at Martha's behest, either Tom Milani or Lyle West were roused and ordered to visit the nursing homes in person. She always insisted they go in uniform and, because she was Martha Cook, both did.

The nursing home staff member was then roundly dressed down by the Chief of Police for laziness, the dying patient was whisked off to the hospital and inevitably lived to enjoy Martha's next visit.

None of Martha Cook's requests were foolish and both men had a special respect they reserved only for her.

"Tom," Lyle West said when Milani answered his private line. "Turn off your recorder."

"Okay, it's off," Chief Tom Milani said, putting the receiver to his ear.

"You have another 'Martha Cook' in your district."

"You mean besides Harriet Locke?" Tom asked, taken aback.

"Yep. Aleta Locke Praetzel."

"The granddaughter?"

"She saved Mayor Liston's life today. Car bomb. Old Herbert wouldn't move on it, so I had to go over."

"You crossed the line?"

"I gave him a heads up. Told the mayor it was a joint effort. Liston didn't buy it."

"You expect trouble?"

"I embarrassed the old man. What do you think?"

"I think I would've let Liston die."

Lyle laughed. "You would not!"

"Don't you dare tell that little gal to call me, you hear. She's your friend. Yours and Lauren's. I don't care where she lives."

"I've already got Martha Cook," Lyle pointed out. "I've got my share of prophets. It's time to share."

"And I've got Harriet Locke. So we're even. Aleta is yours."

"She lives in your district," Lyle countered.

I'll get the mayor to move the boundary so Harriet's new house is in your district," Tom commented wryly.

"Does your wife know about those cookies in your desk drawer?" Lyle asked.

"I thought we were friends."

"Touch that boundary and we won't be."

"Okay. Okay. I probably couldn't get the mayor to go along. He wants that subdivision in his town as much as Councilman Phillip Fleming wants a new school. Boy, nobody better get in the way of either of those guys."

"You coming to Lauren's party?"

"My wife's bringing the lasagna."

"My folks will be glad I invited them."

"How many are going to be there?"

"Well, Lauren doesn't like to leave people out. There'll be a lot."

"Is Martha Cook coming?"

"Her job is to make sure Aleta stays put. Lauren is afraid Aleta will jump up to help and hurt herself. And only Martha is a match for her. I think you should tell Martha about today," Tom said.

"Why?"

"Because…"

"You're right."

The party was held at the half-finished home of the Stanley Praetzels. Since most of the women were providing some dish for the meal, everyone came early. They were all invited to wander out to the barn a couple hundred yards away to view what water and heat had done to Bessie Dobbins' artwork. An appraiser had visited earlier along with the director of the gallery that handled Bessie's work and both agreed that the damaged paintings had an ethereal quality that was not only unique but captivating. Coupled with their limited number the two experts agreed the value of those paintings had increased a hundred fold.

The guests enjoyed their journey out to the Praetzels' newly restored barn which had been carefully pieced together after the fire to resemble the original. Aleta's father had absented himself from his firm in the Bay Area and spent a month working with Ed Ornstein on the project. They scoured the countryside finding materials from barns being torn down and giving Stanley back the barn he remembered playing in as a child. It had been his neighbor's barn then. Now it was part of his extensive acreage which included an apple orchard and several wheat fields. The house was being rebuilt.

When Stanley and Aleta met, only the master bedroom and bath had been completed. The bedroom stood on the site of the old kitchen. Stanley lived on take-out and slowly laid hardwood flooring and built his massive stone fireplace.

However, before she would marry him, Aleta insisted he finish the kitchen. The architect had already drawn the plans, and Cook Construction, on Martha's orders, rushed to complete the kitchen and large family room before the wedding date. They did it in a month. Harriet Locke and Martha Cook were old friends and the two had planned this match and were determined to facilitate its consummation.

The finishing of the rooms was still not done when Harriet Locke had moved her living room furniture from her large Northern California home into her granddaughter's large living room to store until her own home was completed in a new subdivision on the outskirts of Willow Glen. Aleta liked the touch of the familiar having her grandmother's furniture gave her. Harriet slept in her Winnebago parked next to the apple orchard; but, she spent her days in the house which was generally empty as Aleta, who had four corporate clients spawned from the original Tontine Trust, was as busy as Stanley who had a flourishing practice as a child advocate especially among the indigent. Stanley was wealthy in his own right and because he was one of them, the rich sought him out too.

When Aleta arrived home from the hospital, she was escorted straight to the couch where Martha Cook sat waiting to do her duty.

"I hear you joined our ranks," Martha said without preamble.

Aleta wasn't surprised that her grandmother had told her. She wasn't upset either.

"I think it was a fluke," Aleta said. "God wanted the little boy to live."

"It wasn't a fluke," Martha declared. "It will happen again."

"I can't see into the future by design, you know."

"I know."

"Grams has visions," Aleta elaborated.

"I don't," Martha stated.

"Oh," Aleta said in a small voice.

"God doesn't have a procedural text book," Martha said.

"Grams has nightmares."

"She's killed a couple of men. Self-defense may be a legal excuse; but, one's heart is a different matter."

"I've killed too."

"Again self-defense."

"Is this ability punishment for taking a life? I mean, are we now supposed to save lives to pay for what we did?"

"You know better," Martha Cook said softly.

Aleta hung her head.

"Oh, I do. And I'm glad I saved two lives; but, it was so scary. Suppose I'd been wrong?"

"You'll soon learn to trust yourself."

"But suppose I tell someone to do something, and they do it and nothing happens. I mean, suppose I'm the only one who knows what the alternative would have been?"

"As I said, you need to trust yourself."

"I'm really feeling strongly that Stanley shouldn't leave the house tonight," Aleta said. "But it's just a feeling. And I don't have anything more to go on."

"The choice is yours to make," Martha said, "but if it were me, I'd trust my feeling."

"Suppose I'm just letting my imagination see danger when there isn't any?"

"It's not the worst mistake one can make; but, you could always ask for a second sign."

"Will God do that?"

"I believe He will," Martha said. "But you could miss the second sign."

"You're making it hard."

"I always found the opposite works better," Martha confided. "I tell God to stop me if I'm making a mistake."

Four women approached the two and the conversation stopped. Two TV trays were set in front of them and plates loaded with a bit of every offering from the buffet table were placed on each tray.

Without thinking both women simultaneously bowed their heads briefly and prayed. Martha's was one of thanksgiving, Aleta's was a plea for help.

After praying Aleta began to relax. There was really no reason for Stanley to leave the house. It was full of people and he was the host. There was more than enough to eat and drink, so there'd be no reason to run out for more. She'd let her imagination run wild. She wasn't going to have to say anything.

Were it not that two police chiefs were among the guests, the police sirens coming closer would have caused more alarm among the guests than they did. Milani and West, however, both knew that none of their men would have approached in that fashion.

"Ramage," West muttered.

"He's in my territory," Milani said. "He's going to regret this."

"What do you know?"

"He's here to make an arrest," Tom replied. "Bessie Dobbins. Give your dad a heads-up. He's the best criminal lawyer in the room."

Lyle slipped quietly to his father's side. "We may need you to step in on this one. Ramage has it in for me. I embarrassed him today. It's payback time."

"Who is he after?"

"Bessie Dobbins."

"Meet him out front," Kurtz West suggested. "Give me time."

Lyle shook his head regretfully, "Can't impede him in anyway."

Kurtz West slipped over to Stanley, "Tell Bessie I'm her lawyer on this one."

Stanley didn't need to be persuaded. But Bessie did.

"You're my lawyer."

"He's better at this type of law," Stanley said. "Besides you don't want us to stop working to get your property back, do you?"

"Can't you do both?"

Aleta interrupted.

"No, he can't. He must stay here. If it makes you feel any better, a couple months ago when I needed a criminal lawyer, I hired Kurtz West."

The first part of Aleta's argument brought Stanley up short. She'd used the word 'must'. It was not something she normally did. Something was wrong.

The door was opened at the first knock. Ramage charged in with several officers. Mayor Basil Liston followed with Justin Conway, the young black Tri City Register reporter. He had a TV cameraman with him.

When the mayor had first spotted the plethora of shiny new luxury cars surrounding the modest appearing house of Stanley Praetzel, he'd experienced a sinking feeling in his gut.

"Damn Ramage!" he'd muttered under his breath as he'd pulled up behind the patrol cars and in front of the newsman. "That fat bastard didn't check out who was going to be at the party."

Ramage had waited for him to exit the car. The TV cameraman turned on his lights and started filming.

Chief Ramage had assured him that his proof was irrefutable, so Liston stepped out of his car boldly and kept his face emotionless. This was the proper expression he counseled himself.

He hoped Ramage would handle the arrest with professionalism. Ramage, however, was here to embarrass West. He was actually delighted there was a big crowd.

As Ramage ordered Bessie cuffed, Kurtz West counseled her in a loud voice. "This is a bogus arrest Bessie. We all know that. Now you are to say nothing to anyone unless I'm with you. If you do as I say, we can sue for false arrest."

Stanley whispered in Bessie's ear. "Say nothing, this can work in your favor in my case. Do you understand?"

Bessie nodded. She realized that she had two of the county's best lawyers on her side. As outspoken as she usually was, she pressed her lips together. Kurtz West's first words had quieted her urge to proclaim her innocence. It felt good to hear someone else protest for her. It was a new experience.

Mayor Liston knew it was time for his statement.

"We apologize for the intrusion," the camera swung over and focused on him. He smiled at the unseen audience. "My police chief moves swiftly when apprehending a felon.

And I back such zeal. Arrests should be made speedily without regard to social standing or the convenience of the accused."

"I agree," Tom Milani said. The camera swung over to the Willow Glen Police Chief who nodded at one of his officers standing in the doorway. "Obviously, he has set an example and is challenging me to do the same."

He turned toward the mayor. "Basil Liston, you're under arrest for conspiracy to commit murder."

The TV cameraman caught the mayor's open-mouthed grunt of surprise.

Liston, however, recovered quickly. "Do you have a warrant?"

Tom Milani reached into his breast pocket and produced one. Willow Glen's black lieutenant stepped forward and made the arrest. The camera caught Liston's discomfiture at being cuffed by a black officer. His face spoke volumes. Subtle as he thought his reaction was, the black populace in the area would read the expression as blatant.

Liston turned to Kurtz West, "Get me out of this! You're my lawyer."

"Sorry," Kurtz West said. "You're accused of trying to kill another of my clients. I can't represent you in this. Conflict of interest you know. In addition, you interrupted my daughter-in-law's party on the very day my son risked his career to save your life. Not a wise move."

The cameraman caught the whole speech and not a word of which was cut later during the broadcast.

After the police left with the suspects, Kurtz West apologized to Aleta for having to leave the party. "Bessie's not too strong. She needs to see me at the police station when she arrives."

"Hey, Mr. West," Ed Ornstein said. "I got proof she didn't do it."

Kurtz West turned to face the short, rotund man.

Aleta inserted an introduction, "I hired Ed to investigate the fire after Bessie called."

"You predicted this?"

"No, I didn't," Aleta retorted sharply and when Stanley squeezed her hand, she realized it was an innocent query. "I just knew how much the city council wanted the property and Bessie's reason for holding on was because she couldn't paint anywhere else but in that house and, well, I thought someone might be trying to move things along. I suspected arson."

"Well, she's right," Ed said. "But it ain't Bessie and it ain't the mayor. It's the fire chief."

"Maybe they're in cahoots," Kurtz West suggested.

"It ain't panning out that way."

"That makes sense," Stanley said. "The mayor may have made a mistake tonight; but, he's been following the letter of the law on this take-over of Bessie's farm. He wouldn't need to burn down the house."

"Who's the fire chief working with?" Kurtz West asked Ed.

"No clue, yet; but you wanna know what I got?"

"Give," Kurtz West said and Ed took him off to the side and laid out his proof.

"Time of the fire Bessie was on her way home from Praetzel's office. She was too far away to have set it."

"Anything else?"

"Pictures taken immediately after the fire before the fire chief changed the scene."

"He planted evidence?"

"Yes."

The party continued. Kurtz West's statement had set everyone at ease with regard to Bessie, and Tom's arrest of Mayor Liston had been fun to watch. There was a lot to talk about.

Lyle West pulled Tom Milani aside. "You had an arrest warrant in your pocket?"

"Convenient, huh?" Tom grinned.

"Who told you?"

"Justin."

"The reporter?" Lyle asked.

"You know I figured out something about our new resident prophets . They only predict murder."

"Well, at least they didn't predict any murder tonight," West said. "It would've ruined Lauren's party."

"And this didn't?"

"Thanks to you, no."

"It was fun," Tom admitted. "Liston's such a windbag."

Lyle glanced toward the people crowded around Aleta. "What's with Stanley? He seems on edge."

"Didn't you hear Aleta say he 'must stay here'?" Tom replied.

"You read anything into that?" Lyle asked.

"Nothing more than a wife insisting her husband put her first."

"So the honeymoon's over?" Lyle asked.

"It had to happen sometime," Tom sighed.

"She took a bullet to save his fish."

"That probably had something to do with it."

"That or the fact that she just found out she can't show dogs for a couple of months?" West added.

"Honestly, what's with you dog show people? There's a lot more to life than dog showing."

"You better not say that here. You're surrounded by people committed to that sport."

"Stanley and Aleta don't even own a dog."

"They've ordered two. A Lab from Ed and a Bulldog from George Sciretta, both show quality," West said.

"Not the George Sciretta!" Milani exclaimed.

"The same."

"I didn't know the mob boys showed dogs."

"He does," West said. "He watched Aleta when she first arrived at the Arborville show and decided he wanted her to handle Maggie. Aleta put eight points on Sciretta's class bitch in two shows and got her majors out of the way in the process."

"I don't understand half of what you're saying; but, I gather she won big." Tom said.

"She's getting pick bitch from Maggie's first breeding," West said. "Stanley's going to show the Bulldog."

"Stanley?"

"Aleta's changed him," Lyle grinned. "Wives do that, you know. Your wife keeps you thin; mine keeps me fit running after kids."

Ed Ornstein joined Tom and Lyle and added his take, "And mine makes me happy."

"You're a newlywed," Tom quipped. "You don't get to weigh in yet."

Ed acknowledged his status and rushed on to voice a personal concern. "Lyle, our dog sitter says Emma's about to whelp. What do we do?"

Lyle smiled, "Relax. Emma's a sensible girl. She'll be fine."

"Well, you're the father," Ed stumbled. "I mean your dog is. Shouldn't you be in on this?"

"Well, Morgan did this pretty much by himself."

"I'm worried," Ed said, obviously distressed.

"Lauren's the one you want. She handles that part."

"But, she's so busy."

"There are half a dozen women here who'd be glad to step into the kitchen and take over hostessing. Only Lauren can help Emma," Lyle said. "Hey, Stanley, you want to come along. Emma's going to have your pup."

Aleta blanched.

Martha Cook spoke up, "I'm not sure Aleta is feeling well."

Stanley glanced down at his wife.

"I'm fine. Really," she protested, and then added, "We'll come over in the morning to see our chocolate boy."

"Chocolate?" Stanley gasped. "I want a black."

"You want one that looks like Morgan."

"Right."

"So, that's what we're getting."

Stanley let out a sigh. "I'm glad that's settled."

"Of course, he might be wearing a chocolate coat."

"But..."

"One thing you need to understand is that when you pick a show dog, you need to disregard color and look for structure."

"But, you've already decided on a chocolate."

"Not really. Just wanted to get you thinking."

"Aleta, with you, my brain is always working hard."

"Good! It'll keep it fit. I hate a lazy brain."

Tom chuckled. "And I thought I had it hard with my wife insisting I just don't change my belt size."

Chapter 9

After everyone was gone, when Aleta and Stanley were alone in their bedroom, Stanley gazed at his wife, her auburn hair framing her lovely face and he wanted her to know how important she was to him.

"Chocolate is fine," he said by way of telling her that.

"To eat or as the color of a dog?"

"Both," he responded gently sitting beside her on the bed. "Now tell me why it was so important I stay home."

"I had a feeling. Martha Cook said that that's all she gets half the time."

"Just a feeling?"

"I wasn't sure it meant anything, so I asked God to stop me if it didn't."

"How exactly was He supposed to stop you?"

"I didn't give Him directions if that's what you're asking."

Stanley chuckled. "I guess I was, wasn't I?"

"Why didn't you ignore me and go?" Aleta asked.

"And wind up dead? No, thank you!"

"That attitude deserves a reward," she said curling her finger motioning him to come.

"You're injured," he whispered as he lay down beside her.

"Not everywhere," she said softly and he leaned over and kissed her gently.

At seven the next morning he brought breakfast on a tray and set it down on the bed.

"You don't cook," she observed.

"Your grandmother came over early. She was worried."

"A premonition?"

"Grandmotherly concern. She was hoping you had a peaceful night."

"Were you…?"

"I was up and dressed. I needed to restudy the laws on eminent domain to see if we missed anything."

"How long have you been up?"

"Since four."

Aleta sat up. She spread jam on her already buttered toast. Her grandmother knew what she liked.

"Did we miss anything?" she asked, biting into the warm crunchy bread.

"No. It's economically beneficial for the city to develop this property and the courts allow that as a reason to take-over someone's land."

"Even at the expense of a private citizen."

"That's how cities redeveloped areas of blight. Otherwise single individuals could hold up a whole project. They could, in effect, hold the city's future for ransom."

"Whose side are you on?"

"If you can't argue their side, you can't win yours."

Aleta took a second bite and grew thoughtful. "But where is the line to be drawn?"

"I believe that's our task."

"So we aren't going to pin our case on the mayor's alleged misbehavior."

"No, we aren't, because neither of us believes he's guilty. He's a puffed-up blow fish of a man, but if we win on a false basis, it could come back and bite us in the end."

"He won't be grateful," Aleta said, downing half her orange juice.

"Well, at least, we won't be disappointed," Stanley said. "You done yet?"

"Why? Where are we going?"

"To see our pup."

"Don't you go falling in love with any until we have the litter graded."

"Lauren said there's an outstanding boy. And two super girls."

"What did Emma have?"

"Five girls, three boys, one chocolate."

"Has the chocolate got a sex or is it unisex?"

"He's the show male," Stanley said, a ripple of excitement in his face.

"Is Lauren still there?"

"She's not certain Emma's done. There could be one more."

"Aren't you due in court today?"

"I got a continuation on all my cases. My mom contacted the judges for me. Sometimes it pays to have a mother that's a judge. I need to work on Bessie's case.

"So why are we going to see our puppy?"

"Because Ed won't calm down and get back to work until Emma's done whelping, so we may as well go there to toss our ideas around. I won't get another excuse as good as today's to get a free day."

"Oh, you foolish man," Aleta exclaimed. "You think we won't be talking dog talk the whole time."

"You and Lauren and Beatrice will, but Ed and I won't."

"What about Bessie? Is she out of jail?"

"Kurtz West had her out of jail before she was even booked. We persuaded Ramage she had a solid alibi."

"Where'd she go?"

"She stayed at West's house. She said we needed the house to ourselves."

"When did you know this?"

"Last night."

"When were you going to tell me?"

"When you asked."

"You don't believe in volunteering information?"

"Not when it's unimportant. My mind was otherwise occupied."

"To say nothing of other parts of your body."

"Careful. Your grandmother is still here."

"Tell her to go walk her dogs."

Lauren met them at the door to the Ornstein's house. The furniture in the dining room had been moved back against the wall to make space for a large child's wading pool littered with clean strips of newspaper.

Emma was lying in the middle of the pool, several pups sucking on her nipples. The rest were sleeping in a nearby incubator. She was panting lightly and Ed was sitting on the floor stroking her back.

As stressed as a new-time father, Ed searched the faces of the two newcomers for some assurances. Aleta was up to the task.

"What gorgeous, healthy puppies!" she exclaimed. "What a good girl you are, Emma."

Stanley studied the tiny squirming pups and gorgeous was not the word he would have chosen. He wisely said nothing as Aleta pointed at two of the plumpest females and asked Lauren if they were her pick.

"You have a good eye," Lauren said.

To Stanley they were just two of the biggest so he thought it was a size thing. The chocolate male was the biggest pup of all, so he was sure he was right.

"What about her?" he ventured, pointing at a large black girl.

"Too long," Lauren said. "She'll make a nice pet. She has a lovely head."

After another quarter hour, Ed reluctantly agreed to leave Emma's side. Beatrice assured him they'd call him if she began to whelp another pup.

"Show me the pictures, Ed," Stanley said. "And tell me what you saw."

"I got hold of the pictures Chief Wicks took."

"How?"

"Let's say Dean found someone who needed a cash boost."

Ed cleared the coffee table and spread the two sets of photos. Stanley studied them for several minutes.

"Clever manipulating of the debris. Each tells a different story," Stanley concluded.

"I can trace almost every item to its original location. One of the reasons Captain Wicks had his men stomp around so much was to disguise his footsteps in the ash. Without a set of photos to compare, he would have gotten away with it."

"The bookcase was the target," Ed went on. "Only no one wanted us to know that. If Hallihan's crew hadn't arrived on the scene so early, there would have been no books left."

"Actually, there are none," Stanley said. "What the fire didn't destroy, the water did. Look at the mess."

He pointed to the pile on the floor. Wicks's men had pulled them all off the shelves. They lay in a heap, their backs broken and their pages torn and wet.

A voice from the other room called to Ed. "It's coming!"

Ed popped up and ran into the dining room.

"Can I help?" Stanley heard Aleta say. He tossed Ed's photo of the bookcase wall down and rushed into the dining room.

"Be ready to clamp," Lauren said.

Fascinated, Stanley watched Lauren stick her hand into the birth canal and slowly ease the puppy out. Beatrice, seeing Stanley's puzzled expression explained that this was a big pup, and if they pulled on the legs, they might break them, but that Lauren's fingers were slim enough to reach up to the pup's shoulders.

"Will it live?" Stanley asked.

He saw the shock of horror on Ed's face and wished he hadn't spoken.

Aleta's answer was calm, "The chances aren't good; but…Oh, good lord!"

"What?" Ed said, panicking.

"Go ahead and pull," Aleta said. "It's dead."

"How do you know?" Ed asked.

"We thought it might be," Lauren said pulling out the pup. "That's why it took so long for her to whelp it. Dead pups don't move. The movement stimulates the mother's uterus to contract."

"Grams always said that a long delay meant a big head, a breech birth or a dead pup," Aleta remarked.

Stanley stared at the pup as it lay comatose on the paper. "How come it's so greenish?"

"It's been dead awhile," Lauren said.

"You can't resuscitate him?" Stanley asked knowing Ed wanted to ask that question.

"It died in the womb several days ago," Lauren said. "I'm sorry, Stanley. There was no way we could have saved this one."

Lauren rolled the dead pup in newspaper and set it aside. To just toss it would have upset Ed even more. All the women could hear his sobs much as he tried to stifle them.

"We can bury it in the yard later," Beatrice said, putting her hands on her husband's hunched shoulders.

Lauren put her hand on Emma's stomach and rubbed it gently, murmuring, "Such a good girl, you are Emma. Sorry about that one. It was a nice one. All your pups are…"

She stopped speaking and changed positions.

"What?" Ed asked, fright overtaking his sorrow.

Lauren smiled. "There's one more."

"One more?" Ed muttered with suspended belief. "I thought you said you only had one left."

Lauren laughed. "So I'm not infallible."

"Will it be dead too?" Ed choked out.

"Not if the cord is still attached," Lauren said. "Here she comes, sack and all. It's looking good."

The pup emerged seconds later. Lauren swiftly tore the sack from its face and Aleta clamped the cord. The women were taking no chances.

The little black one emerged squalling and squirmed its way out of Lauren's light grip and fell between its mother's front paws. Emma finished the cleaning, rapidly eating the after birth. Aleta removed the clamp so Emma could chew the cord closed. Cords chewed by the mother rarely had to be hand tied. It was nature's way of sealing it.

The pup fought its mother's ministrations and went straight toward a nipple, latched on and began sucking.

"Do we know if it's a boy or a girl?" Beatrice asked.

"Has to be a girl," Lauren said. "Boys are never this feisty."

"She wanted her brother to get out of her way," Aleta chuckled. "Being dead is no excuse in her eyes."

Ed managed a smile. "She is a pistol, isn't she?" His tone was that of a proud father.

"She's a beaut!" Lauren said. "I think she's your pick."

"Unless she's a boy," Aleta said. "She's so big. Turn her over."

Lauren turned the pup.

"A girl!" she announced. "I knew it!"

A short time later Emma was taken outside to relieve. Then her legs and tail were washed in the tub. She was rubbed dry with a towel and finished with the blow dryer. Aleta replaced all the soiled papers with fresh ones. The pups snuggled next to one another in the warm incubator, their wet fur slowly drying.

Stanley watched his chocolate pup as it slept. He was rather pleased his pup was unique.

"How come only one was chocolate?" he asked Aleta.

"Statistics," Aleta replied proud to use her newfound knowledge of Lab genetics. "There was only a twenty-five percent chance for a chocolate. That would mean two out of eight; but that doesn't happen in every litter. But now you have aroused my curiosity. Slowly she unrolled the newspaper with the dead pup.

"It would have been another chocolate," she announced. "Statistically every litter should be half male, half female. This one had six girls and four boys. The next one might swing the other way."

"Next one?" Ed gasped. "Emma's not going through that again!"

"I'm glad we're getting a boy," Stanley chimed in. "I'm not going through anything like this ever."

Aleta grinned. "We're getting a female Bulldog, remember?"

"Can't we just show her?"

"I guess I could have babies instead," Aleta teased.

"I'm going back to work!" Stanley said. "You women are so perverse."

"Just because we sing when the birth is done?"

"How can you forget?" Stanley asked as Lauren led Emma to the pool. Aleta began laying the pups in the pool and Emma laid down and gave each pup a lick.

"We don't forget," Lauren said. "But such a reward!"

Ed watched Emma fussing over her pups. "She seems happy."

"Why shouldn't she be?" Lauren said. "Just look at what she did!"

Beatrice served hot cardamom seed rolls with strawberry jam and hot coffee. As they ate, everyone stood around the pool and watched the pups nurse. It was a pleasant interlude of comradeship and celebration.

"Well, maybe, just maybe, we could have one baby," Stanley said pensively.

Aleta laughed. "Don't worry, guys. After he has one, he'll want another."

"You're lucky if I give you one!" Stanley declared firmly.

"You already have," Aleta said, smiling.

Before Stanley could get a grip on what his wife had just told him, Beatrice gushed out an enthusiastic congratulation and Lauren asked, "How far along?"

"Let's say we had one great honeymoon."

"I thought you were on the pill," Stanley said. He was having trouble grasping the reality that his wife was pregnant. In his mind, that was a future event.

"Why would I be?"

"I thought all women were."

"Women who don't want to have children are."

"You wanted a child so soon?"

"I wanted to have your child," Aleta said. "And I didn't expect it to happen so soon. I thought it would take a while. Grams said it took a couple years before she conceived Dad."

"What about your mother?"

"They had to use a fertility clinic."

"So you weren't worried," Stanley assessed aloud. "That's reasonable, I guess. But couldn't you have been careful for a couple of months, just in case."

"Why?"

"You know why. People will count," Stanley declared.

"Yes, we will," Lauren joshed. "Down to the day."

"Why are you worried?" Aleta asked her husband. There was more to his reaction.

"I watch a dead puppy being born and you ask me that? Your timing couldn't have been worse."

"Take another look," Aleta said. "This room is full of the celebration of life. My timing, as usual, is perfect."

"You should kiss her," Ed coached.

Aleta laughed, "He's angry because I caught him off guard. It's difficult to do. I have to work at it because he's gotten to know me so well."

"You planned the whole morning?" Stanley asked annoyance mingled with surprise.

"Well, not the dead pup part," Aleta confessed. "That was a set-back; but then you walked right into it."

Slowly, Stanley began to smile. "I did, didn't I?"

He took her hand and pulled her toward him. "Come here you minx."

His kiss was long and sweet.

"I like that name for our girl," Beatrice said. "Minx. What do you think, Ed?"

"Well, she is that! Look at her pushing her sisters out of the way."

Chapter 10

Stanley took Aleta back into the living room with him. He pointed at the photos scattered on the glass coffee table.

"What do you see?"

Aleta looked at the top photo. "Some books are missing."

Ed and Stanley stared at the glossy print.

"That's what's wrong," Stanley agreed. "The framed picture doesn't belong in the bookcase. All the rest of her photos are scrunched together on that roll top desk of hers."

"It could be a special photo."

Aleta pointed at the picture of the roll top. "There's a space on top of the desk."

"Why move it?" Ed asked.

Stanley meanwhile punched in a number and asked if Bessie was up yet.

"You know Kurtz West's number?" Aleta asked surprised.

"You aren't the only one with a penchant for numbers," Stanley rejoined.

Aleta moaned, "We're going to give birth to an actuary."

The conversation was cryptic. Ed and Aleta had to be content with watching Stanley scribble down book titles on Beatrice's flowered stationery.

He handed Ed the list. "Here are the books I want your associate to bid for on eBay."

Ed made the call.

"Aleta asked, "How did she know which ones were stolen?"

"The photo was stuck where her rare books were."

"Why eBay?"

"Just a hunch."

"So that means the fire was supposed to cover up the robbery? What a rotten thing to do!" Aleta exclaimed, then, after a short pause, asked, "How does this tie in with my getting shot?"

"It doesn't," Stanley said.

The phone interrupted them. Ed answered it.

"Two books have shown up on eBay. Dean's submitted a bid."

"Tell him to keep bidding. I need to call West and ask him what to do. I'm not sure we can avoid having to work with Ramage on this."

"Isn't Bessie's farm in an unincorporated area?" Aleta asked.

"Yes," Stanley replied slightly puzzled.

"Then technically, she's under the County Sheriff's jurisdiction."

"If that's so, how do you explain the Arborville Fire Chief telling Bessie that her house was in Oakwood's jurisdiction?" Stanley asked.

Aleta thought a moment. Her long hours of study in the hospital was paying off. "Technically it wasn't yet; but, it definitely wasn't in Chief Hallihan's jurisdiction either. And the fire was out. Rather than argue he put his men to work saving what Bessie asked him to save."

"So, a robbery at Bessie's house would be the sheriff's case," Stanley concluded. "Do we know anything about the sheriff?"

"He can't be any worse than Ramage," Aleta said.

"I think I'll ask West what to do," Stanley said. "Once it's out of our hands, it's out of our hands. We have too big a stake in this to let go."

"So technically," Aleta mused aloud, "Ramage had no legal right to seize Bessie in the first place. It was the sheriff's call."

"It's a technicality," Ed put in.

"The law is built on technicalities," Aleta said. "He may not have hired the men who shot me; but, he personally invaded my home to arrest an innocent woman. That's harassment."

"You'll need a stronger argument than that one," Stanley noted.

"I need to study Illinois law," Aleta said. "That's what I need to do."

"Come home with me," Lauren said. "Lyle has a whole law library in his den. It's up-to-date too. It'll be quiet. The kids are with their grandparents. When his parents found out I'd be up all night helping with Emma, they had Lyle bring the kids over to their house this morning. Lyle is always thoughtful when I'm pregnant. He guards my sleep zealously. I think he wants me strong enough for all those night feedings."

Aleta looked at Stanley. "Take notes."

"You want to go to bed again?" Stanley queried wryly.

Aleta blushed and Lauren laughed.

"Ed, let's go to your office," Stanley said slightly abashed himself.

"Will Emma be okay?" Ed asked his wife.

"You gave her a whole litter of pups to fuss over. She won't even miss you," Stanley observed.

"She'll be fine, Ed," Aleta chimed in. "And nobody should worry. Stanley will pay for that remark."

Chapter 11

Lyle West came through the door to his large two story house on one of Arborville's tree-lined streets. His dogs scrambled down the stairs from the bedroom and greeted him so effusively that Aleta's tiny sliver of fear when she heard a key in the lock disappeared. She rubbed her eyes and leaned back ready to explain her presence to Lyle when the light tap on the den door told her he already knew.

"Been hard at it, huh?"

"You've got a great library."

"Please use my den for the next few days. Tom Milani wants you to stay away from your office until he nabs whoever's behind the attack."

"If he doesn't think Mayor Liston had anything to do with it, why'd he arrest him?"

"He's hoping whoever is after you will think he's safe to come out of whatever hole he's in."

"I'm bait?"

"We don't work that way," Lyle said. "You're safe here. Morgan won't let anyone get near you. And you have my private number as well as Tom's. Call if anything strikes you as odd. It may be our only chance to catch him."

"Lauren's still asleep," Aleta said.

"She had a long night. I hear you're taking the chocolate boy. Have you named him yet?"

"Scooby."

"How'd you come up with that?"

"Stanley will insist on serious names for our children, so we need fun names for our dogs."

"I hear congratulations are in order," Lyle said smoothly.

"Lauren told you?"

"She had to tell someone."

"And whom did you tell?"

"Tom Milani. It's too delicious a news bite not to share. Heard you knocked Stanley off his pins."

"I guess I did."

"How's the case coming?"

"It's not," Aleta declared. "I can't get past the public use statement even though I think they could develop the subdivision elsewhere, the court apparently doesn't listen to such arguments. It doesn't try to second guess the city governments."

"True."

"And it allows a broad interpretation of public use as well. Economic redevelopment covers a broad spectrum of projects, even private ones."

"I assume you came across the SWIDA case where the Illinois Supreme Court reversed itself and stopped Southwestern Illinois Development Authority which had condemned the property owned by the National City Environmental to give it to Gateway Race Track to be used for a parking lot."

"I read it; but, it would be a stretch in this case. There it was a blatant attempt by one neighbor to acquire the land of another for his own profit."

"And you don't think this case is the same?"

"Taking Bessie's land and building houses or stores on it will help the town economically. Even if Liston makes money under the table that wouldn't cause the court to halt the condemnation."

"You're missing my point."

"What point?"

"Read the decision again," Lyle said. "You'll get what I'm trying to say."

"Why don't you just explain it?"

"If you don't discover it on your own, you won't be able to argue it," Lyle commented as he closed the door. "Have fun!"

Aleta picked up the Law Journal and read aloud the 2002 decision by the Illinois Supreme Court that the law of eminent domain "...requires that the use for which the land is taken shall be public as distinguished from a private use..."

She read on, "...it is incumbent upon the judiciary to ensure that the power of eminent domain is used in a manner contemplated by the framers of the Constitution..."

She closed the Journal. "This is no good. The project is a good one for everyone but Bessie."

She pondered her own statement. "For everyone? Suppose there's someone besides Bessie that will lose something. But what? It has to be money. Everything like this is always about money. Who would lose money if Bessie loses her land?"

Aleta called Stanley. "Who would lose money if Bessie loses her land?"

"The gallery that sells her paintings. But they might not believe that Bessie can't paint elsewhere once settled in."

"Anyone else?" Aleta pressed.

"Maybe the farmer who leases her land for his wheat crop."

"Anyone else?"

Stanley turned to Ed and asked the question. They were in Sheriff Toby Kern's office.

The sheriff answered the query himself, taking the phone from Stanley. "The neighbor to the south, Huck Dirkson. He's got a commercial stable. He boards and trains horses. If Bessie's land becomes a subdivision, Huck's worried about being next, even though the mayor says he won't because his daughter boards her show horse there. Bessie doesn't mind the smell. Reminds her of when her folks were alive and theirs was a working farm. Huck says Bessie might even rent him some of her land as pasture next year so he can expand."

Stanley took back the phone and his voice was replete with authority, "We'll look into it, Aleta. You go back to your books."

"Trying to hogtie the little woman?" Sheriff Kern joshed, a twinkle in his eye. He was a genial man, older than either West or Milani and much more casual.

"She was shot and she's pregnant and she doesn't use any common sense when it comes to her own welfare," Stanley purported. "And she's a redhead."

"West has got one of those," Kern chuckled. "Me, I got me a brunette. They're much tamer."

Ed's cell phone rang and everyone waited. He interrupted the conversation to report, "Dean sealed the deal for twelve grand. That's double what it's worth. Can we get that kind of cash quick?"

"Tell Dean to set up the exchange," Stanley said. "I can have the money within the hour."

Bessie described the book in detail over the phone and Howie Pappas was arrested immediately after he accepted the money. Subsequently his house was searched. Seven of Bessie's prize volumes were found.

Sheriff Kern, suspicious that many of the items in the house were stolen, was about to have his men confiscate them when Ed suggested that lifting prints off the items could prove ownership. Sheriff Kern then turned the whole matter over to Hawkins Monroe, the area's top forensic expert located in Willow Glen.

Stanley was curious. "You use Willow Glen's lab?"

"We don't have a lot of crime in the farm area of the county. We don't need a full time lab guy. We could use the state lab, but Hawk gives better service and he doesn't make mistakes."

"Whose lab is it?" Stanley asked, curious.

"Willow Glen and Arborville support the lab."

"Not Oakwood?"

"Ramage is not what you'd call the cooperative sort."

"So who does he use?"

"The state boys, of course. It's his way of thumbing his nose up at West."

"What's with him and West?"

"Enemies."

"Why?"

"West is too good at his job."

"What are you going to do about Oakwood's fire chief?" Stanley said.

"Well, if this Howie Pappas rolls over on him, I'll arrest him. Otherwise I haven't much of a case," Sheriff Kern replied.

"He rearranged the evidence."

"But not to cover up the fact that it was arson," Kern explained. "I need to connect him to Pappas to charge him as an accessory to robbery."

"Too bad," Stanley said. "His arrest might have helped Bessie's case."

"Sorry," Kern said. "But I tell you what I will do. I'll delay letting the media get hold of this. I owe the Register's editor a favor and he'll keep the story under wraps so he can have an exclusive. This'll be good payback. On top of that, I'll monitor Pappas' incoming email."

"Wicks won't be foolish enough to contact Pappas," Stanley protested.

Ed inserted a comment about criminals not trusting each other. The way he said it told Stanley that he had an idea.

They left shortly after that.

"So what's your idea?" Stanley asked. "I can't be party to anything illegal."

"How about an ad campaign?"

"Go on."

"Dean just bought a book for twelve thousand dollars on EBay. He is a satisfied customer."

"How will Fire Chief Wicks get wind of this?"

"We get EBay to tout the sale on their website. Dean told me one of the guys at the fire station is a big computer geek. I bet Wicks is keeping tabs on Pappas through him?"

"But a lot of firemen know Dean."

"Dean used another name," Ed said. "He paid cash. The seller didn't ask for ID."

"It just might work," Stanley said. "Can Dean take care of this on his own. I need you to canvas Bessie's neighbors. Talk to all of them so Huck Dirkson won't know we're targeting him."

"Are we?" Ed Asked.

"In a way. He's a piece of the puzzle," Stanley replied. "I just don't know where he fits yet."

Chapter 12

At six Stanley drove to Lyle West's house to fetch his wife.

"Take a round-a-bout route home," West said. "This is our safe house for your wife for a few days. We expect our attacker to fall into one of our traps. He's got to move soon. You'll be in court on Bessie's case next week."

"Lyle's got an idea as to which decision we should base our case on," Aleta said. "But I don't see it."

"Really?" Stanley queried. "I thought the 2002 SWIDA case would be our best bet. One can always make a strong case based on Illinois Supreme Court decisions."

Aleta turned on Lyle. "You told him!"

"No, I didn't," Lyle replied. "Great minds…," he began and then he spotted his wife standing in the doorway and amended his statement, "…we…men's minds work alike."

Aleta laughed. "Good wiggle, Lyle. I dare Stanley to tell me what you two geniuses see that I don't."

"I'm more curious as to why you don't think that case applies," Stanley said.

"Not as good a wiggle," Aleta declared.

"But I'm not trying to wiggle," Stanley said. "I need to find the loopholes before I go into court and you're just astute enough to point them out."

Lauren clapped hands. "Great recovery!"

Aleta smiled. "I agree. Pointing to my brain so positively does erase a lot of errors made today."

Stanley took Aleta's hand. "Let's go while I'm still ahead."

"We still have work to do," Aleta pointed out. "We should take some stuff with us."

"Mothers-to-be need rest," Stanley declared.

Lauren laughed. "Told you!"

"I guess men do think alike."

"We'll be busy enough arguing the SWIDA decision," Stanley proclaimed. "You can dig back into the law books tomorrow."

"Did either you or Ed have any luck today?"

"So-so," Stanley replied.

He was pretty sure Lyle knew about the arrest of the robbery suspect by the sheriff; but, to say anything in front of Lauren might not be a good idea. He didn't know how much of his work Lyle shared with his wife. He'd ask him sometime.

"Are you going to the show this weekend?" Lauren asked.

"She can't show," Stanley stated flatly.

"She can watch," Lauren said. "I thought you might be keeping your grandmother company. It'll be her first Illinois show."

"Oh, Stanley, I have to go!" Aleta exclaimed.

"I don't trust you. You can't get near a ring without wanting to go in."

"Grams'll make sure I behave."

"It might even be a good idea," West said. "We can set up a decoy in your house over the weekend."

"I don't want my house shot up," Stanley declared.

"And I don't want an officer hurt," West countered soberly. "Let me work on this with Chief Milani and I'll get back to you."

Stanley needn't have worried about Aleta prying about that day's activities; she was all hyped up about attending the dog show.

What he didn't know is that she hadn't called George Sciretta and told him she could show his dog because her shoulder was feeling better by the hour. Tom Wilson would bring Sciretta's Bulldog in his RV since he had been showing her the past month. Tom had been told Aleta might take over, but Sciretta promised payment even if she did so Tom went along.

The little fat man was new to the dog show world; but, he wasn't afraid to pay for services, so Tom felt he was nurturing a new client. Maggie would be ready to special in a year and he was a pro who went on circuits every weekend. Eventually, Sciretta would begin using him all the time. It was a matter of priorities. He was a full-time professional handler. Aleta was a gifted beginner whose full-time profession was as a lawyer. Tom didn't think she'd join his ranks; but, if she did, he wanted her as a friend. Maggie was her first professional handle. She would naturally feel a bit possessive.

Aleta had opened the door to the tight-knit group of long-time breeders who rarely used a handler, and Tom was way ahead monetarily. The Danielsons had given him Drummer to handle since August, and except when he went head to head with Lyle West and his big black Lab, Morgan, who sired Drummer, Tom and Drummer won the Breed consistently and placed in Group half the time. The Danielsons were delighted. Drummer was moving up in the national rankings and he was suddenly being considered as a stud worthy of consideration.

Aleta had called Tom Wilson and told him about her injury and they discussed her showing Maggie. She told him her doctor would tape her shoulder so she didn't wrench it, but showing Maggie was all she could manage.

Tom responded positively. "I have a conflict between Afghans and Bulldogs again, so I'd welcome you on Maggie. She hasn't shined up to me yet."

Aleta was surprised and said so. Tom shrugged it off.

"It happens."

"I'm sure I can hitch a ride with someone. All I need is Stanley's permission."

"Permission?" Tom laughed. "Since when?"

"Since I got married; but, don't worry. I'll figure out something. I'll call you if I don't."

"I'll see you Saturday. Bulldogs show at nine."

After that conversation, Aleta had been determined to show Maggie. She couldn't touch a big dog, like her grandmother's Chessies or Evelyn's Goldens. But Maggie, while solid and heavy, was short-legged and moved slowly. She never pulled on the leash. She just trotted nicely by her side as long as she didn't walk too fast. Maggie didn't walk fast, period.

Aleta knew she wouldn't have to lift her onto a table as she would one of Beatrice's Scotties or Madge's Doxies. Maggie would walk up the ramp under her own power. Stacking was eliminated as Maggie self-stacked and Aleta always stood in front of her when she presented her. The arm would be tightly strapped in place so she wouldn't hurt it when she walked fast. She wouldn't need to run at all.

Every one of her friends would understand. And all she needed was to show one dog to feel included. Watching was not for her.

She knew Stanley realized this; but, maybe he would reason that her grandmother could control her. He definitely understood Aleta wanting to support her grandmother at her first Illinois show.

"You need to share me," she posed. "And I need to tell Grams the good news."

"You don't need a dog show to do that," Stanley teased.

He was going to let her go. Her grandmother was the reason he had her. And Stanley still felt he owed the older woman.

"Okay," Aleta acquiesced, "but, I do need to go to support her."

"That one's your best argument. I'd stick with it."

"Is it good enough?"

"Yes."

When Stanley drove into their drive, no dogs barked. Aleta saw the huge earthmoving rig parked to the right of the house.

"What's the digger doing here?"

"We need to start on the foundation for the nursery before the ground freezes."

She looked around. The Winnebago was gone.

"Where's Grams?"

"She took the dogs over to Beatrice's to wash them for the show."

Aleta opened the car door and got out.

"You knew about the show?"

"Yes," he replied as they walked toward the house.

"You knew I'd want to go?"

"I was pretty sure."

"If West hadn't said something, were you going to remind me?"

"But West did say something," Stanley teased.

"So why were you waiting?" she asked as Stanley opened the front door for her.

"For you to ask me."

"So I can go?"

"I wasn't ever going to stop you," Stanley said gently. "I was going to voice my opinion as strongly as possible; but, your life is your life. You don't make stupid mistakes. I trust you."

Aleta began to cry.

Stanley put his arm around her. "I know about Dr. Cook agreeing to tape your arm. He thought you were going to try to drive and he called me to tell you not to."

She cried ever harder. "I don't deserve you," she sobbed.

"Sure you do," Stanley whispered as he drew her to him. "You deserve me. And you are the best thing that has ever happened to me. Your shoulder is your shoulder."

Aleta snuggled in her husband's arms and asked coyly, "Dr. Cook told you it'd be okay, didn't he?"

"Close," Stanley admitted. "He told me pain would stop you from hurting it too seriously."

"You want to come along, don't you?"

"Yes, I do."

"You know if we borrowed Beatrice's RV, we could stay on the grounds and have a home base of our own."

"Isn't Beatrice going?"

"And leave Ed and the pups alone? Not after she saw how emotional he was. Even the best directions wouldn't get him through a weekend alone."

"Doesn't she have dogs entered?" Stanley asked, his tone slightly suspicious.

"Don't worry. I can't show them."

"Could someone else?"

"I'll call and ask."

"I'll put the lasagna in the oven."

"What lasagna?"

"Tom Milani's wife brought a huge dish. She left us the leftovers."

"Did everyone leave leftovers?"

"They left everything you asked for seconds on."

Aleta's mouth dropped open, "They kept tabs on what I ate?"

"My mother always keeps tabs on what I eat. I think it's an inherited trait in females that comes into full fruition as soon as she has a child."

"That's crazy."

"When I ask you what our baby ate three years from now, you'll tell me exactly how many peas he swallowed," Stanley remarked smugly.

Aleta busied herself with her phone call.

Chapter 13

Joey Crowder had spent most of the day staking out Stanley Praetzel's office waiting for the lawyer to show. He'd watched a woman moving around in the office; but, he didn't know who she was. He wasn't going to kill a secretary by mistake. He prided himself on hitting his target on the first try.

He'd driven through the parking structure looking for a beige Lexus with the license he'd been given. It wasn't there. It wasn't parked behind the office nor anywhere along the street near the office.

He'd left the downtown area briefly to scout out the house tucked at the end of a long gravel drive with an orchard on the left and a plowed field on the right. It had looked abandoned so he'd started up the drive. The sound of several large dogs barking bade him to back up and leave. He'd have to stick with a car bomb. The dogs weren't going to let him near the house.

As he was driving down the road he saw a line of earth moving equipment turn up the same gravel drive he'd just exited. He couldn't think exactly how to use them; but, their appearance made him pull over and stop to think.

Looking back over the plowed field, he saw a woman call three large dogs into her Winnebago and then drive off the property.

The equipment was parked and the operating engineers climbed off their rigs, lit cigarettes and chatted as they waited. They didn't need to wait long. A truck drove up and two men in shirts and ties under their jackets stepped out, put on hard hats and began barking orders. Cigarettes were snuffed out, engines revved up and two shovels began digging. Haulers moved in to receive the dirt from in back of the house while a scraper began work on the long driveway.

Joey Crowder had seen all he needed to see. No one was coming or going to that house for several days.

He quit waiting at six and went to McDonalds and ordered two Big Macs, fries and coffee. He wanted to go to the pizza joint and order a supreme and a pint of beer. He didn't dare. He got too friendly after a pint.

Where the hell were these people, he wondered.

He ate in his car in the litter strewn parking lot and stared at a lonely crooked tree. He closed his eyes for a few minutes and dozed. When he woke, his coffee was still warm. It was still light and he decided he needed to head for his motel. He couldn't afford to zonk out in a parking lot.

He drove out sipping his coffee. He decided to take one more run past the house.

Inside the house, Aleta put down the phone and told Stanley that the ladies had congratulated Grams upon her arrival at Beatrice's house and had eagerly shared every word spoken between the two prospective parents. Harriet had told her Beatrice's rendition had them all in stitches.

"How do most men act?" Stanley asked, annoyed.

"Just like you," Aleta grinned. "She is really happy. And Beatrice says we can use her RV. She asked if we'd transport her Scotties. She's going to talk to Tom Wilson about showing them."

"Suppose he can't?"

"Grams and Evelyn will work it out," Aleta predicted. "And you can hold dogs for them if necessary. Lauren and Lyle will be there too. And I think Madge and Nathan are going. It will be his first show since he got out of the hospital. She's going to make him take it easy though so we can't ask either of them to help."

"You are too, you know. Taking it easy, that is," Stanley put in.

"There's no way I'm going to upset a man who's going to let me show Maggie two days in a row."

Stanley put his arms around her and kissed her tenderly.

"The lasagna's ready," he whispered.

Aleta burst out laughing. "That's the best you can do with a romantic moment."

Stanley grinned. "If I didn't break the spell you cast, we'd wind up in bed hungry. And that baby needs lasagna."

"We aren't going to bed afterward either," Aleta announced lightly.

"You want a bath first."

"Love it when you read my mind," she said. "Let's eat. It's been a long day."

"There's whipped cream in the refrigerator," Stanley said.

"Any dessert to put it on?"

"I can think of one."

"After my bath," she said her lips twitching as she tried to repress a smile. "My you have come a long way in that department."

"Well, tonight's the night to play. We have the whole place to ourselves."

Chapter 14

Lauren called Beatrice that evening to check on the pups.

"They're doing fine," Beatrice said. "Harriet and Evelyn are here, so you can relax. We washed Harriet's three Chessies today. Tomorrow we're going to do Evelyn's Goldens and Friday we'll do the Scotties. Tom Wilson thinks he can fit them in."

"Remember you can call me any time if you're worried," Lauren offered.

"You can rest, dear," Beatrice said. "Harriet's not going home. Stanley's putting in a new drive and digging the foundation for the nursery. She says her dogs wouldn't be able to stay out of the way."

"Good idea," Lauren said. "Where are Stanley and Aleta staying?"

"At the house. The concrete trucks are scheduled for Friday morning according to Harriet."

"They'll have fun," Lauren giggled. "Stanley was back in Aleta's good graces when they left here. Who's taking your Scotties? We could find room in our rig if you need."

"Stanley's taking my RV. Evelyn's putting Topaz in with the Scotties. Harriet's not sure Stoney will accept his presence in her RV"

After she hung up, Lauren repeated the conversation to Lyle who frowned part way through.

"What's wrong?"

"You mean Stanley and Aleta are on that property with no dogs."

"Well, yes, I guess so. But the dogs sleep with Harriet."

"They bark at anything strange. I don't like them being there unprotected."

Lauren handed her husband the phone. He called Tom Milani who said he'd post two men on the property immediately.

"Call first," Lyle said. "Or you're apt to panic them."

After Tom radioed dispatch and sent two men to Stanley Praetzel's house, he rang Stanley.

Stanley didn't answer him right away and Tom worried that he was too late.

"Where were you?" he demanded when he finally reached Stanley.

"Giving Aleta a bath," Stanley blurted out.

"Oh," Tom replied sheepishly.

"What's up?" Stanley asked, recovering his equilibrium first.

"I'm sending over two men to guard the place. West said the dogs are gone."

"You're sending them over now?"

"They should be there before you hang up."

"Can you tell them not to…oh to hell with it… Aleta, we're going to have company."

Tom chuckled when he heard Aleta shout, "Now?"

"Thanks, Tom," he said as he hung up. Before the phone went dead, Tom heard Stanley say, "Aleta, where's my robe?"

He relaxed. They were safe.

Joey Crowder slipped behind the wheel just as the first police car came up from behind him lights flashing. A second followed the first within seconds.

He sat until they passed and realized that his sitting at the side of the road wasn't suspicious in their eyes. Cars were supposed to pull over and stop when police approached with lights or sirens.

He'd finished just in time.

He decided to skip the motel and head home. He didn't need to be anywhere in the morning after all.

Chapter 15

At five the next morning, Harriet Locke awoke with a start. She turned on the bedside lamp, put on her glasses and picked up the phone. She glanced toward the window. The drapes were open, it was still dark out.

It has to be done, she realized.

I thought I was done with these, she pondered. Maybe I am. Maybe it's my imagination. Maybe deep inside I don't want to give up that ability, as troublesome as it is.

Besides, she argued internally, it's too early. I don't need to wake anyone up. Neither Stanley nor Aleta will be up this early. And even if they are, neither would go anywhere.

I could wait, she concluded.

Her stomach churned.

A thought crossed her mind. Suppose Aleta is having a miscarriage. Stanley would rush her to the hospital. How dare she decide on the timing? She woke up now for a reason.

If I call Stanley and Aleta, they'll understand.

But wouldn't Aleta want to check it out before engaging the police? Sure she would. But suppose opening the car door set it off. Or what if raising the hood or slamming the hood shut was the trigger?

Why am I assuming the bomb this time is as rudimentary an affair as the one under the mayor's car? West had said that one was the work of a rank amateur. Somehow that fact had made it into the paper. Suppose whoever is after Aleta upgraded his attack force.

She punched in Milani's number.

A sleepy voice said, "Milani here."

"You're awake," Harriet said. "Good!"

"Who is this?" Tom Milani asked glancing at his clock. "It's five AM!"

"I know. I didn't like being awakened either. There's a bomb planted in Stanley's Lexus. It's not like last time. It's hidden."

"I've had men posted there all night," Milani protested.

"Were they there when Stanley and Aleta got home?"

"No, they arrived a little later," he admitted.

"Maybe too late."

"You're sure about this?"

"We know they're targets," Harriet said, her voice shaky with trepidation. She was praying silently as she was speaking. "If it's a false alarm, I'll never make another prediction. But, please, this time, take me seriously."

Tom swung his legs down onto the floor. He was grateful for the soft carpet. The feel of the softness underfoot told him this wasn't a dream. This was real. He was being asked to trust a prophet again.

"They are targets," he repeated to convince himself that action should be taken. "I guess I can have my men guard the car until I get there."

"No!" Harriet shouted. "I don't want you killed either. This is a job for the bomb squad."

"I have to call the county for that."

"Do it."

Milani ran through the explanations he could use. They all seemed inadequate. There was no explaining what was happening and why he believed this woman.

"Okay, I will," he said finally.

"And you'll keep everyone away until the bomb squad gets there?"

"Who's everyone?"

"As soon as it's light the work crew will arrive to finish the foundation. They can't start work until the bomb is disarmed."

"I'll see to all of it," Chief Milani said.

His tone told Harriet that he would.

Stanley woke at quarter to five. He dressed quietly and gazed at his new wife as she lay sleeping. The light poured onto the bed from the bathroom. It was a soft light and suddenly he had the irresistible urge to make love to her again.

He pulled back the light cover and sat beside her. His hand roamed up the outside of her thigh to her breast. It took her nightgown with it. He remembered how difficult the nightgown had been for her to remove the day before.

The loose sweatshirt she wore had been easy for her to slip on. She just left the left sleeve tucked inside and pulled it on over her head. Her pants were spandex. She hadn't wanted to be hampered by zippers which took two hands half the time, so she pulled them up her slim hips with the zipper closed and locked.

Gently, he slipped the free arm from the gown and the gown barely brushed her face he was so careful. The shoulder wrapped in the bandage that bound it to her chest was last. Why she insisted on wearing a gown when they were alone, he couldn't fathom.

He kissed her lightly on her nipple and she stirred.

"I'm going to meet Ed," he said softly. "I need to do some more research before court. It just occurred to me that

Cook Construction might have bid on the Oakwood project…"

She grunted sleepily.

"We'll talk later."

He pulled the cover back over her naked body telling himself he could wait.

It would be better tonight. Tonight he'd give the guards specific instructions to steer clear of the bedroom window. Aleta's modesty the night before had inhibited her from engaging freely in sexual activity. Having guards outside was worse than having a grandmother in an RV nearby.

He picked up his cell and his briefcase with his notes for today's cases. There were two this morning and two this afternoon. If he didn't check out his hunch this morning, it'd be another day before he knew if he was on the right track or not in the Bessie Dobbins case.

He turned on the coffee so it'd be ready for Aleta. He'd catch some on his way over to Ed's.

As he exited, he greeted the cop at the door, "Hi, Rob. I'm going in to work. Take good care of her."

"Will do," Rob said.

"Carl still on?"

"He's at the side of the house near the car."

Stanley headed for his bronze Lexus. Aleta's matching Lexus was in the shop. It would be delivered this morning.

He rounded the corner and greeted Carl and then clicked the remote to unlock the door.

"Thanks for protecting us," Stanley said. "I'm glad it was a slow night."

"Me too," Carl said. "Take care, Sir."

Stanley threw his briefcase onto the passenger seat and climbed in. He opened his cell phone and punched in Ed's number.

"Hi," he said. "Sorry to get you up so early but I need you to help me do a computer search."

"I was getting up anyways. Emma needs to go out a lot. The early morning shift is mine."

"How're the pups?" Stanley said closing his door and inserting his key in the ignition.

"All gaining weight. Harriet and Evelyn say that's a good sign."

"Is my chocolate boy still the biggest?" Stanley asked turning his key. The engine purred awake.

"Scooby? Yeah, he's the biggest."

"Scooby?" Stanley said, shoving the automatic gear into drive.

"That's the name Aleta gave him. Kinda cute, ain't it?"

"I wonder why she chose that one," Stanley puzzled aloud.

He put his foot on the gas, drove around the house and down the driveway.

"Said you get to name the kids; but, she doesn't want the dogs to have serious names," Ed replied.

"She said that?" Stanley said as the two officers' shouts reached his ears.

He jammed on the brakes and opened the door.

His first thought was Aleta.

He ran toward the house. He only got two strides from the car when it exploded. The blast pushed him forward hard. His chest plowed a furrow in the hard ground.

Aleta woke at the sound, threw back her covers and ran straight toward the front door, screaming, "Stanley!"

She yanked open the door and saw the flames rising toward the dark sky.

"Stanley!" she yelled as she ran past Rob who put out a hand to grab her but hesitated when he realized she was stark naked.

Carl, who'd run straight toward the man lying prone on the ground, found himself teamed with a totally nude woman in pulling Stanley away from the burning car.

Milani shouted over the radio and Rob answered. "It blew about thirty feet down the driveway. Mr. Praetzel wasn't inside but he's down. He could be hurt bad."

Milani, who'd hesitated when Rob had told him Stanley Praetzel was driving down the drive, now cussed himself for that split-second doubt that there was a bomb.

Once out of danger from the burning car, Carl turned Stanley over.

"He's not breathing!" Aleta exclaimed.

Carl immediately began mouth-to-mouth resuscitation as the naked woman sat on her heels her only concern for her comatose husband. She gripped his hand in hers and prayed.

Rob kept Milani informed even though he heard the two sirens coming down the road. He wasn't quite sure what to do about the naked woman. She appeared to be oblivious about her state and, on top of that, she was praying. How do you tell a praying person to get dressed?

Milani's car was the first official vehicle to arrive. A second squad followed his and parked at the entrance to the driveway.

Tom screeched to a halt as close as he could get and leaped from his car. His first thought was that Aleta's clothes had been blown off. His second, more rational assessment was that she'd flown from her bed straight through the door at the sound of the explosion.

Stanley coughed and Milani realized he was alive.

Milani's eyes took in Aleta. Oh to have a wife who sleeps in the nude, he thought and yanked his mind back to business.

Stanley opened his eyes to see Aleta, unclothed, bending over him, tears streaming down her face.

"Why aren't you the one kissing me," he coughed.

"Change of pace," she quipped, and then suddenly became aware of her state of undress. "Where's my nightgown?"

Tom Milani dropped his coat over her shoulders and told his men to close their eyes.

Aleta ran back into the house.

"How'd you know?" Stanley asked.

"Aleta's grandmother woke me."

"So she can still prophesy."

"Seems so."

"Why didn't you call me?"

"Your phone was busy."

"Why didn't it explode when I turned on the ignition?"

Milani smiled. "Your questions tell me your brain still works. The answer is I don't know. Harriet Locke said the bomb was not simple like last time. I'd say it had a delayed timer."

Stanley tried to push himself up. Milani insisted he stay still until he was checked out, but Stanley argued with him.

"Aside from not hearing too well, I'm okay," Stanley said.

A hand on his chest restrained him as he tried to rise. "We do this my way," Milani said.

"I have to be in court at nine."

"By then I'll know if you're okay," Milani said. "So lay back and relax. Think about your wife. Mine would have dressed first."

"I took off her nightgown before I left. She needed help with that yesterday."

Milani chuckled. "Aren't you a considerate husband."

"Don't laugh," Stanley remarked. "She may never forgive me."

"You're right," Milani agreed with a snicker. "But, wow, what a vision to wake up to."

"You saw way too much!" Stanley exclaimed, irked. His vexation gave way to his own plight as he thought about Aleta.

"Oh Lord, I'm in deep shit."

Inside the house, Aleta dressed as hurriedly as she could with only one workable hand and debated the whole while whether she could face the men who'd seen her naked. It was her worst nightmare come true. When she slipped on her shoes, she spotted the chief's coat. He needed this. It was cold outside. She had no choice.

Coat in hand, she emerged from the house. Her head was down. The men were still gathered around Stanley. He was still on the ground.

Immediately, her worry over him pushed her into a run. "Is he okay?" she called. "I thought he was okay."

She threw the coat at Chief Milani and dropped to her knees beside her husband.

"You're awake," she looked confused. "What's wrong?"

"It's my idea he be checked out," Chief Milani said. "I don't want him keeling over later of internal bleeding."

"He's bleeding?"

"Not that I know of," Milani said. "But you and your husband won't sit still unless I present the worst case scenario."

Aleta was immediately concerned. "It could happen, Stanley. You're alive. Let's keep you that way."

"Only if you promise to forgive me."

"Forgive you?" Aleta looked startled. "For what?"

"Promise first," Stanley insisted.

The corners of Milani's mouth twitched. This guy had the husband thing down cold. He could take lessons from him.

Exasperated, Aleta said, "I promise. So what am I forgiving you for?"

"I undressed you before I left," Stanley said softly. "I remembered how difficult it was for you to get out of that gown yesterday. I wanted to help."

"Wow!" Aleta exclaimed.

"So you forgive me?"

"I promised, didn't I?"

"Yeah, but do you forgive me?"

"You owe me," Aleta decided.

"Anything!" Stanley said. "I'm so sorry."

She leaned over and kissed him lightly. "It's going to be something big. It may take me years to come up with a payback sufficient enough to make up for this."

Stanley groaned and Tom Milani smiled. It was what he thought all along. Stanley had met his match. He was forgiven; but, he would pay a penance.

Dr. Wayne Cook met the ambulance at the door. Martha Cook's only son and his wife had died in an auto accident and Martha had raised her only grandson. Despite his natural business talent, Wayne left his grandmother to continue heading the family business and entered medical school. After a short stint in an HMO in Rock Island, he came home and joined the ongoing practice of his grandmother's doctor until she underwrote a free clinic. As soon as the building next to the hospital was finished Dr. Cook took over. He also was on call for emergencies at the hospital. His clinic relieved the hospital of many emergency drop-ins who didn't have a family doctor to consult when they were ill.

Both Tom Milani and Lyle West beeped Wayne Cook when a case was coming in they wanted him to take charge of. This was one of those. Wayne left his warm bed, his red-headed wife and his twin boys and raced toward the hospital. He arrived just minutes before the ambulance.

"You two can't seem to stay out of harm's way, can you?" he asked jovially.

"Milani said he could be bleeding internally," Aleta reported as she hurried alongside the gurney.

"We'll check it out," Dr. Cook said. "How's your shoulder?"

"Fine," Aleta responded dismissing her injury as inconsequential.

"While you're here, let me have a look, okay?"

Reluctantly, Aleta agreed and while her husband was being prepped for an MRI, she found herself in an examination room and her shoulder wrap being removed carefully by a nurse. She was draped in preparation for Dr. Cook, a minor procedure, for which she was unduly grateful.

The wait was exceptionally long and Aleta found herself watching the wall clock wondering what was taking so long.

A nurse poked her head in the room. "Dr. Cook's been delayed. I have a person who says he was talking with your husband when the explosion occurred. He says it's important he talk with you."

Aleta checked her status. She was covered.

Ed came in the room. "How is he? How are you? Were you in the car too?"

She explained that Dr. Cook wanted to examine her shoulder. Stanley was having an MRI to see if there were any internal injuries.

"So, he's okay?" Ed asked, his brow clearing. "I thought he was dead when I heard that blast. Then the phone went dead. I rushed right over. The county bomb squad was there."

"Any idea who set it?"

"Didn't get much," Ed said. "But the guy was a pro."

"Why did you need to see me?"

"Stanley wanted me to do a computer search. He said it was very important. I'd like to get right on it but I don't know where to start."

"I was half asleep when he left. I vaguely remember him saying something about Cook Construction and Oakwood but not what. I don't see the connection."

"I think I do," Ed said. "When you see him, tell him I'm working on it."

Chief Tom Milani woke Chief Lyle West. "We had a bombing at Stanley Praetzel's place."

"Anyone killed?"

"Stanley was injured. It was a car bomb. I called to let you know Harriet Locke is back in business. She woke me up. When my man told me, Stanley was driving down the drive, I almost let it go; but, I yelled at them to make him get out of the car. I was so sure she'd made a mistake. He'd taken only a few long strides when it blew."

"How'd you get him out so fast?"

"He thought his wife was in trouble."

"They are pretty committed," Lyle observed.

"You'll never know how much."

"Yes, I will, because you're going to tell me," Lyle said knowingly.

He was right. He got the whole story.

"He'll never live it down," Lyle commented wryly.

"Him? What about her?"

"You know what this means, don't you?"

"What?"

"She's no longer the primary target," Lyle said.

"Why do you say that?"

"She can't drive."

"They're usually together," Tom pointed out.

"I think the target has switched to him," Lyle countered. "And I think it happened when he got the continuance. She'd have to drop the case if he were injured or killed. She can't appear in court in his place."

"I'll assign him a bodyguard," Milani said.

"Her too," West said.

"I guess I can manage that. The decoy obviously didn't work," Tom Milani said with a sigh of resignation.

"That's because it was a car bomber. He was looking for the car not the person."

"How do we get around that?"

"Use police cars to transport them."

"Become a cab service?"

"Just for a couple of days. Friday they're leaving for the dog show in Beatrice Ornstein's RV. And I'll be parked right next to them."

"You're leaving town?"

Tom sounded vexed.

"It's your case," Lyle responded calmly, "both attacks have been in your town. Besides I'll be guarding your two main targets. You know they're going to the show."

"After this?"

"They're alive, aren't they?" West said with a light tone.

Tom shook his head. "I never will understand you dog show people."

"It's a perfect hiding place," West said. "Someone else's trailer, someone else's space on the grounds, someone else's dogs with them. We couldn't set it up better."

"Okay. Okay. You're right," Milani acceded. "I'll do it the regular way until they leave. Then they're yours."

"Thanks for the story," Lyle said. "It was a good one."

"Which you won't tell Lauren, right?"

"Absolutely, I won't tell Lauren. She's Aleta's best friend. Somehow I'd wind up at fault."

"Gotcha!"

Chapter 16

Aleta heard Dr. Cook talking with someone outside her room. She didn't recognize the man's voice. Within seconds, Cook pushed through the door.

"You've got a bodyguard."

"Me? Stanley was the one who was almost killed."

"He's got two."

"Oh."

"I didn't get back as quickly as I thought I would."

"How's Stanley?"

"If you'll watch him for me, I can let him go home."

"He's got several court appearances," Aleta put in.

"He can do those. His hearing in the one ear will come back eventually. He's going to be sore as hell tomorrow though."

"Nothing broken?"

"No. Just got the wind knocked out of him. Slight concussion. If he doesn't fall asleep or doze off today, I'll check him again tonight. If he does either, call me."

"You're sure he's okay to go to court."

"He needs a clean shirt."

The car bomb incident made the seven o'clock television news. The fire was out, but the camera caught the paramedics loading Stanley into the ambulance.

Joey Crowder stayed glued to the set. Was the man dead or alive? By nine he knew that Stanley Praetzel had survived the explosion. The photos showed the totally demolished Lexus and Joey waited for an explanation.

By ten he had his answer. Stanley Praetzel had gotten out of the car just before the bomb went off. It seems he thought his wife needed him. Seconds later he would have been dead.

Joey Crowder had been promised a good piece of change for this job. He'd been paid a measly five grand up front. He kicked himself for his foolishness. The amount at the other end had swayed him. It alone was three times his normal rate.

While he was good, Joey Crowder didn't yet fully appreciate what price a contract killer could charge. He sat in his overstuffed chair in the middle of his sleazy apartment and dreamed of what he could have done with the cash.

The more he thought, the more he felt the intended victim owed him. Three beers later he was talking to the walls. He turned up the television so he could cuss louder.

A knock on the ceiling from the guy upstairs only made him turn the volume up, then he turned on his stereo. The booming base pounded on his eardrums but he didn't care. Screw the guys upstairs. They had no business being home in the middle of the day when regular people were supposed to be at work. A loud banging on the door brought him to his feet. He swaggered to the door and pulled it open and swung wildly.

The huge man caught the swing and then caught Joey as the drunken man lost his footing and fell forward.

"What's going on here, Buddy?" the big man said. "Sounds like World War III. Come on, let's cut down on the explosions."

He dragged the limp man back into the room, and with one arm around Joey's chest, he turned off the stereo. Next he lowered the TV volume.

He didn't turn it off. The newscaster was talking about the man who'd escaped being killed by a bomb that morning. He stuck Joey in the big chair, pulled the last beer from the second six pack, snapped the tab and took a long swill.

"Some guys have all the luck, huh? Born rich, gorgeous wife and some son-of-a-bitch tries to off him and fouls it up."

"I didn't foul it up!" Joey grunted. "The bomb went off. The goddamn guy left his car halfway down the driveway because he thought his wife needed him. What chicken-shit kind of man jumps when his wife calls. He was halfway down the driveway for God's sake!"

"Tough shit alright. You get paid up front?"

"Just a measly five grand," Joey snorted.

"You gotta go back," Tag Burrows said firmly. "You gotta finish the contract or nobody'll hire you again."

"They'll be looking for a bomber," Joey complained.

"So you take him out another way. Lookit this. The guy's father is a rich sonofabitch. Bet he'd give you a hundred grand not to kill his son."

"You think?"

"Yeah. Only you gotta be clever."

"What about the contract?"

"Shove the five grand down the guy's throat. You got a better offer."

"Won't that ruin my rep?"

"Hey, I'd bet he'd go even higher. We could both retire somewhere warm, set us up in a nice apartment with a pool and get outta this crappy city."

"That might work."

"Hey get a load of that wife of his. We should nab them both. We could have some fun with her."

"Too risky," Joey said, his mind coming into focus. He always hated the fact that it took him so long to get drunk enough to forget what he wanted to forget. Some guys couldn't handle two drinks, but he was a regular beer keg on legs. Now he was glad. This project sounded too cool to pass up.

"Not if we plan it. We don't even gotta kill them; but, we gotta be ready to do it if we gotta."

"How much?"

"For both—a million maybe." Tag decided. "Yeah, definitely a million."

"If we do that, we need a house or a van," Joey reasoned. "We gotta have some place to stash them. You really think we can get a million?"

"Yeah, sure. Why not?"

"Yeah," Joey said, his mind already at work.

Chapter 17

Stanley's briefcase had been blown clear of the fire and lay under an apple tree. It blended in with the ground and had been thrust under tree leaves by the force of the blast so it wasn't found until Stanley's second case in court was underway. Milani sent an officer to the courthouse with it.

The judge declared a twenty minute recess so Stanley could review his file. Ordinarily, the judge would not have done this; but, he'd heard about the car bombing. It was a miracle the man was standing.

Aleta told Stanley she was going to use the restrooms. Her bodyguard cleared it first and Aleta stood waiting, head down blushing. This was turning out to be a day of embarrassment.

She had hoped to bury herself in Lyle's study. She was worried that she was falling way behind. If she knew which cases she needed to study, she could have asked Lyle to bring the books to the courthouse; but, that wasn't the way it worked. One case referred to another that referred to another. She needed to be in a law library to do the job. Stanley had given her a direction; but, she had some ideas of her own.

During the second case involving a nearby destitute mother who was fighting to keep her two children, she watched with increasing interest as Stanley insisted that the two children be heard. Social services objected saying all they would hear was the kids testifying that their mother loved them. Stanley insisted that the children's own description of how she manifested that love was critical, and the judge, perhaps out of sympathy for Stanley's near death experience, decided in his favor.

Aleta was surprised at how artfully Stanley led the children into expressing themselves. Even so, Aleta didn't think he'd won until he made his argument. Not only did the children stay with their mother; but, social services was ordered to give supportive services.

"I would have lost that one," Aleta confided when they headed out for lunch.

"No, you wouldn't have," Stanley said.

"Yes, I would have thought removing the children was the right thing to do. They'd be fed, clothed and warm."

"Those are incidentals," Stanley said.

"Is that your wealth talking?" Aleta snapped.

"No," Stanley said evenly. "But tearing a child from the arms of his parent is a deeply traumatic event and many children never recover."

"Well, you did convince me," Aleta said. "Do you win all your cases?"

"I wish I did."

Ed Ornstein met them before they left the courthouse. "Will you be done by three?"

"Probably. Why?"

"Mrs. Cook is going to take us to the main office of Cook Construction. I found the Oakwood bid and it was like the other bids but there was a note at the bottom of the last page 'VAR 2 not shown.' I asked Mrs. Cook about it and she wants to see what that variation is."

"Therein may be our answer," Stanley said. "It won't explain the attacks on us though; but one thing at a time.

Aleta who was used to imposing buildings wasn't prepared for the Cook Construction complex. There was even a helicopter parked alongside a building and a small airstrip in the field beyond. A fleet of limousines and company cars was in a long row of open garages.

Spread out over considerable acreage were half a dozen three-story buildings in park-like setting. Willows dipped their branches over a small offshoot from the Des Plaines River. The creek wound through the maze of buildings.

"My, this is pretty," Aleta observed as Mrs. Cook's Lexus parked in front of the main entrance. Her arrival with three civilians and three uniformed police officers shocked everyone into pretend business at their desks. No one could have explained what they were working on had they been asked. Everyone greeted Mrs. Cook by name as she passed.

Aleta was taken aback by the deference shown this woman who two days ago had been assigned to keep her in her seat. No wonder Martha Cook had everyone's respect. She wasn't just the head of a small-to-middling construction company, she was the commander of a giant corporation.

The embarrassment from the morning's escapade began to fade as she walked alongside Martha Cook absorbing some of the respect being showered upon her.

When they were in the elevator, Martha turned toward Aleta and said, "Have you put this morning's embarrassment behind you?"

Aleta blushed. Does everyone know?

"What happened isn't generally known," Martha said kindly.

"How?"

Martha smiled. "I just wanted you to know that I'm about to be embarrassed; however, we do what's right regardless of our personal discomfiture."

Startled, Aleta asked, "You?"

"Something is going on that I believe will embarrass me as head of this company."

"It was only a bid. And you didn't get the job."

"Our plans were used to sell the project and they weren't real."

When they left the elevator Aleta would swear that everyone was standing at attention figuratively speaking.

"The plans for the Oakwood project," Martha ordered.

A young woman rushed over to a bank of file cabinets and Martha stopped her with a query, "Why aren't they in pending?"

"I was told the contract was signed on this variation," the clerk replied hesitantly. "We were the low bidder on the second variation. That's the one I am handing you."

"Really?" Martha said taking the roll of blueprints from the woman's hand.

Without opening the roll, she said, "I want the other variations, as well.

The woman went to a separate cabinet and pulled out two more sets of blueprints. Martha rolled open the first of the rolls she had been handed on a large tabletop.

"Where's the school?" Martha asked.

"The elementary school isn't in this variation," the clerk said. "But it's in the other two variations."

Having said that, the clerk unrolled one of the blueprints.

"This is the first variation," she explained. "It has the elementary school on the site of the old farmhouse and barn."

"This is the one I approved," Martha said. "I approved the bid on this one as well."

"The city council decided to explore a couple other options. In the second option they eliminated the elementary school but kept the middle school, and we bid on that option and were the low bidder."

"You said there were three bids?"

"Yes," the clerk said. "The third variation we didn't underbid the competition."

"Who handled the bids?"

"Elliott Duffield."

Martha studied the blueprints to the second and third variation briefly then gathered the three sets of prints and told the woman to send Mr. Duffield to her office. She departed as quickly as she came and the whole group ascended to the top floor.

Elliott Duffield, a distinguished looking, older man entered immediately after they arrived. There were plenty of chairs, but no one sat.

Martha Cook rolled open the blueprint to variation two on top of her huge desk and asked Elliott about the chances that this would be the project the town would go ahead with.

"Ninety-seven percent," Elliott replied, slightly uncomfortable over the presence of the three strangers.

"I understand the contract has been signed."

Elliot hesitated for a split second before responding. "It's in the works. Our bid has been accepted."

"You realize, Elliott, that you are fired."

"Whatever for?" Elliott sputtered. "You can't do that just because I successfully bid a project you didn't."

"I wish that were what you had done. If that were true, I'd have promoted you."

"I don't like your insinuation."

Martha eyed him coldly. "I'm insinuating nothing. You made an unauthorized deal with Mayor Liston. This house surrounded by the century old oaks is going to be his personal residence. What were you going to trim to give him that house at well under the construction cost?"

"I have no idea where you got your information; but, it's not correct. No personal deal was struck."

"Where did you cut costs then? This bid is far too low," Martha said.

"You've only glanced at my bid," Elliott charged. "It's legitimate."

"No, it's not," Martha Cook declared with finality. "I know exactly how much building that middle school will cost. My guess is that you planned to charge overages once into the project."

"We always have overages."

"But we don't plan them. That's dishonest."

"Everyone does it," Elliott said defensively. "You're behind the times."

"Well, as long as I'm in charge, we stay behind the times," Martha said adamantly.

"You can't just fire me outright."

"Read your contract," Martha said, buzzing the in-house security. "You have fifteen minutes to clear out. I'd hurry if I were you."

When Elliott Duffield rushed out, Aleta asked, "You don't think he was responsible for what's been happening to us, do you?"

"He's just greedy. He knew the mayor had the court decision in the bag no matter how good your arguments were."

"Why the third variation?" Aleta asked.

Stanley answered his wife's query.

"In case there was an outcry about the elimination of the elementary school. The mayor's house would still be where he wants it."

"Where'd they put the school in the third variation?" Aleta asked.

Martha unrolled the blueprint. Aleta bent over and studied it carefully.

"The school's been moved to the other side of the project. Why?"

"Guess the mayor don't want playground noise to interfere with his afternoon naps," Ed quipped.

"Something else is different," Aleta said.

Martha rolled out all three plans and studied them.

"Where'd this land come from?" she observed. Her comment caused all three to study the blueprints again.

"They added land," Stanley said. "They condemned another parcel for variation three. Why not leave Bessie where she is?"

"Because the mayor wants to build his home on her land," Aleta concluded.

"Unfortunately, the courts don't care," Stanley reminded her.

"Well, they should!" Aleta declared.

"They only look at the larger project. Whose house goes where is not a detail that the courts concern themselves with."

Aleta turned to Ed. "Can you find out who owns the land at the other end of the project?"

"Sure. You want I should find out how he feels about selling it?" Ed asked.

"I want to know everything," Aleta said.

"It's a dead end," Stanley said. "He doesn't figure into this at all."

"Hey," Ed broke in. "A good investigator follows every lead. He don't say in advance whether the lead is good or bad."

Stanley shrugged, "I know when I've been outvoted. I take defeat gracefully."

Aleta kissed him lightly on the cheek. "Thanks. I know how hard it was for you to do that."

Stanley turned to Martha, "May I borrow these? I want to study them."

"I could make you copies," Martha offered.

"There's something about presenting original plans in court that makes whatever I say seem more legitimate."

"Will they help?" Martha inquired hopefully.

"They might."

"Take them for as long as you need them."

"You realize that you're legally bound to honor the second bid."

"It won't be the first time we suffered a loss," Martha said.

Chapter 18

Ed hit Jerome Lutz's farmhouse at a little after five. He quickly assessed the wrinkled, weathered face and penetrating eyes as belonging to a man of experience. He came straight to the point.

"I work for Bessie Dobbins' lawyer."

"Come on in," the older man said. "How about a cup of joe?"

He opened the new storm door, a bit out of sync with the weathered appearance of the old house. The porch was old, but solid. The railing had new boards in it. Someone was keeping this place repaired.

Ed removed his cap as he entered the house, a gesture of politeness not lost on Lutz.

The living room furniture was old, but clean. Not a thing was out of place.

"People call me Jerry," Lutz said fetching two mugs of coffee from the kitchen. Ed noticed the knobby joints characteristic of arthritis.

"You were one of those who spoke up for Bessie to keep her farm," Ed opened.

"Yep. Is it gonna happen?"

"Might," Ed said. "She's got a sharp lawyer; but, there's not much chance."

"So that sonofabitch's gonna win?"

"Don't you like the mayor's plan?"

"Bunch of crap. And he don't care nothing about anyone but himself."

"Why's it crap?"

"'Cause it ain't the plan that's gonna be used. And the bidding on the real plan was rigged."

"Rigged?"

"Yeah, the mayor got a payoff," Lutz commented bitterly. "No loyalty."

"To who?"

"To local contractors what bid fair and square on the job," he replied heatedly.

"You know any?" Ed asked knowing he'd touched a nerve.

"Yeah, my son, Gene," he replied. "C&G Construction. Cole's my son-in-law. They do good work."

"They were low bidders on one of the plans," Ed said.

"Yeah. They learned real quick that that damned Cook Construction Company ain't the honest folk ole Martha Cook claims they is," Jerry Lutz said. "I told them to play her game, so's they did on the third bid."

"So the projects were changed and the bids opened up again?"

"You got it. Don't know why Cook didn't bid low the last project; but I think they thought the council would go with the one they could get the cheapest. The damned mayor isn't gonna build a school. That's just ad talk."

"Does Oakwood need a school?"

"Hell, yes! Phil Fleming knows it. He's got little kids. Mayor's kids are older."

Ed decided not to play dumb, "If they go with the third plan, they gotta have more land, don't they?"

"Yeah, my farm was next up."

"How do you feel about that?"

"I wouldn't mind a school being built on it. I'm ready to retire. Been farming a long time. My hands ain't what they was once."

"And live in town?"

"Not on your life!" Lutz said. "I'd get me a small cabin somewheres north and hunt and fish all the live long day. Don't that sound great?"

"Yeah, sure does," Ed said honestly.

"But ain't gonna happen," Lutz said bitterly. "Not as long as Liston's the mayor."

Chapter 19

Nine o'clock that night, Stanley phoned Ed Ornstein.

"I'm maybe onto something," Ed said. "Can you come down to my office?"

"Sorry, I can't," came the reply. "Remember I had an appointment with Dr. Cook at the hospital? Well, he snagged me and stuck me in bed. Milani took away my clothes personally. He's determined I'm not going home tonight."

"Can they do that?" Ed asked aghast.

"I guess Wayne was breaking some sort of law letting me go home after a concussion. It's not a regular law, mind you, but a hospital rule."

"I can go over what I found with Aleta and…"

"She's asleep."

"Nabbed her too, huh?"

"You got it. Milani says he wants a good night's sleep for a change. Wayne even gave her a sleeping pill to make sure she'd stay down."

"Heck!"

"Tell me what you've got."

And so Ed repeated the entire interview with the aging farmer with remarkable accuracy. At the end, Stanley asked, "The porch railing that he fixed, how was it done?"

"If the spokes was painted, it'd look like new. But he didn't fix it himself. His hands is shot. But it weren't being fixed to sell."

"Maybe they were fixing it for the appraiser," Stanley pointed out. "Wouldn't you put in a couple day's work to realize an extra thousand or two?"

"New railings won't do that."

"Oh, I think they probably fixed more than the railings; but, that isn't what's made you return to the office instead of going home to check on Emma."

"The old man's angry. How much you wanna bet the son is too? And construction workers have access to explosives."

"I should call Milani," Stanley said.

"Why him? The county bomb squad has both bombs."

"Well, I think I should wake him up. This is an important break."

Ed quickly got the picture.

"How many times do you plan to wake him up?"

"Only two or three," Stanley smirked, then returned to seriousness. "The bomb squad said the two bombs were the work of two men. I guess bombers leave signatures. So why use a different guy?"

"Different perp. Different motive. Different method," Ed replied. "Lutz wants Liston gone. He said that as long as Liston is mayor, there ain't no hope the council will buy his land."

"He could sell it privately," Stanley said, then went on, "However, if the town wins, then what happens to his property. A private sale might bring him even more; but, that could be complicated. If a developer does a bit of research and finds there's not going to be a school built as originally planned, the deal could fall through. The city council could throw up roadblocks until they decide what they want to use the land for.”

“He's screwed.”

“Not if he has time to wait,” Stanley said. “How bad are his hands?”

“He ain't got a winter left in them.”

“I got it!” Stanley said suddenly. “You call Milani. If I call him, he'll remove my phone.”

Ed brushed aside the suggestion by ignoring it and finishing his report.

“I thought maybe the two rotting in Milani's jail might be on one of the construction crews that did the bidding. C&G Construction wasn't second lowest on the bid on the second variation, Scanlon Construction was. I asked around. Scanlon's not beyond making ridiculously low bids and then piling on the overages after the job's his. If you the customer won't pay the overages, he quits part way through. He can prove you got your money's worth.”

“So we got two angry construction firms; but, losing a bid happens all the time.”

“Yeah, I know. You want I should quit?”

“Except for Cook, the others are small time construction firms, right?”

“Yeah. C&G is just getting started. It'd be a big boost for them to land this one. Scanlon could retire on what he'd manage to overcharge on such a long project.”

“Milani needs to get the work history of the men he's holding.”

“You want me to call, huh?”

“Yes. Twice. Once about the bomb. Once about this.”

“Tell you what,” Ed said. “You call. I'll call you in an hour. If I don't get through, then I'll call him and say I need to reach you.”

“That's even better!” Stanley exclaimed. “Put me in a hospital gown will he. That he needs to pay for. A man has limits.”

Stanley heard Milani's phone ring once.

"If you're calling to protest, you're wasting your breath," Chief Milani said gruffly. "I'm in bed, practically asleep."

"I'm not taking this lying down," Stanley began, "but…"

"Knowing how you're dressed," Milani chuckled, "I'd say that's exactly how you're taking this."

"As I was saying, Ed came up with a new lead. What if our bomber was a member of one of the construction crews that lost the bid."

"We've identified the man who set your car bomb. He's a pro. The bomb squad has seen his work before."

"And he's still loose?"

"It's hard to convict without motive or witnesses or some piece of evidence that ties the bomb to him."

"Are they going to arrest him?"

"If they can find him," Milani said. "Looks like he's moved."

"Any clue as to where?"

"All we know is he traded his car in for a used gray Dodge van as is. I guess it's not much to look at. We've got the license number."

"Is that why you put us here?"

"I figured he might head straight for your house. I have men waiting."

"So you aren't in bed, are you?"

"No, I'm not."

Stanley set aside his pique at his predicament.

"Ed thinks that the other two may be construction workers or were in the past."

"We'll check that angle," Milani said matter-of-factly. "Ed must have uncovered a motive."

"Construction workers have access to explosives," Stanley added. "One of them could have been responsible for the bomb under the mayor's car."

"Thanks," Milani said simply. "Good lead."-

"No, thank you," Stanley said with sincerity.

"So I take it you aren't planning to call me every hour," Milani quipped.

"Me disturb your sleep? Never!" Stanley retorted with humor. "But as Dr. Cook has the nurses waking me every hour to check on me, you can call me."

"The man has a sense of humor."

"It's not funny."

"Sure it is."

Tag Burrows drove the van past the Praetzel house without stopping. Joey had him continue driving out into the country. They turned onto a north-south highway and headed north.

"What are we doing?" Tag asked.

"We picked up a tail," Joey said. "It was a set-up."

"What was?"

"The house. They aren't there."

"How far do we go?"

"To the Wisconsin border if necessary," Joey said.

"How do you know it was a set-up? I didn't see no cop cars."

"That's why," Joey said. "I just missed getting caught when I set the bomb. Why would they not be guarding them now?"

"Maybe they figured you wouldn't be back?"

"What about that car following us?"

"It ain't a squad car."

"They drive around in plain cars too."

"We didn't pick him up for couple miles."

"Cops is smart," Joey said.

"You're paranoid. I'm going back to the house. If the car turns around, I'll believe you."

The car kept going.

"See!" Tag gloated.

"I don't care," Joey said as they continued on without a tail. "That was too close."

"You're paranoid."

"Go back to Oakwood. I'll feel better when this van is inside the garage."

"How come he give you the house?"

"I told him the cops would check the motels."

"Oh yeah," Tag returned. "But them beds ain't no good. I'd rather be in a motel."

"Stop jabbering. We gotta stay hid."

Chapter 20

Dr. Wayne Cook breezed into the room shared by the Praetzels and found both in one bed pouring over blueprints.

"I guess I could have saved you the cost of a bed," he joshed.

"You probably saved our lives last night," Stanley said. "Milani told me his man followed a gray van but the license plate was the wrong one. He figured if the men weren't stopped, they'd relax and try again today."

"Why not stop the van anyway?"

"He said he needed a reason to search the van. If it had turned onto my property, he'd have had a reason."

"So can we have our clothes?" Aleta asked.

"Tom's bringing them. He wants you to stay here until he gets here."

"We have things to do," Aleta protested.

"You're free to go," Wayne smiled. "But it's raining and you'll have to leave the gowns."

Aleta looked at Stanley, "You up for a nude dance in the rain or should we wait?"

"We wait for umbrellas. We can't get the blueprints wet."

"Okay, now show me the change in the property lines," Aleta said.

"In the third variation, a section of Bessie's land is separated and attached to Huck's land. Maybe that's how whoever conceived of this planned to equalize the difference in land cost."

"It also brings Huck Dirkson back into the picture."

"Whoever did it wants the stable to stay put."

"What council members have girls that ride horses?"

"Ed can find out," Stanley said picking up the phone. As it rang he leaned over and kissed his wife. "We make a good team."

"All of them," Ed answered. "It's a keep-up-with-the-Jonses thing."

"They all have daughters that ride?"

"Fleming has a son. I hear he's pretty good," Ed replied.

"So, it could be any of them."

"Tell him to find out what kind of houses they live in," Aleta said.

"The laundry has arrived," announced a cheerful voice from the doorway. Milani entered with an armload of neatly folded clothes. "My wife says there was no way a woman would wear underwear two days in a row, so she washed just about everything."

Aleta squealed delightedly, "I love your wife!"

"These will have to do you for a couple of days though," Milani said somberly. "You can't go home and you can't go shopping."

"I keep spare clothes at my parents' house," Stanley said.

"I didn't know that," Aleta charged.

"I didn't think about them until now," Stanley apologized. "Tell them I'm going to court today and…"

He stopped when Milani shook his head. "No court?"

"No court."

"Tell my parents I'm going to a dog show. They'll know what to pack."

"What about me?" Aleta asked.

"Borrow," Milani said casually.

"I'm showing a dog. I need to look really good. Besides Beatrice isn't my size."

"What about your grandmother?" Stanley asked.

"Her clothes are old." Aleta protested.

"She's bought a lot of new outfits shopping with your mother."

"Old lady clothes. She and I don't have the same taste."

"You'll have to make do," Milani said, knowing no woman wanted to hear those words. "We're taking you straight to Beatrice's house. You're staying there until you leave in a caravan with your grandmother and the Wests. I'll have people in the house and outside. After you're out of Willow Glen, you're West's responsibility."

Aleta's distress was real. "What am I going to do all day?"

"West brought over some case studies for you to study. Ed says you can use his computer. He'll be at the office."

"What about Stanley?" Aleta pressed.

Milani grinned. "Unlike you he didn't get much sleep and he'll need it. He's got a lot of driving to do. How're those ribs today?"

Stanley grimaced, "Pretty sore."

"You've got it all planned out, haven't you?" Aleta snapped.

"I'd better have," Milani said soberly. "Your lives depend on it."

"We'll do as you ask," Stanley said firmly. "Aleta, let's get you dressed."

Aleta grunted her acquiescence. She hated being told what to do. She wanted to declare that she could do it herself, even though she couldn't; but her wedding vow popped into her head.

"Stanley has the final word," she said. "I go along with what he says."

Milani's surprise was evident. Stanley had tamed his redhead. Lyle was still working on his.

While in the clothing store as Harriet Locke was trying on a rust-colored jacket both she and Beatrice agreed would look good on Aleta, Harriet saw two quick scenes in the mirror in front of her. In both Lyle West was drawing his gun. In both he was shot dead. She blinked to see if she could get the vision to return; but, she couldn't.

They were separate incidents. In one he was shot in the head; in the second, he was hit in the chest. But where and when were not clear.

She walked out, her face drawn and pale.

"What's wrong?" Beatrice asked.

"Nothing," Harriet murmured. She turned slowly. "It looks good doesn't it?"

Beatrice's focus returned to the garment Harriet was wearing.

"If Aleta doesn't like it, it's perfect for you," Beatrice said. She held up three skirts and Harriet said, "Find me a couple of blouses."

Harriet went back into the dressing room. She tried on the gold and wondered if Aleta would like it. She didn't. She could always take it home and return it next week if Aleta didn't like it either.

She changed into a dark green skirt and looked herself in the mirror. This is better, she thought. Definitely this one. Aleta can choose. I can at least bring her skirts that fit. As she unzipped the zipper she checked the pockets. There were two. She felt something in one.

She pulled out a tiny bit of paper. It was blank. She scolded herself. What was she expecting? Written instructions? The answer was yes. She remembered the shock of seeing Lyle West in a crouched position, pull his gun and fire. The bullet hit him an instant later.

She shook her head as she dropped the green skirt and reached for the dark brown one. She glanced in the mirror as she bent over.

"Quite a spare tire I'm developing," she muttered. "Just what I don't need."

Beatrice poked her head between the curtains. "What don't you need?"

"A spare tire."

"You're thin as a rail!" Beatrice observed. "I'm the one with a spare which reminds me, I bought a new one for the RV. Don't let me forget to have Ed stow it in the space."

Harriet handed Beatrice the green skirt. "This one's nice. Don't like the gold. Are there any other choices?"

"I'll look," Beatrice said. "Here are a couple of blouses."

As Harriet handed Beatrice the skirt, the slip of blank paper fluttered to the floor. Beatrice bent to pick it up.

"Don't worry. It's blank," Harriet remarked.

"Yep, it is. Why do we always figure there's a message?"

She was gone before Harriet could respond.

I was hoping too hard I guess. You gave Aleta a whole news article. How about an auditory hallucination this time. Psychotics don't usually get both. At least I don't think they do.

Her cell phone rang. She picked it up.

"Hello," she said as she stepped into the brown skirt.

"Yeah, there's a spare. Ed put a new one in before we left."

It was Stanley's voice. Flabbergasted Harriet couldn't find her voice for several seconds. A second voice came on line.

"You stay there."

It was Lyle West's voice.

"Nobody saw us leave," Stanley rejoined.

"You've been driving," came the response. The bushes rustled. Then came a single shot.

Harriet pulled the phone from her ear and dropped it on her purse as if it were a snake.

"Don't like that method either, God," she growled. "We need a new way to communicate."

"Who are you talking to?" Beatrice said pulling back the curtain. "Hey I like that skirt. See how the gold blouse goes with it."

Harriet put her arms in the sleeves and buttoned the blouse, her hands performing the task without any conscious orders from her brain which was still trying to hear the last words of a man about to die.

Impatiently, she turned to Beatrice. "I like all your choices. I know at least one outfit will fit. Aleta can try them on and choose. We can return the rest next week."

"Sounds good," Beatrice said. "Do you know her shoe size?"

"I have shoes. Let's go."

"What's wrong?"

"I received another prophecy," Harriet said. "I can't think anymore. Aleta can borrow whatever else she needs from me."

"Who this time?"

Harriet shook her head.

"He should be warned," Beatrice said.

"I know how to prevent the first death."

"There were two?" Beatrice gasped. "You got two visions."

"I need to go home now," Harriet said.

Beatrice gathered the blouses, the two skirts and the jacket and hurried toward the cashier. By the time Harriet emerged from the dressing room, the purchases were being packaged.

"I'm sorry," Harriet said contritely.

"Hey, if it had happened to me, I'd be pretty shaken up too. And in a clothing store. I might never go shopping again."

Harriet took her friend's arm. "I'm glad you were here. There are only a few people that would have understood."

"I thought you weren't getting visions anymore."

"I thought so too. I'm not a happy person right now. In fact, I need to go home and cry."

"Cry in the car. You'll just upset everyone if you arrive home in this state, especially if you won't give us a clue. Speaking of which, here we are. You just sit down and I'll pack up and get us home."

"I don't have the last piece of the puzzle," Harriet said. "I don't know when or where the second death will happen."

"If you don't prevent the first, will it matter?"

Harriet shook her head. "No, no it won't matter at all. Not at all."

Beatrice shut the car door, walked around and climbed into the driver's seat.

"Everything in its season," Beatrice said. "That's the way nature works."

She drove out of the parking lot without waiting for a response.

Of course, Harriet thought. I only need to take one action right now. In fact, if I knew the circumstance I might take such drastic action so as to change too much.

Harriet was surprised at her own reasoning. Where did she come up with that answer? It was the perfect answer. She didn't recollect ever having that thought before; but, it made such perfect sense. Why hadn't she ever seen that concept before?

I should be grateful that He trusted me with saving Lyle's life the first time. There must be a reason why He showed me the second vision. Stop trying to explain it to your brain. How can you explain what you can't possibly know? God may not even think in such a straight line. So many lives are intertwined. Lyle needs to survive the first attempt. And I need to know about the second. But why? Why not show that one later? That makes no sense.

"I need to talk with Aleta alone," Harriet said out loud.

"Take her to your room to try on the outfits we bought. I'll see you aren't disturbed."

When the two walked into the house, the smell of baking hit them.

"Evelyn made pies," Aleta announced. "She loves your kitchen."

"We were successful," Beatrice announced. "Aleta you go up with your grandmother and try on the outfits. I'm going to get on with the lunch to go with this dessert."

"Where's Stanley?" Harriet asked.

"Upstairs sleeping."

"Don't wake him," Beatrice said. "Use my bedroom."

"Isn't the front bedroom empty?" Aleta asked.

"There's a policeman parked in it. He has a full view of the street from there," Beatrice replied smoothly. "Evelyn, help me set up the lunch. You'll see Aleta in all her splendor at the show."

"Hurry," Harriet said. "We haven't a lot of time. We still need to pack for you. How did Dr. Cook tape your arm? We bought a coat. I hope you can wear it."

"He taped it so as to restrain movement but not make it impossible for me to put my arm in a sleeve like before."

Harriet carried the hangers with the coat and skirts while Aleta carried the blouses. As soon as they were in the room, Harriet locked the door.

"We need to talk," Harriet said. "I can't be interrupted."

"Should I sit and listen or…"

"Try on the clothes. Maybe you'll get some of the puzzle I didn't get."

"What does that mean?"

"I saw someone die twice."

"The same person? How can that happen?"

"I have no idea because if he died as I saw in the first vision, why would I get the second?"

As she spoke, all her old worries flooded back.

"When did you get the vision?"

"When I was trying on the coat and one of the skirts."

"Which ones?" Aleta said striping down to her panties and bra.

Harriet handed her the dark brown skirt and held out the jacket. She reached for the beige blouse but came up with the pink one instead.

"Oh Grams!" Aleta squealed. "I was sure you'd pick an all brown outfit. I didn't dream you'd dare to buy me pink and rust."

Harriet laughed. "Neither did I. Beatrice selected the blouses and I just took them all. We can return any you don't like."

Harriet helped her into the blouse and then the coat and stood back mouth agape. The combo was electric.

Aleta looked at the outfit from every angle. "Let me show Beatrice."

"Yes, do," Harriet said wondering what piece she expected Aleta to fill in.

The oohs and ahhs from downstairs warmed her. Slowly she realized she didn't need to tell Aleta anything. This was her vision. Aleta had on both pieces of the outfit and she experienced nothing. There was no magic in the clothes.

When the Wests arrived after lunch, there was a break in the rain long enough to load the remainder of the dogs. The lookouts were at windows on each side of the house.

Milani brought West up-to-date and the two of them worried in a quiet corner of the living room. Harriet slipped quietly onto the couch nearby.

The two police chiefs stopped talking, looked at her and waited.

"I was thinking," she said after a period of silent thought, "that Stanley shouldn't drive the RV."

"Aleta's arm won't let her," Lyle commented. "It's too long a trip for Evelyn. We have no one else unless we only take two vehicles instead of three."

"We need three to sleep all of us and to house the dogs." Harriet pointed out. "And this rain could follow us down. We need the room."

"So despite his chest, Stanley has to do it," Tom Milani said.

"His chest?" Harriet asked. "What's his chest have to do with anything?"

"The explosion didn't just knock him down," Milani explained, "it threw him against the hard ground. He's got a set of bruises I don't see on car accident victims without multiple breaks."

Harriet looked shocked.

"You had no idea? You haven't seen his chest, have you? I should have known. If you had, you wouldn't have been making a quiet suggestion."

His response gave Harriet time to recover.

"I was just going to suggest that since the bomber is somewhere near here. and he's looking for Stanley, that we should hide him on the trip south and not put him in the driver's seat."

"She had a vision," Lyle concluded as if it were a common occurrence.

Tom picked up his friend's attitude. "So what do we do to keep someone from dying?"

Harriet was so shocked she laughed.

Lyle smiled and spoke up, "I guess we don't let Stanley drive."

"Then who?" Tom said. "My budget is already stretched to the limit; but, even if it weren't, I couldn't explain turning one of my men into a chauffeur for a weekend."

"I agree."

"We need someone we can trust," Harriet said. "And frankly, there may be a risk, so it's got to be a cop. There isn't any other choice unless…"

Lyle grinned. "I love to watch a woman's mind work, don't you?"

Tom fell into the lighter mood quickly. "As long as it's not my wife. When her mind spins, I'm in trouble."

"Ed's assistant," Harriet suggested, enjoying the lightness of the moment.

"Dean Lundgren?" Lyle said thoughtfully. "That might be the answer. He's young, strong, licensed to carry a gun, and he knows what's going on."

"A gun?" Harriet asked. "We aren't going to need a gun. Nobody should have a gun. Nobody."

Her body tensed. She remembered the second vision.

"Don't worry. We try never to use them," Lyle said, "but since the bad guys carry guns, the good guys need to too."

On the other hand, Harriet thought, since I've changed the first event, maybe I shouldn't try to anticipate the second. I could mess things up. I need to let things unfold naturally. It was part of Lyle's make-up to keep his gun with him. Ordinarily, she knew he wouldn't have it with him at a dog show; but, he was in charge, albeit unofficially, of the safety of two people. It would be foolish for him to come unarmed.

"Well, okay," Harriet conceded. "I'll grant you that it would probably be prudent for you two to have guns."

"You still have your rifle in your RV," Lyle pointed out.

"Well, yes, but…"

"So we can circle the wagons if necessary."

"Okay. Okay, so I didn't even count my guns," Harriet admitted. "I do hunt you know. I'm storing them in the RV until my house is built."

Lyle just smirked. Stanley had room in his house to store Harriet's rifles; but, she liked having them in her RV, as if every hunting trip was not only planned days in advance, but circumscribed by law. Of course, hunting season had just opened. He was a bit surprised she was going to a dog show. Jason Danielson, one of the other members of the Tontine group, was duck hunting with his Labs and two of his sons. If Lauren weren't pregnant, Lyle would be there too. But when Lauren was pregnant, Lyle stayed close.

Aleta's presence would add extra fun. It had been a fast growing friendship that bloomed quickly, partly because both Lauren and Aleta were displaced Californians and partly because both loved to show dogs.

Lyle found Stanley an exciting intellectual equal, one whose early years were similar to his own. He realized they would have become friends had not a five year age difference put Stanley in eighth grade when Lyle was a college freshman. That gap narrowed as more years passed but, without a common interest that brought them together, they remained acquaintances floating on the outer edge of the social circle of their parents. Lyle, as Police Chief, had little in common with his social counterparts and socialized rarely with them. Stanley, a not too gregarious single man, found such gatherings not comfortable either.

Lyle knew he had missed the dimension that having Stanley as a friend would add to his life. He sensed Stanley felt as he did, so he took it upon himself to explain the situation to Stanley.

He sought out Stanley and found him in bed with his wife by his side.

"I hate to order the two of you to share the same bed for the next several hours," Lyle said with a grin. "But Chief Milani and I have decided that because the car bomber is in the area, we want you to hide in the bedroom in the back of the RV during the trip, with the blinds down."

He looked at the snickering pair. "No one is to peek out. We don't want anyone to suspect that anyone is there."

"Who's going to drive the RV?" Aleta asked.

"Dean will drive and help with the set up."

"Who's paying for that?"

"Harriet said the Tontine would pay. I guess it comes under legal expenses. Keeping their lawyers alive is considered a necessary legal expense according to Harriet."

"Does she know what Ed charges per hour?"

"This is Dean."

"If Dean leaves, Ed will have to do his work," Aleta observed. "He'll charge the full amount."

Lyle looked relieved, "Boy, now I am glad Harriet offered to pick up the cost. Neither Tom nor I could ever have explained that much of an expense."

The downpour hit the roof suddenly.

Lyle's response was immediate.

"Come on! Now's the time to get the two of you to the van."

"It's pouring."

"But you can't see ten feet in this weather," Lyle charged. "Let's go."

"Dean's not here!" Aleta protested.

"We're not hiding him. Stop stalling."

Stanley curled up, groaning. "Aleta, I'm up. Let's move."

"Maybe we shouldn't go?" she said suddenly realizing how much pain her husband was in.

"You can't not go!" Lyle protested. "I've got you for the weekend. Milani's got a trap set. He needs you out of town. And Lauren hired a sitter."

Stanley turned at the door and addressed his wife. "I'm going to spend four hours in a moving bed. It's a new experience for me. Want to share it?"

"You don't get seasick, do you?"

"I'll puke on my side of the bed," Stanley promised.

"Well, who could refuse such an invitation."

"Thanks," Lyle said as the group descended the stairs.

"You almost panicked," Stanley said. "Don't you understand these women yet?"

"Thanks," Lyle repeated.

"Look I'm going to be in pain no matter where I am. Whoa! Look at it come down!"

With raincoats hurriedly thrown over the three of them Lyle, suitcase in hand, led the way and was the last to enter the RV.

"I'm going to block the bedroom door with the case to remind you that you aren't to leave the bed," Lyle said. "Is there anything you need before I block the door?"

"Towels," Aleta said. "My pants are sopping wet. Stanley, take off those shoes. I'm not sharing a bed with wet shoes!"

"What about yours?" he countered.

As if in response, he heard two shoes clunk on the floor.

"Can't they stay on?" he pleaded. "They'll dry eventually."

It occurred to Aleta that it hurt him to bend over.

"Lay back," she said.

He did as he was told stifling a moan as he did so. Aleta pulled off both shoes and then his socks. She hung the socks over the towel rack and reached up and unbuckled his belt.

"Hey, what are you doing?"

"Your pants are as soaked as mine. I want to sleep in a dry bed."

"You're not taking off your pants," Stanley stated authoritatively.

"Oh, don't be such a worry wart. Lyle will turn around until we shut the door."

"I want my pants!" Stanley insisted.

Lyle swallowed a smirk.

"They'll be hanging on the outside of the door," Aleta stated yanking them from his feet which were curled to resist their departure.

Aleta dropped hers beside Stanley's. "You'll hang them up, won't you?" she asked as she closed the door.

Lyle heard some grunting and knocking against the walls and then silence. "Are you set?" he asked picking up the pants and hanging them both on pant hangers. Stanley's pockets emptied on the floor.

"What's that?" Stanley called.

"I'll put your stuff in the top drawer," Lyle said. "Don't forget where it is."

The two lying in the bed heard the outside door open and close.

"We're alone," Stanley breathed. "That's a nice sensation."

"Yes, we can do what we want; but we can't do anything."

"Next week this'll all be behind us."

"Grams tried to tell me something."

"She had a prophecy, didn't she?" Stanley said. "I figured as much considering how adamant Lyle was about us not being seen."

"It's not us that's in danger."

"Then why are we lying here in the semi-dark in a coffin-like space?"

"It's not a coffin," Aleta protested. "It's a bed. And it's someone that's with us that's in danger."

"Who?"

"I was trying on my show outfit and she sent me down to show Beatrice and when I came back she had decided not to say more."

"How can you be sure it's not us?"

"I don't know. But when I tried on the outfit I knew it wasn't you or me. It was a strange feeling, but it was the reason I was so giddy. We were going to a show. I had clothes to wear. And neither of us was going to wind up dead."

"Well I'd be giddy too if I had been you," Stanley remarked dryly. "Tell me exactly what she did say."

"Why?"

"Because we're two legal minds used to untangling knotty problems. And we've got hours to think about this."

Aleta repeated every word. Because her grandmother had prefaced her comments by locking the door, Aleta had focused on every word.

Suddenly, the outside door to the RV opened. Both fell silent.

"Hi, you guys. It's me, Dean. We're getting ready to go, rain and all. I brought some tapes to keep me company."

They heard a suitcase plunked on the floor.

"Hey, these are really wet," he commented.

"Are they hanging up?"

"Sure are," Dean replied. "Oh, and I'll have the music loud enough so you can do whatever you want in there."

"Thanks for the permission," Stanley said, "but, in case Lyle didn't tell you, I can hardly move."

"Yeah, I know. You know what they say. Where there's a will, there's a way."

"Oh, go drive!"

"It's gonna be a long drive if we're fighting rain all the way. We can't go fast in these big guys."

"We'll be sleeping," Stanley finished.

"Remember, you don't come out no matter what."

"Thanks for doing this, Dean," Stanley finished.

The music began as the RV engine rumbled awake. The rig trembled slightly and Stanley took Aleta's hand and the two lay staring at the ceiling.

"What were we talking about?" Stanley asked.

"I forget. All I can think about is what he said."

"You mean the 'where there's a will' part?"

"Is there?"

"You want to?"

"We have no bathroom."

"We have towels."

"They're for drying us off," Aleta said.

"Well let's start there."

So that's where Aleta started. It wasn't long before they each discovered what movement caused pain and which did not. Aleta was the one to come up with the idea that eventually worked. It was a slow, relaxed ride and both enjoyed the duration as together their excitement rose to a smooth completion.

When done neither could believe what had just happened. Shortly afterward they fell asleep on their backs their hands clasped.

They woke together to the drumming of the rain on the roof. They could hear the swish of the water as the wheels underneath them hit the water-coated pavement.

Stanley looked at his watch. "We've been on the road for three hours."

Aleta looked over. "You wore a watch to bed?"

"We aren't in bed," Stanley shot back. "Well, yes, technically, we are; but, I maintain we aren't, not really."

"Where exactly are we?"

"In a vehicle traveling down a highway in the pouring rain. That's where."

"What do you think about what Grams said?"

"Oh yes, I remember. That's where we were."

"She seemed relaxed when I came back into the room as if my having a good show outfit was critical."

"Would you have gone without one?"

"Probably not, especially with your chest in that condition."

"So, it was critical," Stanley surmised. "So she wanted us to go."

"With us eliminated, there are only five people left," Aleta put in.

"What five?"

"Grams, Evelyn, Lyle, Lauren and Dean," Aleta answered.

"Not Dean because if he wasn't scheduled to come along until your grandmother's vision radically altered the plans."

"Not Grams. She said 'someone,'" Aleta reasoned. "We're down to three."

"Well," Stanley said, "I can see Evelyn or Lauren accidentally getting in harm's way once, but not twice."

"That leaves Lyle," Aleta murmured.

"So now we know who," Stanley said. "But when and where."

"We know the first killing happened on this trip," Aleta said. "That's why we're locked in this room. Someone must have seen us leaving and Lyle, being our protector, tried to stop them and was killed."

"Your logic is sound. So if we make it to the fairgrounds…" Stanley began then stopped. He didn't want to jinx anything. He laughed at his own thought. How can you jinx a prophecy?

"If we make it to the fairgrounds, what?"

"We put on our pants and enjoy ourselves."

"What about the second threat?"

"We stay on our toes," Stanley said. "Maybe that's all we need to do."

The rain stopped at that instant. The two both automatically believed it was an omen. Neither dared say anything to the other, but both relaxed.

Chapter 21

That evening Aleta took her clue from her grandmother. Evidently the first danger was passed. The group, delighted to be south of the rain, decided a barbecue would be the best way to spend the evening. Stanley tended the fire. When it was ready, he put on the steaks while Lyle and Dean set up the pens. Harriet and Lauren took the dogs to the pens one by one and filled the water dishes. Special smaller portions of food were meted out to some. Others were given a small biscuit. Evelyn set the table and took potato salad and a tossed salad, from the refrigerator. She set out the rolls and butter. Then, she set an apple pie on the table and cut it into eight slices.

The work was quickly done with everyone working. Aleta felt useless, but, Harriet insisted she do nothing and everyone backed up that decision. Aleta made a few attempts, but even Stanley refused to allow her to help. Finally, Stanley told her to go find Tom Wilson and let him know she was here and would be taking Maggie into the ring in the morning.

As the group gathered for supper, the night settled in. Lanterns were brought out and by the time the pie was consumed, everyone was satiated and relaxed. A bit of wine topped off the evening's meal and stories of the trip were exchanged. Aleta and Stanley were silent during the exchange; but, in the end Dean mentioned that it wasn't only their shoes that were parked in the hall. He ended by saying, "They'll sleep well tonight," and the group roared while the newlyweds cast their eyes down, totally embarrassed.

It was Stanley who came to their rescue. He raised his wine glass and said, "A toast to all of you who made this day a good one for us. Thank you."

"You're welcome," Lyle said, lifting his glass. "On the way back, we get the bed."

Everyone laughed and the tension was broken.

Chapter 22

Lyle West called Tom Milani late that night.

"Did our rat fall in the trap?"

"He's been scurrying around all day," Tom replied. "The construction crew poured concrete all morning. Then the rains came."

"What about the concrete?"

"Covered with plastic."

"Your guys were out in that storm?"

"Switched to a different surveillance technique," Tom said. "Necessity dictates change."

"So what did you do?"

"We moved the car so it's opposite the bedroom windows. I've got three inside with the decoys. Two on, one off every eight."

"Sounds good."

"How was your trip?"

Lyle told him about locking Stanley and his bride in the bedroom.

"And they found a way," he added.

"God, do you remember your first couple months?"

"But with that chest?"

"As you said, they found a way."

"You're sure the bomber is still there?" West pressed.

"Someone spotted him just before dark," Milani said. "It may take him a day to figure out a way to get around all that wet cement."

"Well, we're here for two full days."

"Nice to have them safe while we go for this guy."

Joey Crowder and Tag Burrows drove away from Willow Glen to a bar twenty miles out that served decent chili and offered draft beer. They sat in a booth in the back of the dimly lit bar and ate in silence.

"Why not tonight?" Tag asked as he finished and reached for his beer.

"Dark as hell and we don't know how soggy the ground is. We could get stuck."

"We ain't driving in. We already decided that."

"I mean us. You. Me. We could go down and one of them could get away in the dark."

"Yeah, you're right."

"Great night for rigging a car bomb though."

"You think." Tag's eyes brightened. "It'd be a sure twenty-five G's."

"We're after a million, remember?"

"Oh, yeah."

"You ain't chickening out?"

"Me? Naw. Just jumpy. Too much rain."

"What you need...hell, what we both need is a good lay."

Tag looked around. "Ain't nobody good here tonight."

"How about them two broads? We got a van."

"Yeah, okay.

Joey got up and went over to the two women. "Hey, girls, how about joining us at our table and let us buy you a couple of drinks?"

"Sure, why not?" was the reply and the evening progressed from there.

Chapter 23

Stanley rose before Aleta. When he went into the RV's kitchen, he found Dean pouring a cup of coffee.

"Did I wake you?" Dean asked apologetically. He poured a second cup and handed it to Stanley.

"My chest woke me. I turned the wrong way."

"Still hurts?"

"Same as yesterday. I keep telling myself it can't get worse," he said as he took a sip of the hot liquid.

"I can't believe you did it in that much pain."

Stanley smiled, but said nothing. The two sat down at the table.

"Want some pie? Evelyn put the leftovers in our refrigerator. I could heat it in the microwave. It will smell and taste like it just came out of the oven."

"The fire fighters teach you that?"

"Naw. I've always liked to fuss around in the kitchen; but, one crew in particular likes that skill of mine. When they're on, I'm always invited over. They got time on their hands a lot and I'm teaching a couple how to really cook."

"Anyone special?"

"What do you mean?"

"You're gay, aren't you?"

"Ed tell you?"

"No," Stanley said.

"I try not to be obvious."

"You tried too hard last night."

"The joke. Sorry about that."

"You pretty much got away with it; but you're better off not trying to be other than you are with this group."

"You can't mean come out and tell them. They're religious people."

"I wouldn't hold that against them. As for the other question, sexuality isn't something one announces. It's private."

"Does it bother you?" Dean asked with an almost abrasive directness.

"As a matter of fact, no," Stanley replied evenly.

"It bothers most men."

"I'm not like most men," Stanley said. "My appearance set me apart at an early age. The boys kindest to me were gay. They felt estranged as well. They wished they could change their sexuality; but, it was as integral a part of them as my nose was of my face."

"Well, it didn't rub off on you."

"What?"

"Their sexual orientation."

"How do you know that?"

"You…um…did it with a chest like that."

"Only because the pleasure exceeded the pain. I'm no masochist."

"You haven't a gay bone in your body, have you?"

"Probably not," Stanley conceded.

"It wouldn't brother you if you did, would it?"

"Not particularly."

"Man, I like you. I could live in a world full of men like you."

"No you couldn't. Your nose would be all wrong."

"Just tell me if you need help with anything," Dean said.

"One thing I need help with is preserving Aleta's privacy. With her arm she can't completely dress herself and as there will be two of us…"

"I can stand guard outside," Dean offered. "And maybe we should keep the window coverings closed all the time as well."

"Good idea."

"How'd you two meet?"

"It was due to some matchmaking cooked up by her grandmother and Martha Cook. It seems Grams didn't like the life path Aleta was on so she threw a little monkey wrench into the works."

"She introduced you too?"

"Not exactly. Grams asked Martha to recommend a lawyer to help Aleta who was being sent from California as the new in-house counsel. Aleta had a year of corporate work in a prestigious San Francisco law firm under her belt and a boyfriend climbing the corporate ladder in the same firm. She thought of it as a temporary assignment and flew out here with Ed. You know about that part."

"Most of it."

"When she arrived, she went straight to Evelyn's house. Evelyn's nephew and his wife had doped Evelyn up and were trying to get her declared incompetent so they could be appointed her power of attorney and gain access to her money."

"Which is why you were there."

"I walked into the house in the middle of an argument and Evelyn's nephew's wife, a twit of a woman with bleached hair and large breasts, was evidently extolling the virtues of cosmetic surgery."

Dean drew in a deep breath. "To Aleta?"

"I still don't have that part of the story straight; but, to force her side of the argument onto Aleta, she pointed to me and asked Aleta if she didn't think I could use a nose job."

Dean's attention was complete. "What a thing to say!"

"Here was this gorgeous girl," Stanley went on with a touch of humor in his tone. "This practically perfect woman and I was being picked apart in front of her. I don't think I ever hated my nose as I did at that moment."

"So, go on. What did Aleta say?"

"She glanced at me casually, not as if I was a freak or anything, and she said, 'It gives his face character. I wouldn't change it.'"

"And you fell in love."

"I was on my way," Stanley said. "But I thought she was just being kind. And then two more things happened. One at a dog show and one at my home."

"What happened at the dog show?"

"She was showing Maggie, you know, the Bulldog she's going to show today and she said to me, 'Isn't she gorgeous!' Now there are a lot of dogs for whom that word is appropriate, but a Bulldog is not one of them. Aleta liked something else about the dog."

"And the other time?"

"My mother put her on the spot," Stanley said. "She was so afraid of me being hurt. She asked Aleta directly about my appearance."

"Your mother did?"

"Mother was a fine trial lawyer before she was appointed to the bench. She was famous for her unexpected unorthodox questions that startled the witness into telling the truth. So, it was not unexpected that she'd confront Aleta. You have to remember who it was who threw us together in a working relationship. It was neither set of parents. Anyway, Aleta said—and I never will forget those words—I love him as you do."

"Wow!"

"So you'd die for her?"

"Oh, I'd do more. There are worse things than dying. I'd do anything to keep her from suffering."

"You probably won't have to," Dean observed. "She seems like the kind of woman who'd have pushed Christ off the cross and said, 'I'll do my own dying, thank you very much.'"

Stanley chuckled. "She does have that trait in her; but…"

Aleta interrupted. "I do not!"

Stanley grinned mischievously, "Whoops! Caught with foot in mouth."

"How long have you been listening?" Dean asked.

Stanley still grinning said, "She heard about the whole conversation. She has super hearing. She's like a dog that way, speaking of which, we're up and ready to do your bidding. How can we help?"

"I hope you left some pie for me."

Chapter 24

The showing began at 8:30 immediately after the national anthem was played. The show schedule put Harriet in Ring 7 with her three Chessies, Evelyn in Ring 5 with three of her Goldens, and Aleta in Ring 1 with Maggie.

Madge and Nathan had elected not to travel through the storm on Friday, choosing instead to travel the following morning. They weren't due to show their Doxies until 1:00 PM, so they had that option.

Lyle accompanied Harriet, planning to show Stoney in Breed while Lauren was scheduled to handle Keeper in the Best of Breed competition. Harriet took in Babe who needed points. There were only a few Chessies entered and Keeper was entered in Breed to assure that Babe would have a shot at one point at least. As it turned out Keeper's entry made two points in bitches if she were beaten so Harriet didn't want to pull her. Lauren was pleased.

Babe took Winners Bitch over two other bitches and Harriet said to Lauren, "Do your very best."

That pleased Lauren who was half-afraid she might be asked to show less well so Babe could earn another point.

Lyle took the Breed with Stoney. Lauren took Best Opposite with Keeper and Babe had to settle for a single point. To Lauren's surprise, Harriet was ecstatic. All her dogs had won in their first Illinois show.

"I would have been upset if Babe had beaten her mother," Harriet confided in Lauren afterward. "She's not mature enough yet."

Lauren understood that orientation. Harriet wanted the win to be a true reflection of reality.

Because there were so few Chessies, the three were done early enough to move down to Ring 5 where the judging of the Golden Retriever bitches was just getting underway. Evelyn had Carmel's arm band ready to slip on Lauren's arm and Lauren sailed into the ring shortly afterward. There were ten bitches in the open class. There had been two in the puppy class and two in the Bred-By class which meant that two points were at stake.

Carmel had been brushed and trimmed to perfection and her flowing coat glistened in the autumn sun. The coolness energized all the dogs in the ring; but, none more so than the one who'd spent a long afternoon travelling the day before. It was great to be out and to stretch her legs again.

Carmel won her class and then the points. Evelyn's delight travelled down the leash and Topaz, alone in the Veteran's class, was so spritely he seemed much younger. The judge happily handed Evelyn her blue ribbon.

Meanwhile, inside the building, the English Bulldog Open Bitch class had just entered the ring. Outside George Sciretta and Stanley stood together and watched as Aleta's mere presence on the other end of the leash seemed to delight the big cream bitch with the rust-colored patches. While Bulldogs lumber when asked to gait, their bodies rolling with each step so that their movement is rarely described as smooth, nonetheless, Maggie's was. It was its effortlessness that gave it grace. Maggie was the first in line, and she out-moved the dog behind her. Her delight at being in the ring with Aleta was obvious to George Sciretta who stood on the sidelines scarcely breathing. After countless near wins, he was hoping that Maggie would again be the dog that had amazed and delighted him his first two shows by picking up two major wins and Group placements to boot. That had been an exciting weekend. He hungered for another. He'd lost enough now to fully appreciate what Aleta had done for him.

"Did the judge like her?" he whispered to Stanley when Aleta took her place at the end of the line after the individual examination.

Aleta smiled over at the two and Stanley, taking his cue from that, replied softly, "So far, it's going well."

Still the short, fat man couldn't relax. While it was a cool, almost chilly October day, and the building was unheated, he wiped the sweat from his forehead. He ran the handkerchief through his bald pate as well.

"Maggie looks good. You've done a good job with her," Stanley said. He'd heard these words often and they always seemed to please the owner.

George Sciretta was no different. He smiled and nodded, happy with the comment. He was proud of his dog.

While there were twelve bitches, they were scattered evenly through several classes. Maggie won her class and George brushed away a tear.

"She's won the Open Class before," he whispered. "You gotta watch out for the puppies. I think they move better. They aren't so big."

Stanley decided to ask Aleta later if that were the case. As they watched, five Bulldogs filed in behind Aleta and Maggie to compete for the coveted purple ribbon and the two points that went with it. Tom Wilson, a French Bulldog on the other end of his lead, joined the two men standing outside the ring.

Stanley saw the Best of Breed ribbon in his hand and knew Tom had done well, so he nodded his greeting and didn't speak.

Tom leaned over, "Your wife looks smashing today."

Stanley smiled. Now he knew how George felt when he'd complimented his dog's appearance. He gazed at Aleta, her happiness at being able to show adding to her natural beauty. Only he knew her arm was strapped to prevent unlimited movement. Her outfit was a perfect celebration of the colors resplendent in the turning leaves of the trees as winter waggled a warning finger that it was approaching.

She tossed her head as the judge passed down the line and Maggie looked up at her eagerly, as if waiting for her next magic trick.

While Aleta was dressed to stand behind her dog, her dark brown shirt being a perfect backdrop for the multicolored Bulldog, she alone stood in front and let Maggie stand naturally. Down the line, kneeling handlers had posed their dogs and were holding up their heads to make the profile what the judges were looking for.

The judge ran the group around the ring once. While the younger ones were fleeter than the older ones, Maggie out-moved them all. The win was hers and, after that, when she went against the few specials, the breed as well.

George Sciretta was beside himself and shook Stanley's hand twice and Tom's once before dashing to the other end of the ring to make sure Aleta got pictures. Aleta had already asked the steward to call for the photographer.

Tom turned to Stanley and observed wryly, "She has an ability to handle dogs."

"And husbands," Stanley commented. "She shouldn't even be in the ring with that arm of hers."

"Don't think I don't appreciate it. Maggie's still considered part of my string, so I'm getting the unexpected rep as the handler who will find the best person for one's dog."

"That's not the rep you're going for," Stanley observed. "And I'm not going for the rep of being a hen-pecked husband. But, Aleta does things to people."

"Yes," Tom said and pointed at George Sciretta, "she makes them happy."

"She won't put you out of business for a long time," Stanley said. "We're expecting."

Tom's smile had an element of relief mingled in.

"Congratulations! Although I never would have thought you two would jump into parenthood so fast. Usually when people line up to get show dogs, well…I just made the wrong assumption."

Stanley chuckled. "I made the same assumption. Boy was I wrong."

"But you're happy. I can tell."

Stanley didn't even have to think about it.

"Thrilled is an overworked word, but that's how I feel."

"Is she still going to want pick bitch from George's Bulldog."

Stanley looked shocked. "Don't even think she doesn't. Besides I get to show the Bulldog. Aleta's going to show our chocolate Lab."

"A chocolate? I thought you were getting one out of Morgan."

"It seems Morgan carries chocolate. And so does Emma. They had eight black, one chocolate."

"So, Aleta's going to compete against Lyle in Labs. That'll be a match-up to watch."

"That won't happen for several years."

"I guess I'll just have to hang around; but right now I've got to go. I've got an Afghan Special in Ring 8. They should be nearly done with the classes by now."

Madge and Nathan arrived in time for lunch. Madge brought homemade rolls and sandwich fixings and lunchtime was spent talking about the morning successes. Aleta had changed into pants and a sweat shirt and when the mayonnaise she heaped on her sandwich ooze out one end and down her sweat shirt, she laughed and commented that that's why she'd changed.

"So you planned this?" Stanley joshed.

Aleta snapped back, "No, of course not. I'm just prepared."

Lyle swallowed a smirk and Stanley knew Milani had told him about the nightgown incident. It pleased him somehow.

Back in Northern Illinois, in a sparsely furnished dilapidated house in the poorer section of Oakwood, Joey Crowder was working on his bombs when Tag woke up.

"What time is it?" Tag asked.

"Noon," Joey replied. "There's coffee."

"Why are you working on that? I thought we weren't going to rig his car."

"We aren't. We're going to rig the house."

"His house? What's wrong…?"

Joey cut in impatiently, "Not his house. This house."

"Why are we blowing ourselves up?"

"We aren't. We'll be gone."

"Where's the damned coffee?" Tag asked. "You need some."

"After we get our money, we need time to get away, so we blow the house."

"That ain't gonna keep nobody busy but the fire department."

"Well, we don't blow it. We rig it to blow."

"And how's that gonna keep them from chasing us?"

"Stanley Praetzel is going to be inside."

"So one cop gets him out and the house blows, so we got twenty-three cops chasing us instead of twenty-four."

"They aren't going to be able to get him out so easy. The way I'll have it rigged, they'll evacuate all the houses around this one, get the bomb squad here and while half those assholes are trying to figure out how to take the bomb apart, the other half will be busy keeping back the crowd."

"Suppose they get in quick?"

"They won't," Joey said. "I need you to go to the hardware store and get me some stuff. Don't go to one here in town. Go to one next town over, Arborville."

"What about scouting the place out?"

"Yeah, okay. You drive by and see if our pigeons is still in their roost."

"How about breakfast?"

"I ain't hungry."

"I am."

"Then for God's sake feed yourself! Just get outta my hair for couple more hours."

Tag pulled on his coat.

"Hey, don't forget the list," Joey called.

"What list?"

"What you're gonna get me. And don't forget nothing."

Tag decided to eat first. He stopped at Joe's Place in Arborville asked for black coffee and then ordered waffles and eggs even though it was past noon. He sat at the counter and the young counterman smiled at him as he set down the coffee.

"Getting a late start?"

"Yeah," Tag said. Suddenly, he had the urge to talk. "Rough storm yesterday."

"Des Plaines River came up to flood level," the young man said. "They got controls placed now. Pops tells me stories about how it used to take out a slew of houses every couple years."

"October ain't flood season though," Tag said. "I'm from Waukegan."

"Yeah, storm was freaky. We never get storms that bad this time of the year."

"So, the ground should dry fast on account it ain't been soaked in a lot."

"Yeah, I guess."

Two cops came in and sat on two stools nearby. Both ordered sandwiches and coffee.

"Storm cause any problems last night?" the counterman asked.

"Big accident south of here on Highway 10," one said. "We heard it was an RV that skidded and thought for a while it was the chief's RV so a couple units went down to help."

"Wasn't West's RV, huh?"

"We figure he got through before it happened. Nobody got through afterward."

"He off to another dog show?"

"Yeah," came the reply.

Tag's waffles were up and the counterman moved quickly so they made it in front of him with the butter just beginning to melt. Tag dug in.

The list was long and Tag decided to tell the clerk that he was doing a friend a favor and he needed help. He began by reading a couple items.

"Your friend rewiring his house?" the clerk asked.

He's doing repairs," Tag said. "I ain't handy so I gets to do the buying; but, it's gotta be exactly what's writ on this paper."

"Let me read it from the paper," the clerk said. "You just follow me with that basket and I'll put the stuff in."

And that's what Tag did.

While he was loading the stuff in the van, he heard two contractors talking.

"So you put down plastic?"

"Took all I had but we managed to cover the whole damn drive before the rain hit."

"Did it do the trick?"

"Pretty much. The rain pounded on it but the forms held and we uncovered it this morning and it's okay."

"So now what?"

"If we don't get more rain, it'll set okay."

"Bet your customer was worried as hell all night."

"That was the only good part. He's outta town."

"So he doesn't know about the rain?"

"He was here when it started I think. Not at the house. Some other couple was house sitting."

Tag climbed in his truck and headed straight for Stanley Praetzel's house. Everything was just like yesterday only the plastic that had covered the driveway had been rolled to one side and the sun was beating down on the long expanse of concrete. A man with a hose was spraying the top lightly with water. It seemed incongruous to Tag that a man sloshing through mud with calf high boots would be hosing down anything.

He wanted to stop but instead went down a couple blocks, turned around and passed by slowly again. He made two more runs before leaving.

So intent was he on trying to scope out the house, he didn't notice he'd passed a sedan parked in a drive with a man at the wheel several times. The man, however, reported what he saw.

All the way home one thing puzzled Tag. The Praetzel's had two cars. One was destroyed. One was still in the driveway. How could they go anywhere without their car?

He resolved to talk to Joey.

When he carried the packages in the house, Tag said, "I need to talk to you."

Joey looked at the bags Tag set down.

"Did you get everything I had on the list?"

"Yeah, but…"

"No substitutes."

"It's something else," Tag pressed. His gut told him this could be important.

"Did you bring me lunch?"

"Er…no…you said you wasn't hungry."

"Well, I am. Go get me something. And not here. Go to Willow Glen. Take a pass by the house."

"I did. That's what I wanted to talk to you about."

"Are the people still there?"

"Yeah, but…"

"Is the car still there?"

"Yeah, but…"

"Go get me some food. And don't come back too soon unless you want I should blow both of us up."

"When should I come back?"

"Two hours."

"Okay."

Back at the Southern Illinois Kennel Club Dog Show, Lyle and Lauren were at ringside ready to take in two specials. One was Lyle's big male. Morgan's black coat glistened in the bright afternoon sun. The day was crisp enough so the sun's rays bounced off Morgan's harsh outer coat as the next week the water from the lake would as well. Impervious to weather a Lab's coat made him ultimately suitable for hunting in stormy weather as well as mild. Lyle, a crack shot, thoroughly enjoyed hunting over his dog and Lauren never wasted his catch. Next to Lauren stood her champion chocolate bitch Holly. A chunky bitch with a sweet expression, Holly always gave Morgan a run for his money.

Outside the ring the entire group was gathered to watch. Dean had volunteered to stay behind to watch the dogs all of whom were outside in their pens enjoying the sunshine on the brisk day. Winter would soon make such moments rare. The dogs, of course, didn't know this. They only knew they liked the myriad of smells assailing their nostrils, the excitement of people hurrying toward the rings and the satisfaction or sorrow of those returning. These latter emotions were translated into smells that made being outside pleasurable.

At one o'clock Madge and Nathan Tobias showed up at the Dachshund ring to find that most of the class dogs were absent. Anya won a purple ribbon but no points. Lisa had started to limp on the way to the ring and a burr was pulled from between her toes; but, she refused to put her foot down. She was scratched at ringside. Rufus took the breed over his daughter and the sole male class dog.

The Tobiases arrived at the Lab ring before the class competition was over. Lisa, who was Nathan's special dog, rode proudly on her master's lap as Nathan's motorized wheelchair took the short dry grass field easily. The other three trotted happily beside Madge. They liked being out where there were people.

Thus it was that the entire group watched as Lyle and Lauren went head to head against the Winner's Dog, another of Morgan's sons. Tom Wilson was on that dog.

"You could share," Tom said lightly.

"Can't back down. One of us has to beat Lauren."

To everyone's surprise the chunky chocolate bitch took the Breed. Morgan took Best Opposite and Tom took Best of Winners.

"This isn't the kind of sharing I had in mind," Tom said.

"You didn't want to share at all. You wanted to win," Lyle retorted.

"Look on the bright side. It was your wife that won. It should make for a good evening."

"You don't know Lauren. She won't be happy unless she takes the group."

"Beating you and me doesn't count?"

"I'll let you know tomorrow."

When Tom Wilson took off toward the building to show Beatrice's Scotties, Dean accompanied Lauren back to put Holly up and rest before the Group started.

Harriet pulled Lyle aside and said quietly, "I need a favor."

Stanley hung back too. Since Harriet didn't seem to mind he too eventually wound up separate from the group heading for the building.

Lyle stopped. "What is it?"

"I'd like you to show Stoney in Group for me."

"I'm okay with Lauren winning," Lyle said graciously. "And nobody could show that big boy better than you do."

Stanley saw Harriet blush and this surprised him.

"This is not an unselfish, but a selfish request. And I'll understand if you say no."

"How is it selfish?"

"I want you to win a Group 1 with him."

"I'm not that good. Tom Wilson might pull it off."

"Can't use him. Evelyn's going to ask him to take in Topaz."

"I can't beat Tom on a Golden with a Chessie. There will be Setters and Cockers and Brittanys in the ring too you know."

Harriet went on excitedly. "The Group judge gave Stoney his final major and placed him in Group as a class dog. He said then that Stoney was the finest Chessie he'd ever seen. Stoney's even more mature now."

"Then you've got a great chance."

"But I've learned that this guy doesn't reward followers. One of my friends whose dog he did well by travelled to Idaho to show under him again. She was dumped. Stoney doesn't have a chance if I'm on him. And a handler's about the same thing."

"What were you going to do if I won today with Morgan?"

"Ask Lauren, of course."

Lyle laughed. "I'd be proud to take him in."

"I didn't go hunting this weekend just to have a realistic crack at a Group win," Harriet added.

Lyle chuckled. "We're almost in the same boat. We're here because Lauren wanted a crack at the group and she knew the breed judge would put up a chocolate over a black if the chocolate were good."

"Why did you enter then?" Stanley asked.

"Lauren wouldn't be completely happy unless it was a win over me as well," Lyle explained. "Beating Tom too was frosting on the cake."

"But you're going to try to beat her in Group?" Stanley pressed.

"With a Chessie," Lyle said. "She'd never forgive me if I took in a Golden, but Stoney is a beautiful dog. Lauren wouldn't mind as much losing to him."

"So you're going for it?" Stanley pushed.

"I'm giving it my all."

"Remember this, Stanley," Harriet advised. "If there is ever any question regarding Aleta's feelings, remember she would want you to give your all."

After Tom won the Breed in Scotties with Beatrice's Belle, Lyle put in a call to Tom Milani.

"The van cased the place six times early this afternoon," Tom said. "I figure they'll move in tonight."

Stanley was nearby and Lyle shared the news with him.

He told Aleta and mentioned that Lyle was taking in Stoney. Before Stanley could explain Harriet's reasoning, Aleta dashed off to find her grandmother.

"Did you have another vision?"

Harriet looked startled, "No. Why?"

"Lyle's showing Stoney."

"Yes, because I need a local man on him with this judge."

"Why not Tom Wilson?"

"You know why, besides he'll be on Topaz."

"So this has nothing to do with your second vision?"

"No, but I have to say something about that," Harriet said.

"Go on," Aleta said looking around. They were alone.

"I'm going to be asking you to do something that will be nearly impossible for you to agree to do. What I need to tell you now is that I am not exchanging one death for another."

"What does that mean?"

"I'm not sure."

"What is it you'll be asking me to do?"

"I'll know when the time is right," Harriet said, "but I sense it's not now."

"You must know more. You're holding back," Aleta accused.

Harriet took Aleta's hand in hers. "I promise you this. If ever I hold back, I'll tell you I am. You know what Tom Milani said before we left?"

"What?" Aleta asked.

"Well, he didn't exactly make a statement. He included the truth in his question. He asked, 'Who are we supposed to save from being murdered?' It is true, you know, we, or at least me, only get visions that help us prevent a murder."

"Why us?"

"Not just us. Not just now. Before Lincoln was shot, not only did he dream of his death, but a number of psychics predicted his murder."

Aleta didn't want a history lesson. She switched back to the danger at hand.

"Stanley and I figured out it is Lyle who's in danger."

"It is," Harriet affirmed.

"When?"

"I don't know when."

"Okay," Aleta said, "but know this. I will do anything to save him."

"I'll remember you said that."

Chapter 25

Simultaneously with the Group competition getting underway at the Fairgrounds, Tag Burrows returned to the house in Oakwood with several bags of fast foods.

"Was I gone long enough?" he asked.

"Too long," Joey complained. "I'm starving."

"Brought lotsa stuff. Forgot to ask what you was hungry for."

"Just gimme a bag."

Tag handed him one. "The house all set?"

Joey dug out a double cheeseburger.

"Yeah, it is. My best work ever."

Joey took a huge bite.

"Won't he know it was us?" Tag asked.

"Who?" he asked, bits of food emerging with the word.

"The guy that gave us the house," Tag asked.

"He's gonna tell someone he hired us to off a lawyer and we blew up his house?" Joey guffawed. More food spewed out.

"He could," Tag said, leaning back to avoid the spray.

"He won't. He'll say we was squatting," Joey assured him.

"Yeah, maybe."

Joey swallowed the rest of his mouthful and took a long slurp on the straw in the soda.

"Besides we'll be long gone and living large."

"What about Stanley Praetzel?"

"He'll be in a zillion pieces," he said grabbing a handful of fries.

"His wife?"

"I got a special plan for her. After we eat, we're gonna go set that one up."

The fries went into his mouth.

"I learned some stuff today," Tag ventured.

Joey sighed. "Start at the beginning. Don't want your ideas mixed in neither. Just tell me what you heard nice and slow."

Tag put down his sandwich and started talking. Joey didn't interrupt because he didn't want Tag to change his story to make it something acceptable. Besides, what else did he have to do? The house was wired and he wanted to eat in peace. This way he didn't have to answer any questions.

Tag added his question onto the end of his tale. "What's the car doing there if they went somewheres?"

Joey flicked off the query, "They went with someone else."

He punched in a single number on his cell.

"We're set up to move in," he said. "But they're gone. They got house sitters. Where'd they go…? Yeah, I know he's the target—but she ain't around neither, so we can't follow her…. Yeah, you do that."

The man that was called slammed down his phone and tried to think. If they had house sitters, they'd have an emergency number. He couldn't contact Praetzel, but the council's lawyer could.

The lawyer called the house and identified himself. The house sitter referred him to the police. He called Chief Milani and said he needed to reach Stanley about next week's case.

"You can call his office on Tuesday," Tom stated flatly.

The lawyer persisted, "The council has an offer for Bessie Dobbins."

"Call Tuesday."

"I can't believe you don't have an emergency number," the lawyer charged.

"This is not an emergency," Tom said and hung up.

The lawyer reported back to the councilman. "He's out of town until Tuesday. But considering, the secrecy, I'd guess that the police have him sequestered somewhere."

The councilman passed along what he'd found out. "Guess you'll have to wait until Tuesday."

"Shit!" Joey exclaimed, slamming down the phone. "We can't wait. Too much waiting's dangerous."

"So what do we do?" Tag asked.

"Who's the only cop we know that's left town?"

"That chief guy, West. He went to a dog show," Tag said. "Praetzel can't be with him. He don't got dogs."

"But that old lady that lived on his property had dogs. Three of them. Big ones."

"What's that got to do with Praetzel?" Tag asked.

"Can't be a coincidence. She takes her three dogs and gets off the property. I plant the bomb and then the police come. I get it planted between the dogs leaving and the cops coming. They were watching him before the bomb went off. Why not afterward too?"

"So he's got police guarding him. That's gonna make our job impossible!"

"Not cops," Joey said with a new enthusiasm. "One cop. One cop already scheduled to go outta town for the weekend. If the storm hadn't come, we'd of fallen into the trap."

"What trap?"

"The one they set at the house," Joey explained, his words pouring out as he put the pieces together. "Sure, why not figure another hit. The first one didn't kill him. And why not another car bomb? That figures. Cops got no imagination."

"So now what?"

"We go to a dog show."

"What for?"

"Because that's where the Praetzels are and with just one cop to guard them 'cause cops figured we'd never find them there."

"But we don't know where it is."

"We call the pet store," Joey said. "We got a phone book."

"We don't got much, but we got that," Tag said opening a cabinet. The phone book sat on the bottom shelf. Aside from shades on all the windows, the house offered little in the way of comfort: two single beds with thin worn mattresses, an old Formica table with a couple matching chairs and a recliner with a broken arm. There were light bulbs in the overhead fixtures and the electricity and water were both turned on. The gas, however, wasn't, so the stove didn't work and there was no hot water. There was an empty space where the refrigerator usually sat.

Joey called the pet store in Willow Glen because that's where Praetzel lived. The owner didn't know anything about dog shows. He did know Stanley Praetzel. He had supplied him with all of his fish.

Joey asked about the woman living on his property with the big dogs and the pet owner didn't know anything about them, then added that Stanley was getting a puppy for his wife because she showed dogs; but that the pup hadn't been born yet.

He went on to say, "If you want to know about dog shows, why don't you call the Arborville Kennel Club. They're in the Yellow Pages."

Joey called the Arborville Kennel Club and the person who answered was sorry she couldn't supply much information. Almost all the members were at the Southern Illinois Kennel Club Dog Show that weekend. Thus Joey got the directions to the show and the show hours.

He and Tag left for the show after making a stop to set the bomb rigged to finish off the wife.

Chapter 26

With Dean Lundgren assigned to watch the dogs, all but Lauren and Aleta took chairs to the group ring and settled down in the front row to watch the rest of the show. Dogs from their little conclave were in four of the seven group competitions.

Beatrice's Scotty, Belle, showed beautifully under Tom Wilson's expert touch and placed second. The hounds were next. Tom took a first with his Afghan, which was a big Group winner. Madge and her red Doxie, Rufus, walked.

Stanley worried about Aleta making it to the ring but Lyle reminded him that Tom's assistant knew when to bring Maggie and Aleta would not be left behind. Stanley had already helped Aleta change into her show outfit and assured her that she was doing a beautiful job despite her injured shoulder. He then added that her new outfit was stunning.

"Tom even said so," he finished and was awarded with a smile.

Because they were alone while she was dressing, Aleta told Stanley what Harriet had said about them having guessed correctly. Lyle was the person her grandmother had seen die.

"What else did she say?"

"That she would ask me to do something that would be extremely difficult for me to do."

"And it would save his life?"

"I believe so."

"Then do it," Stanley said. "I've never met a man that's been a better friend to me than Lyle. I would hate to lose him unless you're talking about exchanging your life for his."

Aleta looked shocked. "That never occurred to me; but, Grams did say she wasn't going to ask me to exchange one death for another."

Stanley frowned, perplexed.

"She wouldn't say anymore."

"Maybe that's all she knows."

"At least I know I'm going to be asked to do something beforehand," Aleta added.

"Nothing illegal, I hope."

"That would be immoral. Grams wouldn't ask me to do that."

"Then do what she suggests. I promise I'll understand."

Aleta kissed him lightly on the cheek. "That makes it better."

"Now it's time to show everyone how great a dog Maggie is."

"I hope Maggie still loves me."

"Why wouldn't she?"

"Last time we hung out together between showings."

"Last time you had a lovely tree, soft grass and a warm summer day. Today you have dry, prickly grass, no shade tree and it's cold on the ground," Stanley recalled.

"You're right," Aleta said. "I fuss a lot before I show. Go ahead and watch the groups with Lyle."

"You're not coming?" Stanley asked.

"Can't. Too nervous."

"Lyle's showing later."

"Lyle's different. But Lauren isn't going either."

"He said she needed to rest because she was pregnant."

"Hey, that's a reason you can use for me too," Aleta said. "A handler isn't supposed to get butterflies."

"Is that a rule?" Stanley asked straight-faced.

"Just go. Let me be nervous in peace."

Considering her last comment, Stanley was a bit taken aback by how calm Aleta appeared as she approached the ring. She spent a few minutes talking with Maggie and playing tug with her towel before wiping Maggie's jowls one last time. They entered the ring behind Tom Wilson and his French Bulldog.

Aleta looked around and spotted seven that might shove her right out of a group placement. As they were individually stacked, examined and moved, she settled on the Chow, the Dalmatian, the Standard Poodle, the Bichon, and the Frenchie as contenders for the number one spot.

When her turn came, she walked Maggie into a stack and went around and stood in front of her and shook her head. Maggie lifted her head just enough to present a good profile. It was all done quickly and smoothly and the judge, who was accustomed to turning and seeing a handler just finishing positioning a dog's feet, was surprised that Aleta had merely walked her dog into a stack. As a breed Bulldogs didn't stack well. They were large, bulky dogs with wide fronts, roached backs, stubby tails, weak rears and huge heads that defied all possibility of balance, but handlers nevertheless worked at downplaying their dog's faults

The judge was taken with the dog's apparent delight at being in the ring. Bulldogs were a breed generally placid in temperament which didn't bode well in the show ring. That they did well against their sparkly competitors was probably helped by their different appearance. They were generally a crowd favorite and judges were sensitive to the same characteristics that appealed to the spectators.

As Maggie moved down the ring the judge wondered why she hadn't seen this pair before. This was no amateur and she knew most of the pros. Whoever the handler was, she was good. In the back of her mind a small memory tickled her brain. Thoughtfully the judge watched the young Bulldog coming toward her, every move as it should be, but freer.

Then she remembered hearing about a young woman who'd appeared on the scene briefly a couple months ago and won Best in Show, but not with a Bulldog. Then the woman had dropped out of the dog show scene completely.

As Aleta took Maggie around to the end of the line and finished by drawing her into a perfect stack, the judge thought, whoever she is, she's back. And what a stunning display.

Aleta won, and the clapping told the judge that, while she didn't know her, others did.

Aleta walked away with George Sciretta to get a photo of the win and told him that first place meant Maggie had earned five points, not two.

"What can I do for you?"

"Let me show Maggie tomorrow and don't expect a repeat. Winning two days in a row is difficult."

The dark eyes danced. "No, I mean it. What can I do for you?"

"We still want that puppy."

"I haven't forgotten my promise. You want two?" he asked eagerly.

Aleta laughed. "One will be enough. Thank you."

"I want to do something."

"You have. You let me show Maggie. Can't you see how much fun this is for me too, especially since my arm is injured."

"Your arm is hurt. I didn't know that."

"That's why I can't show any big dogs. They'd pull and rip out the stitches."

"What happened?"

By now, the shooting incident had paled after what had happened to Stanley and so Aleta told him she'd been shot. He wanted to hear all about it.

He was such a good listener, she told him about the car bombing as well ending with, "It was the work of a pro."

"You want I should find out who?"

"The police know who. They just can't connect him yet. I told you he was a pro."

"You know his name?"

"No. But they set a trap for him. By the time we go back, he should be in custody."

"That's good," the short fat man said.

In the van hurtling toward the dog show at the southernmost part of the state, Tag Burrows was unsettled.

"We ain't planned this good," he pointed out. "We don't know nothing about dog shows. We'll stick out and get ourselves picked up for something and then what?"

"The lady said it was open to the public. We're the public."

"We can't just grab them and drag them off."

"That ain't the plan. We got a whole day. If it don't work, we come back here and do it. But, it's gonna work. We got luck on our side. If we didn't, we would've been caught in that trap."

"So we come back and do the first plan if it don't look right?"

"You got it," Joey said. "So relax. We're gonna scout out the grounds tonight when the show's over and then go back to the motel, order in some pizza to go with our six-packs and sleep in soft beds with pillows."

"You want to go out and get laid again?"

"Naw. It weren't so good last night," Joey admitted.

"Mine weren't neither."

"We need a better class of whore," Joey said. "With a million bucks we can go someplace and choose."

At the show site, the Sporting Group was the last one and the excitement among the enclave of friends from the northern end of the state rose as they watched three dogs from their group enter the ring. Lyle was first with Harriet's big Chessie male, Stoney. Tom Wilson was next with Evelyn's veteran dog, Topaz. Lauren followed with her chocolate Lab, Holly. The dogs were generally in order of speed with which they could traverse the enlarged ring. As usual the setters led the group. Stoney being so large went before the Topaz who, had he been younger, could have outrun him. That Holly was right on their tail was a result of Lauren knowing that Holly would outreach those that followed her.

The English Setter was an eye-catcher. He was an immediate crowd favorite. Stoney was a Chessie and usually ignored by the crowd. Chessies weren't showy. But Lyle, dressed as usual in his light blue pants and navy coat, added a touch of class to the pair and so eyes watched the pair and noticed the judge taking a bit more time with the big dog. They had to admit he was a handsome fellow and definitely a strong male animal that carried himself with pride. Obviously, the judge liked him.

Tom Wilson, also impeccably attired, showed the Golden, whose muzzle was beginning to gray, with the same smoothness of the prior competitor only this time the dog's coat glistened in the sunlight rather than hide the sun's rays beneath tight curls the color of dead grass. The profile was more pleasing to the eye.

The short, chunky chocolate Lab had a thick otter tail that wouldn't hold still. The eyes sparkled and every contour of the body was in full view. The coat was thick, the eyes soft, the muzzle broad enough to carry a big bird, the feet properly webbed and the chest broad. The bitch was a piece of balanced perfection. Her clean parallel movement placed her at the top of the group in the judge's eyes.

He had his first four places and much as he wanted to stick a small dog into the group, none was good enough to knock out either the English Setter or the three retrievers.

He decided to make a preliminary cut in order to give some recognition to those who came close. He pulled out the Pointer and the black Cocker along with his top four. The others left the ring and from those six would come the winner.

The judge stood back and looked at them, then had them circle the ring. He'd pulled them out in the order they entered the ring so no one knew who had placed until the finger pointed at Lyle and Stoney as they were slowing to a halt.

"One!" said the judge.

His finger pointed at Lauren and Holly, "Two."

Topaz took third and the setter, fourth.

The group outside the ring went wild.

Tom congratulated Lauren who was beaming because she'd placed. She hadn't been sure she would do that considering the competition. Both the dogs excused from the ring were previous Best in Show winners.

Lyle was stunned. Harriet had shrewdly judged Stoney's chances and taken the steps necessary to win including giving up her own strong desire to show him herself.

His wife hugged him and congratulated him and said, "You're a real pro, honey."

And that woke him up.

He couldn't believe it. He was going into Best in Show with a Chessie.

Aleta came up and said, "You're going head to head with Tom again. His Afghan won."

"I know," Lyle managed. "Your grandmother doesn't expect miracles, does she?"

"Always!" Aleta laughed.

The Best-in-Show judge looked around the ring at the seven dogs before him. Tom and his Afghan were a familiar sight at this level. The Chessie was an unusual choice. This one must be special because there wasn't a handler on him. The German Shepherd and his handler were also old hats. Down the line he saw two more familiar pairs. Both the Bulldog and her handler were new. The Pom was new but the handler wasn't.

He watched them circle the ring. The Chessie could move. The Bulldog was no slouch either.

When the judge was going over the Chessie, he asked Lyle, "Where's your Lab?"

Lyle smiled. "Traded him in."

"Why?" the man queried as his hand felt the spring of the ribs and the fingers sought out the shoulder layback.

"Needed a boy that could beat my wife's dog," he returned.

The judge stood back and looked again at this dog. He'd definitely not seen him before. He was a magnificent animal. If ever a Chessie deserved recognition, this one did.

After going over the other dogs he walked between the Chessie and the Bulldog. The latter was a beautiful specimen presented to perfection by an absolutely gorgeous woman. When he turned to walk back to the table for the ribbon, he passed the Chessie again and he stopped. He remembered his thought when he first went over him. If ever a Chessie deserved to win…

He chose the Chessie.

To his surprise, the Bulldog handler whooped, "Stoney, you did it!"

"It's her grandmother's dog," Lyle told the judge before others crowded around to congratulate him.

"I almost gave it to her," the judge said.

"I know," Lyle confessed. "I'm not sure I could have chosen between them."

"Why isn't she on him?"

"She hurt her arm or she would be. Maggie doesn't pull. Stoney does on occasion."

"Where is she from?"

"California," Lyle said. "She just got married, so she's a Midwesterner now."

"A pro?"

"A lawyer."

"She has talent."

Lyle shared the judge's comments when the group gathered around the barbeque. Dean took charge of the cooking and Tom Wilson and his crew were invited to join in.

"I knew he liked Maggie," George exclaimed. "I knew it."

"Maggie's time will come," Tom Wilson said with heartfelt encouragement. "She's still young."

Harriet chimed in. "The judge told me that if ever there was a Chessie that deserved to win, it was this one."

"Did he say anything about Maggie?" George pressed with the eagerness of a newcomer hungry for encouragement after missing the grand prize by so slim a margin.

"He asked me if I taught Aleta to show and he congratulated me," Harriet shared with a modicum of pride. "He also said that a lot of judges would pick that Bulldog; but, not many would chose a Chessie."

"So, Maggie has a shot?" George questioned.

"George," Aleta said quietly, "today Maggie was at her best; but, so was Stoney. There were nine hundred dogs in competition today. You're a man who works with numbers. Maggie was one of the top seven, and, if we believe the judge, one of the top two. Out of nine hundred! That's pretty great in itself. And she's not a champion yet. Someday you'll know how truly great it is for a dog from the classes to make the final competition."

Others quickly delved into how rare that was and George began to realize that Maggie was being recognized by people who knew.

"How many people have asked for a pup from her first litter?" Evelyn asked.

"I got thirteen names so far. Is that too many?"

"You need to find out which ones want pups to show and love, but mostly to love," Evelyn counseled, "like Stanley and Aleta. They'll keep the pup whether it wins or not."

"How'll I know?"

"Start by watching how other Bulldog breeders treat their dogs. Then ask the ones you like to help you pick homes," Evelyn finished.

Slowly the dogs were put up for the night, but the conversation continued until there wasn't enough fire to ward off the darkness.

In the shadows, Tag Burrows and Joey Crowder walked the grounds, impressed with the empty rings spread out on dry grass. The noise and activity had allowed them to walk around the RV's without being stopped. They didn't stop but moved quickly as if looking for a particular RV. This was not unusual. Visitors often sought out handlers after the show.

They found Stanley and Aleta and walked past them as Stanley was telling his wife to sit down. Someone nearby was cooking meat. The smell made them both hungry.

A short, fat man approached from the end of the row and Joey turned away; but, not before George got a look at him.

Joey hurried away and Tag had to trot to keep up with him.

"What's up?" Tag asked.

"Sciretta's here," Joey said.

"Who's he?"

"Tell you later," Joey said. "But we gotta find out if he's connected with anyone here."

"How do we do that?"

"We come back tomorrow and watch."

"Then what?"

"We move in. I've got a plan."

Chapter 27

Stanley was dressed when Aleta awoke. He and Dean were chatting over coffee as they had the day before. This time the smell of cardamom seed rolls wafted past her nostrils. She recognized the touch of Madge's hand.

She didn't notice how Stanley was dressed until she sat down. He had on a shirt and tie and was wearing tan sports pants. They were barely casual being pressed and creased with the same care as the pants to his best suit."

"Where are you going?"

"Tom Wilson asked me last night to help him with Beatrice's dogs."

"But I'll be in the ring," Aleta wailed.

She wanted Stanley watching her.

"Tom says Bulldogs will be done by then. He says he'll take Cassie in for the points, but he needs someone to walk her around during the Breed. He says Beatrice wants him on Belle then."

"I guess that will be okay. The rings are right next to each other in the building."

"Madge asked me to help her too," Stanley said.

"Doxies show at eight thirty. Same as Bulldogs."

"Madge says she'll take Annie in for the points. She's hoping there'll be enough competition for a point," Stanley explained. "She said I'd be done before the dogs get done in your ring. You won't even be in the ring yet."

When Aleta and Stanley arrived at ringside, Nathan and Madge were waiting for them.

"Where'd all these Doxies come from?" Aleta asked.

"Our competitor's RV broke down Saturday morning and they didn't get it fixed in time. They got here too late to show."

Madge looked at Stanley. "Can you still help us."

"Of course, he can," Aleta said. "I just hope I get to see him. But if I don't, you'll record him for me, won't you, Nathan?"

Aleta and Madge had been talking in low tones about the possibility of Annie going Best of Winners and acquiring the dogs' points. Neither of them noticed how intensely Stanley was watching each dog in each class and his attention never wavered even after the winner was declared and Madge entered the ring with Annie.

Before she was given the points, Stanley had sized up her three competitors and chosen her as the best of the four. The judge agreed.

Madge gave Stanley Annie's lead.

"What do you want me to win?" he asked.

It was a serious question.

"Best of Winners will give her one more point."

"Will Best of Breed do the same thing?"

Madge looked at him askance. "Yes, it will."

"So you want me to do my best?"

Madge smiled. "Absolutely!"

Stanley nodded. "Okay, then. Let's do it."

Madge led the way into the ring. Stanley was the last one in. There were five dogs in the ring all hoping for the top prize. Stanley remembered that Aleta had showed this little one to a breed win two months prior. He hadn't known much then; but, he remembered that if Annie was enjoying herself she was naturally showy.

While he was in line before going in, he threw a toy mouse in front of her. She pounced on it and grabbed it, and it squeaked. Stanley snatched it from the floor and stuck it in his pocket. He squeaked it lightly before he went in. Annie was intrigued. She was too inexperienced to be jaded.

He stood at the end of the line playing hide and seek with the mouse while the judge examined the three specials. When it was Annie's turn, she trotted, tail wagging with a lively animated gait. Her long topline stayed even as she moved across the floor.

The judge thought she looked even better than before. He looked at this handler whose attention was focused on the little dog but who seemed to sense his next direction. He could send this pair to the group.

Rufus took Best of Opposite sex and Madge couldn't believe her baby girl had beaten her special. She was both amazed and delighted. And when the judge congratulated Stanley on his handling, the comment was not lost on Madge. Madge insisted he be the one in the photo that was taken.

Nathan recorded it all.

Aleta attired this time in green with the rust-colored jacket still managed to catch the judge's eye. Maggie was as animated as she had been the previous day, the handler being as lively and engaged as the bitch at the other end of the lead. They moved as one and both stood rock still when the judge stood back for a final look. Maggie free-stacked was more beautiful than those that were posed. She won the points and the Breed.

Tom Wilson arrived after winning the Breed with a Smooth Collie male whose ear tip managed to stay down through the judging. His only fault was that one ear rose to a point when he was highly alert. The key was to keep him one step below that. The win was worth two points and Tom was pleased. He breezed into the building to exchange dogs with his assistant who was waiting with his Scottie. He arrived in time to see the end of Stanley's performance.

It was surprisingly good. The man was obviously a quick study. He watched Aleta in the ring and marveled at her skill.

When Stanley came to stand beside him, he said jokingly, "I hope you don't do quite as well with Scotties."

"I remember how Aleta showed Annie," Stanley said. "I copied her."

"Well, Cassie is a good little bitch and as I remember it, Aleta won with her."

"I believe so," Stanley said, "but it was trickier."

"Well, Man, give it your all," Tom said lightly. "Take me on."

"You don't want me just to take her in?"

"Never 'just take' a bitch in. Make her sparkle. That Beatrice isn't here doesn't matter. You give it all you've got. It's the only way you get better."

"But I'm working for you."

"Then brand this in your memory. I expect the best you've got each and every time."

Stanley smiled. "That's not going to be much. Winning with Annie was a fluke. Besides there wasn't a single handler in the ring."

"When we're done, I'm going to give you another lesson in dog showing," Tom said mysteriously.

"I gather that's my pay," Stanley joshed.

"Only if you do a good enough job."

Stanley watched while the Scottie dogs went in. There were only two.

Stanley watched with unabated intensity exactly how Tom handled Cassie. He didn't have time to let the sinking feeling deep in his gut telling him he was over his head rise to the surface. He kept focused on what the handler did that sparked the dog. Again he remembered that Aleta said that puppies should enjoy the ring. He remembered how Cassie liked her space. Tom made certain she had plenty. He remembered that in Breed Aleta didn't. She had let the Specials run up on her. Cassie had challenged them. With Scotties this was a good thing he'd been told afterward.

With Tom handling her, Cassie won the single point over the other two in competition. He came out of the ring, transferred Cassie's arm band to Stanley, handed him a handful of liver bits and Cassie's leash.

"You know what to do," he smiled.

"Except with the liver," Stanley said straight-faced. "Do I eat it?"

"Cassie will want you to share," Tom said smiling.

He liked a bit of banter. It relaxed him.

The two male specials went in first, followed by the two bitch specials, the winner's dog and finally, Cassie. The first circling of the ring told the judge who his three top competitors were—two bitches and a dog. Cassie was one of the bitches.

The judge went over the specials on the table and had them move in a straight line. The first male was the one he'd preselected and so he watched him as he finished his circle and came up behind Cassie who spun in place and pounced toward him. It was an outright challenge. The male took a step back.

When the second male came running around the ring, the handler, not having seen the first challenge saw that the judge's eye was still on him so he purposely overshot the back of the line and stepped into Cassie's space. Again she spun around. Her pounce was more decided and he backed up three steps.

As the judge finished with the group, he pulled out Belle and had Tom move her to the head of the line in front of the first male. Then he moved Cassie up and pointed to the space between Belle and the male special. It was the space reserved for Best of Winners. Stanley politely waited for the two handlers to move. He had Cassie's leash properly taut. Cassie, however, didn't think the dogs moved fast enough. She pounced at Belle who moved forward and then stared at the male who stepped back. Cassie settled between them and Stanley slipped her a bit of liver.

The judge moved the dog in front of Belle and then moved Cassie in front of the dog. He asked them to go around and thus Cassie took the Breed.

"I thought I told you not to do that," Tom joshed as he shook Stanley's hand.

"I want my reward," Stanley retorted, "and it better not be liver."

When he left the ring, Tom asked, "What do you do for a living?"

"I'm a child advocate," Stanley replied.

"You're a quick study is what you are."

"What's your tip?"

"Well, my handing Cassie's lead to you signaled the judge that you were part of my team."

"You still almost won, so that was also the signal that you wanted the win for Belle."

"You do catch on fast," Tom said. "But Beatrice won't be upset. Cassie outshone everyone in the ring. How did you ever know to let her?"

"It's what Aleta did."

"You sure watch that wife of yours."

"Wouldn't you if she were yours?"

"Yes, I would."

Aleta came up, "Would what?"

"Give you a treat for teaching him so well."

Aleta slipped her arm around Stanley's waist. "He was pretty spectacular today, wasn't he?"

"Are you taking the two into group?"

"I know my limits," Stanley said. "I think I'll sit out the group."

"I don't know if he told you," Aleta said, "but he was in an explosion a couple days ago. His chest is black and blue. Lifting the dogs onto the table would be too much for him."

"That true?" Tom asked.

"Pretty much," Stanley responded. "Bending over was tough. I'm not sure I could hold a dog against my chest without wanting to toss it into the next county."

"I'll take Cassie in then," Tom said. "But you get a Breed photo before you put her up."

By the time Stanley and Aleta were finished and out of the building, Lyle had won the Breed with Morgan and then walked over to the Chessie ring and matched that with Stoney. Both would be in the group competition that afternoon. When Evelyn took the breed with Topaz that made it a clean sweep. Everyone in the enclave of friends had a dog that would be shown that afternoon. For them, showing was over until three. They decided to celebrate by having a barbecue. After the Best in Show was finished all would be packing up and heading home. Now was the time to celebrate.

Joey Crowder and Tag Burrows had arrived early enough to see Lyle win the Breed in Labs, but they spent their time looking for some sign of Stanley. They roamed the RV parking lot and saw that his RV was still in place. Joey didn't know there were rings inside the big building. He thought the building was filled with vendors like those crowded along the roadway leading to it. His mistake was in assuming that the ones crowding by the entrance were the excess. He had no idea that at dog shows, the dogs were always first. In inclement weather, dogs were the first to be crowded into the building. Vendors either closed up or huddled under their self-make shelters.

Today was one of those days when the Show Committee was hoping no special arrangements were going to need to be made. The sun shone until around ten when clouds began to crawl across the sky. On Saturday the continued sunshine had blessed their choice to hold the Groups outside where there was more room around the rings. But as the clouds continued to gather, it was decided not to take a chance on the final day of the show. Better to be safe than sorry they told each other.

Joey heard the announcement about the change in the location of the groups as well as the fact that they started at three. He decided that wherever Stanley was, he wasn't in his RV or near the rings, so they might as well split until the big event at three. He'd caught a glimpse of George Sciretta coming out of the big building and that had cemented his decision to vanish for a while.

Joey's presence, however brief, didn't escape George Sciretta's notice. He made a call.

That call started a chain of inquiries. A lieutenant on the Chicago police force, a former partner of Chief Tom Milani, made a call to his old buddy.

"I'm doing a quid pro quo from long ago," he started by saying. "Nothing illegal, but I need your help."

"Stan, if I can, you know I will," Milani said.

"You've got a car bombing case up there. Any clue as to who the bomber is?"

"We do."

"Joey Crowder?" Stan ventured.

Milani neither confirmed nor denied the query.

"I'm supposed to tell you that he's not working for anyone in Chicago."

"Why is that important?" Milani asked.

"The person who put out the contract is local."

"Go on," Milani urged.

"He's a member of the Oakwood city council," Stan said.

"Tell me which one," Milani said. "That would really help."

"The family wants you to lean on the entire council."

"Why?"

"The Family doesn't want Aleta Praetzel or her husband hurt."

"They're safe," Milani said, disturbed that this was the second call about their whereabouts.

His uncertainty that this was the purpose of the call vanished with the next statement.

"Joey Crowder was seen at the dog show. The Family wants him to get a call to drop the contract."

Shocked that the Praetzel's whereabouts had been discovered, Milani spit out the first thing that occurred to him. "Why don't they call Joey themselves?"

"It's got to come from the guy who put out the contract," Stan said.

"I'll give Chief West a heads-up."

As soon as he hung up, Tom Milani tried West's cell, but couldn't get through. He decided to go another route. He called Ed Ornstein, who was at home watching Emma and her litter.

"Joey Crowder is at the show."

"Did you call West?"

"Tried. Can't get through."

"I can call Stanley," Ed said. "Who called you?"

"I got a call from an old friend in Chicago. It seems the Family wants Aleta and Stanley protected. Any idea why?"

"Aleta went down purposely to show George Sciretta's Bulldog."

Milani took a deep breath. "You mean the mob wants her protected because she's showing somebody's dog?"

"Not just somebody. Sciretta is the Family's bookkeeper. He's very low profile; but, my guess is that messing with him isn't wise."

"Does Aleta know all this?"

"Don't think so. West does; but, I don't think anyone else does."

"My caller confirmed that the man that put out the contract is a member of the Oakwood City council."

"We've narrowed the field to three. Our prime suspect is Phillip Fleming. He's been the most outspoken advocate for the building of the school."

"How did you narrow the field?"

"Let's just say we did," Ed said. "I'm sensing that you called for another reason besides just to warn Stanley and West. You want my help."

"The Family wants me to threaten the entire council and scare Joey Crowder's employer to pull back on the contract. I can't lean on the whole council, especially with what little I have. I need you to do a search."

"Search what?"

"Phone records," Milani said. "I received a call from Roger Lascovich, the Council's lawyer, yesterday trying to probe the whereabouts of Stanley Praetzel. I think he was prompted by the council member we're after. I think Joey Crowder pushed him to find out if Stanley Praetzel was in his house. For some reason Joey became suspicious and pressed his employer to verify that Stanley was still in town."

"So you want me to find out who called Roger Lascovich before he called you?"

"I'm going to get warrants for the phone records; but, I'll be hampered by legalities you won't be. This is off the record you understand, but if you discover who it is, I'll lean on him to call off the contract."

"I'll get right on it," Ed said. "And I'll call Stanley and let him know what's going on."

The barbecue was in full swing when a cell phone rang. Both Lyle and Stanley reached for their phones, but came up empty; however, George Sciretta answered his and the other two decided they were near enough to their trailers to hear their phones if they rang. They were both wrong.

Lauren had stuck her husband's phone in a drawer. He was going to enjoy this day if she had anything to say about it. She figured that Milani had Stanley's number. He could reach Lyle that way if it was anything critical.

She didn't realize that Aleta had removed Stanley's phone from his coat pocket that morning when she found out he was going into the ring. If anything critical came up, she figured West would be called. The only other person calling Stanley would be Ed and business could wait until the morning was over.

In the excitement that followed, she forgot she'd tucked his phone under the mattress.

As a result of their identical unilateral actions, neither Ed nor Tom Milani got through. Both gave up relatively quickly and concentrated on trying to uncover the perpetrator of the contract.

Ed had no problem hacking into phone company records. Milani got seven personal calls during the previous afternoon and none of them proved to be from the lawyer in question.

Ed then searched the calls that came in through the switchboard. He had the firm's number; but it didn't show up. There were far too many calls to go through individually.

He called Milani and asked him if he could pinpoint the time.

"I can't," Tom said, "but maybe the people stationed at the house can. Lascovich called there first."

"How many incoming calls do you suppose they received?"

"Maybe a few. It's Stanley's private number. Not too many people have it."

"Searching Stanley's records will be easier. You might start there. Lascovich used a private line."

With the time pinpointed, Ed came up with three calls from that phone one after the other. First was the call to Stanley's house, the second to the Willow Glen police station and the third to an Oakwood City council member—Brandon Webber.

He was one of the three not yet eliminated from consideration; but one considered unlikely. Finding his motive would take considerable digging, Ed reasoned, but first he needed to be stopped. He called Tom Milani.

Chapter 28

Chief Tom Milani changed into his uniform after swiping his rough beard with an electric razor. He always looked like a hood on television. On the short side of average, a bit stockier than he wanted to be, in his uniform he looked trimmer.

Two units had been told to report to police headquarters to accompany the chief.

Justin Conway who was hanging around the station called his friend at the TV station and told him to pack his camera. Justin, while a newspaper reporter, believed that being on scene when news broke was what made a good newsman, and he wasn't going to shut out the future possibility that television might be his future. His editor didn't like him having his foot stuck in two different doors but he liked the copy Justin turned in. Readers liked it as well and the sales increased whenever Justin broke a story.

Milani briefed his two officers, chosen for their imposing appearance as well as their polite demeanor. He needed private time with Brandon Webber to pull this off and they were his assurance that he would get what he wanted.

He would, after all, be in the middle of Chief Herbert Ramage's town arresting one of its chief citizens. And he had no warrant.

At the last minute he decided he needed a driver. He briefed him as he drove. Lieutenant Alan Peets asked why he was chosen to drive.

"Because you're a lieutenant, you're in uniform today, you're tall and muscular, and you scowl good."

"I'm also black," Peets said. "You're sure you didn't want a black chauffeur."

"You were the handiest," Milani countered. "I'm not sure your race is an advantage or a disadvantage in this situation. Your quick wit is, however, so keep it handy."

Peets grinned. He loved to challenge the man. Sometimes it nettled Milani; but, the end result was better than thinking that Milani had stereotyped him.

"You'll be in the room with me," Milani said. "We're not playing games with the guy. I just need a witness in case he says later that I threatened him."

"You don't think the presence of three tall, muscular, armed police officers is intimidating?"

"Two will be outside the office," Milani said a bit hesitantly.

"Let's hope Ramage storms in," Peets said, "so your action will be deemed foresight and not intimidation."

"He hired someone to kill Stanley and Aleta Praetzel!" Milani blurted out. "I've only one chance to prevent their death. Consider this my throwing myself between them and the bullet."

"Chief, I'm with you on this," Peets said. "I promise only to scowl threateningly."

"Good. That'll never appear on the tape."

"What tape?"

"I'm recording the conversation."

"You can't legally do that."

"I can if I put the recorder on the table."

"Don't record," Peets advised. "As a council member he's been put on the spot and been burned by his own responses. You need him not to be worrying about that."

"Good suggestion."

"We're being followed."

"Justin and his TV friend?"

"Yes."

"I expected them. Their presence will work to our advantage if Ramage shows up."

The two marked Willow Glen patrol cars stopped in a no parking zone directly in front of Webber's Furniture Store. The four officers wove through the main floor crowded with couches, tables and chairs to the rear of the store through which they could see Brandon Webber talking with two customers.

Lieutenant Alan Peets encouraged the couple to give way to the Willow Glen Police Chief. As soon as they left the office, Peets closed the door and the other two officers blocked it from the outside.

Brandon Webber sputtered his protests over the presence of the officers in his store.

"We are here to offer you protection," Tom Milani said.

"Protect me? From what?" Brandon Webber sputtered angrily. "If I want protection, I'll call our own chief of police."

Milani smiled. "Be my guest. Call him. We'll protect you until he arrives."

Webber picked up the receiver and punched in 911. He got the dispatcher, who put him through as soon as he identified himself. The alacrity with which she responded produced an onrush of confidence.

"Ramage," Webber said, skipping the title which Ramage valued highly. Ramage's teeth were instantly on edge.

"Yes, this is Chief Ramage," he said loudly enough for Milani to hear.

"I'm in some kind of danger. I want you to come over immediately… No, I don't know what kind… What do you mean you're busy. You're never busy… It is not a waste of time… How do I know? Because the Willow Glen Police Chief is standing in my office telling me, that's why."

Webber held out the phone. "He doesn't believe me."

Milani shook his head and nodded toward Peets who took the phone from Webber's outstretched hand.

"To whom am I speaking?" Peets asked politely.

"Who the hell is this?" Ramage stormed.

"I asked first," Peets said.

"Chief Herbert Ramage, Chief of Police," Ramage said vexed that he had to give in.

"Can you prove it?" Peets asked.

"No, of course I can't prove it. Not over the phone, you dumbass," Ramage charged, "but Webber can tell you it's me."

Peets handed the phone back to Webber.

Webber who hadn't understood what was happening until this minute, suddenly got the picture, "Not so much fun not being believed is it…? I tell you the Willow Glen Police Chief Tom Milani is standing in my office offering me protection… No, he didn't say why I need it… I called you… You're my Police Chief. I expect you to get down here… Why? Because I'm a city council member and I'm telling you to… No, don't send a cop. The store is full of cops, only they aren't our cops. Get the hell down here and tell me why my store is full of Willow Glen cops!"

He slammed down the receiver. "He's coming."

"While we wait," Milani said, "I should tell you about a phone call I received this morning regarding you."

"From whom?"

"A reliable source."

Webber was too intrigued to press for a name. "What did he say about me?"

"He said that the Family doesn't want either Aleta Praetzel or her husband harmed," Milani said. "That's a direct quote."

"What's that got to do with me?"

"My caller said that they'd narrowed the person who put out the contract for the thirty thousand dollars, to a member of the Oakwood City council."

"That doesn't mean it was me!" Webber protested.

"Who do you think it is then?"

"I don't know; but, it's not me."

"Your hired killers are at the dog show."

"What dog show? That proves it wasn't me. I don't know anything about a dog show."

"The Family wants you to call Joey Crowder and tell him that the contract is cancelled."

At the mention of Joey's name both officers noticed that Webber paled and his hands trembled slightly.

"I don't know any Joey Crowder."

"It won't take me long to prove that you do," Milani said. "I can either do it before Stanley Praetzel is killed and you'll be facing attempted murder charges or after he's killed and you'll be facing charges of first degree murder."

"On the other hand," Peets said, "you could chose not to cooperate and we'd be helpless to help. We'd be required to leave you under Ramage's protection. Speaking of whom, I believe he's finally arrived. I'd hate to call for help in this town."

"You can't put the mob onto me," Webber cried. "Cops can't do that."

"We don't have to," Milani replied. "They've got their own sources. And the only way to escape from them…"

A loud clamor just outside the door, shook Webber. "Okay. You win. You guys will protect me if I make the call, right?" he shouted above the protests coming from Ramage.

"Yes, we will. You'll be our prisoner."

"You promise?"

"We want a full confession."

"Yes. Yes. Anything."

"Make the call," Milani said. "Lieutenant Peets, quell the disturbance outside."

Within two minutes, the clamor subsided.

Webber took out his handkerchief and wiped his brow as he made the call. Tom Milani punched the speaker button on the phone and set the tape recorder on the table next to it.

"To prove you cancelled the contract," Milani said. "Be specific!"

Webber nodded agreement.

"Joey," Webber said. "I'm cancelling the contract on Stanley Praetzel."

"I'm ready to move in."

"There's been a complication," Webber said. "It seems his wife has friends that I don't want to cross."

"So no killing, right?"

"That's it," Webber reiterated.

"Neither one, right?"

"The friends mentioned that no harm should come to either one."

"I want the money anyways. I had lots of expenses."

"Not thirty thousand dollars' worth!" Webber argued.

"Don't think you can stiff me!" Joey said. "I'll be in touch."

Milani slipped the tape recorder in his pocket and opened the door. With the TV cameraman filming the ensuring action, Milani said, "Brandon Webber, you're under arrest for conspiracy to commit murder and for the attempted murder of Stanley Praetzel. Lieutenant Peets, please cuff the man and read him his rights."

Peets repeated the familiar words knowing full well he'd be lucky if the side of his face made the evening news. Peets loaded the handcuffed man in the back of the patrol car.

"He's your prisoner, Peets," Milani said. "Rob can be my chauffeur on our return trip."

Milani said nothing about recording the telephone conversation. That recording was made for another purpose.

Chapter 29

The first call Tom Milani made when he got back to his office was to his friend in the Chicago police force. He played him the tape.

The second call was to Ed Ornstein. He played him the tape.

Ed called his assistant Dean and asked if either Stanley or Lyle West was around. He was told they were both watching something called Group. They were all involved somehow. Ed told him not to interrupt them but to pass along the good news when he had the chance.

Dean leaned back in his chair and decided it wouldn't hurt to wait. He wasn't to leave the dogs he'd been told several times, and there was no one around to take his place. He'd tell them all later. It was a relief, however, to only have to worry about the dogs.

Joey clapped the cell phone shut and cursed for several minutes before he was able to tell Tag Burrows what had happened.

Tag having heard the words, 'no killing,' had an inkling that the contract had been cancelled.

"So, now we go home?" he asked.

"Why?"

"We can't kill them."

"So we can't kill them; but we can still kidnap them."

"We was warned to lay off."

At first Tag thought Joey didn't hear him. Joey's eyes glazed over and he slowly began to smile. It was a strange smile, surreal. Tag grew tense. He didn't like the signs. Joey was up to something.

Joey didn't keep him waiting long. "The Praetzels have been told they are safe, so they'll relax. And that cop that's with them will relax too. It's a goddamn stroke of luck!"

"But Sciretta will see us."

"So what?"

"Won't he tell someone?"

"He's already told and you notice he didn't tell the cop."

"Won't he try to stop us?"

"He already did," Joey said. Then his tone became urgent, "Look, there's no danger. Sciretta isn't a hired gun in the first place. Second, he won't even twitch a finger without orders. By the time the Family gets wind of what went down, we'll be long gone and a million dollars richer."

"But how do we get Stanley Praetzel to go along if we can't kill him?"

"He don't know that," Joey declared.

"Suppose he does?" Tag argued.

"He still don't know."

"How do you know they didn't tell him?"

"Don't matter."

"Sure it matters."

"No, it don't. We're doing a kidnapping not a murder. We tell him the plan's changed. He ain't stupid. He'll get the picture."

216 • Susan Davis Sandberg

"So this'll work?"

"Better than before."

"Okay, I'm in."

The two left for the Fairgrounds shortly after. As they were driving in, they saw RV's pulling out.

"Is it over?" Tag asked.

"There's still a lot of RV's left. Let's drive into their lot."

As they drove their gray van down the rows of RV's, they passed the four rigs that were parked to make a rough circle with the pens set up in the middle. Dogs were still in most of the pens and a single man was dozing in a chair nearby.

Tag recognized the guy as one who'd been there earlier. Joey drove around the corner and parked in a vacated space in the next aisle. From where Joey and Tag sat, they had a clear view of the cluster of pens and the entrances to several of the rigs.

Joey killed the engine and they waited.

A short time later, a small, thick-waisted woman came into the area with a short, long-backed dog on a leash.

"She's too wiggly to stay with us," Madge explained as she put Annie in her empty pen.

"I got a message for Stanley and the Chief," Dean said. "Are you going to be here for a while?"

"I need to feed the puppy, so go ahead and deliver your message. I'll watch the dogs."

"I won't be long," Dean called back as he ran off.

"Now's our chance," Joey said, opening his car door. "Bring the tape."

Tag followed Joey as he walked briskly down the road behind the cluster of rigs. Their movement set off the dogs. The woman turned and Joey waved as he walked on. The woman waved back and then entered her RV.

As soon as Joey saw her door close, he cut behind the RV he was passing and backtracked, Tag on his heels. The barking continued as the two crept along the side of Stanley's RV and snuck inside. The barking stopped.

The three big males—Stoney, Morgan and Topaz were at ringside waiting to enter. They would not have given up so quickly.

Madge appeared and the barking started up again. She talked to the dogs, telling them to hush.

Joey separated the bottom slats in the side window and saw her put down a food dish in the pen with the small Dachshund.

All the blinds in the RV were shut tight so it was shadowy and dim inside. There was still enough light to see. Joey cracked the blind over the kitchen sink and opened the briefcase on the table. He pulled out some stationary with Stanley's letterhead.

"This is their RV alright," he announced.

"So now what?"

"We wait."

"That's the plan?"

"Simple, huh," Joey said happily. "The big problem was how to get into the RV so we could surprise them and luck was on our side. We're here."

"I don't like not being able to see out," Tag complained.

"I do. Nobody can see in."

Dean arrived as the judge was selecting the winners of the Terrier Group. He saw the group rise and clap and headed for Stanley.

"What happened?" Dean asked.

"Cassie took third place." Stanley replied.

"Is that good?"

Aleta leaned over. "For a puppy that's great!"

"Madge had a big ribbon too," Dean said.

"Annie won fourth in the Hound Group."

"And that's good?"

"It's great!" Aleta said enthusiastically. "She's a pup too."

"Madge said she was wiggly," Dean said. "She's feeding her so I thought I'd pass along Ed's message."

"Anything wrong?"

"No, it's good news. The man behind the attacks has been arrested. He made a call and the contract has been cancelled. I thought it might help you to relax to know that."

"Thanks," Stanley said, giving Aleta a squeeze.

"I promised I'd get right back," Dean said. "Will you tell Chief West?"

"Sure, I will," Stanley said. "Does Ed want me to call?"

"He said there was no hurry," Dean reported and then began to run back toward the RV parking section.

Stanley walked over to Lyle West and repeated the message. Harriet heard what was being said, but her gut didn't relax. She realized her butterflies could be because she was about to go into the ring. Only time would tell.

Tom took Topaz from Evelyn. The retrievers lined up in the same order as the day before with Harriet and Stoney in front. Tom and Topaz took the spot behind Harriet. and the Lab fell in behind him, only today the Lab was Morgan and Lyle was handling him.

It was another head-to-head challenge. Both men found this personal competition exciting and that excitement travelled down the leads to the dogs. It was not something they could call up at will. It just happened but both knew it usually meant they would be in contention for the win.

Aleta slipped her hand into Stanley's. "It's nice that it's over, isn't it?"

"Wonderful!!" he murmured. "Who are we rooting for?"

Aleta reared back a little bit in feigned shock. "How can you ask that?"

"But Stoney won yesterday," Stanley offered as an argument. Aleta's frown told him that wasn't a consideration.

"Think of it this way. Everything I am today I owe to Grams."

"Including being my wife," Stanley whispered in his wife's ear.

"So who are we rooting for?" Aleta pressed.

"Lyle, of course," Stanley said softly. "We owe him too."

The judge spent extra time going over all three retrievers and the spectators realized that those three were under consideration. When the judge made his cut, it surprised no one that they were included. Also in the group was the black Cocker Spaniel from the day before and two who'd walked the day before, the Brittany and the Clumber Spaniel, both repeat Group winners.

His consideration of the final six was more prolonged than usual. Politically, the retrievers weren't being considered for Group 1. He had three politically powerful candidates in the other three. He was choosing between the three retrievers for fourth place.

As he went down the line, he put his hand on the Chessie's shoulders and marveled at the power he felt as the muscles rippled beneath his touch. No wonder this animal took Best in Show the day before. He deserved a placing higher than fourth.

Tom Wilson had the Golden posed perfectly. He recognized age creeping in by the graying muzzle. He hadn't many wins left in him. He ran his hand down his hind leg. Well-muscled. The dog was in superb condition.

His eyes went to the black Lab and Lyle raised a brow and Morgan responded by raising his. Lyle cocked his head and Morgan added that. It added a touch of the comical which is a prized attribute in Labradors. The judge ran his hand down the back and allowed it to press down lightly. Such a strong topline. He stepped back. The dog was perfectly balanced.

He looked at the Brittany next. The dog looked the same as always. He went on to the Cocker and found himself actually liking the naturalness of the retrievers. The Clumber appealed to him. He was wagging his tail, what there was of it, and looking up expectantly.

The decision was made for him by the dogs themselves. This was one time when he could be a judge and reward perfection. He'd started in the sporting-breeds and he had three superb retrievers to choose from.

Morgan took the Group One; Stoney, Group Two; and Topaz, Group Three. The Clumber lumbered into the final placing. The crowd at ringside roared their approval.

After a wild exchange of congratulations the four who placed went over to the corner ring to have their photos taken while the Working Group was called into the ring.

Stanley decided it was a good time to call Ed and put his hand in his pocket and discovered that the phone wasn't there.

"Aleta, do you know where my phone is?"

Aleta flushed lightly. "I stuck it under the mattress."

Stanley raised a brow in query.

"You were going into the ring. I didn't want it to ring when you were in there."

"That was this morning," Stanley pointed out annoyed.

Lauren was standing nearby and she laughed, "I stuck Lyle's in the drawer under his socks. I forgot about it until this minute. I don't think I'll tell him until he's finished showing."

"I'm going back to get mine," Stanley said hurrying toward the RV.

"Don't forget I'm the Group after this one," Aleta called after him.

"I'll be back," he promised.

Harriet finished her photo shoot and hurried in his wake to put Stoney away.

Stanley opened the RV door and hurried inside without caution. As he turned the corner toward the bedroom, he came face to face with a large man holding a gun. It was pointed straight at him.

A smaller man stepped out of the bathroom after flushing the toilet.

"Lock the door," Joey said.

Stanley reached back and flipped the lock.

"What's the plan?" Stanley asked calmly. His mind was racing over what Aleta had told him. He wasn't going to die. Lyle was. Lyle wasn't here, so for the moment they were both safe.

"I like a man that gets right to the point," Joey said. "We're going to hold you for ransom. We figure you're worth a million."

Outside the thin metal door, Stanley heard a dog growl. He tensed until Harriet called, "The Herding Group is almost done. Non-Sporting is next. Should I wait for you?"

She never waited for him.

"I've got the runs," he called out. "I'll be there as soon as I can."

"Don't forget Lyle," she said, pausing for a while. "If you miss Aleta, you don't want to miss him."

"Thanks for the reminder. I should be okay by Best in Show," he called.

"Come on Stoney. Stop growling at the Scotties," she said. "Let's put you away so Evelyn can keep Topaz with her. She'll like that."

"What the hell was that all about?" Joey demanded.

"My wife is going into the ring next. She'll expect me to be there."

"And if you ain't?"

"She'll come to fetch me to watch Lyle go for Best in Show."

"The cop is going to be showing?"

"He'll be watching Aleta and shortly after she finishes, he'll be going in the ring again."

"Will he come back here first?"

"Probably not."

"How long before your wife is done?"

"Twenty, maybe thirty minutes, depending on whether she wins."

"Okay, take off your pants," Joey ordered.

Stanley unbuckled his belt, unzipped his pants and let them fall. He kicked them off.

"Shoes and socks too," Joey said. "And your shorts."

"Whatcha doing that for?" Tag said. "The tape's right there."

"If someone comes, he's gonna answer the door. Like that he ain't going to open the door too wide."

"I could send Dean to the ring with a note and then we'd be free to leave."

"Why are you anxious to leave?" Joey asked suspiciously.

"Cause he don't want me to bang that gorgeous wife of his," Tag guffawed.

"That it?" Joey asked, not expecting an answer.

"Suppose I can make it worth your while not to rape her."

"Go on," Joey said intrigued. This man wasn't making any move to escape. He hadn't sent any secret message with the old lady that had called to him.

Stanley was about to start when Joey cut in. "We're taking her with us. There ain't no bargaining about that."

"Yeah!" Tag said with the kind of enthusiasm that sent a shiver down Stanley's spine.

"May I sit down?"

"We like you standing right where you're standing," Joey said. His tone sounded too familiar. This was more than just a matter of embarrassing him. These men were enjoying looking at him.

Disconcerted, he spoke quickly. "I can get you two million—double what you're asking."

"Go on," Joey said.

"One for me from my parents and one for her from her grandmother."

"Why are you telling us this?"

"I want you to know she's valuable too."

"So how we gonna negotiate with two people? That's too tricky."

"I write one letter and ask for the two million. I give it to Aleta's grandmother and she arranges to get hold of my parents. In the letter I say that my father is to deliver the ransom. You won't have any trouble recognizing him. He looks just like me."

"How do you get the letter to the grandmother?"

"She's here at the show. I can have the guy watching the dogs deliver it. But it's got to be while everyone is still in the big building or this won't work."

"Will he leave?"

"He's my employee," Stanley said. "He'll do whatever I say."

"Your wife will be back for sure before the show is over, right?"

"Absolutely. She will be angry I missed seeing her and she'll come to fetch me to watch Lyle."

"So after she comes, how long we got?"

"Where's your car?"

"Next row over."

"Well, when we send Dean to Aleta's grandmother, that's when we should transfer to your car."

"Van," Tag said. "We got a van."

"So we get caught before we get ten miles," Joey pointed out testily.

"Not if Dean doesn't see us leave. He's been hired to protect our privacy. If he sees Aleta come in and he doesn't see us leave, he'll assume we don't want to be disturbed."

"For how long?"

"Well, he's already spent several hours outside waiting."

"So, he's like a bodyguard."

"Right."

"Okay, write the letter," Joey said. "Put it on that fancy stationary of yours."

"You want to dictate it?" Stanley asked.

"Yeah," Joey said. "Don't add nothing."

Stanley moved over to the table and sat down before one of them could order him to write it standing where he was. It felt good to sit down. He felt less exposed.

Joey began to dictate and Tag began singing a sexy little ditty about tits and ass that galled Stanley. The man was horny as hell. There was no way he could keep him off Aleta even for an hour.

He forced himself to write what Joey was saying bad grammar and all. He was rather glad for it actually. His father would know he was being forced to write it—not that he would have any doubt. Stanley had half that amount in his checking account.

"Don't sign it," Joey said. "Don't want you giving no clues by your signature."

"No problem," Stanley said. "Now let's address the other problem."

"What other problem?" Joey asked bewildered.

Stanley carefully folded the letter, took a plain envelope from his briefcase and slipped the letter inside.

"No fingerprints but mine," he commented.

"What problem?" Joey pressed.

"We're all men of experience. My guess is that you two have been in prison."

"So?" Tag challenged.

"When men in prison get horny what do they do?"

"You know," Tag said. "They make one of them a bitch."

"Either of you ever been a bitch or used a man as a bitch?"

"In prison you gotta," Tag exclaimed.

"So you know it works," Stanley said.

"What you saying?"

"How about for the next day or two whenever you feel horny you use me as your bitch and you leave my wife alone. I promise I'll be willing anytime day or night and I'll give you a good ride."

"You gay or something?" Tag said, "'cause we ain't."

"I'm not accusing you of being gay. Prison probably made you bi-sexual. You can go either way, so how about it?"

"Why should we do you a favor?" Joey spat out. "I hate your guts! You rich guys have it all. Nothing ever goes bad for you."

"Well, here's your chance," Stanley said.

"Chance to do what?"

"Stick it to a rich guy."

"I'm really horny," Tag confessed. "I'd like some right now."

Stanley couldn't believe he stood up and bent over and said to Tag, "Have at it. You can have me as much as you want. You gotta admit that's…"

His words were cut short by the first thrust of the big man's penis.

He gritted his teeth.

My God, what am I doing?

A large hand pushed his chest against the counter and the pain made him cry out. He grabbed the dish towel on the counter and stuffed it in his mouth.

His agony stirred the big man into thrusting harder. Each thrust brought spasms of pain from his badly bruised chest. The big man thought he was inflicting the distress and it excited him into ejaculation.

"Damn!" he said. "It didn't last long enough."

"My turn," Joey said.

The pain began again. Stanley thought the pain would never end. His chest which he could barely stand being touched was being pummeled against the countertop with each thrust.

I can't do this, he thought. I can't. It's got to stop. I can't take anymore.

Then suddenly, it did.

Stanley took the towel out of his mouth and turned. "Do we have a deal? Me anytime. My wife never."

Tag shrugged. "It was okay for me."

Joey nodded. "It's a deal. You anytime, day or night."

Stanley couldn't believe he nodded. Then he heard the words he hoped he wouldn't hear.

"I want one more go," Tag said. "Maybe in front of the wife."

"No," Stanley said with a firmness that surprised them. "This is our secret. I tell no one. You tell no one, especially my wife."

Joey sensed he had a new bargaining chip. "You do what I say. She does what I say. She don't never have to know. Now, do we got time?"

Stanley wished he could say no, but these guys would only get angry if he did and he was wrong.

"Yes, there's time."

"That's what I wanna hear!" Tag said pushing Stanley's chest onto the counter.

The rape seemed to last forever.

Chapter 30

Lauren greeted Harriet when she returned to the building.   The Working Group was in the final judging stages.

"Where's Stanley? Aleta's about to go in the ring."

"He's got the runs," Harriet said.

"Poor guy. Can I do anything?"

"He took some medicine. He's hoping it will work fast enough," Harriet fibbed. Lauren was not geared to reading Harriet's expression; however, Aleta was. She would spot the lie.

"Should we tell Aleta?" Lauren worried aloud. "His not being here will bother her."

"Run and tell her then," Harriet said, relieved that she didn't have to try to fool Aleta. It had begun. Not the competition inside the ring, but the trial by fire that would test the two she loved most in the world. Not knowing anything except that if she or they asked Lyle for help, he would die. She couldn't see what would happen to them; but, she didn't see death. But then she couldn't see past Lyle's fate.

Still, she thought, I was able to see both of his impending deaths. Maybe that's why I could see both threats to Lyle before, so I'd know that I would see past his death to the death of another if that was going to happen.

It was as if she were looking into a room so dark one couldn't see even the faintest outline of a piece of furniture. There was a future, she knew, but she couldn't discern even a bit of it.

Fine prophet you are, she scolded herself, you can't see a single bit of the future on your own.

She chuckled at her own thought. Of course, she couldn't see the future. Wherever did she get the idea that she had any power?

Aleta caught her smile as she entered the ring and it told her everything was okay. Must've been something he ate. Stanley reacted to certain foods. He always travelled with his favorite diarrhea medicine and usually it worked swiftly. He could easily be here in time to see part of the competition. She and Maggie being among the slowest moving in the group were third from the end. He could still make it.

Harriet sat back to watch. God wanted Lyle to live. He wanted her to make choices depending solely on His will without any assurances that no one would be tested as a result.

It is better I don't know, she realized. I'd never be able to give the advice I need to give if I did. For some reason, she knew she'd touched on the truth. While she was sitting here, Stanley was in hell.

My God, she thought, I'm thinking about myself when I need to be asking God to give him the strength to endure.

The events in the ring were seen and heard, but her brain, so busy with its fears, shut out the messages from both her eyes and ears.

Evelyn leaned over. "I think Aleta's going to make the cut. She's looking as good as she did yesterday."

Harriet nodded perfunctorily. She tried to focus on her granddaughter in the ring, but no sensations were truly registering. Her eyes followed Aleta around the ring, but her mind refused to assimilate what she was seeing. She knew her senses were working. She also knew her brain wasn't. And she didn't even know what she was thinking.

Unnerved by her own mental dysfunction, she sat staring into the ring wondering if anything would ever compute again.

Evelyn nudged her. "She made the cut!" she whispered. "Today has been a good day for all of us. Wouldn't it be something if she and Lyle were both in Best in Show?"

Suddenly, Harriet woke up. She can't win, God, she prayed. Lyle's life is more important.

It was at that moment she realized that she had been praying with all her might that her granddaughter be spared. God had given her a choice.

She stared at the six dogs in the ring. Tom was there with his Frenchie who was standing proudly, his bat ears alert, his front feet planted as if he owned the land he was standing on and all the world around it. He was a marvelous little dog whose short coat revealed every muscle. The weakened light picked up the apricot brindle striping in his coat.

He looked like a little tiger, she thought. The dog turned in place as the judge passed him. His movement brought the judge's eye back to him. He stared at the judge with his large round eyes and seemingly thrust his chin out defying him to look elsewhere.

The Frenchie took the Group. Maggie came in second. Aleta congratulated Tom warmly.

"He sure put on a show at the end," she said. "Once he decided to claim the prize, there was no stopping him."

"It was almost yours, you know," Tom said. "You showed Maggie to perfection. I hope George realizes that placing in Group four times on the way to a championship is rare."

"Tell him for me," Aleta said, accepting the red rosette.

"It was close," the judge said. The two handlers smiled at him and nodded.

Harriet greeted Aleta with a light hug when she exited the ring.

"How's your shoulder?" she asked.

"Where's Stanley? Didn't he make it?"

"Let's get your photo taken," Harriet suggested guiding Aleta to the corner of the building where the photographer was set up. A backdrop had been erected and potted palms flanked the rise on which dogs and handlers posed. A toy was tossed, ears came up and the light bulb flashed. Usually only one shot was needed. The handler knew how to set the dog's feet in place, the judge knew what expression of his photographed the best and put it in place as soon as the photographer stepped behind the camera and the tossing of the toy was timed with the snapping of the picture. It had been done a thousand times and it always alerted the dog.

Aleta handed Maggie back to Tom's assistant who would walk her back to her pen. She gave George Sciretta the rosette and Tom came up and chatted with him about placing in Group four times as a class dog. Sciretta's attention was riveted on what Tom was saying and Aleta slipped away.

Harriet walked with her and as they left the building asked her to slow down. Aleta slackened her pace.

"I can't go all the way with you," Harriet said. "I don't know why but I can't."

"Something's wrong, isn't it?" Aleta said starting to speed up.

"Wait!" Harriet called. Her voice carried the panic she felt.

Aleta spun in place.

"It's happening," Harriet said. "The men have Stanley. Stoney told me."

"You didn't tell anyone," Aleta charged, her ire rising. "You just left him!"

"You can't warn anyone. You need to obey Stanley. He is doing what needs to be done."

Tears sprang into Harriet's eyes and coursed down her cheeks. Aleta moved toward her and put her arm around her.

"Don't cry. I will do as you say."

"Lyle's life depends on it."

"I'll do it."

"Don't think I don't know I'm sending you into hell because I do."

"I know what to do."

"Trust your husband," Harriet said pulling away. "I will be praying."

Aleta rushed off. That her grandmother let her go knowingly told her that she was a vital part of the means necessary to save Lyle's life. People sacrificed for others all the time. And Lyle was someone both she and Stanley loved.

I guess I would die for him as well as Stanley, she thought.

She didn't realized that life is sometimes worse than death. That she was about to discover.

Harriet returned to the group. Lauren asked about Stanley.

"Aleta's going to check on him. She'll be back in time to watch Lyle with or without Stanley," Harriet said, grateful that Lauren couldn't read her as well as her granddaughter could.

"What an exciting end to our weekend."

"Yes, it is," Lauren said. "I'm more nervous than he is I think."

"Come on, sit with me and we'll be nervous together."

Aleta hurried toward the parking lot. She refused to contemplate what waited for her. Her grandmother had told her to trust Stanley. What could she have meant by that? Stanley was a victim. He wasn't in control.

Her heart seemed to leap into her mouth as she approached the RV. She had never been so afraid.

What was to stop her from turning around and running? Her grandmother said she was about to enter hell.

Who enters hell willingly? she thought. No one!

Stanley would understand, she told herself. She could go up to the door and call to him. And she could tell him that she was going back to the show. He would figure something out. He was clever.

She mentally kicked herself for her cowardice.

So you're a coward, she told herself. So what? So you don't want to suffer. Who does? Most people dive into danger without being aware they are and then they react. You know about the danger. You are reacting. One pulls one's hand away from a flame. One doesn't thrust one's whole arm.

There has to be another way, she reasoned. I have a good mind. I should be able to come up with an alternative.

She slowed to a walk. What if she went to get help and told Lyle that he was in danger of being shot. Couldn't she see he didn't get involved? Sure she could. That was a much better plan.

She was at the RV door when she resolved that her alternate plan was better.

She opened the door saying, "Stanley, I have an idea…"

The presence of the man with the gun shocked her. She paled visibly and her voice faltered.

She was surprised at her own surprise.

Stanley was waiting by the sink half dressed. This shocked her as well.

Before she could stop herself, she blurted out, "Where are your pants?"

"Hush, Aleta," he said gently. "And come here. The gentlemen want you naked."

"What?!" she exclaimed.

"Not another word," Stanley said firmly.

Aleta was too shocked at his calmness to speak, so she remained mute.

"May I help her?" Stanley asked the smaller of the two men. "She has an injured arm. If you'll allow me, I'll show you."

"Yeah, why not?" Joey said. "Only hurry."

"Whatever you say," Stanley replied politely. He began by removing Aleta's coat. He knew this was the most difficult garment of all for her. She could have managed the rest.

"Just stand still," he said. "This will all be over in a minute."

Aleta heard the words; but, obeying them was not something she wanted to do, yet she found herself unable to move. Her brain was still in shock. She'd walked right into hell. She'd been so puffed up with her own mental ability, she'd forgotten where she was and walked through the door into her worst nightmare.

She was frozen in place. She felt Stanley undo the buttons of her blouse and all she could think was how can you do this to me.

He slipped the blouse off the good arm first because he could bend the elbow. The bandaged shoulder came next.

"You wasn't kidding," Tag exclaimed. "What happened to her?"

"She was shot," Stanley replied dropping the blouse onto the chair on top of the coat. He made no attempt to lay it down carefully and she was annoyed. They were going to be so wrinkled.

He turned her so he could unfasten her brassiere and she moved as a woman in a trance. Facing away from the men was better somehow.

"Turn her around," the shorter man said.

"Sure," Stanley agreed, turning her so she faced them fully. He dropped the undergarment on the floor and unzipped her skirt. It fell to the floor. He tucked his thumbs underneath the elastic of her half-slip and panties and pulled them both down together.

Then he knelt and freed her legs from the tangled mess at her feet. She felt him remove her shoes and her stockings and she didn't care. She was fully exposed. And without looking into their eyes she knew the men were eyeing her lavishly.

He was offering her up to those strangers. She was expecting everything else; but, not this.

"I'm getting horny," the big one said.

"We got time?" Joey asked.

"Not much," Stanley said.

"Just a quickie."

"Aleta, go to the bedroom and lay down. Don't say a word. I need to have a… er… conversation with these gentlemen."

Aleta ran to the bedroom and closed the door.

"I don't think we have time for both," she heard Stanley say.

Feeling frightened and betrayed, Aleta began to cry. She buried her head under her pillow and sobbed. She didn't hear Stanley's original grunt as he felt the first thrust. She didn't hear anything after that because Stanley, the dish towel filling his mouth, managed to keep his agony controlled. What screams he couldn't hold back were muffled well enough not to make it past the bedroom door.

Aleta's fear and anger poured out in her weeping. Her shame rode with her into the bedroom and whispered degrading words in her ears. Her husband's betrayal was beyond belief. She had half-expected to be sexually assaulted. She had assumed that was the hell awaiting her, the hell that was going to walk through the bedroom door at any moment. What made it worse was that Stanley hadn't even tried to stop them. How could he have so calmly stripped her naked in front of strangers? He knew how devastated she had been when she'd run from the house naked by accident. She woke screaming from nightmares even since. How could he put her through this? Did he think she would ever be able to let him undress her without reliving the humiliation she had just endured?

In the kitchen, Stanley stood up. "Are we ready?"

"Go ahead," Joey said. "No funny business."

"I haven't messed with you yet, have I?" Stanley said. "I want to come out of this alive."

"Yeah, okay. Give him the envelope."

Stanley opened the door and called to Dean. He slipped the envelope through the slot.

"Take this to Harriet Locke. Give it only to her. Wait for an answer."

"Aren't you going to watch the rest of the show?"

"Just take the envelope. It's important. Do whatever Harriet tells you to do. Understand?"

"Yeah. I understand. I guess."

"Make sure she reads it," Stanley said. "Don't leave until she does."

After saying that, he shut the door. Dean hesitated and stared at the envelope in his hand. This was crazy. Still, Stanley and Aleta were here. He wasn't leaving the dogs alone.

As if in answer to his unspoken query, Stanley opened the blind in the door. "I'll watch the dogs," he shouted.

Dean took off.

He found Harriet at ringside and handed her the envelope.

"Sit down," she ordered. "Did he say I needed to open this right away?"

"Not exactly. He said I was to wait until you did."

"And he's watching the dogs."

"Yes. He opened the blinds on that side so he could see."

"He's sick," Harriet said. "That's why he couldn't come out."

"Sick?" Dean queried puzzled.

"The trots."

"Oh."

After a few moments, he asked, "Aren't you gonna open the envelope?"

"Not until after this is done," she said placing the envelope in her lap and holding it down with both hands.

"Should I wait?" Dean asked unsure what to do.

"He told you to, so you wait."

"Won't he be wondering?"

"He wants you here to remind me to open it when this is over. He might have thought I'd forget otherwise."

"This is all making no sense," Dean said.

"Shhh," Harriet whispered. "I'll explain later."

"I think I should go back."

Harriet put her hand on the young man's knee, "You stay where you are. That's an order. And yes it's from the man paying your salary. Your job is to sit right here. You aren't to leave my side until I release you."

Dean settled down. The letter was a ruse. It was a signal of some sort. That he could understand.

The bedroom door opened and Aleta stayed face down. The hand that touched her was Stanley's.

"Time to go."

"Like this?"

"I have a blanket. Tag is going to tape your hands and feet. If you promise not to yell, I can persuade them not to tape your mouth."

"I promise," Aleta murmured. She wasn't going to be raped. He'd talked them out of doing that. She had no idea how; but, she was grateful. And they were going to wrap a blanket around her.

"Keep your pillow," Stanley said quietly. "If you need to cry, use it to muffle the sounds."

Aleta hugged the pillow to her chest. She didn't feel so naked with it close to her body. Stanley pulled a blanket from the cabinet as Tag put duct tape around her ankles. He wanted her hands behind her back, but Stanley protested that that would hurt her shoulder and to her surprise he prevailed.

She didn't understand the strange relationship he had with these two. The blanket was wrapped around her, a large trash bag was pulled down over her head, and she was hefted onto the big man's shoulder. A yelp escaped and she remembered about the pillow.

"You gonna be quiet?" Tag asked.

"Yes," she murmured, burying her face back into the pillow.

She felt herself being carried down the RV stairs. Each jounce forced out a yelp of pain, but she bit the pillow and smothered the sound. She felt herself being pulled from the big man's shoulder and laid down on a hard floor. She was slid along the floor's surface as if she were a bag of dog food.

The door remained open. She could feel the cold air coming through the blanket. She couldn't see anything. She hoped the bag would be removed. She noticed light coming from the bottom of the bag. It wasn't closed tight. She wouldn't run out of air.

Please let Stanley come with me, she prayed. Please, God.

She heard the shuffle of feet and felt the weight of something light being thrown next to her.

"You don't cover yourself," Joey said. "Ain't nobody can see you but me. And I don't want you doing anything underneath the blanket."

"Like what?" Stanley replied as he lay next to his wife. "I haven't hardly a stitch of clothes on. And it's cold."

"That's why we left your undershirt on," Joey shot back. "You give me anymore lip and you'll lose that too."

Aleta couldn't believe how contrite Stanley's apology was. Why was he letting these guys treat him like this over such a tiny complaint?

"Aleta, remember the purpose of the pillow," Stanley said. Remembering her grandmother's admonition, she stuffed it in her mouth to muffle her retort. It was a fortunate placement as the van bounced over a curb and a sharp jolt of pain forced a screech from the pit of her stomach.

As the van hit a series of ruts, Aleta buried her face in her pillow. Each jolt sent a searing pain through her shoulder. She didn't realize how much she had been protected by the smooth cushioning of the bed in the huge RV. Here on the bare steel floor of a van with worn shocks she was feeling every bump in the road.

Grams, you were right, she muttered into the pillow. This is hell.

As she lay with her face buried, her ears picked up a muffled moaning nearby.

Stanley was feeling this too, she realized. His chest could barely stand to be touched. She wondered why he insisted on keeping on his undershirt. He'd told her being bare-chested was more comfortable. Why did he insist on keeping on that bit of clothing?

He was not acting rationally.

Suddenly, Joey spoke, "Don't do that!"

Aleta couldn't figure out what he could possibly have done.

The next sentence surprised her even more. "Come to think of it, do it again."

"Whatever you say," Stanley murmured. "Can I make sure she has some air?"

"The bag stays on!" came the sharp retort. "I don't want her turning you on. This ain't a pleasure cruise you know."

"Just let me flap it a bit, that's all," Stanley asked.

Aleta waited. Why didn't he do it? What was he waiting for? Suppose the men said no.

"You gotta do something for me then."

"Later," Stanley said. "Anything."

"Okay, give her air."

Alta didn't realize how stuffy it was under the bag until Stanley raised the end and forced fresh air in.

She was about to thank him, when he said, "Aleta, the pillow."

Wasn't she going to be allowed to speak to him at all? Maybe it was because he'd promised she would be quiet. She didn't know these men. He did. Was it important to them she obey? She hated that role. It grated on her very nature.

The van hit the highway and the jouncing stopped. She couldn't believe how grateful she was for the smoothness of the road. Her gratitude brought tears to her eyes. She thought herself foolish.

She thought of those back at camp and wondered when they would discover she and Stanley had been kidnapped. They must have by now.

"You drive for a while," Tag said. "I wanna watch."

Aleta couldn't figure out what he was talking about. It might make sense if she was uncovered, but she was wrapped tight in the blanket. Her hands and feet were taped. Weren't Stanley's?

He'd flapped the plastic himself. He hadn't asked them to do it. He'd done it. His hands were free. She sensed that he didn't have a bag over his head either.

"There's a diner up ahead," Tag said. "I'm starving."

"We can't go in and eat," Joey said. "Who's gonna watch him?"

"I won't go anywhere," Stanley said. "I won't leave my wife."

"We can take turns," Tag said.

"Yeah," Joey said. "We can do that, but I got a better idea."

"You thinking what I'm thinking?" Tag said.

"We take turns at both. How about it, Stanley? Will she do what you tell her to?"

"If I ask her to, she will," Stanley said.

"Okay. I'll get the room," Joey said.

The van pulled off the road and bounced over a rough patch of road before coming to a sudden stop. Aleta bit hard into her pillow. What was Stanley going to ask her to do?

She could hear the big man breathing hard. She lay very still. This wasn't going well. She had dreamed of reaching their destination having the wretched bag removed and settling down into being a prisoner. This stop wasn't what she wanted. In fact, this was what she didn't want. They were nowhere. She had hoped that once they reached wherever they were going, which she guessed would be near home, that the kidnappers would be consumed with their plans to get their money and get away.

This stop could only be for recreation, the kind she wanted no part of.

Lyle was safe. Why was Stanley still not showing any backbone? Was not being tied up so important, she thought then let her mind rest on that. Maybe he was planning an escape. If he was, he needed to be free.

She had to admit she liked him saying he wouldn't leave her. It was one of the few things he'd said that had been a comfort. Of course, he might have been told not to speak either. Still, if that were so, he'd broken that rule a couple of times. He'd broken it to tell her to be quiet.

Her grandmother had been right, this was a bad place to be. Even if the pain had stopped momentarily, although her shoulder now ached even when the van was still, fear was riding her hard. Did they cover her up so they wouldn't be distracted? Was she going to be taken into the motel room and unwrapped like a bar of candy and enjoyed?

The door opened.

"We're set," Joey answered. "Room five. Can you remember that?"

"I'm going first," Tag said. "Then I want a second shot."

"Whatever," Joey said. "Okay, Stanley. Give the missus the instruction."

"Aleta," Stanley said quietly but firmly, "Lay quietly and wait for me to return."

"That's it?" Joey asked incredulously.

"She promised to obey when we took our vows. Aleta keeps her word."

Aleta could almost hear a touch of pride in his voice. He was proud of her. She wasn't proud of him, but he was proud of her.

She felt a rush of fresh air as he lifted the plastic and waved it up and down a few times.

"Let's go have that conversation," Stanley said.

She heard the doors slam and she was alone.

He went willingly she told herself and he said he would be back. Waiting alone in the van trussed up and in pain, wasn't pleasant; but, what was waiting was much more unpleasant. The big man wanted to do her twice. How could Stanley ever talk him down from that? And there were two of them.

The air inside the bag was stuffy. They were gone. Why wasn't she taking off the bag? Because she was afraid. That was why. She was terrified over what they might do to her. Stanley had held them off, but it was only a matter of time.

Still, with no one around why not lift the bag? She tried to lift it up and the wave of pain told her why she hadn't tried it before. The onrush of fresh air, however, felt good. She would breathe quietly. Maybe it would last longer.

Take one moment at a time, she told herself. Remember what Grams said. Trust your husband. Except for the shoulder, which was left over from the shooting, she hadn't been hurt. She'd been embarrassed, but not hurt.

The side door of the van opened and the bag was pulled off her head.

"Your husband is a good negotiator," Joey said. "He said to say, 'Pillow' and you'd know what that meant."

Aleta nodded. She could barely see the man leaning over her. She told herself it was better that way. She knew which one it was, but it didn't matter. Rape was rape.

She closed her eyes and stiffened involuntarily.

The van door slammed shut.

Aleta waited for the sound of movement to tell her she wasn't alone. Slowly she opened her eyes. She was alone.

What had Stanley used to negotiate with? Surely the promise of money wouldn't do the trick. And if he promised too much, they'd realize how rich he was. If there was one thing she'd learned about her husband, it was that he knew how to handle money, which means he knew how to guard it from predators.

Maybe he was arranging transportation for the kidnappers. That would make getting a room with a phone a reasonable act. They might not be able to negotiate later. Stanley would be able to charge tickets to just about anywhere. And he had his card numbers memorized.

And fake ID's, Aleta thought. Once on a tangent her mind raced along past all intersecting ideas. And clothes maybe and luggage. Stanley would supply all of these things. No one would stop him. His cards weren't stolen. They were still in the RV. No one knew he had a penchant for numbers equal to her own.

The more she thought about what Stanley could offer, the more she relaxed. Fringes. Who wouldn't jump on that?

Wait. They wouldn't let him make their travel plans. The minute he was found….

Her mind plunged into the dark alternative.

Why can't I see that?

Because I can do nothing to stop it, she told herself. There were a lot of deaths in the world. She was only shown the ones where her action could alter the event. Her own was not among those.

What she didn't know was that when Tag had finished and Joey had entered the motel room, Stanley had worried lest his wife suffocate.

"She can't lift her arm to push the bag up. She could have if you hadn't taped her hands together."

"Those hands stay taped."

"Fair enough, but how about taking the bag off her head?"

"What do I get in return?"

"Anything you want. Ever had a blow job by a man?" Stanley asked, knowing he was treading in hostile waters.

As expected, Joey reared up. "I ain't no fag."

Stanley wasn't one of the county's best trial lawyers without having learned how to put a spin on whatever he was selling.

"Hey, I'm not one either; but, we're both men of the world. We experiment. Not every man is willing to do that. Tag isn't. My guess is you're more sophisticated."

"Yeah, I am," Joey said. "Wait here while I take the bag off and tell Tag to take his time eating."

Stanley laid down on top of the bed spread. He knew this would excite Joey. He'd guessed right about the sexual orientation of these two. He was their rape victim of choice. If he angered them, they'd take it out on Aleta. He was not going to anger either of them.

When Joey returned, Stanley sat up.

"Tag said he'd have two desserts. And I promised him a second go. I told him the longer he waited the better it would be."

Stanley groaned inwardly.

"You ever had a blow job?" Joey asked.

"No."

"How do you know what to do?"

"You're going to tell me what you like and I'm going to remember for next time."

Joey took off his pants and sat on the edge of the bed, Stanley knelt in front of him and began. A rape ended the session.

The side door of the van opened. Aleta realized it was the big man.

"Who took the bag off?" he hollered.

"Joey did."

"What else did he do?" he said pulling apart the blanket and checking her hands. They were still taped and that calmed him.

He stared at the half naked woman lying in front of him. He was really horny. Gingerly, he touched an exposed nipple. An involuntary shudder shook Aleta.

The motel room door opened. Quickly, Tag covered Aleta up.

"Whatcha doing?" Joey charged.

"Just checking her hands," Tag said. "That's all."

"Okay," Joey said. "He's waiting for you."

Tag slammed the door. "What are you gonna do?"

"Get us some coffee and stuff to take with us," Joey said.

Tag entered the motel room and Stanley asked, "Same as before?"

"Yeah, unless you got a better idea."

"Me, no. You're the boss. We do it your way."

The response pleased Tag.

The rape was as harsh as the last time. Stanley didn't dare not give Tag his due. Tag liked to hear Stanley whimper. It wasn't difficult to do considering the pain his bruised chest provided with each thrust.

His mind during the rape was on surviving the next thrust and the next. The chest pain was accelerating with each rape. You can't bruise a bruise without the body screaming at you to quit.

Stanley barely managed to crawl back into the van. Aleta was puzzled by his demeanor, but kept her queries to herself.

Stanley was allowed to curl up this time. Neither man looked back at him. He surreptitiously rubbed Aleta's upper arm. It was a gentle rub, the kind one would give a kitten.

She remembered the pride she'd heard in his voice when he said she would obey and her eyes closed and she fell asleep.

I will heal, Stanley told himself. Lyle is alive. Aleta hasn't been ravaged. The baby is safe. I will heal. In time I will heal all the way.

But deep down, he wasn't sure he'd ever recover.

Chapter 31

Earlier at the dog show, with Dean sitting stiffly by her side, Harriet watched the Best in Show competition. She desperately needed not to envision what was happening in the trailer. If she had been expected to do anything, Stanley would have sent word for her to act immediately.

Lyle, unfettered by worry, showed Morgan to perfection. While Labs rarely were awarded the top honor, the judge hadn't often seen a black in which he could find no fault. Tom Wilson's perky French Bulldog was demanding a look as well. Without Tom on her, the Afghan didn't sparkle as she usually did. The German Shepherd was his usual stunning self. He'd amassed countless Best in Shows and was hitting every circuit to add to that number. The Pomeranian was another repeat winner and was vying for another win with her perky attitude. The judge started with her and backed up. He looked at both the Frenchie and the Pom as if deciding between the two which, in fact was what he was doing.

The Frenchie followed his every move and when he swung his head, the quizzical look moved him a notch above the Pom. He gave a cursory glance to the Irish Terrier and the Boxer and stopped again at the black Lab. He was a magnificent specimen, he thought. He remembered the Chessie that had won the day before. He'd given him a Group One. The Lab wasn't in yesterday. There was a chocolate he'd placed. He remembered his top three as being equal. How had the chocolate bitch won over this male?

He moved on past the Afghan to the Shepherd. The dog was the hallmark of his breed. He'd deserved every one of his many wins. His eye strayed back down the line to the Lab and onto the Frenchie.

One should not have to pick one. So who today caught his fancy. His eye came back down the line. The Lab cocked his head and mimicked his handler's movement. He walked over and looked at the Lab again. Morgan's eyes were fixed on his owner and yet when the judge snapped his fingers, the eyes flickered to his face, a puzzled expression bringing his brows into an odd juxtaposition.

Morgan won Best in Show.

Harriet was among the first to congratulate Lyle. "Stanley couldn't make it," she apologized.

"He's sick," Dean put in. "Sent me up with this note. Congrats, Man!"

"He has a little gift for you back at his RV, so after you finish glowing, go see him. I'll be there." She turned to Dean. "I'm going to need your help packing up."

"Sure thing," Dean said as he walked beside her. "Aren't you going to open the envelope?"

"When the time is right."

"There's nothing inside, is there. My delivering it was a signal."

"There is a letter inside; but, you're right about its delivery being a signal."

"You gonna tell me?"

"After you help me, I will."

Evelyn joined them and Harriet asked her if her two girls could be doubled and the other crate given to Topaz. She agreed; but asked why.

"We can't use Beatrice's RV to haul dogs back. Do you suppose Madge could fit two Scotties in her RV?"

Tom heard the discussion and turned. "Beatrice wants to special Belle the rest of the season, sort of a test run. She says Belle is really upset about Emma and the pups. I told her I'd take her. I thought she told someone."

"She talked about it with me," Evelyn said. "I didn't know she'd decided."

"Belle's entered in all the November shows."

"Well, Madge can take one for sure," Evelyn said.

"I'll pick Belle up right away," Tom said.

"Dean, I want you to help Evelyn and Madge," Harriet said, "but first come with me."

She led the way to the RV that Dean had driven down and told him to wait outside. She handed out his jacket, his CD's and Stanley's briefcase.

"You're going to be driving my rig home," Harriet said.

"Who's driving this one?"

"I'm not sure yet. Lyle might after I talk to him; but you don't say anything to anyone until I tell you you can. Now go on, just put these things in my rig."

Harriet ducked back inside and locked the door. Then she opened and read the letter. Immediately, she called Stanley's father.

"I need to talk with you about your son's kidnapping."

"Who is this?"

"Harriet Locke. Aleta was also kidnapped. I have the ransom note in my hand. They are going to pick the money up from you directly."

"Stanley and Aleta went to a dog show at the southernmost tip of the state," he said, his statement in itself reflecting his doubt.

"That's where I'm calling from."

"Put on Lyle West," Praetzel demanded.

"Listen to me," Harriet said, her voice rising to a new height. "Before I involved West you need to answer some legal questions. First, who has jurisdiction?"

"They do."

"This is complicated," Harriet said. "What kind of jail time would I get if I moved the scene of the crime?"

"Don't do that," Hubert Praetzel said. "We can handle any problems legally. Leave that to us. Follow West's lead."

"I'll do as you suggest," Harriet said. "I think I'm just scared for my granddaughter."

"How much do they want?"

"One million from each of us."

"That little?"

"These aren't bright kidnappers. Stanley wrote the note but someone else dictated it. You're to get the two million in non-sequential, unmarked bills. I think Stanley put in the 'non-sequential'. He probably explained it too. Anyway, one million goes in a back pack, the other in a briefcase. Carry-on luggage is my guess. Again I see Stanley's mind at work. Can you do that? I can write you a check for my half as soon as I get home."

"You're sure they're coming here?"

"Let me read you the note."

There was a knock on the door. "West here," the knocker called out.

"Be right there," Harriet called, then said to Hubert Praetzel, "I'll call you back."

She hung up despite sputtering protests. She unlocked the door and let West in. He could tell by her expression something was terribly wrong.

"I'm in a crime scene, right?"

"Right."

"Murder?" Lyle asked.

"Kidnapping." Harriet replied.

"Both?"

"Yes."

"The bomber?"

"Yes."

"Do you foresee a death?" Lyle questioned.

"Not any more," Harriet responded.

"When did it happen?"

"Death was avoided when the kidnappers snuck Aleta and Stanley out of here while you were in Best in Show."

"You knew?" he accused, his anger rising.

"Yes," she replied matter-of-factly.

"Why wasn't I told?" he demanded.

"Because if you had tried to stop the kidnapping you'd be dead. Aleta and Stanley elected to save your life."

"Dammit! Not at the risk of their own!" Lyle shouted.

"They were risking many things, but they were not exchanging their death for yours. That much I do know."

"We need to notify the authorities right away."

"We need to get our people and their dogs out of here just like everyone else. We know the kidnappers. The fingerprints in the RV will confirm that. We know where they are heading. I need to be there. I'm to pay part of the ransom. You need to be there. Can Lauren drive home if Dean spells her off every few hours.? I think Evelyn can spell Dean for an hour or two."

"Since everyone was at the Group rings most of the time… How'd they get past Dean?"

"He came up to deliver a message to Stanley that Ed called, remember. I think that's when they snuck in."

"Was anyone here?"

"Madge was; but, she would have said something," Harriet said. "We don't need her statement except to prove there was a time they could have snuck into the RV. That's not essential to getting Aleta and Stanley back alive. Somehow I know you're the key to saving Stanley's life. Please believe me, you are essential."

"Mr. Praetzel has a private jet. Have him fly down and fetch us," Lyle said. "I'll get the others on their way."

Harriet picked up the phone and called Hubert Praetzel. "Lyle says you are to fly down and fetch us."

"Where are you?"

Harriet told him and he said, "I'm leaving immediately."

"The money?"

"Women are good at handling money, Lydia told me," Hubert said. "She scolded me soundly for being so provincial."

"I'm used to it."

"Not from relatives, I hope."

"You were a good sounding board. Thank you. I was panicking. Aleta is my favorite person in the whole world."

"As Stanley is mine."

"You've got to make sure West comes home with us, no matter what. Trust me. He's going to save your son's life just as Stanley saved his today."

"How… never mind, tell me when we meet."

Chapter 32

The private jet was on its way home two hours later. Harriet repeated the brief interview they had had with the sheriff before he'd dismissed both of them.

"All he asked was did you personally see or hear anything? Hubert Praetzel asked. "That's it? What about the RV?"

"He said we could drive it home. He said there'd be too many fingerprints to sort through," Lyle said. "I jumped at the chance."

"We parked it in airport parking," Harriet put in. "We'll send Dean to fetch it tomorrow."

"Hawk can go over it," West added.

"What's the sheriff going to do?" Hubert questioned.

"Let me supervise the exchange of the money for the hostages. He doesn't hold out much hope for success," West said. "I think, in essence, he turned the case over to me."

"I can argue that," Hubert Praetzel said. "Any chance we can locate them?"

"I think Stanley has engineered the pick-up," Lyle West said. "Meanwhile, we'll hone in on our belief that they are heading for the place in Oakwood that they used as a home base while scouting out Stanley's place."

"Can we do a house to house search?"

"Captain Ramage doesn't cooperate on any joint police venture, Sir," West replied. "Besides I have a better way."

As the jet was landing at the local airport north of Willow Glen, Tag Burrows was pulling into the garage of the abandoned house in Oakwood that they would use as their home base until they split.

"We ain't turning on any light," Joey announced. "We don't want the neighbors to know we're back."

Stanley stepped out onto cold cement and stubbed his toe on the concrete step from the garage to the kitchen. The street light in front filtered in through the worn slats in the blinds covering the front window as well as through the blinds in the front kitchen window.

Joey opened the first door off the kitchen with a window facing the dark backyard. Stanley entered and stood waiting. Tag came in and dumped Aleta on the floor. She had stuffed the pillow in her mouth when the van door was opened and she was roughly dragged out by her feet. Being carried had caused more pain, but the dump ripped her wound open and, even though muffled, her shriek reached every corner of the house.

"It won't happen again," Stanley promised quickly. "She must've fallen on her injured shoulder. And I've got a foolproof exchange worked out. Should we discuss it now?"

Joey looked at the girl still wrapped in a cocoon of blankets and said, "To hell with it. We'll never be able to find the tape in the dark anyway."

Stanley threw down his blanket and walked through the door. He knew that neither man wanted to talk about anything; but, keeping up the illusion was critical to his tattered self-esteem.

Tag closed the door and Stanley said, "Who's first?" Tag stepped up.

Joey opened the door to the back room and Aleta looked toward the outline of the figure in the dim light. "I forgot to tell you two that I've set bombs at every door and window of this house. You open any of them without using the correct procedure you'll go up ka pow!"

"He ain't fooling," Tag reported, grunting between thrusts. "He spent two days rigging the place."

Stanley was too busy trying not to be heard to respond. His heart sank. Maybe all this was for naught.

He heard the door shut and let his groans escape through gritted teeth. Tag pumped faster.

Stanley just tried to hang on. He'd come this far. Now that he'd aroused two latent homosexuals to the joys of sex with the same sex partner, he realized he'd awakened a desire too long dormant. Maybe the long drive, the heavy meal and a good sexual experience would down them for the night. He didn't know how much more of this he could stand.

It surprised him how quickly his self-esteem had plummeted. He understood now why being caught naked in front of strangers had disturbed Aleta so. We all have our nightmares. She was living hers. He was barely surviving his.

His chest burned with a searing pain. It felt as if his skin had been scraped off. He desperately wanted the pain to stop. His fingers reached forward searching for a smooth surface. Their touch told him the countertop had been roughened by countless knife cuts until the surface resembled a steel file fashioned for the purpose of rough sanding. He grabbed the chrome faucet and tried to keep his chest from sliding back and forth with each thrust. The effort was barely perceptible. The thinness of his shirt provided no protection. His chest still burned. This had to be it, he decided. He had no fortitude left. It hadn't been a day and he was unable to keep going.

Tag was done and Stanley felt the insertion of the larger penis of the two. Joey was taking his turn. The sharp edge of the countertop dug into his groin and cut deep into the skin covering his hip bones.

After a few thrusts, Stanley grunted, "I think I know where this would be more fun."

Joey paused. "Where?"

"The back of the living room chair. The angle would be more stimulating."

Joey stood back and released Stanley who moved to the chair.

Shortly afterward Stanley crawled back onto his blanket and was grateful for its scant softness.

Aleta whispered softly, "I need to go to the bathroom."

"Can't you hold it?"

"I've been holding it."

"They're sleeping," Stanley said. "I don't want to wake them."

"I can't wait," she whimpered. "It's going to come out whether I like it or not."

"Just a minute," Stanley said, rising stiffly. He took his blanket, folded it over several times, then unwrapped Aleta and gently sat her on the folded blanket.

"Go," he whispered.

"It's your blanket," she whispered back. "I can't do that."

"Go. I can sleep on the floor."

"We can share my blanket," Aleta said.

"Then you'll be uncovered."

"We'll be a matching pair," she giggled and felt the warm rush wet the blanket beneath her.

"We're going to get through this."

"The sink," Aleta said suddenly. "Your safety lies under the sink."

"What are you talking about?"

"I can't stop what's going to happen; but, if you get under the sink, you'll live."

"What's going to happen?"

"I think it's an explosion. I don't know any more than that."

"Where are you?"

"Not here," she said. "I don't understand this at all."

"Don't worry. I think it's what I needed to hear."

"What happens during those conversations? You come back less confident after each one."

"You know how a lawyer hates to lose an argument."

"Let's lay close," Aleta said. "I can't touch you, but our legs can touch. I am glad not to be alone."

"I am truly proud of you, Aleta. No man could be prouder," Stanley said quietly not knowing exactly why these words were necessary. "Your body is beautiful, Aleta. Every part of it is lovely. I'm sorry I had to undress you. I thought if they did it they would hurt you."

"I'm glad it was you."

"I'm uncomfortable without clothes as well."

"You don't seem so."

"Men are better at hiding their feelings," Stanley said, "but I do think it bothers you more. I wish I could change things, but I can't."

"Will it get worse?"

"I believe it will," Stanley said honestly.

Chapter 33

It wasn't until almost dawn that Stanley was roused again with a tap on the shoulder and the words, 'we need you.'

"So soon," he said, trying not to let his abhorrence take hold.

"It's almost light out," Tag said. "And we gotta make plans."

Stanley rolled over on his side, trying not to wake up Aleta and pushed himself up. Every muscle in his body screamed at him. A few groans escaped his lips as he stood up.

He walked stiffly from the room. Tag didn't seem to notice. Or if he did, he didn't care.

"Where you going?" Tag asked. His voice woke Aleta.

"Last night Joey tried the chair. It worked pretty well."

"Well, I ain't Joey. I like it like it was before."

"Whatever you want," Stanley sighed.

"You better believe we do it my way or I'll have me a piece of that sweet ass that was sprawled out beside you."

Aleta sat up and drew her legs together. Her fear made her grip her pillow and tuck it under her arms in front of her. The movement caused a sharp twinge and she bit into the pillow before the cry left her throat.

The door had been left ajar and she scooted around so she could see what was happening. The street light was still filtering in through the front windows while she was bathed in darkness.

She saw Tag push Stanley face forward onto the counter and she heard her husband ask for the towel. She heard Tag grumble. She watched the big man reach over and pick up a bit of cloth that looked black in the faint light from the other side of the counter and give it to Stanley.

Then she saw Stanley shove it in his mouth and nod.

She heard a zipper opening and watched the undulation of the big man's rear and suddenly she knew what Stanley was enduring.

Tag's comment told her he'd negotiated himself to stand in her place. Keeping her covered had been his way of protecting her.

She heard the soft cries coming from the mouth into which a towel had been jammed. How many times had they used him? She guessed it had started in the RV. The motel stop. Last night.

The pillow kept her gasp unheard as another man passed in front of the door. He was naked from the waist down. He was waiting.

My God, how she'd misjudged Stanley. Dying for her would have been easy. Living and suffering, that took more steel than she dreamed he possessed. Thank God she had obeyed him and kept silent. She could have wounded him beyond repair with her sharp tongue.

Tears formed beneath her eyelids and ran unhindered down her cheeks. She wanted to cry stop, but she stuffed the pillow in her mouth harder. He had taken great pride in her obedience. It was to him the ultimate gift. And she resolved that he would have it.

Grams had said to obey him. How did she know? Perhaps all she knew was that he would protect her no matter what the cost to himself.

Dear God, give me the chance to tell someone what a brave man he is. That's all.

Joey was now taking his turn. Stanley was still lying on the counter. She could hear the screams through the towel now. He was in agony.

Aleta's tears continued to flow, but she said nothing and she remained in place.

Every ounce of her being wanted to rush in and offer herself in his place; but, she decided her gift to him was to let him make the choices. He had asked her not to speak and, while she knew their whispered conversation was okay, his admonition was still in effect.

She lay back down where she had been when he left and gathered the blanket around her body. They mustn't be tempted by her nakedness. And Stanley must never know she knew. Not yet. Maybe someday. Maybe never.

Stanley crawled in beside her shortly afterward. He left her wrapped up.

"I'm afraid," she whispered.

"So am I, but we will get through this."

Just after dawn, Tag spotted a car cruising down their street and slowing in front of their house. He rushed into Joey's room.

"We've been made."

"Get the girl and put her in the van. We're all set to move. We go before it gets any lighter."

Tag came in and picked up Aleta. "We're going for a ride."

Stanley scrambled to his feet, but Tag put his hand on Stanley's chest and stopped him dead.

"You don't want me to come?"

"You're waiting here," Joey explained. "Aleta is going to pick up the money for us. "You're our insurance that she'll come back with it."

"She has no clothes!" Stanley protested.

"So?" Joey sneered. "She's used to being naked."

"My shirt," Stanley said. "Give her my shirt."

"Tag put the bitch down and take off his shirt."

Stanley heard the moan. "No, don't put her down. I'll take off the shirt."

He gritted his teeth, took both ends of the shirt and pulled it over his head. He couldn't completely stifle his cry of pain as the shirt, bloody from the latest encounter, took loose skin with it. He'd yanked it off as quickly as one would a Band-Aid stuck to hair, still tears sprang into his eyes as his chest screamed at him for his action.

He stuffed the shirt into Aleta's hands.

"Love you," Aleta whispered, breaking his order to be silent. She grimaced as she spoke and her voice was strained. Stanley knew she was in pain too.

"You've got something planned. You're too clever not to have a delaying tactic at both ends," Stanley observed struggling to keep his voice calm. It was a warning to his wife that these men were not to be trusted.

"You're right," Joey bragged unable to keep his cleverness a secret any more. Still, it was important Aleta not hear. "Tag, put her in the car."

While Tag was gone, Joey finished. "We'll leave her alive but with booby traps all around her and her sitting on one. Clever, huh?"

Stanley swallowed hard. Harriet was still out there; but, suppose all she saw was the explosion.

"That'll only buy you a little time," Stanley said, tears of pain running down his cheeks, "but if you leave her mouth untaped so she can warn everyone who comes near, it'll take hours for the police to round up bomb sniffing dogs and find the booby traps. Plenty of time for you to get away."

"You could be right. But, I'll give you a choice. Mouth untaped or the shirt?"

"Mouth untaped," Stanley said.

"Yeah, okay, I'll tell her how you chose."

Tag came in with the tape and Stanley's hands were taped behind him and his feet were taped together. Stanley asked them to leave his mouth untaped so no one rushed the house early.

"If they do before you have the money in your hand, they'll grab Aleta and you won't get the money," he said.

He won that argument.

Joey made the call to Stanley's father as Tag drove the van away from the house. His orders were terse.

"The Fairgrounds. Twenty minutes. You come alone. Stand in the middle of the field past the entrance. We know what you look like so don't send no cop. When we get the money, we tell you where your son is. The house he's in is wired so don't move in early. Aleta will give you the rest of the instructions."

Aleta relaxed a little. The time leading to their release was almost there.

I can do this, she thought, clutching Stanley's bloody tee shirt.

I can pull the shirt down. It's long.

Chapter 34

Milani and West had synchronized their two units into one. Every man was on. West was to concentrate on getting Stanley; Milani, Aleta. The men were briefed in advance as to all the alternative plans and were stationed around the two cities near the possible drop points and the approach they were to take. There were two officers in each car.

West had told the Arborville Fire Chief that he might need him to cross the line into Oakwood. Hallihan had protested that that was Chuck Wicks's district. West had persuaded him to be his back-up.

"I don't know much; but, I do know that this guy loves to blow things up and I think both of you will be needed."

"You'll be there?"

"Yes, I'll be there."

"That'll make the shit hit the fan!"

"It might be worse," West replied. "But I'll cover your tail, believe me."

"You always do," Hallihan said. "How come we know where to go?"

"Brandon Webber owns a lot of rundown property in Oakwood. We scouted out the houses before it was light. Our men think they have a bead on which one, so that's the one we're going to head for."

When Joey's call came through on Hubert Praetzel's speaker phone, Milani sprang into action.

He radioed his men. "Group A you're it. Group B, back them up, Group C, stand ready for a switch." Then he issued a warning that the kidnappers had wired the house where the victims were with explosives. All doors and windows, he reported. Then repeated the warning along with the admonition that no one attempt to enter the house until the bomb squad cleared it. And just so there would be no doubt in anyone's mind, Milani added that Chief West was in charge of the Oakwood detail.

One of Chief Ramage's men called his chief at home and reported the transmission. Ramage sprang from his bed and yelled, "Find that house! No one comes into my town and takes over. I'll have West's job for this!"

He dressed quickly and called the TV station. He was going to rescue a kidnap victim and he wanted coverage.

Tag drove onto the fairgrounds through a hole in the fence that he and Joey had cut earlier.

Aleta gripped Stanley's shirt. It was sticky but she didn't care. It would cover her.

The van bumped over a lot of rough ground and Aleta yelped into her pillow. Now was no time to anger the men. This was so close to being over.

The van stopped. She heard one of the two scramble up on top. Then she felt the blanket being pulled out and opened. The tape on her ankles was cut off. She was yanked to her feet. The shoulder was wrenched in the action. Her yell was buried in the pillow which she was clutching as it left her with a modicum of cover as the blanket fell at her feet. The pillow was torn from her grasp.

The shirt was yanked away.

"I'm supposed to wear that!" Aleta protested.

"Ah, the woman has a tongue!" Joey exclaimed climbing down from the top of the van. "It's him alright. He's got the money."

"You told Stanley you'd let me wear it," she persisted, her voice quieter.

"Well, he changed his mind at the last minute," Joey said. "I give him a choice and he chose him over you."

Aleta was bewildered. What could Stanley want? Or need?

Clothes maybe, she thought. He'd hate to be found naked.

"I'll do without," she said stoically. Stanley had his reasons.

She looked at the shirt on the ground. It was bloody. She stared at the hand of hers that had held it. It was also bloody.

"Go get the case and the back pack. Come straight back here," Joey ordered. "They gotta not follow us or Stanley is dead. You see this?"

Aleta nodded.

"It's a remote detonator. We get caught and my finger hits the button and BOOM. No more Stanley."

"Where's Stanley?"

"I'll call and tell Mr. Praetzel when I'm safely away with the money. He's to wait right where he is. Now go!"

He gave her a little push. The sticks and stones made walking difficult. She looked down trying to find smooth ground and saw Stanley's blood on her hand.

It would take her forever to do this if she inched along.

"Get going!" Joey shouted. "Or you'll take the money from Mr. Praetzel's dead hand."

The thought jarred Aleta into action. She straightened up and began to stride boldly across the rough ground. Sharp stones pierced her tender feet. Dry twigs poked at the cuts.

This is nothing she told herself, gritting her teeth, remembering Stanley in the dark kitchen the night before. Tears came to her eyes and she let them flow. She couldn't halt the cries of pain that leaped from her throat; but, she kept her lips sealed and those cries resounded more in her ears than in the listening ears surrounding her on all sides.

This is truly nothing, she repeated to herself, over and over as she placed one foot down after the other. Her pain faded from her thinking as she saw the shock on her father-in-law's face and remembered she was naked.

A rustle in the bushes told her she had company. Of course, the police were here. He wouldn't have come alone.

Stanley's words rang in her ears. Remember you are beautiful, but somehow they didn't help assuage the embarrassment she felt as she walked onto the large expanse of mowed grass.

Unfortunately, while it was short, it was also dry and prickly. While easier to traverse than the sticks and stones, the tiny stiff blades jabbed at her sore and bleeding feet. Then her foot hit something soft and squishy and she realized at once what she'd stepped in. The foul smell accompanied her as she walked; but, the stool protected that foot from the pricks of the dry grass.

She chuckled at the irony. Wait until I tell Stanley. Talk about putting your foot in it.

And with that thought, she momentarily forgot her own embarrassment and remembered that it was not only the house that was a danger to Stanley, it was Ramage. Who could stop a chief of police?

Another one, she thought.

As she approached her father-in-law, she asked, "Is Milani or West in earshot?"

Hubert Praetzel was bewildered and didn't know how to respond. He didn't want her to know there were a contingent of police watching her.

"Milani!" she shouted. "West! Who's in charge here?"

"I am," Tom replied. "West is at the house."

"The one where Stanley is?" she asked as Praetzel helped her slip on the backpack. She grimaced as he tried to slip the strap over her injured shoulder.

"Yes," came the response.

"It's wired," Aleta said loudly.

She lowered her voice to instruct her father-in-law.

"Don't try to put the other strap on. The shoulder won't take it. Slip the strap over my head instead."

"We know," Milani responded. "The bomb squad is on its way."

Hubert Praetzel quickly slipped the strap back down Aleta's arm and put the pack strap over her head. The pack hung down covering her breasts.

"Move it to the back," she whispered. "They'll be angry if I'm covered."

Her statement was said with remarkable calm.

"You're bleeding," Hubert Praetzel said.

"Not as badly as your son, believe me. A braver man has never walked this earth. You wouldn't believe the sacrifices he made to protect me."

"We know where he is," Milani said. "You don't have to go back."

"The kidnapper has a remote," Aleta said. "I do have to go back."

She picked up the case and said, "Tell West that Ramage is going to blow the house and kill Stanley. It's his turn. Oh, and Mr. Praetzel, you must stay put."

Hubert Praetzel watched her walk away his mouth agape. What kind of woman was this his son had married. As a testament to her authority, he didn't move a muscle.

Milani spoke into his radio mike. He hated using Ramage's name over an open radio, but he had to be direct.

"Lyle, Aleta said that Ramage is going to blow the house. She said it was your turn."

"I understand," Lyle said. "Another source told me the same thing earlier."

"I understand," Milani replied then added. "To all units on this frequency. West's orders are to be obeyed immediately and without question."

Hubert Praetzel stood like a statue and watched his daughter-in-law take a side step and then go on. He couldn't see that she'd deliberately stepped in the same horse dropping that she'd accidentally stepped in before.

The sticky stuff clinging to her feet picked up dry grass as she was walking and, as she walked, it put grass-soled shoes on her feet.

"Thanks God for the shit," she said. "And thanks for letting me tell Stanley's dad how brave he was."

The pack was heavy and the strap choked her; but, it didn't cut off her air completely. She found she could breathe easier if her body was erect.

Why not? she thought. Everyone can see everything now. And Stanley would be proud if he knew I wasn't cowering like a whipped dog. At that moment, making him proud became important. Her walk became surer. When she reached the spot where the kidnappers waited, Tag tore the back pack from her neck. Joey threw the case in the van.

"Ain't we gonna count it?" Tag said.

"It's all there," Joey said. "Get the tape."

"You aren't letting me go?" Aleta asked. Her voice came out unusually soft. The question was just that. There was no hint of accusation.

"We got a little surprise for you," Joey said.

Tag grabbed her arm and Aleta stumbled along the rough path to a stall in a nearby stable. He held her at the

268 • Susan Davis Sandberg

entrance while Joey uncovered the metal tip of a small anti-personnel mine. Aleta gasped.

"So you know what it is," Joey said. "There's a bunch of them all around here."

Tag handed him the tape. First Joey taped her hands and then her feet. Then he slapped tape across her eyes.

All she could do was pray that he wouldn't tape her mouth. And to her relief, he didn't.

Tag spun her around.

"We don't want you remembering where you saw this one," Joey said. "Okay Tag avoid these two and set her down."

Tag moved her in a zigzag pattern and plunked her down on a piece of cloth on top of a flat piece of wood.

"It's armed," Joey said. "You move off that board and it will blow. Oh, and, you're sitting on your husband's shirt. I kept my promise. I let it cover a part of you."

Tag and Joey laughed as they walked away.

She heard the van's motor turn over and she reached up and pulled the tape from her eyes. The spin of its wheels on the dry earth and the tiny pings the stones made as they hit the tailpipe told her that her captors had left.

The anti-personnel mine whose location she was sure about was the one near the entrance.

It wasn't long before she heard the sound of feet converging on her location. She wondered what man would see her first.

It was Stoney, however, who appeared at the entrance to the stall.

"Stoney, sit!" she ordered.

Her voice carried and brought several armed officers into her area.

"There are bombs in here!" she shouted. "I'm sitting on one."

One man took a step toward her and Stoney growled.

"Get that dog outta here," another yelled.

"You don't touch the dog!" Aleta exclaimed.

The men hesitated.

"Call Milani," Aleta ordered.

"No need," Tom said. "I'm here."

"She says there are bombs all around," one man reported.

"Then there are," Milani said decidedly.

"When did he have time to plant bombs?" the man asked. "We had him in our sights the whole time," added another. "He never left the truck."

"I can tell you where one is. He showed it to me," Aleta said.

"Men, back away and set up a perimeter. No one comes near until the bomb squad gets here."

Harriet arrived in time to hear the end of the exchange. "Stoney, come here," she called.

The big dog didn't move.

Two men shouldered their guns and aimed.

"No need for that," Harriet said.

"Put them down, men," Milani said.

"He could set one off," one of the men protested, keeping his rifle leveled at the dog.

"You're one of West's men, aren't you?" Milani asked. He then spoke into his radio. "What's the situation over there?"

"We're waiting on the bomb squad," West replied.

"You got the right house?" Milani asked.

"Stanley answered. He's tied up, but he's alive."

"And Ramage?"

A siren could be heard.

"He just got here."

"We need the bomb squad here. Crowder set Aleta up as well."

"No don't!" Aleta yelled. "Don't pull them off the house. Save Stanley first. Nothing will happen here as long as I stay sitting."

"She says Stanley first," Milani said. "But I need you to tell your men my orders are as good as yours."

"Shoot him," West said and clicked off.

"What'd he say?" the Arborville officer asked.

"He said to shoot you," Milani said. "And if you don't lower that gun this instant I will."

The officer glanced down and saw a gun pointed at his mid-section. He looked around and saw several more.

He dropped the rifle and put up his hands.

"Sit him over there," Milani said. "He waits with the rest of us."

Harriet again called Stoney but again he refused to budge.

"He's guarding her," Harriet explained.

"I see that," Milani said. "Can you get him to stop?"

"I can," Aleta said. "Stoney, go."

Harriet called Stoney at the same time and the huge male Chessie left his post.

"One crisis avoided," Milani said. "I wish I could free you."

"Hey, I've been tied up like this from the beginning. It's no big deal."

And as she said it, she realized it wasn't.

In Oakwood, Chief Ramage charged up to Chief Lyle West. "What are you doing here?"

West decided to treat him as a fellow professional. "We were hoping to get here before the kidnappers left with one of the hostages; but, we were late. However, we've cleared the houses around this one and called the bomb squad."

The television cameras were focused on the pair. West didn't care. The longer he kept Ramage away from the house the better.

Ramage's men arrived.

They created a cordon around their chief as he walked toward the house. The TV cameras followed the movement. West saw an opportunity to engage him. He was still a long way from the house.

"The house is wired to explode if any door or window is opened."

"And who told you that?" Ramage asked derisively. "The perp who wanted time to get away?"

His voice carried into the house. Stanley suddenly remembered what Aleta had said last night.

The sink. He had to get to the sink. He first tried wriggling along the floor. The pain kept him from moving more than a few inches. He couldn't reach out to push himself up without his hands.

He fell back and accidentally wound up on his back. Lying on his taped hands was too uncomfortable. He began to roll back over on his side when it occurred to him that his feet could push him anywhere.

He bent his knees and pushed. His hands scraped along the floor, but he ignored the discomfort and bent his knees and pushed again. He could hear West arguing with Ramage.

A few more pushes and he was in the kitchen. He pushed himself toward the sink. The cabinet doors were closed. He spun around on his back. Lifting his legs, he used his toes to grab hold of the knob and pull. He knocked the second door open with his foot.

What was Aleta thinking? How could he fit in that space? Maybe his head but not his whole body. He scooted over and stuck his head inside. Okay, I've saved my brain.

He inched forward until his head touched the wall. He bent his neck and his shoulders hit the back.

His chest screamed as torn flesh touched torn flesh. He couldn't bend. He just couldn't.

Outside West stopped arguing.

"I'm sorry, Chief," he said. "But I'm going to ask you and your men to step away until the bomb squad gets here."

West nodded and several of his men moved in, grabbed and disarmed three Oakwood officers positioned the furthest from the chief. The men were caught by surprise. Their drawn weapons were for show. None of them had ever fired one. They were frankly glad to be pulled away from the house that might explode and so gave up easily. They practically led their captors to the yellow tape marking the periphery.

Two men were left. They fingered their weapons nervously.

Lyle West put out his hand toward the men behind him and one of his men handed him his rifle.

He shouldered the gun. "Back away," he ordered. "Or I'll shoot."

The two remaining Oakwood officers backed up. Neither was ready to shoot the Arborville Chief of Police, not with a dozen men with drawn guns aimed at them.

Neither could remember seeing the guns drawn. How had they missed that motion? How had Chief West gotten his men to back him without saying a word?

Two pairs of hands went in the air. The guns held loosely by the tip of the barrel until one of West's men took them. The men scrambled behind the yellow tape.

"Cowards!" Ramage shouted as the men gave up. "Cops don't shoot cops!"

"We wait for the bomb squad," West called. "Step away from the house."

The TV crews, forced to stay behind the yellow tape, were able to zoom in on the man standing near the door at one end of the boxy tract house. The door would open in and swing against the inside wall.

Chief Ramage had yet to take the step up onto the small porch although he was near to doing so.

"Come on, West. We both know this is a bid for TV attention."

"You brought the cameras here," West said coolly. "I will shoot if I have to."

"Like hell you will!" Ramage shouted scrambling up the single stair and reaching for the knob.

West pulled the trigger.

Ramage grabbed his arm and yelled, "You sonofabitch! You can't shoot a police chief. I'll see you in jail!"

"Back off!" West ordered.

Ramage was too furious to back off. "You aren't the boss in this town. I am!"

He looked around as he grasped his forearm.

"You," Ramage shouted at an officer in a Willow Glen uniform, "Milani's man. Arrest that man. Take that gun!"

Milani's man never wavered. He kept his gun trained on the potbellied Oakwood Police Chief. He adjusted it slightly to bring the second arm into focus.

Meanwhile, inside the house West's rifle shot had propelled Stanley into action. It was as if he'd been personally shot. He shoved himself in a curl around the sink and screamed from the pain as his chest scraped on the pipe.

His scream put resolve into Ramage's words.

"There's a man in pain in there. There is no bomb."

His left hand reached out. West fired again. Milani's man got off a round as well. Two bullets hit Ramage in the shoulder but sheer determination forced him to turn the knob in his hand.

"I'll see you all…," he began.

The explosion threw him back onto the dried weed-ridden grass.

Hallihan's men turned on their hoses as the front window blew. Then the kitchen window went. Simultaneously all heard a third explosion from inside the house. It was the door to the garage. One by one the back windows followed.

Each explosion was only seconds behind the prior one. Stanley drew his feet further into his hole as the flames from the rear windows raced up the wall to the roof.

Hoses began spraying water immediately. Minutes later the firemen chopped the remainder of the frame around the living room window and entered. The room was filled with smoke. All knew there was a man trapped inside. No one was leaving without him.

Stanley coughed. His cough was weak, but it was heard.

Two fire fighters ran into the kitchen, moved aside some debris and a heavy beam which had fallen after the last blast. One leaned over, saw Stanley's bloody chest and decided he was too injured to move. He took off his mask and put it over Stanley's nose and mouth. Stanley sucked in the oxygen gratefully.

West appeared almost immediately. He squatted down.

"How're you doing, Buddy?"

Stanley put up a thumb. He started to remove his mask so he could speak; but, West put it back over his face and answered his unasked question.

"Aleta's in a bit of a pickle. I'm sending the bomb crew over there now that Ramage managed to blow up this place."

Stanley didn't look surprised.

"You knew?" Lyle asked. "Of course, you knew. My guess is she told you to crawl in here."

Stanley nodded.

"How the hell did you manage to do it?"

Stanley lifted his mask. "Your first shot scared me all the way in."

"Well, then it did some good."

Stanley removed his mask. "You saved my life."

West put the mask back on. "If you don't leave this mask in place, you'll lose the life I just saved."

Stanley nodded.

West ordered the tape cut on his hands and feet and told the firemen to cut away the plumbing. Then coughing he left.

One of the firemen laid a blanket over Stanley's legs and groin. The other put plastic over his chest. A third began to cut the pipe.

The pipe vibrated and Stanley clamped down his jaw and took a deep breath.

This is nothing, he told himself. It's almost over.

Back at the Fairgrounds, Aleta was becoming increasingly uncomfortable. She wanted to spread her feet a bit for balance but she couldn't.

The group had heard the explosion. What no one knew is what had happened.

"Ramage opened the door," Aleta said. "I guess Lyle couldn't stop him."

Milani asked West for an update.

"We pumped three rounds into him," West reported. He knew they'd heard the explosion. "I should have shot him dead."

Milani relayed the bare skeleton of what West said. "They shot Ramage three times. He still managed to reach the door."

"How about Stanley?"

"The firemen are going in now," Milani said.

Milani heard the crowd yell. "I think he's still alive."

Aleta smiled. "He crawled under the sink, didn't he?"

Harriet's shout brought everyone back to the situation in hand.

Aleta started, "What?"

"You were leaning over."

"My butt's asleep. I can't keep my balance."

"How soon will the bomb squad be here?"

"They're on their way. Fifteen minutes."

"We got someone who knows where the bombs are planted," a strong male voice announced.

Tom Milani looked over. His men had their guns trained on a big man holding the arm of a smaller man whose hands were taped in front of his chest.

"Joey Crowder, I presume," Chief Milani said, smiling. "Have I got a job for you."

The big man threw him on the ground at Milani's feet. "He's yours."

A second man was thrown beside the first.

"He's a bonus," the big man said. "What about her?"

"We're waiting for the bomb squad. There are bombs planted all over and we can't go in and get her."

The big man pulled Joey up by the hair. "Where are they?"

Joey pointed to the one at the entrance and two more in the pathway to her from the middle of the entrance.

The big man ordered Joey to crawl in and show him. Slowly, hands still taped, Joey crawled toward Aleta carefully brushing the straw aside as he went. He uncovered the first and then moved over slightly and uncovered the second.

"Are there any around Aleta?"

"No," Joey said and he pointed at the others.

"Aleta, can you hang in there one more minute?" Milani said.

"If you cut me loose, I can manage longer than that."

"I'll go," a man named Jesse offered.

He then threaded his way down the clear path and knelt beside Aleta and freed her feet and then her hands. She moved her feet.

"Are they asleep?" Jesse+ asked.

Aleta nodded.

"Your hands okay?"

She nodded again.

"Put them on the board to steady yourself and I'll rub your ankles."

"I can only put one down," Aleta said. "Just do one foot."

She lifted her leg and the man began to massage the ankle.

Joey meanwhile was inching his way around the area, uncovering his carefully placed bombs.

"Feels good," Aleta said.

"You've given me an idea," Chief Milani said. "Jesse, tell me, if I asked you to, could you carry her out.

"Sure," Jesse said. "Be best on my back so I can see where I'm going."

Milani looked at the big man who'd thrown Joey at his feet earlier. "You look big enough to carry Joey."

The man grinned. "Put him where she is?"

Milani nodded.

"Sounds good to me. Give me a minute to get Joey ready."

Joey looked up, pale-faced. He had just reached the entrance.

Before he could utter a sound the big man grabbed him, handed him to a cop nearby.

"Hold him," he said and pulling the tape from his pocket wrapped it around Joey's body plastering his arms to his sides.

Milani called out as soon as he finished. "I'm coming in, Jesse. I'm going to hold down the board with my hands. You lift Aleta onto your back and haul her outta here."

Jesse squatted down and had Aleta put her good arm around his neck. He grabbed it with his hand.

"When Milani tells you to, put your legs around my waist and hang on."

"Ready," Aleta said.

Milani took the cleared pathway and went around behind Aleta and Jesse. He put his hands on both sides of her bare thighs and pushed down on the board.

Perspiration beaded up on his forehead. He hoped he could put enough pressure on the board.

"Lift," he said, pressing down as Aleta wrapped her legs around Jesse. He braced himself for the sudden spring when Jesse stood up and Aleta's weight left the board. Milani put all of his weight on his hands as if he were doing a push-up. The board rose slightly.

The big man, holding Joey in front of him, hurried to the board Milani was holding down. He sat Joey on it. Milani slipped his hands out from under Joey's rear. He ran out after the big man.

He breathed a sigh of relief. "Now if it blows it won't matter much."

"You can't do this. This is abuse!" Joey yelled. "I'll have your badge."

The big man stepped up. "No, you won't. You was told to lay off Aleta. You're lucky you ain't dead."

Joey clamped his mouth shut.

Chief Milani turned around to find Aleta talking with her grandmother. She was still naked.

He called for a blanket.

"The paramedics are coming," Aleta replied. "Thank you for your concern; but it's a little late to protect my modesty. I lost that over an hour ago."

She turned to her grandmother, "Don't worry, I'll find it again."

Harriet smiled. "You've never done anything inappropriate in my eyes. And I include today."

Aleta squatted down and ruffled Stoney's one ear with her good hand. Stoney sniffed her bandage and she pushed his nose away. "Not today. But when I'm well, you and I will go for another Best in Show."

"Bet you haven't heard. How could you? For you our world was a long way away," Harriet said. "The show. You know, the one you were at before you dropped into Hell. Lyle won Best-in-Show."

"Sorry I missed it."

"I am too," Harriet said. "Was I wrong? Was there another way?"

"If Lyle had died, we'd be in a hell with no end," Aleta said. "Now I need to see Stanley as soon as possible. Can you make sure Dr. Cook sees me before he sees Stanley? It's critical.

"I'll call," Harriet said. "Now you relax. The paramedics are here."

Chapter 35

Dr. Cook took Harriet's call. She repeated what Aleta had told her.

"I've got a gunshot wound coming in."

"Chief Ramage. He blew up the house and almost killed Stanley. West shot him."

"Our West?"

"Long story, but Aleta says it's critical she talk with you. She was alone with Stanley in the hands of these men. Something must've happened. Something serious."

"I'll be busy with Ramage."

"That's what interns are for."

"Where was he shot?"

"Shoulder and arm."

"Okay, my interns can practice on him."

"And you'll see Aleta?"

"As soon as she arrives."

"She's been through hell."

"I can imagine."

"No, Wayne, you can't," Harriet said. "No two people have ever needed you more."

The first ambulance arrived as Harriet was speaking. Wayne rushed out, his interns at his back. He listened to the vitals being rattled off by the paramedics, then turned to one of his interns.

"Todd, you take this one. Jason, you assist. I have two more coming in. Garrett, you're with me."

Ramage protested. "I deserve the best!"

"I'm giving you two of my best interns," Cook said as the gurney was pushed into the first examining room.

"I want a real doctor."

"They are real doctors."

"They aren't to operate on me."

"As you wish," Dr. Cook said. "Todd, you and Jason x-ray his arm, prep him for surgery. See who's on call."

"I want you."

"Two of my regular patients are coming in. They are my first priority," Dr. Cook said as a second ambulance screamed to a stop.

The two interns transferred Chief Ramage from the gurney.

"Sir," Todd said, "who's your regular doctor? We'll call him."

"Skip him. He's a quack. I want Cook!"

Cook shook his head and rushed out, prepared to meet Aleta. However, it was Stanley who was rolled in first. He came accompanied by paramedics spitting out his vital signs with machine-gun rapidity.

Cook looked at Stanley's chest.

"My God, Stanley, you've got to stop trying to take the hair off your chest with a sander."

Stanley started to laugh then grabbed his stomach.

"Where else does it hurt?" Cook said as they rolled him into the second examining room.

"Everywhere."

"Your wife was supposed to beat you in," Wayne Cook said. "I guess you won the race."

"Doc, she's had a rough time. Please take care of her personally."

"Garrett, I want an MRI right away. I don't want to be surprised by a hematoma later," Cook said.

He looked directly at Stanley. "Your vitals are good for a man in such bad shape; but, I don't want to be fooled by a bleed somewhere. Explosions are tricky things. They cause weak vessels to break as well as bones."

"Can we do me from the waist up?"

"Why?"

"Because I ask it."

"It won't hurt your reproductive organs, I promise you."

"It's not that."

"Garrett, go arrange for the MRI," Cook ordered.

Cook excused the nurse next.

"Okay, what is it? What happened that you don't want me to know about?"

"Nothing," Stanley said. "Chalk my request up to a quirk."

"You don't have quirks. You could have, but you don't."

"You can't do it without my permission. I am a lawyer. I don't have to explain."

Cook eyed Stanley coolly. "You were raped."

"No. I wasn't."

"How many times?"

"I said I wasn't."

"How many partners?"

"I said I wasn't."

"It's possible to get certain sexually transmitted diseases from small tears in the bowel," Wayne said. "You don't want to pass any on to your wife and child, do you?"

"I'll stay celibate!"

"Stanley, you're reacting like a rape victim," Cook said.

"I wasn't raped."

"It wasn't your fault," Wayne Cook declared adamantly.

"Yes, it was!" Stanley countered.

"It was you or Aleta, right?"

Stanley nodded.

"I'm not sure I would have done it; but, for you with the chest injury you had... well..."

"I let them do it. Over and over again."

"And their alternative?"

"It seemed right at the time; but, now I'm wondering if there was another way."

"Of course there was another way. You could have gotten shot, and then they would have done to Aleta what they did to you. Or they could have tied you up and made you watch. Or they..."

"Stop! Stop!" Stanley said. "Do your tests all of them. Don't tell Aleta, please."

"I won't," Wayne said. "I can do a wide spectrum of tests without raising any red flags."

"What about the tests for sexually transmitted diseases?"

"I'll do those separately and privately."

"Thank you," Stanley said, tears welling up in his eyes.

Wayne handed him a Kleenex. "Can't have my intern think I hurt you."

"What about Aleta?"

"I'll tell her no sexual activity for a week at least. Your whole body is too bruised. I'll blame it on the explosion," Cook said, then left.

Stanley heard Cook tell the nurse to tell Dr. Armstrong that the patient had agreed to a full MRI, then Stanley heard the doctor greet Aleta.

"Stanley is here, isn't he?" Aleta asked. Before he answered, she raced on, "I had Harriet call. Why didn't you wait to speak with me?"

"Whatever you had to tell me could wait until I had an MRI done. I really had to move fast."

"An MRI?"

"To catch a hematoma or any other bleed or fracture he might have sustained in the explosion. I don't want him bleeding out on me while I'm tending to his chest wounds."

"Did he tell you how it got so bad?" Aleta asked.

"Not exactly."

"Can you send the nurse out?" Aleta asked.

Dr. Cook waved her out.

"They raped him. Over and over. They even stopped on the way and rented a motel room and they took turns."

"You knew?"

"Not then. Not until the end when I saw them. They were causing him so much pain, I wanted to scream at them to stop; but, Stanley had told me not to say a word; but that's no excuse. I was scared to death they'd do the same thing to me. And Stanley was doing something so brave, I couldn't jump in and rescue him. It would have…"

Dr. Cook nodded. "It would have destroyed what little pride he had left. You did the wise thing."

"You won't tell him?"

"No, I won't," Dr. Cook said. "That's for you to do."

"I won't ever tell him. I'm so ashamed."

"My advice is to tell him."

"But, I failed him."

"The truth will set him free," Dr. Cook said. "Right now he's lonely and frightened that you'll find out and want nothing to do with him."

"But he did a brave thing. Doesn't he know that?"

"He thinks he should have stood up to them."

"And instead he used his wit and his cunning and persuaded two men not to rape me. And then he suffered unspeakable agony repeatedly so I didn't have to suffer it even once. I am so grateful. You don't know how brave I know he was. It took guts not to abandon me by dying for me."

"He needs to hear that."

"But then I'll have to confess my own cowardice."

"But you would help him to heal. Rape victims are more than just physically damaged. Psychological healing takes a long time."

"He'll hate me for being such a coward."

"Aleta, he loves you with as deep a love as any man could have for a woman. Embrace it. Embrace him, but not for a week.

"Why?"

"I will be running tests."

"Oh, no."

"Talk to him before the results get back."

"Hurry and fix me up."

Dr. Cook began to remove the bandage.

"I don't want to hurry too much. Chief Ramage wants me to take out the bullets in his arms. I told him I was going to be busy with you two. Now have you any complaints other than your shoulder?"

"Sorry, Doc, only my shoulder; but it's a mess if that'll help.

When Cook removed the bandage, he groaned.

"Well it's messed up alright. I have to operate."

"Stanley first."

Chapter 36

Late the next morning, Dr. Wayne Cook walked into the hospital room of Stanley and Aleta, "How are my two favorite patients?"

"Thank you for putting us in the same room," Stanley said.

"If I hadn't one of you would be sitting next to the other and I wanted both of you resting for at least a week."

"A week?" Aleta questioned her mouth agape.

"Your shoulder was worse than I thought. You tore out all the stitches and managed to tear some ligaments and muscles as well. Six weeks with your arm in a sling. No driving. No physical activity. No sex."

"Come on, Doc. No sex?" Aleta questioned.

"Not if you want to use that arm normally again."

"The nurse said no visitors and no phone calls. What's that all about?" Aleta asked switching topics.

"That's West. Evidently there's still someone trying to kill you."

"Another person?" Aleta gasped.

"He can tell you all about it when he comes. But getting back to Stanley's condition. He needs to be here. We need to treat his skin as if he were burned. Fortunately, he has enough healthy skin so we may not need to do grafts; but, he is vulnerable to infection right now."

"So that's why this contraption?" Stanley asked.

"It's to keep the sheet off your skin."

"What about his hospital gown?" Aleta countered.

"He has no gown on," Dr. Cook said with a wry smile.

"It's beginning to feel natural," Stanley commented.

"This week is going to make confirmed nudists of both of us," Aleta quipped.

"Well, that'll be a plus for the rest of us."

"Tell him about the shit shoes," Stanley said.

And Aleta did.

"I sense a lightness of spirit in here," Dr. Cook said.

"I repeated the conversation you and I had yesterday, word for word," Aleta said.

"I can't even remember what I said."

"Aleta has an excellent memory for words as well as numbers," Stanley said proudly. "You gave excellent counsel, Dr. Cook."

"So how are you feeling?"

"As if a huge weight has been lifted from my shoulders."

"I hope you didn't quote me to her."

"One conversation was all we needed to start a conversation of our own."

"Well, as long as I'm being listened to—not as common an occurrence as you might think. Here's one more piece of advice. Use this week to heal more than your bodies. You were both affected deeply. You are past the first layer. It's time to explore the next."

"You haven't told anyone else, have you?" Stanley asked abruptly.

"I didn't tell Aleta. She told me. What happened is between you two," Dr. Cook said. "Be grateful that West is keeping all family and friends away for a week. The psychological wounds are fresh. You don't need anyone, however innocently, to poke at them."

A voice from the doorway said, "I heard the 'be grateful to West' part. The rest I ignored because it wasn't about me. I don't know why he didn't stay with a good subject when he had hold of one. Did anyone tell you I pumped two rounds into the potbellied pig? Milani's man's bullet hit so close to mine, I think he should get a medal for sharpshooting instead of facing a review."

"I'll leave you alone with these two. They have lots of questions."

West held up a bag. "That would be a mistake. I come bringing gifts. Four slices of Beatrice's famous chocolate cake."

"Four?"

"Well, I was hoping to come during Aleta's bath time and reward the nurse for letting me watch."

"In your dreams!" Aleta quipped.

"Don't dare. Lauren is too close to me when I'm dreaming. She can practically read my mind."

Lyle opened the bag and pulled out four plastic containers each holding a serving of cake. He then produced four forks and four napkins.

"You're going to spoil us," Aleta said.

"No one is allowed to send gifts, flowers or cards," Lyle said. "You are to eat nothing that hasn't been handed to you by me personally."

"We're going to starve!" Aleta wailed. "Lauren told me about you. You get so busy you forget to eat."

"Lauren is taking care of the acquiring part. I'm just her delivery boy."

"The hospital does feed it's patients, you know," Dr. Cook commented wryly. "Most expensive meals in town."

"Stop looking my gift horse in the mouth!" Aleta declared. "Those women are great cooks!"

As he finished his cake, Stanley said, "I need a phone. I need to stay in touch with Ed."

"You can use my cell when I'm here," West said.

"You could bring me mine," Stanley said. "It's under the mattress in the RV."

"So your wife hid yours too," Lyle smiled.

"By the way, congratulations on Morgan's win. Wish I'd seen it."

"Who was your biggest competition?" asked Aleta, eager for dog talk.

"Tom Wilson and that Frenchie of his. He had it up until the last second. At first I thought the Shepherd would get it and then the judge settled on comparing Tom's Frenchie with the Pom and I thought that was it, so I played face games with Morgan. He likes to mimic me. Evidently, that caught the judge's eye and he came over to take another look. He snapped his fingers and Morgan gave him that quizzical look Labs are famous for and I guess the choice was closer than I thought."

"How delicious!" Aleta said. "I can't wait to see Scooby in the ring."

"Scooby?" Stanley queried a trifle annoyed. "You named him without me?"

"I name the dogs. You name the kids."

Stanley was surprised. "Really?"

"You don't want a person who calls her first dog Scooby to name our son, do you?"

"I wouldn't answer that," Lyle advised. "Just go with it. And, of course, check every name out until you choose one she likes."

"Why not let her choose?"

"Redheads don't like the word no."

"And you're an expert?"

"Ask Wayne. He's married to one too."

"If you guys form a club," Aleta warned, "we wives will form one too."

Stanley quickly stated, "No club. Now, Lyle, where are you in the investigation?"

Cook rose and left quietly.

"Ed's narrowed the field to two construction crews. Both employed our perps as laborers. Both have people working with explosives, but the obvious suspects have alibis. He's out nosing around the sites now."

"So the mayor's clean," Aleta concluded. "I was hoping he wasn't."

"Do me a favor and don't take him off your suspect list," Stanley said.

"You aren't planning to attack him in court, are you?" Lyle asked.

"I want his counsel to think that's the way I'm going."

"Well, you're fortunate because Milani and I aren't taking anyone off our suspect list just yet."

"Do you still have a job?" Stanley asked abruptly.

"Well, Martha Cook is Harriet Locke's friend and Aleta is Harriet's granddaughter and you are Aleta's husband, so the answer is I've got connections… Actually, it's a mess but I didn't kill Ramage, the TV crews got lots of footage of me trying to dissuade him from killing himself. Of course, he doesn't see it that way. He claims I was baiting him so I could shoot him. He says I could have had my men take him down the way they took down his men. He says I have a vendetta against him which is why I didn't treat him with any respect."

"And people are believing him?"

"Well, there's some truth in what he says," Lyle said. "I don't respect him. And I thought he'd mess things up, so I acted pretty high-handed. And yes, it may cost me my job. Today's hero is tomorrow's villain."

"Not to us," Aleta said.

"What would you do if you weren't chief?" Stanley asked.

"Join the rest of the villains," Lyle grinned. "Be a lawyer."

"You can join our firm," Aleta offered. "Praetzel, West and Praetzel."

"I haven't been fired yet."

"I gather Mayor Liston is backing Chief Ramage," Stanley said.

"One hand washes the other," Lyle said. "Two of Ramage's men have applied to join the Arborville force. Young guys who want to be real cops not just traffic ticket dispensers."

"Are you taking them?"

"Not at this time. I sent them to Milani. He's got an opening."

"Sorry about the trouble," Stanley said.

"Hey, it felt good at the time. I'm a grown-up. I had a choice. I chose to act like a kid and show off. And now I have to face the consequences of that choice. The thing is, I really enjoyed shooting him."

Aleta spoke up. "You know when Chief Milani offered to get me off the mine and put Joey Crowder there in my place, I was so eager to do it, I didn't even think about how dangerous it was for him. That board could have broken. Crowder's lawyers have one helluva case, and I think Milani knew that; but he wanted to get back at the guy. And when that big guy plunked Crowder down on the bomb and Joey wet his pants, it was a satisfying moment.

"Joey peed?" Stanley said.

"Not only that, but the bomb guys insisted on going over every inch of the ground and then disarm each mine and dig each one up before they'd tackle getting Joey off the throne," Lyle reported. "Tom decided to go for gold. Joey was near fainting when they finally rescued him. His legs had gone numb it seems."

When Lyle left, Stanley turned to Aleta, "What did you enjoy the most about that time?"

"The look on your father's face."

"The what…?"

"He was shocked but in a good way. It was as if someone had handed him a million dollars. It was some sort of affirmation of me as a person. I don't know how to explain it."

"He didn't look at you as if he were ashamed?" Stanley asked aghast.

"He knew I had no choice. My whole life before that day told him I was chaste, and he was the first to see the sacrifice. I will always appreciate that."

"You said he was speechless."

"That was the first level. This is what I sensed," Aleta explained. "I guess we're on the second level now."

"I think I can face him now," Stanley said.

"Okay, tell me how you felt when you found out I knew."

"I was so grateful you didn't try to rescue me. It meant you respected my choice, appalling as it was to you."

"I thought you'd think I was a coward."

"That thought never crossed my mind," Stanley said. "But I told you this already."

"I guess we're on the next level," Aleta said. "And much as I hated what those men did to you, I don't hate you for your part."

"At least not at this level," Stanley remarked.

"Well, then let's start peeling away the layers and shake off the effects of this hell we both lived in for such a long time."

"It was only a day," Stanley said.

"I bet you didn't think that way when you were being raped. I bet it felt like it would never stop."

"You have no idea!" Stanley said.

"No, I don't," Aleta said. "So tell me."

"It's too…"

"Horrible?"

"Yes."

"You think I'll cry?"

"I think you'll never want anything to do with me again."

"Why on earth would you think that?" Aleta asked shocked.

"Because I endured such degradation and didn't fight back."

"It was done to me too," Aleta said. "We are as one now. So let's get the monster out of the dark and destroy him."

"There are some things one shouldn't share."

Aleta's voice was firm. "But this isn't one of them. God put us here, flat on our backs staring at a hospital ceiling, and nothing to do but dwell on what happened. So let's dwell together. If I have a limit to my love I'm apologizing right now; but, at least let's see if it matches yours."

And so Stanley told her.

And she listened. The tears came but she let them roll onto her pillow and gave them no heed. There is a time for grief. This was that time. Later she could rejoice in their survival. Right now they needed to grieve over the loss of a precious piece of their very souls.

The next day Lyle brought pie baked by Evelyn. Dr. Cook came in and the four shared the four pieces.

"I can't get over your timing," Stanley commented to Dr. Cook."

"It's not lucky timing," Lyle said. "He called to find out when I was coming."

After the men left, Aleta asked her husband what level they were on.

"I'm not sure I'm up for digging any deeper."

"We haven't even touched on the rage you buried deep down."

"I'm afraid to go there."

"Well, that's a beginning," Aleta observed. "You know we're going to do this, don't you?"

"And you'll know if I'm not dealing, won't you?"

"I told you God put us here. He gave us seven days. We rest on the seventh just as He did. We work the other days."

"I could be preparing for the trial," Stanley hedged.

"We need more facts. When we have the complete picture, we can discuss your argument."

"You are determined, aren't you? Suppose we talk about you."

"We can start there," Aleta agreed. "How did you feel undressing me in front of those men?"

"We're talking about me, not you. How did you feel?"

"You first," Aleta said with authority.

There was no denying her. He started slowly, remembering the mixture of feelings. Loving the feel of her soft skin, hating not being able to explain what he was doing, fearful she would become angry, rebel and ruin his tenuous hold on the situation and his plan to protect her, worried because he was giving her no choice, because he had to shut her out and shut her down, treat her as if she meant nothing to him when every fiber of his being wanted to hold her and comfort her.

"I would not have allowed you to make that sacrifice," she remarked. "You know that."

Stanley smiled as a thought struck him.

"What is it?" Aleta pressed.

"I guess we're at the level where I imagined what my life would have been like had they tried to rape you and succeeded."

"I would have handled it," Aleta huffed.

"I'm not sure I didn't choose the easy way out."

"I'm not a difficult person to live with," Aleta charged.

"I like spicy food," Stanley replied evenly.

Aleta laughed. "You are probably right. I could barely handle being undressed in front of those two. I know I could maybe have suffered through the rape and that I probably would have made that walk; but, it would have been so much shame piled on shame that when Joey Crowder set me on that bomb, I would have risen immediately and taken that stinking bastard with me."

"Now I do feel better," Stanley said. "Still ashamed, but better. I don't understand your shame though. Enlighten me."

And so went the afternoon and evening of the second day.

The third day Lyle brought Rachael Milani's lasagna and cookies baked by Madge.

As usual Wayne Cook joined them.

"How about stopping the treatments?" Stanley asked. "They're damned uncomfortable."

"If I don't, you'll take away my lasagna?" Cook probed.

"If I thought that would do it, believe me, I would."

"Glad to see you're still thinking straight," Cook said.

"Lauren says to tell you the pups are cute," Lyle reported. "Your boy is still trying for two nipples every chance he gets. He's really growing."

"Good for Scooby," Aleta commented, her mouth half full.

"So Stanley, have you thought of a boy's name yet?" Wayne asked.

"It could be a girl," Stanley hedged.

"So you haven't?"

Later, when they were alone, Aleta asked, "Why are you worried it might be a girl?"

"A girl who looks like me?" Stanley said. "As long as we're on this honesty kick. Be honest. You don't want a girl that looks like me."

"Well, I must admit I don't want a girl with a penis," Aleta confessed tongue-in-cheek.

"Keep going," Stanley pressed.

"Well, I'd rather she didn't have hair on her chest."

"What else?"

"Well, your waist doesn't have a feminine look to it."

Stanley exploded, "Of course not! I'm a man!"

"Exactly," Aleta said. "So she won't have a nose like yours. She'll have a feminine version and that's okay by me."

"Speaking of looks," Stanley said, "considering how beautiful you are, why was walking naked such a problem?"

"You used to shower with other boys after gym. You shouldn't have had any problem running around nude in that Oakwood house; but, you did."

"It wasn't the same," Stanley said. "They were dressed."

"Exactly."

And so went the afternoon and evening of the third day.

Madge sent home-cooked roast beef on homemade bread the next day. Beatrice sent brownies.

"I may keep you two another week," Wayne Cook commented after his first bite. "The meals are getting better and better."

"No you won't," Stanley said. "One week of treatments is all I'm allowing. After that my skin can rot for all I care."

"The judge granted another continuance," Lyle announced. "Your court date is set for next Tuesday."

"How close are you to finding the last man?"

"We know who it is. We just have to come up with the proof. And we suspect there's someone behind him. We can't move in until we find out if that's so."

When Cook and West were finished, they departed more quickly than usual.

"We're getting close to the end of this," Aleta said.

"I feel we've pretty much exhausted every possible feeling we could have had also," Stanley rejoined.

"That just means we've finished on the third level," Aleta put in.

"I think we're done."

"Now I know we're not."

"Go on," Stanley said. "I dare you. What area haven't we discovered."

"Your latent homosexuality."

"My what?" Stanley gasped.

"It's what you've been most ashamed that someone would find out about," Aleta went on. "It's normal you know."

"Homosexuality is normal?"

"Sure. Why not? I believe our sexuality is on a continuum. Some are outright homosexual. Some are outright heterosexual. But most of us fall between the two. In other words, we aren't pure."

"I'm not a homosexual!" Stanley declared.

"And I'm not saying you are; but, all of us—men and women—have strong sexual feelings and our genes determine which way we go; however, two heterosexual parents produce a homosexual. Now how could that happen if genetically there were absolutely no homosexual predispositions in all of us."

"You have no idea what you are talking about."

"Sure, I do and you know it."

"I grew up with gay friends. Believe me, I had a support group waiting if I had wanted to go that way."

"I believe you," Aleta said. "And I've never touched another woman sexually, but I know what I like in breasts."

"But that's because you like your own body."

"And you like yours," Aleta said.

"That doesn't make me a homosexual."

"I'm going to go out on the limb here. It's so much easier because I'm staring at a ceiling with a crack in it. You know we could do a Rorschach with that crack if you want."

"No. I don't need an amateur psychoanalyst interpreting my fanciful imaginings over a crooked crack any more than I need one to interpret my dreams."

"So, you're having dreams?"

"Nightmares," Stanley said. "Aren't you?"

"Yes, I am."

"It's nothing more than leftover dread of a repeat of the horror," Stanley announced. "That's it. End of story.

"Freud had a theory about dreams."

"Freud had a lot of theories about sex."

"I read his book about dreams."

"No wonder you're so obsessed."

"I'm not obsessed. I think he had hold of a bit of the truth. He said dreams are wish fulfillment."

Stanley almost rose into a sit but his chest rebelled when he started to and, so he let his voice carry his anger. "That's rubbish! I'm dreaming about being raped because I want it to happen again? Is that what you're saying?"

"Exactly!" Aleta said.

"Damn it, Aleta. You are so far off-base we should stop here before you go over the line."

"I'm already over it," Aleta said. "People make the mistake you're making. Dreams are never what they seem."

"That I will agree to," Stanley said, letting himself lay back figuratively.

"When I dream of someone dying, I'm not hoping that they die. I know that because I never dream about enemies dying only those I love the most in the whole world. So if I'm not wishing them dead, what is my wish. The dreams are always very sad and I can't handle what's happening and I wake up and call it a nightmare."

"Go on," Stanley said intrigued.

"So what if the wish was to be able to handle such grief. It's brought on by the fear of that very thing happening and not being able to cope. The wish is for coping skills not the death of a loved one."

"That could be," Stanley agreed.

"So, your nightmares are the same thing," Aleta said.

"I'll agree that I could be reliving the nightmare wishing I could have coped better."

"You coped just fine. Your goal was to save me. You saved me. The problem was you felt degraded. Yet you didn't do anything wrong."

"I let them…"

"And that is the key. You feel as if you let them. You had a choice which means you allowed it to happen. Sometimes we don't have a choice between good and evil. Sometimes we chose between two bad choices. That was the choice you had. You chose between you and me, and you chose you; but, because you had so many close gay friends when you were young because they felt as alone as you did, because of that you came away feeling that everyone who accused you of being gay when you were a teenager, all those hateful people who rejected you, that they would believe they were right. Deep down, you know that there is might be a modicum of truth in such an accusation. And if that were so, you feel that would destroy you."

"You… you…," Stanley began his fury shutting down his brain.

"I'm glad you're over there and your chest hurts," Aleta said.

"I wouldn't ever hit you!" Stanley declared knowing he'd like to.

"No, you wouldn't; but, both of us know that the thought crossed your mind."

"But I wouldn't do it."

"What if they had told you that if you hit me they wouldn't rape me."

"Well, maybe then."

"So what they asked you to do was bend over and let them hurt you instead of me."

"And I would do it again."

"That was the driving force that made you submit over and over again."

"That's right."

"And you hated every minute of it."

"Absolutely!" Stanley declared, settling back. How could she understand some parts of his experience so completely and miss by a mile on other parts.

"I like our sexual relations," Aleta said softly. "I love it every time you touch me."

"I feel a 'but' coming," Stanley said warily.'

"No 'but' is coming."

"Okay," Stanley said tentatively.

"So, you understand that because I like what you do, I don't want a stranger to do the same thing."

"I see where you're going," Stanley said. "I'm not a homosexual."

"The problem is not whether you are or not, but that you can't accept the possibility that you could be."

"But I'm not," Stanley said suddenly near tears.

"I'd love you if you were," Aleta said. "I love you as you are."

"My mother said that to me once."

"She thought you were a homosexual?"

"She didn't think I was interested in girls."

"Were you?"

"I was afraid of them."

"Well, I'm glad you got over that," Aleta quipped.

"So's my mother."

"Stanley, you had gay friends when you were growing up."

"That doesn't mean I was gay or am gay."

"I think you have to fight so hard not to be gay, you never accepted the possibility you might be. You never experimented. A lot of men do you know."

"I couldn't. They would have swallowed me whole."

"So this was your experimentation," Aleta said. "So how was it?"

"I was raped," Stanley declared flatly.

"So they ruined you for other men," Aleta said. "That's too bad."

"No, it's not. I don't want…"

Aleta interrupted. "Tonight when you sleep and you dream, allow yourself to want to experiment. Relax into the experience."

"It…"

"Can't hurt. It's only a fantasy. Learn something about yourself."

"I know all about me."

"You are a more complex man than you know. I fell in love with the homosexual part of your being as well as the heterosexual part. Dream knowing that."

Stanley said not a word. This woman was reaching into areas he had kept private for a lifetime, even from himself.

The fourth day finished with him having the same nightmare again. He woke up sweating, afraid to sleep again. Surely she couldn't be right. He decided to try it her way. What could it hurt? It was a fantasy.

The fifth day Lyle arrived dressed in rain gear that was still wet when he walked into the room.

"Dr. Cook is coming," he announced, "but he's got an emergency, so we just have to wait."

"What did you bring us today?"

"Evelyn made candy. Beatrice wanted you to know she could make something besides desserts so she baked chicken pot pies which in my book is half dessert," Lyle explained. "We arrested the construction guy. He was acting on his own.

He thought that if he killed the mayor, Philip Fleming would take over as mayor. He has filled in as acting mayor so that makes sense. But here's the strange part. He didn't care if you quit or not. He was only out to eliminate the mayor. He wanted the project to go through; but not the one without the school. He wanted the school built. He had nothing to do with you; but, it was the action of those two in your office that let him believe he could get away with it."

"But they were caught," Aleta pointed out.

"He thought they were stupid."

"It's a mess," Stanley said.

"Which is why they all might have gotten away with it." Lyle summed up. "So many guys with motive."

"So were the first guys working for the mayor?"

"We think the man behind them was someone who was afraid the case wouldn't be won in court with you two on it. Stanley's rep scared him. It points to a council member who wanted to blacken the mayor's name just enough to step in and take over."

"Philip Fleming?"

"Ed is working on that angle now."

When the men left, Aleta said. "I've been waiting all morning. Did you have a nightmare last night?"

"Yes."

"Why didn't you tell me about it?"

"Because then you'd want to go to another level."

"I don't think there are any more levels," Aleta said. "We have unexplored rooms in each level but we're on the ground floor."

"Okay then. I did have the nightmare."

"And?"

"I didn't follow your suggestion…"

"Ok…" Aleta said in a small voice.

"…the first time. I did the second."

"And where are we?"

"I'll know tonight."

"Remember I love you no matter what," Aleta said. "I'd love to come over and kiss you."

"Leave the gown behind," Stanley said.

"We can't…"

"I know…"

"We're in a hospital room."

"Doctors and nurses are used to naked people."

Aleta got up, dropped her gown on the bed, went over and kissed her husband lightly on the forehead.

"What a feast you are," he said.

"You don't get away that easy," she quipped. She pulled back his cover.

"What are you doing?"

"We are starting our own nudist colony," she said as she removed the contraption that kept his skin open to the air.

"I found out something," he said quietly as he lay exposed gazing at his nude wife. She took his hand.

"I liked my gay friends' attitudes. They were gentle and caring and accepting…"

"And…"

"I'm not homosexual. I've had fantasies but last night I let them out and that's all they are."

"We all have fantasies."

Stanley squeezed her hand lightly and pulled her toward him. "I prefer reality."

"No sex."

"I haven't touched you for days. Let's begin there. It'll be sweeter on Tuesday."

"What's Tuesday?"

"The seventh day."

"You go to court on Tuesday!"

"Tuesday begins at 12:01 AM."

She kissed him lightly on the forehead and then the mouth.

And that was the fifth day.

Monday Lyle walked in with a small bag.

"Fudge," he said.

"That's our entree?" Aleta asked, surprised.

"You are spoiled!" Lyle exclaimed.

Dr. Cook entered. "What's the food doing outside the room?"

Aleta laughed delightedly. "So there is a real entree."

"Why do you think I'm here?" Dr. Cook said. "I don't check on patients every day. I like to let them rot a while. So today's your last treatment, Stanley. You two can go home tomorrow."

"You kept us here just for another meal." Aleta asked.

"I know when I've got a good thing going," Cook said. "And from the size of the containers I think the ladies went all out."

"Roast turkey and stuffing. Evelyn says it's the one thing she makes well."

"It's not Thanksgiving," Aleta mentioned.

"Evelyn knows that but she said they are all thankful you two are alive and okay."

"Well, they will be if they obey their doctor's orders."

"What orders are those?" Stanley asked.

Wayne grinned, "No activity for Aleta that would strain her shoulder."

Lyle suppressed a smile begging to burst forth. "Like what?"

"Oh you know, the usual things," Dr. Cook said.

Stanley burst in, "No driving, housework or…"

"Sex?" Lyle finished.

"Serve the food!" Stanley said brusquely.

Lyle handed Stanley his cell. "You've got three minutes."

"Oh, for heaven's sake," Stanley said. "You're just lucky I'm getting out tomorrow."

"Call," Lyle ordered.

Stanley made the call.

Ed answered, "You'll never guess what else I found out."

"Go on."

"Bill Makovsky, the other council member we were investigating. Well, he's got a motive. He's going to sell his property to the city and buy the mayor's house. It's near his office and it's a step up for him."

"Is Makovsky's property valuable?"

"Poor location for a business, not residential enough for today's buyers, too old to be a profitable rental property. Still Brandon Webber made an offer. The council knows Webber has got shitty places all over the city. They don't want him to own one next door to the town hall, so, they decided to buy Makovsky's house and expand the town hall. They say they need more office space."

"What am I not seeing?" Stanley asked.

"Brandon Webber made an outrageous offer on the Makovsky property and that's what the town will have to pay."

"Is there any way you can get a realistic appraisal?"

"You need more than one, and we gotta get our guys in the house."

"Work it out; but, get me those appraisals," Stanley said. "I need them first thing in the morning."

Aleta spoke up as soon as Stanley disconnected.

"Give Lyle back his phone and eat."

"Are you going to boss me the rest of today?"

"You should be so lucky. I'm going to boss you the rest of your life."

"You're in for it," Wayne said.

Stanley smiled. "Not really."

"Oh, come on," Lyle said. "You're talking to two long-time married men."

"But I have power now," Stanley said.

"What power?" Aleta said. "You don't…"

Stanley cut her off with a single word, "Pillow."

Aleta didn't say another word for the rest of the meal. The three men talked and Aleta listened without comment.

"Aleta and I thank you for bringing us this fantastic lunch," Stanley said. "It was quite wonderful. Please tell the ladies we will never forget their thoughtfulness nor their great cooking. It has made our stay so much more enjoyable."

"Lauren wants you over for supper soon."

"Tuesday will be good. Aleta shouldn't be cooking yet."

"She'll be delighted," Lyle said. "She's been dying to chat with Aleta, that is, if Aleta ever finds her tongue."

"Oh, it'll be back by then," Stanley said. "Aleta come give me a kiss."

Holding her short gown closed, Aleta left her bed and came over and kissed Stanley lightly on the cheek.

"Are you angry with me?" Stanley asked bluntly.

Aleta took his head in her hands and kissed him fully and completely on the mouth. Her grown opened in the back; but, she ignored it.

Stanley whispered in her ear, "I do love you."

"I know," she said softly. "I know."

The visitors left shortly afterward.

"One word," Lyle said. "If I said that to Lauren when she was spouting off, I'd get a pillow in my face."

"Well, they're obviously connected at a deeper level," Wayne Cook said.

"What do you know that I don't?"

"Not nearly enough, it seems," Cook responded. "If I did, I'd use the same technique on Yancey."

"Think Stanley will ever share it?"

"Not a chance!"

Once alone in the room, Aleta asked, "What was that about?"

"I wanted to see if you still loved me," Stanley said. "I thought you'd think I was asking you to perform a parlor trick."

"I did," Aleta confessed.

"But you obeyed anyway."

"I figured you had your reasons."

"I did."

"You realize they got a show, don't you?"

"Dr. Cook got the show, and he's seen you before. Lyle will still have to hope to come in during bath time."

"You fox, you!"

And that was the sixth day.

On the seventh day they copulated just after midnight delighting in the slow gentleness required by Aleta's shoulder and Stanley's only partial healed wounds.

Eight hours later, after Dr. Cook had retaped Aleta's shoulder, Stanley's father showed up with Stanley's best suit and a silk shirt.

"Dr. Cook said 'silk'," he explained.

"Would you like me to join you as co-counsel?" Hubert Praetzel asked.

Stanley welcomed the suggestion and his father felt a new warmth coming from his son. Aleta hugged the older Praetzel spontaneously and he marveled again at the strength of this woman his son had married.

Harriet brought Aleta's green show outfit and Aleta decided it was appropriate for the day and told her grandmother so. Then she kissed her lightly on the cheek.

"Shall I help you dress?" Harriet asked.

"That's Stanley's job," Aleta said demurely and the elder two people excused themselves.

That both had seen Aleta unclothed was forgotten. That was part of the past. The couple had moved on to the present.

Harriet wished she could tell her parents how proud she was of the daughter they raised. But it was too private a pride to be shared.

Chapter 37

When Judge Arthur Green entered his courtroom, he was surprised to see it packed. After he sat down, he looked over toward the diminutive octogenarian seated at the table not only with a young lawyer who spent most of his time in Juvenile Court, Stanley Praetzel, but also with Hubert Praetzel, a criminal attorney of considerable note. Then he glanced at the people behind the pair and did a double take. Most of the people in the first row of spectators he recognized.

Next to an unknown young woman with her arm in a sling sat the Honorable Judge Lydia Davis. The next person in the line was the prestigious criminal lawyer, Kurtz West. Beside him in full uniform sat his son, the Arborville Chief of Police Lyle West.

To his left was the richest and most powerful woman in the county, Martha Cook. An older woman sat beside her which was unusual because Martha was not someone anybody sat next to casually. The older unknown woman had an aura about her that told Judge Green that she was a power in her own right. This was confirmed by the fact that the

Willow Glen Chief of Police Tom Milani was seated on the other side of her. That ended the line of noteworthy faces. He didn't recognize the rest of the people in the row, but it didn't matter. Those he knew were important enough. Why were they here? Was something important about to happen? The presence of several reporters told him it was.

Roger Lascovich, Oakwood City Council's lawyer, made a brief presentation. He opened with the statement that the city council had acquired Bessie Dobbin's land under the laws regarding Eminent Domain. That was fact.

Lascovich carefully outlined the steps that had been taken. Everything was in order. The final step in the process was the adjudication of the amount of compensation due Miss Dobbins.

When Stanley Praetzel rose and stated that, while his expertise lay in the area of child advocacy, he knew what stage in the process they were in, Judge Green relaxed. He could let this young man have his say.

Stanley Praetzel began to speak. His tone was settled, calm and firm.

"There were a series of events the first of which caused me to take this case. I can prove each allegation and I will present the proof verified by the witnesses seated in the first row behind Miss Dobbins at Your Honor's pleasure.

"The criminal actions to which I refer will be addressed in another court but will be mentioned here only as essential background information.

"A fraud has been perpetrated on this court. It was done because the 2002 decision handed down by the Illinois Supreme Court forbids one neighbor from acquiring the property of another under the provisions of Eminent Domain simply because he wants it. On that basis I ask that the court allow me to present my case for reconsideration of the original decision made because it was reached on the basis of false information. May I continue?"

Judge Arthur Green, a man of considerable years, was by nature of his age a man from the old school. The young lawyers polite respect was not lost on him.

"This court will listen to all information pertinent to your allegation that fraud has indeed been committed."

Stanley continued.

"First, two construction workers were hired to threaten me not to accept Bessie Dobbins' case which I wasn't planning to take. The two men had guns. They shot my wife. Chief Milani has the two men in custody and a recording of the statements made at the time of the shooting wherein they named Mayor Basil Liston as the man who hired them. This action aroused my suspicions as the court had already decided in favor of the City Council with regard to Bessie Dobbins' property. The only portion of the case remaining was the amount of compensation to be awarded to Miss Dobbins.

As an aside, let me state that Mayor Liston's involvement is under investigation at this time. The men later identified council member Bill Makovsky as the man who actually gave them the guns and the money; however, Bessie Dobbins had told only Mayor Liston that she had hired me as her attorney in this matter. This fact points to the probability of a conspiracy.

"Objection, Your Honor. Irrelevant," Lascovich cried.

"Overruled. The Court is curious. Proceed, Mr. Praetzel."

Stanley picked up this tale smoothly.

"At approximately the same time that my office was invaded, Bessie Dobbins' house was set on fire.

Lescovich rose.

"Your Honor, please. What has arson to do with the reason we're here?"

"A little leeway, Your Honor," Stanley Praetzel requested. "I can tie it together with a few more sentences."

"See that you do," Judge Green ruled. "Objection overruled."

"Oakwood's Fire Department was late to the scene of the fire. Arborville's Fire Department had already brought the fire under control by the time they arrived. Chief Wicks of Oakwood insisted on taking over. Despite Bessie Dobbins' protestations that the fire couldn't have been caused by the wiring because the fire marshal had removed the fuses, Chief Wicks ordered his men to chop up Bessie's house to ascertain that no hot spots existed. Chief Wicks's actions rendered the house unlivable."

"Your Honor," Lescovich pleaded. "This is a matter for another court. What the fire chief did or didn't do is not relevant. He is not a member of the City Council"

"Mr. Praetzel, can you tell me why Chief Wicks's actions are relevant to the matter before this court."

"You mean besides reducing the value of the property before compensation is decided?"

Judge Green smiled. "Point made. Objection is overruled, however, Mr. Praetzel, move on."

"Subsequently a bomb was planted under Mayor Liston's car by a member of the C&G Construction Company who wanted to see Philip Fleming take over as Mayor. Councilman Fleming has been a proponent of the building of new schools which was the basis for the Resolution of Necessity voted on at the fifth public hearing on the subject of acquiring Bessie Dobbins' farm. This incident was the last piece to the puzzle. Someone knew about the fraud.

"Objection!" Lescovich bellowed. "So far we have seen no evidence of fraud. We are not going to listen to the crazy delusions of a bomber, are we?"

"Mr. Praetzel?" Judge Green asked.

"Actually, they weren't crazy. And I am done with the preliminaries. I am ready to expose the fraud. May I continue?

"Objection overruled. Proceed.

"The City council had three plans drawn up. The first showed the elementary school located on Miss Dobbins' farm where the house and barn now sit. This was the plan presented in the public hearings and to this court."

Lescovich started to rise, but Judge Green glared at him and he sank back down.

Stanley continued after a brief pause. He waited until Mr. Lescovich was again settled.

"Changes can be made after the presentation of a plan for any number of reasons," Stanley said. "This does not constitute fraud. This is not what happened in this case."

"It was at this point that another contract was put out on my life, by yet another member of the city council, Brandon Webber. But I digress. It's just that these attempts are what induced me to dig into this matter more thoroughly.

"That bids were being entertained for the construction of the schools on Bessie's property was appropriate at this juncture. That the council had the architect draw up variations to the plan is not in itself unusual. What was unusual was the radical departure from the plan publicly presented. That plan, for the sake of clarification I will refer to as Variation One. It called for two schools to be built on Bessie Dobbins' property—an elementary school and a middle school.

"Variation Two called for the construction of a new house for Mayor Basil Liston instead of the elementary school on the site where Bessie Dobbins' house now stands. The elementary school does not exist in Variation Two.

"It appears that the main purpose of obtaining Bessie Dobbins' land was so that Mayor Basil Liston could build a house on it. In order to do this, he not only needed the cooperation of the majority of the council, he also needed to hide the truth from the court, given the 2002 ruling by the Supreme Court. And he used good old-fashioned greed to persuade his compatriots to support his plan. His is a complex plan."

Lescovich was on this feet.

"Your Honor, please. This is no time for speculation. So there were three plans. So what! Let's move on to the business that brought us here today."

"Mr. Praetzel, I see no proof of fraud." Judge Green stated. "Or for that matter conspiracy. Do you have proof of bribery?"

"Not in the usual sense, Your Honor." Stanley Praetzel replied. "But permit me to lay out what I can prove. I believe Your Honor will reach the same conclusion I did."

"Objection, Your Honor," Lescovich cried. "This is a waste of the court's time."

"Overruled. I will allow the presentation of proof to the allegations made by Mr. Praetzel."

"Thank you, Your Honor," Stanley said, opening the folder in front of him.

"First, Bill Makovsky has already contracted to buy Mayor Liston's house at a considerable discount. The sale is in escrow as we speak. It's size and location is a step up for him. Mayor Liston has not bought another house. He is building one. It's completion is the caveat that rules when ownership will change hands."

He turned over a sheaf of papers and continued.

"Second, Bill Makovsky plans to sell his own property, which is located next to the town hall, to the City of Oakwood to use for much needed office space.

"Brandon Webber has made an offer to buy Makovsky's property at a highly inflated price.

"We have two appraisals in hand verifying the true worth of the Makovsky property."

He turned over another group of papers, then continued.

"The City Council plans to vote on matching Webber's offer for Makovsky's property at the next council meeting. It is on the written agenda of which we also have a copy."

He held up a single sheet of paper.

"I have with me the original contract between Cook Construction Company and the City of Oakwood, signed by four members of the council who constitute a majority and a former vice president of Cook Construction Company which Mrs. Cook plans to honor. The contract is for Variation Two."

Another set of papers was turned over in the folder and a scroll of blueprints was held up.

"Finally, I have with me the original plans for Variation Three which rearranges property lines and adds Farmer Jerome Lutz's acreage to Bessie Dobbins' acreage, thus allowing the construction of the elementary school as well as the sale of the eastern portion of Bessie Dobbin's land to the commercial stable that borders it.

"Also on the agenda for the next council meeting is the rezoning of the eastern portion of Bessie Dobbin's land as pasture.

"The fourth signer to the contract for Variation Two, which puts Mayor Liston's house on the site originally designated as the site for the elementary school, is Phillip Fleming, the vocal promoter of the need for a new elementary school. His signature can only be explained by the council's plan to build the elementary school on Farmer Lutz's land, which Mr. Lutz is willing to sell. An appraiser is scheduled to visit the Lutz farm this week and report back to the City Council. Mr. Lutz is present in this courtroom today to verify this.

"Variation Three was bid on by three contractors; but Cook Construction was not the low bidder. I strongly suspect that the exceptionally low bid on Variation Two was a ploy to promote the quick destruction of Bessie Dobbins' house and laying of the foundation for Mayor Liston's house while the council completed the steps necessary for Variation Three which would then be considered a mere expansion of a project which was already underway.

"Huck Dirkson is also present in the courtroom and will testify that he was approached and asked if he would be willing to buy the pasture to the right of Bessie Dobbin's house and agreed to pay the appraised value. From the sale of this acreage, the council could afford the extra money it would take to buy Farmer Lutz's property.

"Bessie Dobbins made a mistake when she didn't hire a lawyer sooner. She firmly believed her land couldn't be taken from her without her consent. She made an error in judgment.

"However, the Oakwood City council members who thought they could take a person's property under the Eminent Domain provision also made a mistake. They conspired to hide the true facts from the court. And once they did that, they knew they had to force Bessie to move before anyone got wind of what was really happening. That's why I was a threat.

"Earlier I mentioned the fire, and my opponent wondered why that was relevant to the matter before the court. It wasn't just the fact that Bessie's house would be valued at less than it would have been if it hadn't been ravaged by fire and by Chief Wicks's destructive action. I mentioned it because, one of the Oakwood firemen told my investigator that they were there to save the trees—not her house, not her rare book collection, not her paintings, but her trees.

"That, Your Honor, is why the court was presented with a fraudulent basis for taking over Bessie Dobbins property.

"The farmer down the road is eager to sell his land for the building of a school. What he doesn't have are century old oak trees on his property, oak trees planted by Bessie Dobbins' grandparents, which Mayor Basil Liston covets. One can build many things, but not a tree."

Stanley picked up two folders from the table in front of him, handed one to opposing counsel and gave the other to the clerk to hand to the judge.

"Both counsels in my chambers," Judge Green ordered.

Once the door closed behind them, Green removed his robe and sat down. "Roger, tell me that you didn't know what was going on."

"No, Sir," Roger Lascovich declared.

He turned to Stanley and asked him if he thought Roger was involved.

"No, I don't, Sir," Stanley said.

"So now what do we do? Where's the Resolution of Necessity?"

Stanley flipped through the pages quickly and located it.

"Looks like everyone signed it," the judge said scanning it. "What about the building contract?"

"Only needs a majority of signatures," Stanley said. "There are four."

"Mr. Praetzel, did your investigation uncover any collusion on the part of the remaining council members? There are two, I believe."

"Correct," Stanley said. "Louise Oppenwall and Jurgen Swanson. And we found nothing to connect these two with the fraud. Our investigation shows they were not aware of the signed contract. In fact, although I didn't include the minutes from the council meetings, Louise Oppenwall objected from the beginning to the taking of Bessie Dobbins' land. She did not object to the building of the school. She supported Philip Fleming's efforts to build the schools. "

"And this other council member?"

"Voted with the majority. He's a rubber-stamp kind of guy."

"Thank you both. You're excused."

The two lawyers left and returned to their places.

Aleta who had moved up to talk with Bessie returned to her seat as soon as Stanley appeared. He sat down, patted Bessie's hand and said nothing.

It could go either way. Oakwood had a legitimate need for the land. That couldn't be denied. The judge could rule that despite the manipulations of numerous council members, the city's needs should be served. No one disputed the need for ground on which to build a school. Judges didn't deal with alternatives. It was generally accepted that they didn't have all the facts that the city council was privy to.

Stanley could see the judgment going against Bessie Dobbins. A little old lady and a few trees didn't weigh much when a whole town had a need.

Aleta wanted to clue Stanley into comforting Bessie who was wilting with the wait. She looked at her husband. He was deep in thought. That's when she decided not to interfere. Bessie needed a lawyer focused on her case more than a comforting hand.

She noticed that the three lawyers to her left remained motionless in this interim. On the other side of the aisle Lascovich was busy talking with his clients.

After forty minutes Judge Arthur Green reappeared. He wasted no time.

"It appears that a fraud has indeed been perpetrated on this court as well as on the City of Oakwood. I take the voluntary presence of the holder of the building contract as a verification of the authenticity of that document. I will not comment on any allegations of criminal behavior presented to this court; however, it is the judgment of this court that the fraudulent representation to this court was deliberately conceived and perpetrated by certain members of the Oakwood City Council. While it would seem that the entire council be held accountable, it has been brought to my attention that one member opposed the council's decisions with regard to this matter; therefore, the court will not charge Louise Oppenwall and will, in fact, designate her Acting Mayor of the City of Oakwood until such time as a new council can be elected. As for the rest of the council I am issuing a warrant for the arrest of each council member on charges of fraud.

"As fraud was involved, the City of Oakwood's current petition to acquire Bessie Dobbins' property under the rules governing the acquisition of property by right of Eminent Domain is denied. However, the government has an obligation to serve its citizens as a whole; therefore, the Oakwood City Council may reapply to acquire the land it needs."

Bessie Dobbins, whose face had lit up when the denial was announced, now paled in dread. It wasn't over. She was going to be worn down by the government machinations which she had spent her whole life trying to avoid.

Stanley took her hand and squeezed it gently as the judge continued.

"The government also has an obligation to guard the constitutional rights of its individual citizens. One individual cannot take the property of another for personal aggrandizement. The court finds in favor of Bessie Dobbins. Any future plan for development by the City of Oakwood is not to include Bessie Dobbins' property."

Bessie collapsed into tears. Her home was still hers.

Stanley gathered her in his arms and held her. Aleta realized that this was physically painful for her husband and came over and gently pried Bessie from his grasp and hugged her with her one good arm.

Bailiffs guarded the doors as court officers took the city council members into custody.

Hubert Praetzel shook his son's hand and Stanley could tell he was pleased. "Simple is best. It represents solid underpinnings. You did a superb job."

His mother wanted to hug him but his father whispered, "A handshake, Judge." The term told her that a certain decorum was called for. Stanley saw the pride in her eyes. That was better than a hug.

He then began thanking the rest of those in the first row. Their presence gave everything he said veracity.

"You pulled out the big guns in this one," Martha Cook said. "Two police chiefs no less!"

Lyle West leaned over, "And in uniform!"

"As they should be," Martha exclaimed.

"You were great," Harriet said enthusiastically. "I'm so glad you're a member of my family."

"My pleasure, I assure you," Stanley said his eyes twinkling.

He would have thanked Tom Milani next but he was talking with Louise Oppenwall. Lyle soon was asked to join the two. Their conversation was brief and Louise Oppenwall, the new mayor, approached Martha Cook and said she was going to entertain bids for a fourth variation minus Bessie Dobbins' property. The women shook hands.

Martha turned to Bessie. "One of the men who bid the town job is an excellent carpenter. He could rebuild your house quickly. He has the crew. And he has a knack for restoration."

Stanley took West aside. "What did Louise want?"

"A recommendation for an interim police chief. He suggested Peets."

"Ramage would hate that!"

"She liked it. She was impressed with his background."

"Did you have anyone?"

"I didn't suggest anyone. Peets is a good choice," Lyle said. "If any of my men are interested, they can apply."

Aleta approached the two men boldly. "Stanley I need to go home and go to bed."

Lyle West arched one brow and Stanley laughed. "We'll be done in time for supper at your house."

"How about lunch?" his mother asked. "We'd love to celebrate with you."

"Aleta needs to rest," Stanley said. "And home is the best place for that. We'll take a rain check on your invitation."

"How about Sunday?" his mother said.

"Perfect!" Stanley replied with such enthusiasm his mother was warmed by his response.

Then he led Aleta straight through the door.

"You want to see the puppies?" Beatrice asked.

"Tomorrow, we'll come for supper," Stanley said.

"Six o'clock," Beatrice called after them.

She turned to Ed. "Where are they hurrying off to?"

"Who knows?" Ed said. "She got to him before I did and said she needed to go home."

"I hope nothing's wrong."

"Ask Lyle," Beatrice urged, so Ed did.

"Where would you go if you were young newlyweds that had been confined to hospital beds side by side for a week?" Lyle smiled.

"So nothing's wrong?" Beatrice said, still unconvinced.

"Well, he said they would be at my house for supper tonight," Lyle said. "But I'll tell you this. The two have been acting strangely since the kidnapping."

"He invited himself to supper tomorrow," Beatrice said.

"You were going to invite them, weren't you?"

"Of course."

"They're taking shortcuts; but, let's face it he managed to pull it all together for Bessie today. That was quite a feat considering all they're been through."

"Yes, it was."

Harriet and Martha walked out together.

"They were really tested with that kidnapping," Harriet said. "Wayne insisted on no visitors and I gathered their wounds were more psychological than physical, although they did have both. He put them together and this morning I walked in on a different Aleta."

"Better or worse?" Martha asked.

"Different," Harriet said. "I think walking naked through the fairgrounds affected her profoundly although by the time she was rescued she seemed to be at ease or maybe it was shock. This morning she was more like the girl I remember, but yet not like her at all."

"Did you get a bad feeling or a good one?"

"Strange," Harriet confessed.

Neither Aleta nor Stanley spoke as he drove home. Once inside the house, Stanley asked softly, "Now what was that all about?"

"The same thing as the hospital kiss in front of your friends."

"I don't think so."

"I know so."

Aleta pulled him toward the bedroom. "I need your help undressing so I can lay down."

Stanley helped her lift her arm out of its sling, then slipped the jacket off the good arm first, then the injured one. He began unbuttoning her blouse.

"This time hang up the clothes," she said, then grinned impishly, "Mine and yours. We're going to need them later."

"And we don't need them now?" he asked as seriously as he could.

"We'll muss them and I can't iron."

"What are we going to do?" he questioned, maintaining his poker face.

"I'm going to thank you," she replied still smiling.

"For winning?" Surprise tinged his tone.

"For putting me first when I asked you to."

Stanley slipped the blouse off her shoulders and started to put her arm back in the sling.

"You're not done," she said.

"All?"

"Yes," she said.

His hands worked slowly as he undid the clasp behind her back. He slipped the bra straps down her arms and then restored her left arm to the sling gently.

"Now you," she said.

"But there's nothing sexy about watching a man undress," he protested.

"You say that because you're a man," Aleta said. "I enjoy watching you more."

"You aren't disgusted when you think about what you saw in that kitchen?" he asked, his voice turned bitter. "Now why did I bring that up."

"Because we still have rooms where residual fears dwell," she said. "This is going to be with us both a long time."

"I expected more."

"Sit down," she said.

Half-clad he did so. Maybe she couldn't stomach him after all for all her brave talk.

She came over and sat in his lap, put her good arm around his shoulders, and kissed him tenderly. "Thank you for loving me enough to bring me home."

Suddenly, he realized she hadn't been testing him. She actually needed to come home.

"You were terrified?"

She nodded. "It was alright as long as we were all quiet and concentrating on the case; but, when it was over, I realized I wasn't ready to face people yet. There were too many. I had to escape before anyone asked me anything."

"So neither of us is over it," he mused aloud.

"It would seem not."

"Well, let's say we enjoy our misery together all afternoon," he grinned.

Aleta kissed him again. "You are my strength."

He returned her kiss and then whispered, "And you restored my soul.

Chapter 38

The next stage of their life began a mere six hours later when they rose, dressed and drove to Arborville.

Lauren and Lyle West were welcoming, and the dinner was lively with a lot of dog talk. Then Lyle mentioned, "We know the sex of our baby."

"When did this happen?" Aleta asked.

"This afternoon," Lyle went on enthusiastically. "At first we decided we didn't want to know and after five minutes we couldn't stand it anymore."

Lauren laughed, "You couldn't stand it anymore." Then she sobered and finished, "but, maybe this is a bad time considering."

"Considering what?" Aleta asked.

"What happened to you," Lauren returned.

"I wasn't…," Aleta began to protest.

"Pillow," Stanley said abruptly.

That single word stopped her mid-sentence. Lyle, who'd seen this happen before, waited for Aleta's verbal protest. That Stanley got away with it once was a phenomenon that Lyle was certain would never be repeated.

It surprised him that Stanley dared do it in the middle of dinner in front of Aleta's best friend. He watched and waited.

Aleta bowed her head and silently cut her meat. She ate a forkful while Lauren's mouth hung open.

It was Stanley who spoke first. "Aleta wasn't raped or sexually molested. You two are our best friends. We won't lie to you. But, know this; we were in a dark place for what seemed to us like an eternity. Neither of us is ready yet to talk about it."

"Aleta," Lauren said, addressing her friend directly, "Talking about bad stuff with friends is therapeutic. You need to talk stuff out."

Aleta did not acknowledge the truth of Lauren's statement in anyway. Stanley has his reasons she told herself. Always before he had been right. She couldn't see his reasons this time, but then she hadn't any of the other times either until much, much later.

Again it was Stanley who spoke. "She has a good therapist as do I. We are talking things out."

"But you told me what I wanted to know, so why did you stop her?" Lauren charged, annoyed at Aleta's silence.

Stanley was aware that Lyle was letting his wife talk because he wanted some answers himself.

"It was necessary," Stanley stated flatly.

"She's a woman with a mind of her own," Lauren protested again. "What she says is her choice to make, not yours."

"You are absolutely right," Stanley said calmly. "Right now she chooses to obey me."

"That's it?" Lauren gasped. "This isn't the middle ages. This is the twenty first century!"

Stanley turned to Lyle and said, "We have a special request to make of you."

Lauren's vexation dropped back a notch as Lyle nodded his acquiescence.

"I know most of the prosecutors in this county but none in the southernmost part of the state. Can we get the trial moved up here?"

"We're working on it," Lyle said. "We have Crowder on attempted murder up here so we have some leverage especially since we have the man who put out the contract. What else?"

"The prosecutor is not to ask us why we allowed ourselves to be kidnapped."

"I thought he had a gun," Lyle commented.

"Harriet knew there was a stranger in the trailer."

"She told the sheriff down south that."

"We don't want that to come back to haunt us," Stanley said.

"How's that going to haunt you?"

"Aleta knew the men were there. She never saw the gun."

Lauren burst in. "Then why didn't she run out to get help?"

Lyle replied for Stanley, "Because she also knew that if I got involved someone would be killed."

"How'd she know that?"

"She has her grandmother's gift for prophecy," Lyle stated flatly. "Chief Milani knows it, I know it, Harriet knows it, Martha Cook knows it and, now, you know it."

"Well, I guess it makes sense," Lauren said. "I know I'd do anything to save your life."

"Aleta knew you felt that way," Lyle continued, "which is why she closed the door and complied. It wasn't Stanley's life at stake, it was mine."

"Yours?!" Lauren breathed, blanching. "You didn't tell me."

"I didn't know beforehand. I found out later and, by then, it was too late."

"No wonder you shot Ramage!" Lauren exclaimed. "You're usually much cooler than that."

"So, Stanley, you don't want to testify?" Lyle questioned, changing the direction of the conversation.

"I doubt that that's possible," Stanley said, "but maybe my testimony will be enough. Aleta should not have to relive any of her experiences at the hands of those two. I need an advocate to argue for me."

"I can do that."

"And warn the prosecutor to stay away from anything that happened during those hours," Stanley said. "We need to let some of those memories die. But more importantly, we need to keep Aleta's prophetic power private."

Aleta rose from the table and walked to the other side and, while Lauren watched, Aleta kissed her husband fully and completely on the mouth.

Lyle grinned. This act alone would spark some great conversations between him and his wife. It wasn't a fluke. The experience had changed Aleta.

Aleta returned to her seat without saying a word; and, Lauren, who thought this was a signal, was surprised when Aleta remained silent.

Lyle knew it wasn't. He picked up the talk where it had been stopped by Aleta's act. "I'll talk to Tom and I think between us we can persuade the DA to do it your way," Lyle went on.

Stanley nodded and then said, "So, it's going to be a girl?"

"I didn't tell you," Lyle remarked.

"Your enthusiasm gave you away."

Aleta smiled in agreement.

"I'm not sure I want a girl," Stanley said. "Tell them Aleta."

Aleta's laughter was spontaneous. "He's sure she'll have his nose. I'm sure she won't. His nose is too masculine. Besides I have some pretty dominant genes of my own."

"That's why we're going to breed Bulldogs," Stanley said, "so the kid will be able to face the world knowing his mother has a crazy sense of what's beautiful. When his friends meet our dogs and say, 'What an ugly dog,' he'll be ready with some profound statement like, 'you take that back or I'll punch you in the nose'!"

Lyle roared. "That's profound all right."

"We're raising Labs too," Aleta said. "Labs get along with everyone. Can't mix Chessies with other dogs. Grams will have to keep the corner on those in the family."

"So you're looking for a female Lab too?" Lyle asked.

Aleta shook her head. "Not yet. We're taking our dogs one at a time, just like our children."

"How many do you plan to have?" Lyle asked.

"We aren't stopping until we get one that looks like me," Aleta said.

"What if the first one looks like you?"

"Then we keep going until we get one that looks like Stanley," she responded.

"Does Stanley have any say in this?" Lyle joshed.

"He gets to choose the names."

"Suppose he picks a name you don't like?" Lauren probed.

"He won't."

"Are you telling me you'll like any name he chooses?" Lauren pressed.

"I think that's the bottom line," Aleta replied thoughtfully. "He'll have considered it carefully and he makes wise choices. I trust him."

Later that evening, Lyle motioned Stanley to follow him into the den and closed the door. "What kind of deal should we be willing to make?"

"None."

Lyle took a deep breath and then plunged in.

"They didn't rape Aleta because they raped you. I'm right, aren't I?"

"Yes," Stanley said.

"I assume you told Dr. Cook, but he didn't say a word to me. In fact, until this evening, I wasn't really sure."

"What gave me away?"

"Nothing really," Lyle said. "It was Aleta's attitude. Then I knew I was right about you. You would never have allowed anyone to rape your wife even to save my life. I figured you'd made a deal; but, with animals like that your promise of more money wouldn't have been enough. They'd have taken it and then raped her anyway. So you offered them a sexual alternative. Not only that, they must have accepted it or she never would have gotten through that door."

"Maybe I shouldn't have been so quick to acknowledge your guess."

"It was smart to tell me. I can really help now," Lyle said. "And you stick with the truth."

"I'm having a lot of trouble handling this right now."

"I'm amazed that you are handling it at all. Does Aleta know?"

"Yes."

"Don't worry. Lauren won't unless you tell her," Lyle said. "It's a good thing you stopped Aleta when you did. Fortunately, Lauren'll be distracted by Aleta's prophetic abilities. In fact, I'm sure that's what she's asking Aleta about now."

"Aleta can handle that," Stanley said. "Will other people guess the truth?"

"I doubt it," Lyle assured him. "Remember I saw your clothes on the floor of the RV. I found you naked in the house after the bomb. And I know you. No one else has those three things to go on. Your secret is yours to keep."

"And Milani?"

"This is just between us."

"I'm glad you didn't see Aleta naked. She wouldn't have been able to come here if you had."

"You know I almost caught a glimpse of her when she kissed you in the hospital."

"If there were any danger of that, I wouldn't have asked her to do it."

"You let Wayne get a look."

"As if he hasn't seen all of her more than once."

"That was a sexier view." Lyle pointed out.

"She was in a hospital gown. Doctors turn their sex drive off when they see a hospital gown," Stanley declared.

"You're sure?"

"Yep."

Lyle clapped Stanley on the shoulder. "Thank you for my life."

Stanley felt satisfied. Lyle knew the truth. It felt right.

"You're welcome."

Later. on the drive home, Stanley said, "He knows."

"Did you tell him?" Aleta asked.

"He guessed. He said that I would never have let you enter the RV unless I'd guaranteed your protection somehow."

"This was a wonderful but scary evening. I'm not sure I can face tomorrow night with Ed and Beatrice."

"We'll take our camera, take lots of pictures of the puppies and talk about dogs all night. They will steer clear of the subject," Stanley assured her.

"How can you be so sure?"

"Ed doesn't bring his work home with him. He may guess, but he won't ever mention it to me or you or Beatrice."

"You know him that well?"

"Yes," Stanley affirmed. "But you have a real test coming up. Your mother called Grams and said she was coming out here."

"No!" Aleta exclaimed. "Please tell me you persuaded her not to."

"We're flying there Thursday morning."

"You bought the tickets without telling me?" Aleta gasped.

"My father is flying us out. Your grandmother is coming. This way we won't be bound by flight schedules. We can leave anytime you say, absolutely no questions asked."

"Mother will start right in."

"We start by telling her about the baby. That should get us through lunch. I will be hungry you know," Stanley said, his tone growing lighter as he talked.

"I do want to see my father," Aleta confessed. "I want to talk with him without my mother around."

"Your grandmother is indeed psychic," Stanley chuckled. "She said you'd want that."

"She isn't being psychic. She knows how close I am to him."

"You want to tell him," Stanley asked somberly.

"You may stop me anytime you want."

"This is important to you?"

"Please let me do this."

"Your father only?"

"And yours."

This time it was Stanley who gasped in surprise.

Thursday Stanley took the co-pilot's seat and Aleta asked, "You can fly?"

"I could have taken you alone, Aleta," he replied. "But it's a long trip and this gives all of us a little time to relax."

"You didn't tell me you could fly!" she scolded.

Stanley grinned and winked at his father. "It never came up."

"What else about you never came up?"

His father interposed. "Did Stanley tell you he's an expert skier?"

"No, he didn't tell me that," Aleta shot back.

"Dad, leave me a few things to surprise her with," Stanley said.

His father nodded.

The plane landed at a small airport thirty minutes north of Aleta's parents' home in Sausalito, a town north of San Francisco where each large hillside home had a spectacular view of the Bay.

Stanley had arranged for no one to meet them. He rented a car and Aleta climbed into it, relieved that her confrontation with her mother was postponed. She had dreaded the long ride with her father driving and her mother plying her with questions.

Instead the foursome was greeted effusively by Robert and Marian Locke and ushered immediately to the patio where, under the warm late October sun accompanied by a light breeze from the Bay, a lovely array of fresh seafood and fruit was balanced by hot French bread baked a second time with garlic butter melted into every tiny pore. Iced tea and wine completed the meal. Dessert and coffee would be served mid-afternoon.

Stanley and his father were openly appreciative not only of the succulent food but the beautiful view before them.

Stanley took advantage of the first pause in the small talk to announce that he and Aleta were expecting.

As predicted, Aleta's mother said, "So soon?"

"I guess I don't take after you and Grams," Aleta laughed. "Who would've thought I wouldn't be like one of you?"

Harriet laughed, but Aleta's mother scowled. It was a private family matter.

Stanley's father said, "My wife and I thought we'd never be blessed and then we were surprised when Stanley arrived after we'd about given up. You are fortunate, Marian, to have been blessed with three daughters. We had to wait until Stanley grew up and married. He was so particular about whom he was going to marry we thought he'd never find anyone. I'm as surprised as you to face grandparenthood so soon after acquiring a long-wished for daughter; but, I can't help but be thrilled."

"As are we," Aleta's dad remarked. "Congratulations, you two. This is the best news ever!"

"Mother, I was hoping that when I was here, you and Grams would shop for maternity clothes for me. I'd like to wear outfits different from what everyone else in town is wearing."

"There's time," her mother began.

"For me, maybe, but Lauren needs clothes now. She's my best friend, Mom. I want to take her back an outfit as a gift. She's done so much for me. When Stanley and I were in the hospital…"

Marian interrupted petulantly, "We were told we couldn't visit!"

"There was still danger," Aleta said smoothly. "We were under protective custody. Even Grams wasn't allowed to visit."

"That's true," Harriet chimed in. "Only the doctor, a couple of nurses and Lyle West, of course."

"Who's that?"

"The police chief, one of them anyway," Aleta replied. "Lauren's husband. As I was saying, Lauren arranged for friends to bake us goodies and Lyle brought them to us every day. It was the high point of the day."

"But we're family," her mother insisted still perturbed by that being considered of no consequence.

Hubert Praetzel cut in. "As were we, and in our case, a family with a great deal of local political clout; but West is immune to such forces."

Stanley's father had managed to switch the subject with that last comment. Robert Locke saw the ploy and took the bait purposely.

"Why is West immune? I would think his job would depend on the goodwill of the local politicians. It is an appointed position, isn't it?"

"It does and he is; but, I think we all like the fact that he isn't political. He's rich in his own right, yet he gives more than a hundred percent to his job. That's why he brought goodies to these two each day. Nothing is too lowly a task for him."

Aleta giggled. "It was something to see a chief in his uniform bringing us lunch. Martha insists he wear his uniform practically every time he leaves the office, and since she's the powerhouse in town, he does."

"Martha's like that," Harriet said.

Not to be denied her fight, Marian pushed into the conversation. "Well, I think something else was going on. I think that West guy was trying to hide the fact that you were raped. I think that's what everyone is trying to do. And I won't have it!"

"I wasn't raped, Mother," Aleta said firmly. "And the baby is fine."

"I don't believe you," Marian countered angrily. "We're family. You can be honest with us."

"I am being honest," Aleta shot back angrily, "Stan…"

Stanley interrupted before she'd even finished the second syllable of his name.

"Pillow," he said quietly.

The words stopped Aleta cold. Her mother looked at Stanley with fury. How dare he interrupt with a nonsensical word.

Marian went on with her tone falsely conciliatory, "It's nothing to be ashamed of, Aleta. And to say the baby wasn't affected is wishful thinking. You need to be seen by a specialist. Were you examined by a specialist?"

Aleta remained mute.

Her mother pushed harder. "You weren't, were you? Well, I don't think much of a police captain who would keep your mother from you at a time when you need her the most."

Stanley cleared his throat. "Aleta wasn't raped, Mrs. Locke."

"I don't believe you either!" Marian declared. "She's a gorgeous woman and she wound up naked in front of God and the whole world and you did nothing to prevent it. And I think whatever hold you have on her you'd better release it or I'll…"

Stanley interrupted. "You'll go shopping as Aleta asked," he stated with authority. Then he softened his tone. "Grams can tell you a few things privately. How does that sound?"

"I want Aleta to talk to me." Marian persisted.

"That's not going to happen." Stanley stated flatly.

"You can't stop her." Marian charged.

"I already have," Stanley said politely. "As soon as you leave to do what she requested, I will permit Aleta to speak again."

"Permit her!" Marian Locke exclaimed. "She doesn't need your permission. She's an emancipated woman. This is the twenty first century!"

"She takes her wedding vows seriously, as do I," Stanley said.

Harriet rose. "Come on, Marian, let me fill you in on a few things while we shop. You can talk again when you get back if you like."

Marian gave in reluctantly. She was receiving no back-up from anyone in the room. She needed to regroup, maybe get Aleta alone. Yes, that was it. She'd get Aleta alone and she'd get the whole story.

When the two women left the house, Aleta asked Stanley, "Does Grams know?"

"No."

"Know what?" her father asked gently.

"I want to talk with you and Mr. Praetzel in the den where we can't be overheard."

Without further ado, the three men followed Aleta into Robert Locke's study. Robert brought in a dining room chair so everyone could sit.

It was a small room whose window overlooked the rising hillside of ivy beyond the stone walkway and wall. Aleta had always liked this room and even now it made her feel safe.

The men waited quietly for her to speak. The fathers both searched her face. Stanley's head was bowed.

"Stanley knows what I want to say. He has my permission to stop me anytime. I've not been brainwashed. I just wanted you to know that."

"That never occurred to me," her father said. "You chose to obey as you promised you would when you were married. I can't say you have ever done anything that has made me prouder."

Stanley lifted his head and smiled at his wife. His face showed his deep satisfaction that Aleta's father understood her. Her father saying this would tell his own father what was happening. It warmed Stanley that her father knew the truth.

"What I am about to tell you is not to be shared with anyone else," Aleta said firmly.

Stanley's head dropped again and his eyes stared at the carpet.

"Believe me when I tell you that a woman might trivialize what happened. I'm taking a chance you won't. If I'm wrong, I'm wrong and that's that. Stanley is going to allow me to make this mistake…"

"Go on, Aleta," her father said. "Take a chance on us."

"Yes," Hubert Praetzel agreed. "Please, do. There is nothing you could say that would change my mind about the courage it took for you to pick up the ransom money, stripped as you were of all dignity, in order to save my son's life."

Again Stanley felt a warm glow. His father understood Aleta's sacrifice. He hoped Aleta realized that.

Aleta scarcely heard the words although later she would remember them. She was too intent on her own message.

"I wasn't raped," she stated. "The men planned to rape me. Stanley stopped them. You need to understand that Grams and I receive visions at times. This time we both had the same one. Lyle was going to be killed if either Stanley or I warned him about the presence of the men. Stanley believed Grams. But it wasn't in his nature to let the men rape me. So he chose the only alternative he could think of that would protect me and Lyle both. He offered himself. He didn't die to save me. That would have been an easy way out. Instead, for my sake, he chose to save himself so I would have a husband and his child would have a father. He allowed the men to rape him instead of me. Because of him only one of us was violated. Not that I knew about this. Over and over they kept coming to get him for what they called 'negotiations' and 'conversations. Stanley never told me. He just insisted I not speak. I had no idea what was happening; but, when I did, I remembered that I'd promised to obey him and, Dad, you taught me to keep my promises. But the point I'm making is that Stanley protected me. He is still protecting me. I am allowing it. I always thought of myself as a strong, independent woman. I think I still am; but, even the strongest person can be broken. That Stanley wasn't still amazes me. I wanted the most important men in our lives to share my pride and joy in the man I married. Stanley knew how important this was to me and despite his fear, he allowed me to share this."

After she finished, the room remained silent.

Aleta decided to wait quietly. Stanley had taught her that sometimes silence is what is called for.

Her eyes were downcast so she didn't see the tears streaming down the faces of the two fathers. Neither spoke. Neither moved.

Stanley, however, sensed their shock and their strong emotions pinned him to his seat. Overwhelmed, he too remained silent.

Quietly, Aleta's father rose. Putting his hand on Stanley's shoulder, he uttered his thank you to a bowed head.

Stanley couldn't bring himself to look at the man.

Hubert Praetzel rose as well. He came over and knelt down so he could see his son's face. He took the bowed head and lifted it as he spoke.

"I've never been prouder, Son. You are a man above men."

Tears streamed down Stanley's face, and he leaned over and cried on his father's shoulder.

Aleta fell into her father's arms, and he held her close as he used to do when she was a child, and she cried on his shoulder.

Afterward, the four talked for a long time. When they heard the car enter the driveway, Aleta paled. Her father took her hand and squeezed it.

He greeted the two women as they entered. Harriet immediately sought out Aleta while Robert Locke detained his wife.

"What did my mother tell you?" Robert asked.

"Absolutely nothing!" Marian said, annoyed. "But I aim to get the truth out of Aleta."

"No you won't," her husband said firmly. "If you ever approach the subject, I'll send them packing."

"You wouldn't!" she challenged.

"Marian, you don't know me if you don't know how far I will go to protect Aleta."

"I don't understand."

"I know you don't. In this you'll just have to trust me. Aleta has been hurt. Please don't poke at the wounds."

"I need to know," Marian insisted. "She needs my help!"

"If you want to help, start thinking of baby names."

"At a time like this? That's crazy! I won't do it."

"Then I'll send them off," Robert said. He stepped away, and Marian saw the set of his shoulders. He meant to do it.

"Wait," she whispered. "I'll do it."

Robert approached the group.

"Your mother has ideas about baby names," he announced. Aleta relaxed.

"That's Stanley's department," she said, pulling out a packet of pictures. "I get to name the dogs. He gets to name the kids. And here's Scooby."

She passed around the pictures. "His eyes have just opened. He's a chocolate Lab. Isn't he cute?"

"Scooby?" her mother exclaimed. "That's a crazy name. I'm glad you aren't naming your children."

Stanley laughed. "And she didn't even ask me! But Mrs. Locke, I love the name you gave Aleta. I'd love to hear your ideas on a name for a girl."

He turned to his father. "You did a good job with my name and you've lived with our last name a long time, so how about you naming the boy?"

What a negotiator! Robert Locke thought as he hugged his daughter around her waist and whispered, "Personally, I like the name Scooby."

"You get to think of a name for our Bulldog then," Aleta giggled.

"I thought you were getting a Lab."

"That's for me. The Bulldog is for Stanley."

"Won't he name him?"

"It's going to be a girl Bulldog and I get to name all the dogs. Fair's fair."

"So there's more than one dog in your future?" her father queried.

"And more than one child," Aleta said gaily. "Did you ever think I'd marry a man rich enough and loving enough to give me both?"

"I didn't think you'd settle for anything less. I just didn't think your ideal man actually existed."

"Pretty lucky, huh?"

From across the room Stanley overheard the conversation. He was the lucky one. How did she ever know what he needed most of all?

His father put his hand on Stanley's shoulder and gave it a light squeeze. For a second Hubert Praetzel didn't speak. Then he asked quietly, "You really like your name?"

"Yes, I do, Dad," Stanley said softly. "Thanks for understanding."

"Don't underestimate your mother," he said noticing that the others were busy. "She was able to read this situation better than I was. Thank you for including me."

"I didn't; Aleta did."

"You did indeed marry an amazing woman," he whispered. "If she were mine I'd buy her a hundred dogs."

"Don't even say that in a whisper," Stanley said a little too loudly.

Aleta looked over questioningly.

Stanley hesitated. He realized that Aleta might think it was a comment about their earlier discussion. It was, of course, but he couldn't say that.

"He said I should let you have as many dogs as you want since they make you so happy."

Aleta laughed happily. "I'm planning to do that; but, don't worry, Stanley. You'll want each one."

They stayed for two days.

Aboard the plane going home when father and son were sitting side by side in the cockpit, Hubert said, "I am left with a lot of questions; but the one I'd really like an answer to is whatever led you to hide under the sink?"

Stanley called back, "May I tell him, Aleta?"

"There is nothing you can't tell him," Aleta replied.

"What's that about?" Harriet asked quietly.

"About my prophetic abilities is my guess."

"Oh," Harriet whispered. "I hope he understands."

Stanley heard the whispers and guessed what the conversation was about. He returned to his father's query. "Aleta told me to hide under the sink."

"So you did?"

"Not until I heard West arguing with Ramage, then I remembered."

"So you believed her?"

"I'm alive because I believed her," Stanley said. "And, Dad, despite the fact that you don't believe we saved Lyle's life, we both believed that prophecy too."

"Be sure to tell me if there ever comes a time when I should," Hubert said.

Harriet and Aleta looked at each other and smiled. Being a prophet wasn't so bad when your predictions obviously came true as Aleta's had with Stanley and the sink.

Both realized again that most times, if people changed their behavior and the danger disappeared, that people would doubt that the prediction had any validity. If it didn't happen, it wasn't going to happen.

Both of them wished fervently at that moment that these prophecies would be the last they would ever receive.

They did not pray openly because they knew God could read their hearts.

Deep inside those same two hearts, each woman sensed that while God was pleased, the answer was no.

They sighed simultaneously and looked at each other. They held hands the rest of the way home.

Sunday morning as Stanley began to dress Aleta for church, he mentioned that his dad had asked his permission to tell his mother what had happened to him.

"Did you give it?" Aleta asked as he finished easing her feet into her stockings.

"No. I don't want her to know," Stanley said as he pulled the pantyhose gingerly up one leg at a time.

"She's your mother," Aleta said by way of argument. "I think it would be wise."

"You didn't want to tell your mother," Stanley countered reaching for Aleta's skirt.

"That's because she would have trivialized it because you're not her son."

"Dad said I should trust my mom."

"He knows her pretty well," Aleta said as Stanley slipped one sleeve up her injured arm and helped her into the other.

"I can't do it," Stanley said.

"Do you want me to?"

"Absolutely not!" he exclaimed fervently.

"It could be awkward at dinner," Aleta suggested.

"I'll take care of it," Stanley assured her as he fastened the last button on her blouse. "There, you're done."

"We have nothing to distract her with," Aleta worried aloud. "Baby talk won't do it this time."

"I said I'd handle it," Stanley snapped.

It wasn't until the end of Sunday dinner during which the talk had been light and inconsequential, when the maid was clearing the plates, that Lydia announced that they'd have dessert and coffee in the living room.

"I have something serious I'd like to talk with you about," Lydia said, rising.

Stanley rose as well and positioned himself behind Aleta's chair.

"The events of the last few weeks made me realize that you two need help," Lydia began.

Aleta shook her head, then a sudden spasm of dizziness hit her. "I… I'm not feeling well."

"Would you care to lie down?" Lydia asked noting Aleta's sudden paleness.

"I think maybe some fresh air," Aleta said, trying to rise. Stanley barely caught her in time. He held her by her waist expecting her to regain her balance.

"I think we'd better go," he said. "Too much traveling has taken its toll."

"I'll drive you," Hubert Praetzel offered. He fetched his coat from the hall.. He held out Aleta's coat and Stanley threw it over his wife's shoulder.

Stanley didn't believe Aleta could stand on her own. What surprised him more was that she had trouble walking even with support.

He bent down and picked her up and carried her. Hubert ran before them and opened the car door.

Lydia punched Dr. Cook's number and quickly told him about Aleta's collapse as she reached for her own coat.

She ran to the car as Hubert was about to drive away, and he stopped and waited for her to climb in.

"The hospital!" she ordered. "Dr. Cook will meet us there."

"I'm just exhausted," Aleta said weakly. "All I need is a nap."

Stanley cradled her gently in his arms and comforted her. "Better to be safe."

"This is embarrassing. It was just a spell of dizziness."

"Aleta dear," Lydia Praetzel said forthrightly, "You're having a stroke."

Dr. Cook managed to arrive the same time Hubert pulled up to the emergency entrance. The staff, warned in advance, was waiting with a gurney. Stanley followed the gurney inside but Dr. Cook made him wait outside the examination room.

"Go sign her in," he ordered. "I'll be out in a few minutes."

Stanley stood outside the door, confused and upset. His parents found him there.

"Dr. Cook won't let me in," he said, his voice cracking. "He told me to go sign her in."

"Let's do that then," his father said putting his arm around his son's shoulder and guiding him to the nurses' station. "She's in good hands."

Dr. Cook called for an IV to be started as he took Aleta's pulse. "Tell me what's going on," he said calmly.

"I'm just tired," Aleta said haltingly. "This is so… so… I need a sleep. I shouldn't be here."

"Your mother-in-law is the panicky type?" Cook questioned gently.

"She's a judge."

"Glad you know that," Wayne Cook smiled. "I'd hate for you to be the only one who didn't."

"But it was contagion," Aleta said. "All of them gave it."

"Nurse, get me a consent form," Dr. Cook said.

When the nurse left the room, Dr. Cook queried quietly, "What frightened you so to make you dizzy."

"Stanley's mother was going to the bathroom and talk."

Dr. Cook took a wild guess at what the problem was. "He doesn't want to tell his mother about his experience."

Aleta nodded.

"What about his father?"

Aleta shook her head.

"He told his father?"

"No. I did. And my father. Stanley let me."

"Who else have you told?"

Again Aleta shook her head.

"But…," she began and then words failed her.

"Someone else knows?" Dr. Cook asked.

Aleta nodded.

The nurse returned with the consent form. Dr. Cook handed it to Aleta. "Sign here."

Aleta tried to form the letters of her name but her hand while it could move the pen along the paper could manage to produce only a wavy line that didn't conform in outline to the undulation of the handwritten letters that would form the name she'd written her whole life.

"Betray…," Aleta uttered, dropping the pen.

"Never heard it described that way before," Dr. Cook said, "but it's an apt description."

He took her hand. "You appear to be having either a TIA or a stroke. The initial effect is the same. A TIA disappears within twenty-four hours and no permanent damage is done. A stroke leaves damage. I'm going to do a CAT-scan and we'll go from there."

Aleta, now thoroughly frightened, uttered one word, "Lyle."

Dr. Cook guessed again. "He's the one who knows?"

Aleta nodded.

He patted her hand gently. "You relax. I'll tell Stanley what's happening and that he should call Lyle."

A faint smile appeared. It was all Aleta could manage. She was beginning to understand that her inability to find words was not merely from fatigue. What she didn't know was that she was substituting other words for those she meant to say. That Dr. Cook chose not to tell her. He did, however, tell those waiting outside the room.

While Aleta was wheeled away to get her CAT scan, Dr. Cook told them what he'd already told her, finishing with, "Her ability to receive information appears unimpaired; however, I suggest when you talk with her later, you don't correct her. To work her way back, she needs confidence."

"I need more of an explanation," Stanley said.

"Earlier she said that your mother had said that she wanted to go to the bathroom and talk," Dr. Cook said. "I assume 'bathroom' was incorrect."

"I said 'living room'," Lydia said.

Dr. Cook continued, "Here's the consent form she just signed."

Stanley stared at the form with the penned jagged line.

"This isn't a signature," he protested. "It's a scrawl."

"People often say that doctor's signatures are scrawls; but, there's always some semblance of rationale in the configuration. This is a true scrawl," Dr. Cook explained. "Aleta used an interesting word to describe her inability to form the letters of her name: 'betray'. It's the most appropriate word I've heard used to describe the feelings of a person having a stroke."

"When will you know how serious this is?" Stanley asked.

"Soon," Dr. Cook said. "Aleta told me to tell you to call Lyle."

"Lyle?" Lydia said, puzzled. "Why Lyle?"

Dr. Cook didn't respond. He was hurrying down the hall.

Stanley's mind raced. Why did she come up with the word betray? It was an odd word.

"I'm going to call her grandmother," Lydia said. "Maybe she meant to say Locke and it came out Lyle."

Stanley didn't say anything. The suggestion was reasonable; but, somehow he knew Aleta meant he should call Lyle.

He decided that maybe she was right. Lyle was sharp. Maybe he could help him figure this out. He went outside and opened his cell and punched in Lyle's number.

"Sorry to disturb you," he opened, "but I need a favor."

"Shoot!" Lyle came back.

"Aleta's in the hospital. She's had some kind of stroke and…"

"I'll be right there," Lyle said. "Lauren will want to come. Is that okay?"

"Of course," Stanley said. "She's Aleta's best friend. And, Lyle, tell Lauren all you know about the kidnapping."

"Everything?"

"Aleta's words are coming out mixed. She told me to call you. Mother thought she used your name instead of her grandmother and said Lyle instead of Locke. Using that reasoning she could have meant Lauren and said Lyle by mistake. That makes more sense to me."

"Or she knew you'd need a friend," Lyle suggested.

"So let's cover both bases."

"Are you sure you want me to tell Lauren?"

"I think my secret is at the bottom of Aleta's problem. I don't know how exactly; but somehow it feels right that Aleta have a friend she can talk freely with."

"I don't want you to regret this later," West cautioned. "We could wait on this."

"Aleta already told my father and hers. I think she needs to talk about this. I trust Lauren."

He heard Lyle shout, "Lauren throw on your coat and call Margery to hop over here and watch the kids, we're going to the hospital. Aleta's had a stroke."

When Stanley turned around, he saw his father standing behind him.

"Dad," he stammered. "I... I..."

"May I tell your mother? It's your choice—yes or no?"

"Yes."

"We'll be in the lunch room," he said. "You wait here for Aleta's grandmother."

Lyle and Lauren arrived first.

"Mother called Grams," Stanley said. "We need to wait near the door. My parents are in the lunch room. Dad's telling my mother what Lyle just told you."

"How's Aleta?" Lauren asked.

"I haven't seen her; but, I'll tell you what I know."

The two listened until he ended by telling them the word she used just before telling Dr. Cook to have him call Lyle.

"It's the word 'betray' that bothers me," Stanley said.

"Maybe she's afraid she might betray you accidentally," Lauren observed.

"Dr. Cook says she doesn't know she's substituting words," Stanley countered.

"Well, she's afraid of your mother," Lauren said. "She's not sure you aren't too. So if it's not future betrayal, how about past?"

"Past?"

"You said you were leaving the table to go into the living room to talk. Maybe she was afraid you wouldn't do that thing that you do."

"What 'thing'?"

"That power thing. I mean, I'm not your mother and it riled me; but, Aleta liked it. And now I think I understand better. Aleta made it okay for me by kissing you in front of us; but, she wouldn't do that in front of your mother. She was probably scared stiff."

"I wouldn't have cared what my mother thought!" Stanley declared vehemently.

"Wouldn't you?"

Lyle interrupted. "Here comes Mrs. Locke. Does she know?"

"No. Just my parents and Aleta's father," Stanley answered.

"Not her mother?" Lauren asked.

"No, she didn't want her to know," Stanley said. "Aleta tried to tell her mother she hadn't been raped, but her mother refused to believe her. I stopped her then. She was being hurt by her mother's disbelief."

Harriet Locke rushed through the door that opened automatically at her foot tread. "What happened to Aleta? How is she?"

"Lyle, fill her in," Stanley said turning and hurrying away.

"Where are you going?"

"To find Aleta!"

Lyle quickly turned to his wife. "Tell Mrs. Locke everything. I'm going with Stanley."

Thus it was that Harriet Locke found out what neither Aleta or Stanley had intended she ever find out. When Lauren finished, Harriet remarked that she could use a cup of coffee and the two went into the lunch room where the Praetzel's were seated.

Harriet studied the mother's face. "You just found out I gather."

Lydia nodded.

"I wasn't told until now either," Harriet said. "And Lauren found out only a few minutes ago herself. It seems your son had a penchant for keeping secrets."

Lydia smiled. "That he does."

"It was Aleta who told me," Hubert said. "I doubt Stanley ever would have."

"Aleta doesn't like to keep secrets. It tears her up inside." Harriet commented.

"She didn't tell her mother."

"She didn't refuse to talk with her about what happened to her personally, just what happened to Stanley," Harriet explained. "Marian was pretty hostile as if Aleta was somehow in control of what happened. The nude thing bothered her. She made assumptions and refused to believe anything Aleta said. Stanley got Aleta to stop talking somehow and wouldn't let her talk again until Marian and I left the house. When we came home, Robert talked with Marian briefly and Marian never brought up the topic again. I'm sure he didn't tell her. I think he threatened her somehow. All I heard was her saying, 'You wouldn't dare!' and him replying, 'You have no idea how far I will go to protect Aleta'."

"Seems like she means a great deal to him."

Harriet grinned. "Remember when Stanley asked Marian to come up with a girl's name?"

"And he asked me to think of a boy's name," Hubert added with a modicum of pride.

"Well, Aleta asked her father to name her next dog. If ever she asks you to name a dog, you'll know you've made it in her eyes," Harriet said with a wry smile. "I'm still waiting for her to ask me."

"I wonder if she'll ever ask me," Lydia mused.

"Oh, she's going to ask you for lots of suggestions," Harriet said positively. "She believes you two raised a perfect son. She wants to do whatever it was you did."

Lydia laughed. "We always said Stanley pretty much raised himself."

"Aleta pretty much did that too. Her mother threw her hands up in the air when Aleta was two. Her dad brought her over to my place a lot. She had a real feel for dogs right from the start. We became good friends."

"I'm not a real dog person," Lydia confessed.

"You don't have to be. Her father isn't. With me it was a way to connect. She's already got a connection with you— one even more precious than any dog."

"She tried to save Stanley's fish," Lydia pointed out.

"Because they were Stanley's."

"Does he realize how deep her commitment is?"

"I think he's beginning to," Harriet said. "I think today might just enlighten him completely."

"Where are we going?" Lyle asked as Stanley and he entered the elevator.

"I told you. To find Aleta."

Lyle pressed a button. "We'll start with the floor the CAT scan is on."

"What do we do if we're stopped?"

"Nobody stops the chief of police," Lyle smiled. "There are multiple advantages to being my friend."

"I'm beginning to get the picture," Stanley said. "Lead the way."

They searched several places on three floors before winding up on the surgical floor.

"Why here?" Stanley asked.

"I'm guessing Wayne put her in her old room. The familiar is good when one is frightened."

"I think that room's this way," Stanley said attempting to pass.

"Who do you think visited you every day?" Lyle quipped. "Follow me."

Lyle led the way through the door. Dr. Cook turned around.

"Brought the cavalry, I see," Wayne Cook quipped.

"He's under protective custody," Lyle said. "Only it's your hospital that's in danger. He was planning to tear the place apart."

"She's alright?" Stanley asked his worried expression telling the two men what the fear was that was driving him.

"Why not sit next to her and hold her hand," Dr. Cook suggested. "The arm's got an IV in it, so be careful."

Stanley dragged over a straight chair. "Oh, I will, I will."

"Lyle, got a minute?" Wayne Cook asked as he hung Aleta's chart at the foot of her bed.

The two men walked out.

Stanley leaned over and spoke softly even though no one was in the room.

"You could never betray me," Stanley said.

"I was… scared."

"Of my mother?"

"Of hurting you," Aleta said.

"I'm so sorry I imposed my will on yours. I should have let you speak after we were again safe."

"No. No. Wrong."

"I know it was wrong," Stanley said.

"No. It was good."

"Good? How can you say that? Your whole body is telling me it wasn't."

"Scared."

"I know you were."

"Scared I would… um…," tears of frustration rolled down Aleta's cheeks, "talk wrong."

"Well, I guess we're crossed that bridge, haven't we?" Stanley said with a new buoyancy. "Lauren guessed correctly. You were afraid of saying something that would cause my mother to begin to ask questions about what happened."

Aleta nodded. "More. Pillow word."

"You were afraid I'd use it?"

Aleta nodded. "Opposite too."

"That I wouldn't use it to stop you?" Stanley guessed. "There was no way out was there?"

"No way out," Aleta repeated.

"Dad is telling my mother as we speak. Lyle told Lauren on the way over. Oh my gosh!"

"What?"

"I told Lyle to tell Lauren everything and he did…"

"So?"

"Lyle told Lauren to tell your grandmother everything. Suppose she did."

"Then you can hate her," Aleta said.

"You mean love her," Stanley said, "because Grams is close to both of us."

"Grams will tell Martha," Aleta warned.

"And Martha will tell no one."

"You did nothing wrong," Aleta stated, her brain settling into a familiar thought pattern. "I liked your protecting me. I was afraid you'd stopped."

"You didn't think I'd stand up to my mother?"

"Yep."

"Oh, Aleta, you walked naked past an army of men to save my life. Facing my mother is not nearly as formidable a task for me as that was for you. I would gladly protect you anytime I can. Don't you know that you mean more to me than any secret I might want to keep? Never, never worry about telling the truth."

"What about the power of the pillow?"

"You tell me."

"We keep it. It's our special secret cov…"

"Covenant?" Stanley questioned softly.

"Yes." Aleta agreed.

"You aren't worried?"

"Never will."

"Never will what?"

"Is that what I said?"

"Yes."

"Kiss me," Aleta ordered.

He kissed her hand.

"You angry?" she asked.

"You minx you!" he exclaimed as he shoved the IV stanchion out of the way and leaned over and kissed her gently on the lips. It was a long kiss.

When he finished, he sat back down in the chair and took her hand. He watched her eyelids close and gazed at her features relax as she drifted off to sleep. After a few minutes he let go to readjust his chair.

She woke up with a start.

"Stanley?"

Quickly, he took her hand again. "Just moving the chair a bit," he explained.

"Don't leave," she whispered. "Please hold on to me."

"I've got you, Aleta. Go back to sleep. I'll hold onto you until you wake."

At home, three days later, Stanley woke to the alarm and shook his wife gently. "We need to hurry. You have to begin interviewing housekeepers at eight."

"We have plenty of time," Aleta assured him with a smile.

Stanley scowled, "Aleta, you have got to stop monkeying with the clock."

"I knew I'd want a leisurely bath this morning," Aleta said. "I missed those in the hospital."

"Okay. Okay. I'll draw it," Stanley said. "How much extra time have we got?"

"Thirty minutes, more or less," Aleta said. "I set the clock ahead thirty minutes."

Fifteen minutes into the bath ritual, there was a loud knock on the door.

"That's her," Aleta said. "You answer it."

"I'm not dressed."

"Your robe's on the bed," Aleta said. "Just let her in and be nice."

"She's early."

"I told her to come early," Aleta said. "I thought I'd have a more interesting interview if we started off casually. Now go. If she goes away, I'll never forgive you!"

Stanley rushed to the door. When he opened it, after tying his robe closed, the woman looked at her watch.

"Did I make a mistake on the time?"

Stanley studied the plump middle-aged woman with brown hair streaked with a few strands of gray, who was wearing an obviously new tan uniform underneath a worn black cloth coat. She was clutching a soft leather purse that had seen better days.

"My wife is expecting you," Stanley said with all the dignity he could muster barefoot and with only a robe to protect his dignity. "Please come in."

"Where is your wife?" the woman asked in a pleasant voice.

"I'm bathing her at the moment," Stanley replied. "You were told she has an injured arm."

"I'm a licensed practical nurse," Bertha Carlson stated. "I could do that for you."

"Thank you, but no," Stanley responded evenly.

"I understand I'm the first applicant," Bertha said.

"My mother sent you?" Stanley asked. It was a rhetorical question, so he followed it with a suggestion as he moved into the large living room. "Please sit down.

Bertha sat down on the tapestry-covered couch.

"You have dogs?" she queried.

Stanley sat down carefully opposite her.

"Not yet."

Bertha picked up a tuft of hair. "Looks like Chessie hair."

"You know dogs?"

"I was raised with Chessies."

"I assume my mother checked your references," Stanley said, his curiosity finally overcoming his discomfort.

"No," Bertha said. "That's why I think I've been sent here to break the ice, so to speak."

"Break the ice?"

"Not to be hired; but just to give you practice interviewing."

"Aleta doesn't interview," Stanley said matter-of-factly.

"Your mother's words exactly."

"She doesn't pick out her own clothes or shop for groceries. She expects others to do this for her."

Bertha's face fell. She reached for the purse that she'd laid down beside her on the couch.

"I'm sorry, Sir," she said with a firmness that surprised Stanley. "Much as I need this job, I don't do well with spoiled, pampered women."

"Stanley, are you interviewing my housekeeper?" Aleta called from the bathroom.

"She says she doesn't like spoiled, pampered women. She's turning you down."

"Raise your salary offer," Aleta called.

"I didn't offer her a salary yet," Stanley said. "I didn't get that far."

"Well, get there!" Aleta ordered. "And don't you lose me my housekeeper because I embarrassed you."

"She thinks you're spoiled," Stanley repeated. "I don't think money is an issue."

"Of course, I'm spoiled. And who's fault is that?"

"Your father's?"

"And money is always important, so stop acting as if she's going to donate her services."

Bertha began to smile. The banter was light and lively. This could be a good place to work.

"I make good coffee," she offered. "Your mother said that was important."

"Go make a pot while I dress my wife," Stanley decided. "Make a full pot."

"Aleta, how many interviews do you have lined up?" Stanley called as he walked back into the bedroom.

Bertha heard her reply, "One."

She lingered in order to hear his response.

"She's it?" Stanley asked, obviously annoyed.

"I hate to shop."

"Your taste and my mother's aren't the same," he said as he entered the bedroom.

"We both like you," Aleta declared.

Bertha left to make the coffee. She didn't care if the woman was spoiled. She had a terrific sense of humor.

"Do you like her," Aleta asked as her husband toweled her dry.

"As a matter of fact I do, but, Aleta, check her references. My mother didn't."

"Really?" Aleta grinned.

"You know something I don't know," Stanley charged.

"She didn't come from the agency."

"So who sent her?" he asked, rubbing her legs dry.

"Martha Cook."

"Okay, what's the catch?"

"She's battling the insurance company who doesn't want to pay her husband's death benefit. She needs work."

Stanley dropped the towel and stood up.

"Tell me you didn't promise I'd represent her."

"How could I? I haven't met her yet," Aleta said picking up the towel and handing it to him. "Besides I'll do most of the work. And insurance companies don't shoot people."

Stanley toweled her back a second time as he tried to be his most persuasive self.

"Aleta, I'm a child advocate. I like being a child advocate. I don't want to expand my horizons. I like my horizon the way it is."

"I'm not asking you to do anything," Aleta said then paused and added, "well, maybe just a few things."

"You only have three months to get ready for the bar," Stanley pointed out. "You haven't time to take on a case— any case."

"Are you going to dress me? I'm really dry, you know."

"Now I am late!" Stanley exclaimed.

"I'll be easy then. Just a sweatshirt and jeans. No buttons."

He began to help her into her clothes. Despite being short of time, he was gentle with her.

"I have to shower, shave and dress," he lamented. "You didn't leave me any time."

"You're in training now," Aleta quipped as he adjusted her arm in the sling.

"For what?"

"Parenting," Aleta giggled.

"I don't need to be trained!" Stanley declared adamantly "What I need is not to be late for court."

Aleta urged him to hurry as she ran from the room. She flew into the kitchen.

"Quick!" she said to Bertha, "Scramble two eggs and make some toast. Get out a tray. He gets an egg sandwich, a small glass of orange juice and coffee. The coffee you'll put in his thermos mug. We'll have a hard enough time getting him to eat at the door as it is."

Bertha looked at Aleta askance. "At the door?"

"He doesn't get out without breakfast," Aleta said.

"Won't he just brush past you?"

Aleta laughed and Bertha hurried to complete the task. She figured she was hired; but, she wanted to hear it. Then she realized that she was being tested. Judge Davis had said that her daughter-in-law's interview method would be different.

When Stanley emerged from the bedroom, Aleta said, "You better have left a mess. Bertha needs to demonstrate her cleaning skills."

Bertha smiled as she stood next to the front door with a tray. So it is a test after all. This was one clever lady. She liked her already.

Stanley spotted the tray. "You don't expect me to eat?"

"In three minutes, I'll give you your coffee mug and you can go."

"This is crazy!" Stanley said.

"Orange juice first."

"I just brushed my teeth."

"You can do it again at the office. You always do," Aleta said. "Drink."

Stanley downed the small glass of juice and picked up the egg sandwich. It would be faster not to argue with Aleta.

"This is good!" he commented.

"Two minutes, forty seconds," Aleta announced. "That leaves ten seconds for my kiss."

"You timed me?" Stanley gasped.

"If you talk it comes off your time, not mine."

Stanley looked at his redheaded wife with the impish grin on her face. He put down his briefcase and gently took her face in his hands and kissed her for much longer than ten seconds.

"I love you," he said softly.

"I know," she responded with a gentle tone. "I love that you're so much fun to live with."

"Nothing else?"

"Well, you are the handsomest man on the planet."

Stanley laughed as he looked at Bertha. "She thinks Bulldogs are gorgeous. See you both later."

And that's when Bertha knew she was hired. There was no test. Aleta had hired her the minute she gave her her first order. She had accepted her mother-in-law's judgment. What a unique woman Aleta was. Bertha remembered both Martha Cook and Judge Davis had used just that term to describe her. How right they were. Working for her was going to be fun.

The Prophet Series

to be released

www.ingramcontent.com/pod-product-compliance
Lightning Source LLC
Chambersburg PA
CBHW050913250626
47155CB00001B/210